CW01478598

Praise for
PALACE OF TEARS

'A wonderful historical novel . . . The Blue Mountains is a place ripe for fiction, iridescently spooky and timeless.' —*Sydney Morning Herald*

'A rollicking, epic tale.' —*Adelaide Advertiser*

'A tap-dancing debut novel, beautifully and lyrically written.' —*Australian Women's Weekly*

'Passionate palatial page-turner . . . a Gothic fiction masterpiece.' —*Tasmanian Times*

'This big, sprawling saga . . . brings together the sophistication of global modernity and the Australian bush, and combines the glitter and glamour of consumer culture with the homeliness of a small regional community.' —*Newtown Review of Books*

'An entertaining, colourful and informative novel . . . Leatherdale brings to life the grandeur and flamboyance of the pre-war and post-war eras.' —*Write Note Reviews*

Julian Leatherdale's first love was theatre. On graduation, he wrote lyrics for four satirical cabarets and a two-act musical. He discovered a passion for popular history as a staff writer, researcher and photo editor for Time-Life's *Australians At War* series. He later researched and co-wrote two Film Australia-ABC documentaries *Return to Sandakan* and *The Forgotten Force* and was an image researcher at the State Library of New South Wales. He was the public relations manager for a hotel school in the Blue Mountains, where he lives with his wife and two children. The bestselling *Palace of Tears* (2015) was his first novel.

www.julianleatherdale.com

The
OPAL
DRAGONFLY

A Tale of Sydney

JULIAN
LEATHERDALE

ALLEN&UNWIN
SYDNEY • MELBOURNE • AUCKLAND • LONDON

First published in 2018

Copyright © Julian Leatherdale 2018

All rights reserved. No part of this book may be reproduced or transmitted in any form or by any means, electronic or mechanical, including photocopying, recording or by any information storage and retrieval system, without prior permission in writing from the publisher. The Australian *Copyright Act 1968* (the Act) allows a maximum of one chapter or 10 per cent of this book, whichever is the greater, to be photocopied by any educational institution for its educational purposes provided that the educational institution (or body that administers it) has given a remuneration notice to Copyright Agency Limited (CAL) under the Act.

Allen & Unwin
83 Alexander Street
Crows Nest NSW 2065
Australia
Phone: (61 2) 8425 0100
Email: info@allenandunwin.com
Web: www.allenandunwin.com

Cataloguing-in-Publication details are available
from the National Library of Australia
www.trove.nla.gov.au

ISBN 978 1 76029 307 9

Typeset in 12/17.5 pt Minion Pro by Bookhouse, Sydney
Printed and bound in Australia by Griffin Press

10 9 8 7 6 5 4 3 2 1

MIX
Paper from
responsible sources
FSC® C009448

The paper in this book is FSC® certified. FSC® promotes environmentally responsible, socially beneficial and economically viable management of the world's forests.

For my daughter

This book is a work of fiction but has its roots in historical research. In the service of fiction, I have taken some liberties with real events, dates, poems and journal entries. For those readers who are interested, I explain this adaptation of historical sources in detail in notes at the back. Aboriginal and Torres Strait Islander readers should be aware that this book portrays and names deceased Aboriginal people.

Her poor mother now did not look so very unworthy of being Lady Bertram's sister as she was but too apt to look. It often grieved her to the heart—to think of the contrast between them—to think that where nature had made so little difference, circumstances should have made so much, and that her mother, as handsome as Lady Bertram, and some years her junior, should have an appearance so much more worn and faded, so comfortless, so slatternly, so shabby.

JANE AUSTEN, *MANSFIELD PARK*

An example and chastisement to the debased populace of Sydney Town.

GOVERNOR RALPH DARLING ON HIS
NEW SYDNEY SUBURB OF DARLINGHURST

And the sunny water frothing round the liners black and red,
And the coastal schooners working by the loom of Bradley's Head;
And the whistles and the sirens that re-echo far and wide—
All the life and light and beauty that belong to Sydney-Side.

HENRY LAWSON, 'SYDNEY-SIDE'

An opal-hearted country,
A wilful, lavish land—
All you who have not loved her,
You will not understand—

DOROTHEA MACKELLAR, 'MY COUNTRY'

ISOBEL

27 SEPTEMBER 1851

Chapter 1

LANE'S TELESCOPIC VIEW

Isobel slept badly.

Again and again she startled awake, staring at her moon-drenched room as if she had never laid eyes on it before. She could hear the familiar chimes of the library clock downstairs and the groans of her wardrobe close by but something was not right. Her bed floated, rocking from side to side in the darkness. Or was it the whole house that had slid into the harbour and drifted out to the Heads on the tide?

Isobel's head nodded again but sleep offered no refuge as she was instantly pulled back under the dark waters of a nightmare. This time she was alone on a beach. Rain fell in torrents from a storm-bruised sky and the ocean seethed, grey and white-capped. Above the din, Isobel could make out a man's voice, carried on the wind. *Help! Please God! Help me!* Blinded by rain, she stumbled along the beach, calling in response.

But the drowning man was nowhere to be seen.

She listened to his pleas grow weaker, more desperate. *Please God! Help me, please!* At last there was only the roaring of the wind and waves. He was gone. Isobel fell to her knees and wept, convinced she could have saved the man if only she had tried harder. And then the scene began again, repeating in an endless loop.

It was a long night. Adrift on her bed, Isobel thrashed about like a swimmer herself in a choppy sea. She felt the drag of the bedclothes twisted round her limbs. Her moans grew so loud it was a wonder they did not wake her sisters next door.

Miss Isobel Clara Macleod, youngest of the seven children of Major Sir Angus Hutton Macleod, Surveyor-General of the colony of New South Wales, had the singular misfortune to know that at seven o'clock that morning her father was going to die.

To make matters worse, she suspected that half of Sydney knew it too. Isobel understood better than most the impossibility of keeping anything secret in this town. A permanent cloud of gossip hung over the place. Scandals could be whipped up as easily as dust devils on the street in summer. As one of the colony's most senior public officials, her father was not frightened of the town gossip or even the vile scribblings in *The Monitor* or *Bell's Life in Sydney and Sporting Reviewer.*

Isobel's father was not frightened of anything.

She woke again to hear the chimes from the library. This time they were answered by five bright pings from the mantel clock in her father's dressing-room. Surely he would be out of bed by now, assuming he had slept at all. What man sleeps peacefully on the eve of his own destruction? Not even her father was *that* stoic.

Out of habit, Isobel unlaced her nightcap, tucked it under her pillow and straightened her blankets and bolsters. She pulled back the curtains that enclosed her narrow four-poster and looked out the window. The moon hung low in the pre-dawn sky, as small and pale as a pearl. Its extravagant show of glitter on the black water hours earlier had died down to a few sparks. Isobel had loved this view since she was ten but this morning it provided none of its usual solace or pleasure. She was haunted instead by the image of her father in his dressing-room next door, paused halfway through unbuttoning his nightshirt or bent over his washstand, looking at this same moon for the last time.

When the Major moved his family to Rosemount Hall seven years ago, Isobel had shared this room overlooking Elizabeth Bay with her two middle sisters, Grace and Anna. This arrangement had been her parents' choice and not one Isobel favoured though she bore it stoically. While she had been close to her two sisters when she was small, relations with them had soured over the years; the best she could hope for was to be ignored and spared their cruel taunts. Her only comfort in this cramped front room was falling asleep to the distant lullaby of the waves and waking to a room filled with the dazzle of morning light off the harbour and the prospect of a day's beachcombing along the bay or an amble in Rosemount's gardens. Or, if she was lucky, there would be a picnic outing on a beach with Mama.

There had been many changes since those early days. Two years ago, Isobel's eldest sister, Alice, had married and moved to England with her new husband. In January of the following year, Sir Angus's youngest son, Richard, was killed in a horse riding accident on the family farm at Camden. And then, just over a year ago, their blessed mama, Winnie, had died of dysentery. Isobel's favourite brother, William, now lived out of town but kept a room at Rosemount where he came and went as he pleased, unlike Joseph, whose long-running quarrel with Father had led to his banishment.

Rosemount was not the same. Sir Angus still had callers and entertained close friends but, with so many departures and absences, the great house felt half-empty. Several of its rooms were permanently closed up. The Major lived here with only a handful of servants and his three daughters for company. At times he talked of getting rid of the 'wretched thing' altogether, though Isobel knew that the idea grieved him terribly.

It had fallen to Grace to take on their mother's role of managing the house. Anna helped her as best she could, given the burden of her affliction. To everyone's surprise, the Major submitted happily to the new regime. Isobel was not so compliant. She thought Grace was a tyrant. A suspicious and jealous tyrant at that, at least where Isobel was concerned.

There was one positive in all this change. As the new mistresses of the house, Grace and Anna had been given their own rooms, leaving Isobel with this smaller front room all to herself. She cherished this refuge, even more now as she approached her seventeenth birthday. Here, late at night or first thing in the morning, she could sit quietly, writing her journal or sketching.

Isobel saw the first blush of orange on the horizon. She knew her father always consulted his *Old Moore's Almanac* and she had done the same with her own copy in the morning room. Sunrise was due at 5.32 a.m. If only a bank of storm clouds like those in her nightmare would bring a downpour of rain her father might still be saved. But the 'red sky' of yesterday's sunset had foretold the clear skies of this morning's 'shepherd's delight'.

Father had chosen a fine day to die.

In the pre-dawn gloom, Isobel fumbled to light the lamp on her washstand. Her hands were trembling so violently it took her several attempts to perform this simple task. She then removed her night jacket and washed her face and hands. There was not a moment to lose. She listened carefully for the creak of her father's door and his tread in the corridor. The servants would have started their chores downstairs by now but the house remained silent.

On a normal weekday morning Isobel would rise around nine, depending on how late she had danced or taken supper at a party the night before. She would ring for Sarah to bring muffins and hot chocolate or a tray of toast and tea. Father usually ate early in the breakfast room and was long gone by the time she and her sisters arose for their daily round of German, French, music, dance and drawing lessons.

But today was far from a normal day, Isobel reflected as she brushed her hair, trying to calm the terror that bubbled up in her breast with each vigorous stroke. Her face in the glass looked paler than usual, almost luminous, no doubt due to her night of tortured sleep but also exaggerated by the contrast of her charcoal black hair, which she tied up with ribbons in two plump wings just above her ears. She checked the precise middle parting that showed her scalp, as white and fragile as an egg.

Everything about her seemed fragile this morning, thought Isobel: her pale face, her leaden limbs, her aching chest. Unlike Grace, suffering did not improve Isobel's looks. Where her sister's features were sharpened and ennobled by sadness, hers merely looked pinched. Her own plainness relative to her sister's haughty loveliness made Grace's jealousy all the more difficult to understand. And to think they had once been so close as children.

She finished her toilette and took a deep breath. It was time to unlock the wardrobe. With every passing minute, the strangeness of this day engulfed her. The doors swung open and she stared at the bundle she had placed there late last night: her brother William's spare trousers, shirt and jacket, all folded neatly beside a pair of leather riding boots and a cabbage-tree hat. They looked so outlandish here among her dresses and bonnets.

What on earth am I doing? She could not decide if her hastily made plans were brave or lunatic. Trespassing into secret male territory, the only way she could. Disguised as a man. It outraged all decorum. She risked making a mockery of her family name. She risked her father's scorn and fury. She might even be risking her own life. How could she possibly justify such madness? The answer was simple. To do nothing was worse. After all the ill fortune her family had suffered, Isobel was not prepared to stand by and let her father destroy himself. And destroy this little world she treasured. So she picked up her brother's hat and thought about how to pin all her hair up inside it.

The previous evening, Sir Angus had invited Captain and Mrs Bradley, and Dr and Mrs Finch and their three daughters to dinner. The Bradleys and the Finches were old friends of the Macleods, going as far back as Sir Angus's arrival in the colony nearly twenty-four years ago.

The Finches had come bearing a gift to entertain their hosts. Last week the long-awaited signal had gone up at Flagstaff Hill to let all of Sydney know that the mail ship was in. News from Home! An anxious crowd had formed at the dock and some poor postmen were even pursued on their rounds. The Finches had a bundle of letters from their eldest son, Aloysius, in London. He had dedicated many pages to his impressions of Prince Albert's 'Great Exhibition of the Works of Industry of All Nations', which had been opened by Her Majesty in May. Dr Finch shared several passages describing the wonders of the Crystal Palace and its panoply of thirteen thousand exhibits from around the globe.

'There were many remarkable innovations from Europe and the Americas,' he read, 'such as Mr Brady's daguerreotypes, Mr Jacquard's loom and Mr Colt's revolvers. But visitors were left in little doubt that Britain was the undisputed leader in industrial technology and design. The building itself is a testament to British engineering and architectural genius.'

This patriotic observation was greeted with cheers. The Major proposed a toast to 'Her Majesty, the Prince Consort and the Empire' and the diners raised their glasses in unison. The young women at the table became even more animated when Dr Finch produced the novel souvenir his son had enclosed, called a ' Lane's Telescopic View'. Isobel thought it ingenious. Ten hand-coloured lithographic prints were cut out, pasted on board and arranged like a tableau, one behind the other, in a stiffened cloth tunnel. The whole device could be folded flat, concertina fashion, for mailing. To Isobel it resembled the toy theatres her brothers had played with as boys, staging the Battle of Waterloo in miniature.

Dr Finch set up the View on the sideboard and invited the Macleod girls to 'take a peek'. Isobel went first. Through the peep-show lens she discovered a view stretching the full length of the Crystal Palace's Great Hall. She laughed with delight. For a moment she could easily imagine herself as one of the guests strolling among the gushing fountains, the fully-grown trees and the giant show-cases. 'It's as if you were actually there,' she sighed.

For Isobel, London existed only in her imagination as a bright vision of order and splendour created by poets, painters and her parents' memories. Like so many others, her father had come to New South Wales as a young man, with a wife and three children and plans for rapid advancement and easy wealth before escaping back home to England. Despite these good intentions and several trips to the Old Country in the meantime on matters of business, Sir Angus had remained in the colony as its hard-working Surveyor-General. His beloved Winnie had reconciled herself to their term of exile but filled her daughters' heads with nostalgic yearning. At least Alice had her prayers answered in the form of a rich husband with a townhouse in London and a manor in the country. There were times when Isobel also craved to be at the centre of the civilised world rather than here on its outer edge.

As Isobel watched her sisters bent over the Telescopic View to spy on the Lilliputian world within, she was struck by the oddest notion: was this how our little lives appeared to God, she wondered, no more than miniscule tableaux spied through a peephole? To think that all our travails and suffering, our feverish hopes and desires, must seem so comically insignificant to the Omnipotent.

The *Herald* and the other Sydney papers had carried reports of the Great Exhibition but Dr Finch's son had also sent clippings from *The Illustrated London News*. Grace was fascinated most of all by the pictures of the Koh-i-Noor, the world's largest diamond and the undisputed star of the show. Once the possession of a maharaja, it had been surrendered to Queen Victoria two years ago as a spoil of war following her conquest of the Punjab. Inside a red cloth tent, it sat on a silk cushion, illuminated by gas jets, with a concealed iron box below, set on a hair-trigger to swallow the diamond whole at the slightest touch. Police struggled to control the restless throng that queued for hours to be admitted to its hallowed presence.

'Have you ever seen anything so beautiful?' gushed Grace.

There had been fears that such a huge gathering of the general populace—estimated at some fifty thousand visitors a day—face to face with these extravagant trophies of wealth and machines of profit would lead to rioting. As it turned out, these fears proved groundless. For the price of a shilling, the working masses came as humble pilgrims to Prince Albert's glass cathedral to worship at these shrines of industry.

'Thank God for the stout hearts of Englishmen and women,' said the Major, taking a sip of his lobster soup. 'Still, one can never be too careful. We live in unsettling times.'

Indeed, they did, thought Isobel. These last three weeks, the streets of Sydney had borne witness to its own rowdy multitudes, stirred up by the shrill campaign speeches for the Legislative Council elections. Isobel had been tempted to go down to George Street to see all the excitement for herself but she knew her father would never allow it. To the consternation of many older and wiser heads, the majority of votes had gone to demagogues and rabble-rousers like Reverend Lang, who spoke openly about the virtues of 'democracy'.

Mercifully, there had been no acts of violence in Sydney despite the rich squatters raising the spectre of mob rule and the terrors of 1848. Who could forget how, only three years earlier, Europe had been narrowly saved from the bonfires of revolution thanks only to bullets and bayonets on the streets of Paris, Vienna and Berlin?

All discussion of politics was soon eclipsed by more cheerful topics and laughter, a pleasing accompaniment to what, in Isobel's estimation, was as perfect a dinner party as could be hoped for. The Finches and Bradleys had made excellent company. Grace was in a lighthearted mood for a change and Anna did not disgrace herself with any unpredictable behaviour. In this harmonious scene, Isobel detected only one discordant note.

During their talk of the Great Exhibition, Isobel saw how Papa fidgeted, nervously fingering his wine glass and shifting about in his chair. This was not like him at all. There was a credible explanation for his unease but only Isobel and her sisters could have guessed what it was. Some four years ago, Sir Angus had patented a design for a new type of ship's propeller, modelled on the shape of the 'boomerang', that curious flying weapon he had seen used by Australian natives on his expeditions. Despite sinking large sums into prototypes and sea trials, his invention had not been ready in time for the Great Exhibition. He still had hopes for its future but for now all he had to show for his troubles were debts.

Sir Angus may have been financially stretched but he was well known for his generous table. With the help of two domestics, Rosemount's butler kept the guests' glasses charged with fizz and claret and ferried dozens of dishes back and forth from the servery. Cook had even been prevailed upon to prepare a collared eel, such an elegant spiced delicacy coiled into a tight spiral inside its own ceramic dish. The richness of the meal combined with the sumptuousness of Rosemount's dining room induced a glow of warm self-regard in all present. The Finches, Bradleys and Macleods counted themselves fortunate to be among the privileged beneficiaries of the Empire's munificence and loyal instruments of her power and prestige. At that moment, Isobel felt especially blessed to live in such a golden age of invention and enlightenment. Who could tell what the future would bring? Ideas as yet undreamed of to expand the sum of human happiness beyond imagining.

By eleven o'clock, the party was over. The guests had been farewelled and the servants were clearing away the remains of dessert. Isobel's sisters had retired to their rooms and their father to his study. Though tired, Isobel lingered a moment in the hall with her night candle. Her father had looked fatigued and distracted towards the end of the evening and she couldn't help being worried about him so she decided to bid him a final goodnight with a kiss on his brow, just as she had always done as a child. Her father indulged such sentimentality in his youngest daughter, and even at times her good-natured teasing.

Crossing the saloon, she noticed that the study door had been left slightly ajar. Again, this was not like Papa at all. He guarded his privacy jealously. As she was about to knock, she spied him seated at his desk. In a circle of lamplight, his face was grim with concentration, absorbed in the task of cleaning something with a cloth. He paused for a moment and held the object up to the light.

Isobel stifled the gasp that rushed to her lips. There was no mistaking what he held in his hands: one of his prized pair of French duelling pistols. It shone with a holy lustre.

When she was younger, Isobel had been allowed into the inner sanctum of her father's study now and then to sketch some of the specimens in his nature cabinets. Shells, fossils, insects. He encouraged this precocious talent in her and her curiosity about botany ('a fit science for a woman's sensibility,' he was fond of saying). On one such occasion, Isobel had been shown one of these pistols, nestled in their velvet-lined case like gems in a lady's jewellery box. While Isobel had no fondness for guns, she had to admit to their masterful craftsmanship, even their unsettling beauty. The pistol's octagonal barrel, trigger guard and percussion lock had been fashioned from brilliant silver-blue steel, intricately etched. The handle of polished walnut, mottled honey-brown and black, was carved in deep, elegant flutes and the stock engraved with a scroll of leaves and flowers.

Isobel was in shock. What could this mean? She did not utter a sound but withdrew quickly, leaving her father to his preparations

14

in private. She tried to stay calm but sobs broke from her as she hurried across the main hall towards the stairs.

Passing by the dining room, she overheard Sarah, the parlour-maid, talking with someone. It was James, Rosemount's groom. The two servants had recently given notice, informing Grace of their intention to marry and seek their fortune at Bathurst. In four weeks they would join the great human flood that had been flowing west since the discovery of gold was officially proclaimed in May. At the request of Governor FitzRoy, Sir Angus had travelled out to the diggings himself in the winter to survey the extent of the newly discovered fields that threatened to drain Sydney of every single able-bodied man and woman in pursuit of a quick fortune.

'Do you think the Major will be killed?' Isobel heard Sarah ask.

'Who knows?' replied James. 'A duel ain't meant for killing. A light wound usually satisfies. But accidents do happen. Now and then.'

They both heard Isobel's cry of distress and saw her pale face in the doorway. Her colour was so deathly they feared she was about to faint. They both looked a little shame-faced, James hurrying to fetch a chair and Sarah a glass of wine.

'We meant no 'arm, Miss,' murmured James.

Isobel thanked him. Only two years older than Isobel, James had served at Rosemount since he was a stable boy. He had always been respectful and pleasant without being familiar and regarded Isobel as the most considerate of the Macleod women, unlike her mother and sisters who treated servants with contempt and suspicion, insisting on their invisibility. When Isobel entreated the young groomsman to reveal the truth, James told her everything he knew.

'Sir Angus is having a big public stoush with Mr Simon Davidson, Miss.' Everyone knew the name of Davidson, a Lancashire-born 'exclusive' with a 250,000-acre slice of New South Wales for his 34,000 sheep. He was one of the most ambitious young men in the colony and had just been re-elected to the Legislative Council. 'Two weeks ago Mr Davidson made a speech on the hustings and said your father had wasted a great deal of public money. Sir Angus demanded an apology, of course, but Mr Davidson refused to give it.'

How had this news escaped her? Isobel knew that such an accusation would wound her father deeply. He was very proud of his record of service to the colony. 'My father was made a Knight of the Realm,' Isobel had recorded in her journal when she was only eight, 'because he is good at drawing maps.' The year Isobel was born, Sir Angus had completed his painstakingly detailed (and, Isobel later discovered, quite beautiful) Nineteen Counties map that documented the boundaries of the entire colony and all its districts and parishes. He had paid over nine hundred pounds out of his own pocket for the engraving of the copper plates. He had also accommodated the engraver, a gifted deaf mute, in his house for two years and, at his own expense, bought up all the copper in the port of Sydney that was stored for ships' sheathing. As a little girl, Isobel had loved that story about her father's single-minded determination.

'Your father 'as challenged Mr Davidson to a duel,' James told her. 'It will be fought with pistols at seven o'clock tomorrow morning at the Lachlan Swamps.'

Isobel fainted.

Thankfully, James caught his mistress before she hit the floor. Sarah hurried to the pantry to fetch the *sal volatile*. Once revived a few moments later, Isobel stared at them both as if in a trance. She could not comprehend what she had just heard. Yes, her father was known for his outbursts of temper. And yes, he had made enemies over the years. But a duel? That was impossible. Her worst fears were now confirmed. She pressed the groomsman for more details. 'Please, James. What is going to happen?'

'Sir Angus 'as asked me to saddle up Pompey for six o'clock. Then 'e will ride out to the duelling ground with 'is seconds, Miss. Lieutenant Manning and Lieutenant Godfrey, I believe. Their job is to make sure everything is done according to the rules.'

'Rules?' Isobel looked bewildered.

'The Major 'as the choice of weapons, which gives 'im the advantage, Miss,' counselled James, trying to calm her. 'And 'e is a very good marksman.'

Her mind a storm of thoughts, Isobel thanked them again for their care and hastened to her room. On the stairs she hesitated. Even if he had thought to spare her feelings, Isobel could hardly believe her father had kept this secret from her. Should she go to the study right now and confront him? But she knew him better than that. She might well be his favourite daughter but she was in no doubt that none of her tears or pleading would change his mind. He would either be furious at her interference or deflect her concerns with hollow reassurances. Once her father set his mind on a course, nothing and no one could dissuade him.

She did not share James's confidence in her father's chances of survival. He was now sixty-two, and his exertions as a public servant and an explorer had taken a heavy toll on his nerves. Then there was the gout and arthritis in both his legs, and his eyesight had deteriorated so that he often wore glasses in private. She knew he would be too proud to wear glasses to a duel.

A duel? For a moment she wondered if a fever had afflicted Papa's brain. Or was there something else at stake, something shameful and secret that drove him to such a desperate course? In the quiet of her room, Isobel tried to calm herself. There was no point in speculating about the whys and wherefores. Her choice was plain. She had to stop this duel or her father would die.

Who could she approach for help? If the servants knew about her father's plans it was possible—even likely—that everyone did. Most galling of all, if Grace and Anna knew, why had they said nothing? She hoped their silence was a sign of ignorance and not complicity. Or, even worse, indifference. 'It is not our place to tell Father how to conduct himself,' she could hear Grace lecturing her. Isobel did not trust either of them to be any use.

What about her father's friends—Dr Finch, Judge Dickerson, Captain Bradley? On this moonlit night, she could walk over to one of their houses in under an hour if needed. But she knew her father would never forgive her for raising the alarm in this way. And who knows, they might already know all about the matter and had refused to meddle in the Major's private affairs. They may even approve of his decision to defend his honour. She had learned that grown-ups always behaved unpredictably, men most of all.

Where else could she seek guidance? She had not seen her estranged brother Joseph in two years and did not even know where to find him. Her eldest brother William would know what to do in such circumstances. He always did. But there was not enough time to warn him. Even so, she penned a short note for Sarah to take to the post office first thing in the morning.

Dear W—

Tonight I have discover'd that our father has lost his mind. He is to fight a Duel with his French pistols tomorrow morning and I am firmly convinc'd he will be killed at the hand of that arrogant lout Mr Simon Davidson if nothing is done to stop him. Papa is no longer the man he once was. Richard and Mama's deaths have undone him. I wish I had learn'd of this Duel earlier as I am sure Father would listen to you. So it is left up to me alone to save him. Desperate times justify desperate measures. You know I am not foolhardy but if any dire Fate should befall me in this venture, I beg you to please forgive me and pray for my wicked soul.

Your affectionate & obedient servant,
  Isobel

Was God watching over this little drama tonight through his heavenly peephole? Would He give her any sign of His providence apart from the urgent whisperings of her own heart? Not since her mother's death had Isobel felt so alone and fearful. She could not shake her conviction that her father would be killed at seven o'clock tomorrow morning if nothing was done to save him.

Isobel knew her father was regarded in some quarters as an impulsive, ill-tempered and arrogant man, the object of both common gossip and official opprobrium. She feared that it was possible, even likely, his political enemies would make use of this duel to harm him; that his reputation would now be permanently stained whether he lived or died; that her own prospects would be damaged if not ruined; and that her family's name would be so traduced that they would pay for this shameful episode for generations. She had to act whatever the cost.

All these reasons outweighed her fear of danger and social disgrace. And there was one other reason she would risk everything to save her father.

She loved him.

Chapter 2

TIME TO GO

There it was, his tread in the corridor as her father passed by her door. Isobel assumed he carried his precious pistols in their velvet-lined case, tucked under his arm. She did not know anything about duels. Would Papa put on his dress uniform as he did for public ceremonies? He cut such a striking figure with those magnificent martial side-whiskers of his and the lavish trimmings of his great-coat with its tasselled epaulettes and campaign medals pinned to his left breast. She loved seeing him dressed up so splendidly.

Behind her door, Isobel had almost completed her own trans-formation into a man. Her hair was pinned up beneath her brother's hat. It had taken three thicknesses of stocking for her slender ankles and small feet to fill out his boots. Thanks to William's slight build and similar height, she had no trouble concealing her womanly silhouette within his trousers and shirt. His cord jacket completed the deceit. But there was no room under these clothes for a corset or the usual layers of feminine undergarment and the lack of crinolines and multiple petticoats was—well, there was simply no other word for it—*exhilarating*. Her body moved differently, even oddly at first, and then with an unaccustomed sense of freedom. She loved the feel of cotton and moleskin against her bare flesh. The sensation scared and delighted her. She was so *wicked*! Surely she would be punished for this sinfulness, and prayed for God to forgive her such unnatural feelings.

Isobel had heard the salacious rumours years ago about the French aristocrat and navigator Louis de Freycinet. It was said that he had disguised his young wife Rose as a man for his voyage of exploration aboard the vessel *L'Uranie*. She had even dined with the Governor of Gibraltar dressed in a blue frock coat and matching trousers! The French authorities, unable to act at a distance, finally chose to overlook this breach of naval law when the expedition returned home. It seemed to Isobel so very French to break rules for the sake of romantic love. Would a British navigator do such a thing? She did not think so.

Isobel examined her new male guise in the mirror. Would she pass for a man as Rose had? Before her stood a slim, awkward youth with delicate hands. Dear me, what would her sisters say? She could not help smiling to imagine their comic expressions of disbelief. How on earth could she smile when her heart was gripped with terror?

It was time to go. Closing her bedroom door gently, she tiptoed past Grace and Anna's bedrooms. She looked over the staircase railing but did not see or hear anyone in the saloon below. It would be embarrassing to say the least if she ran into one of the staff.

Above her, the rising sun shot rays of rose and amber through the skylight in Rosemount's elliptical dome, the house's crowning glory. Beneath this dome was the house's other architectural centrepiece, the staircase. Mirroring the ellipse of the dome, it curved in on itself like the inside of a seashell. Its broad mudstone steps and iron banisters made the descent perfectly safe, but Isobel always felt a twinge of vertigo at the top, and today was no exception. The drop to the saloon floor was over sixty feet and the staircase created its own centripetal force, hurtling you forward faster and faster, like a drop of oil spiralling down a funnel. This was fun when you were a child. It was a different matter in a ball gown that hid your feet, or in a pair of your brother's riding boots.

Isobel reached the bottom without incident and snuck across the saloon, still half in shadow. What was that? She could hear voices in the breakfast room opposite. She froze. Had her father stopped for something to eat? Was he in there now taking his soft-boiled eggs and kippers? Surely not. Her pulse raced at the thought of him discovering her dressed like this. But the voices were women's, the parlourmaid Sarah and Mrs Bedford, the housekeeper.

Isobel crept to the back door. There was not a soul about so she crossed the courtyard at the rear of the house as fast as she could. And there, waiting for her by the service wing, was James with two horses, bridled and saddled, ready to ride, just as she had asked.

'I'm so sorry, Miss, but all the ladies' saddles are being repaired,' James informed Isobel as she approached. 'Have you ever ridden astride before?'

Two years ago her brother William had forgotten to collect Isobel and her mother in the gig from Appin rail station. They had been forced to borrow two horses and ride to the family farm on gentlemen's saddles. It had been an exciting and unforgettable experience and one they had kept as a secret between themselves. 'Yes, yes, I have. Once.'

'Well, at least you're dressed for it.' James tried to suppress the subversive grin that threatened to break out across his face at the sight of Miss Macleod in her brother's clothes. Isobel could not blame him. She wished her dressing up was just a childish game to be enjoyed and made light of rather than a desperate resort to spare her father's life. She dismissed the suspicion that James was fibbing about the ladies' saddles as a last-minute ploy to spoil her plans.

'I will be fine, thank you, James.'

Far from being a game, Isobel knew that dressing up as the opposite sex was a breach of the law. Less than a month ago she had read in Papa's copy of *Bell's Life* about the arrest of a sailor off *HMS Pandora* for the criminal offence of 'appearing in female apparel' near Church Hill. The man had fought off the arresting constable and then ran into St Philip's Church nearby to harangue the congregation! It took six constables to finally take him down to the police watch house on Cumberland Street where a large angry mob, outraged at this injustice, had gathered and beaten the police with bludgeons and fence palings. What a city, thought

Isobel. Sodom under the Southern Cross. Was London such a pit of depravity and lawlessness?

Isobel approached her lovely chestnut mare. She had ridden April many times and was familiar with her temperament. The mare seemed to study Isobel curiously as she climbed into the saddle but did not shy away. 'There, there, good girl,' Isobel crooned.

Isobel was a good rider. With her right leg hooked over the high pommel of a lady's side-saddle, she knew the correct way to sit squarely across April's back and keep the reins even so as not to unbalance her horse's muscles. But this! This straddling, with both feet in the stirrups and her knees and thighs gripping April's flanks, this felt so different. The flesh-and-blood engine of her horse thrummed through her body as she had never experienced before. She was in control of April in a manner not normally conceivable as a lady rider.

James mounted the piebald gelding and they cantered out together along Rosemount's grand carriageway. The crenellated roof of the stables could be seen in the distance, obscured behind a grove of oaks. Isobel looked back. A flock of roseate clouds loomed over the harbour and the façade of the great house was painted gold by the rising sun.

Rosemount's estate had been carefully planned so that when visitors approached it from the front gates they passed through a landscape of tall trees and boulders that blocked views of the water. The carriageway then turned sharply out of these woods to reveal the full panorama of house, gardens and harbour in one moment of epiphany. The visitor beheld a white mansion facing the sea as starkly beautiful as an Apollonian temple on a clifftop above the

Aegean. From the ridgeline down to the beach, the estate was a wedge of startling emerald green, flanked by olive-grey eucalypt forest and pale sandy scrub on either side.

Isobel felt the sting of tears in her eyes. This place had been her home since she was ten and yet she never tired of its beauty. But today the act of looking back had its own peculiar poignancy. Would her father ever lay eyes on Rosemount again? Would *she*? She could not decide if this glorious vision of her home bathed in fire was an apocalypse or a beacon of hope.

'Come on, girl, no time to waste,' she whispered in April's ear as she leaned into her neck and, with a sharp prodding of heels, goaded the mare into a gallop up the last stretch of driveway before they melted into the blue shadows of the forest with James close behind.

Chapter 3

LACHLAN SWAMPS

The sun was now well above the horizon as James and Isobel cantered along the Old South Head Road, their shadows close beside them. Between the trees, Isobel caught glimpses of the harbour, sparkling silver in the morning light, and heard flocks of parrots explode into the sky with their noisy hosannas.

Though the muscles of Isobel's thighs and knees ached with the uncommon exertion, she barely noticed, so elated was she by the sensation of freedom in the saddle. For minutes at a time she forgot her fear, lost in the rhythm of riding and the rush of wind in her face. But then she would suddenly be filled again with dread and sorrow, her heart galloping inside her chest and her mouth dry from surges of panic at the thought that she would arrive just in time to hear the fatal shot.

'Over there!' shouted James, pointing to where some twenty or so horses were tied up beneath a clump of paperbarks. Further up the road they could see at least a dozen cabs parked on the turf with their drivers standing in a circle, smoking. Isobel was outraged.

'It seems like half of Sydney has turned out for this show!' she cried, choking back tears.

They rode in under the trees about thirty yards down the road from this gathering.

'You can go back now, James,' said Isobel. 'I don't want to get you into trouble.'

'With all respect, Miss, I think it's a bit late for that,' grinned James. 'It is just as well I am leaving for the goldfields in a few weeks and will not need your father's reference. I've come this far. I'm not leaving you alone now.'

Isobel did not have the heart to argue. She nodded her assent as they dismounted, tethering the horses out of sight, and made their way into the bush.

Lachlan Swamps formed part of a large low-lying marshland with a chain of freshwater ponds, close to Sydney Town. With the Tank Stream now too polluted and small to adequately supply Sydney with clean water, Governor Darling had commissioned an engineer, Mr Busby, to superintend the digging of a bore from the swamps to Hyde Park to feed the town's water carts.

The ground sloped away sharply from the road, thickly wooded with paperbarks and tea-tree with a profuse undergrowth of swamp grasses, bracken and palms. James went ahead, scrambling down the slope, and began to clear a path as best he could. In her usual female garb Isobel would have made slow progress, but in trousers and boots she easily managed to keep up. They soon found a winding narrow track through the undergrowth but the ground grew soft underfoot as they advanced. In places it was impassable, flooded by stretches of dark tea-coloured water, and they were forced to turn back. Flashes of sunlight winked as they passed under the forest's canopy that arched over them like a vaulted cathedral ceiling. Isobel's nostrils were filled with the tang of tannin, mulch and decay.

Away to their left they heard men's voices and spied a party of six moving through the trees in single file. It was obvious these men had found a sturdier track heading towards the duelling ground. Isobel and James changed course to follow them. The track came out into a grove of old paperbarks, their soft bark flaking away like dead skin. The thick liver-spotted trunks leaned drunkenly at all angles, tethered only by twisted roots in a flat sheet of swamp water stretching as far as the eye could see. In this unruffled silver-green mirror, amid islands of waterlilies, a second identical forest hung upside down. The place struck Isobel as eerie, almost holy, with the occasional screams of waterfowl and their panicked flurry of wings breaking the deep silence.

Then they both heard a murmuring of voices ahead. Through the congregation of ancient trees, Isobel spotted a group of men moving about on higher ground. She saw Dr Finch first, smoking a cheroot, laughing and talking with the seconds, Lieutenants Manning and Godfrey. She presumed the good doctor was present in his capacity as surgeon. Isobel was astounded. To think she had dined with him only the night before and he had not said a word about this morning's fateful event. There were about a dozen other men milling about in frock coats and high hats, chatting amiably. A manservant had set up a camp stove and was serving cups of coffee. This hardly seemed the setting for a deadly contest; it had the pleasant, unhurried air of a country race meeting.

And then Isobel saw the two men at the centre of the drama. Mr Davidson sported a black Prince Albert hat, dark blue jacket and gold quilted waistcoat. He wore his hair long touching his collar and smoked a cigar. Such a dandy! She sneered at his vulgarity. Her father was dressed in his finest green frock coat, mustard waistcoat and favourite brown felt bell-topper. He stood alone, his face unnaturally white. To Isobel, he had aged a hundred years.

Crouched behind one of the paperbarks with James, Isobel gradually became aware that the entire grove had now filled with onlookers. 'What's that?' she whispered, motioning towards a knot of men to their right who appeared to be exchanging handfuls of silver and notes.

James's face flushed red. 'I'm afraid they're laying bets, Miss.' Isobel stared in horror. How could men be such monsters?

She looked back at the duelling ground. Up on the hill there had been a sudden shift in the temper of the scene. The milling crowd of men had split into two groups who now stood in silence watching the main actors.

Her father, the challenger, and his enemy, the respondent, stood back to back. Isobel saw the seconds each holding one of her father's French pistols. In a stiff clockwork manner they approached each other, swapped the pistols over and closely inspected each other's weapon. Satisfied that both pistols were properly primed and cocked, the seconds handed them to the duellists.

'Are you ready, gentlemen?' a voice commanded. The two men, still standing back to back, nodded. 'Very well then, on my signal.'

'It has begun,' James exhorted his mistress in an urgent whisper.

Now, now, now. It was time for Isobel to act, to put a stop to this obscene farce, to save her father's life. But she could not move. She was stuck inside a whirlwind of pure terror.

Chapter 4

THE SECOND SHOT

Isobel heard the first shot ring out through the paperbark grove. Only then did she realise that she had closed her eyes. A return shot followed. She opened her eyes again to see her father and Mr Davidson standing some twenty paces apart. There was a sharp burning smell in the air. The pistols hung limply by their sides.

'Two misses,' shouted the same voice that had opened this deadly drama.

Here was Isobel's opportunity. Her plan from the start had been to shame her father and all these men into abandoning their horrible ritual. She had managed to come this far disguised in male clothing but now she would reveal herself. Flinging aside her brother's hat, her beribboned hair would be unveiled as she dashed up the hill. 'Stop, stop this at once!' she would scream at the top of her lungs, running to embrace her father.

She had played out this scene in her head many times. It would require great courage, she made no bones about that. But she hoped that at the critical moment the heat of her anger would melt away any scruples or fear and impel her forward with the force of a steam locomotive. Isobel understood, perhaps for the first time in her life, how her father's righteous temper empowered him to take on all the fools of the world.

But she had underestimated the power of her *fear*. It was simple enough to rehearse acts of courage in your thoughts. But when it finally came to the deed itself, that was a different matter. What held her back? Shame. Shame that blazed inside her like a bonfire. Oh, how utterly wretched it was to be a weak, defenceless woman, valued only for her ornamental education and not her convictions! Tears of impotent rage burned in her eyes.

The men on the hill had reloaded the pistols and now checked them as before. 'What do you want to do?' whispered James urgently. Ever since his elevation to the position of stable boy at one of the grand houses on Woolloomooloo Hill, James had taken a practical interest in the sports of his gentlemen superiors: fox-hunting, trout fishing, kangaroo shooting, even the twenty-five rules of the Irish Code Duello. James had explained to Isobel that if a dispute about which party had given first offence could not be resolved by the seconds then the matter must proceed to two shots, or to a hit, if the challenger required it. He suspected the Major, as the challenger, had insisted on a second shot, and possibly even a hit to conclude the matter with honour. Once the battle was joined, neither man could honourably walk away without firing his weapon. In a pistol duel, 'dumb shooting'—or firing in the air—was strictly prohibited.

'If no apologies are offered,' James had explained, 'then any wound that agitates the nerves and makes the hand shake must end the duel for that day.'

What utter foolishness this all seemed to Isobel. Was it possible that women would resort to such nonsense if they had the choice? She hoped not. Women expressed their public displeasure with the slightest arch of an eyebrow or blush of a cheek. Or they communicated through a coded language of folding or unfolding fans, or the strategic placement of their cutlery at dinner parties. Then there were the elaborate rules that governed the endless rounds of visiting, leaving one's card and being 'at home' or 'not at home'. Women's business was not conducted on the field of combat but at the card or tea table, in the sitting room and drawing room. Isobel could not imagine women ever taking up pistols and swords to settle their differences.

'At your pleasure, gentlemen,' announced the voice, inviting them to take their second shot at their own discretion. The reloaded pistols had been returned to the duellists. Isobel saw her father's face, as grave and deathly white as the profile of a marble statue. Who would fire first? If the Major missed then he must stand and receive the second shot from his opponent. The same went for Mr Davidson, who no longer looked so cocky. His face ran with sweat and he hunched his shoulders as if he might pull his head inside his collar like a tortoise. The scene would be comic if it was not so deadly serious.

Both men raised their arms and took aim. 'You are a rascal and a blackguard, sir!' the Major barked at his opponent.

'And you are a bully and a fraud!' shouted the other, his voice squeaking like an off-pitch violin.

Isobel could see the tremors that passed through the bodies of the two men like galvanic shocks, their legs and arms shaking as if palsied. This spectacle was unbearable to watch: Isobel's proud father reduced to quivering humiliation. She felt her blood begin to stir. To think that Papa was willing to face death, to place his own honour above the welfare and love of his family! How could she ever forgive him?

And that was the spark that lit the wick of her rage. Before James had time to say anything more, Isobel broke cover from the paperbark grove and charged up the hill. Her brother's hat flew off without any assistance from her and she felt the morning air cool on her scalp. The next few seconds were a blur. Voices shouted distantly like the sound of surf pounding on a beach. Her own ears were deafened by the crashing tide of her pulse. The trees, the sky and the absurd tableau of her father and his friends and enemies standing in a swamp were smeared across her vision as she hurtled onto the duelling ground.

At the last moment she saw her father's face tilted towards her, his eyes wide with shock. Did he know it was *her*, his favourite daughter, Isobel? The pistols both exploded, the roar and stink of the gunpowder overwhelming at such close range. Isobel saw her father's head snap back, his bell-topper falling to the ground as his body reeled and crumpled, a jet of blood springing from his throat.

Mr Davidson too was wounded, the shot grazing his skull and puncturing his hat. But Isobel saw nothing but the body of her father on the ground. The scream from her own throat sounded like nothing she had ever heard before, a cry of such pain it was enough to sunder her whole world in two.

ISOBEL

1838 TO 1849

Chapter 5

A BIRTHDAY PICNIC

JANUARY 1847

The day before Isobel turned thirteen, her mother's gift to her was a precious hour or two ('Just you and me, my sweet') enjoying a picnic in Rosemount's gardens. The Major was away in England again, this time to oversee the sea trials of his new 'boomerang' screw and lobby the Colonial Office for more pay. Despite Papa's promise to bring her a present from London as compensation for his absence, Isobel was disappointed, and she knew this picnic was her mother's way of assuaging her feelings.

It was perfect picnic weather, a hot summer's afternoon without a scrap of cloud in the boundless cerulean. With her brothers and sisters otherwise occupied, Isobel had her mother's undivided attention, a rare treat. The servants had laid out the rugs and hamper in the shade of Rosemount's grotto: rhubarb pies, macaroons, cream puffs, lemon-cheese tarts, sandwiches and, as a birthday surprise,

Isobel's favourite—lollipops. The cool alcove was the family's favourite refuge from the summer heat and provided a royal box view of the harbour with its leisurely parade of yachts, luggers, cargo ships and paddle-steamers. The grotto took advantage of a natural sandstone overhang at the water's edge, with its seats and ceiling artfully carved by the architect Mr Verge's masons. Over the brilliant jade waters of Elizabeth Bay, the two low-slung green islets Clark and Shark lay permanently at anchor in the middle distance, with North and South Head, majestic gateway to Port Jackson, framing the ocean beyond.

Neither Isobel nor her mother spoke for a while, absorbed in the loveliness of the scene. Isobel had her journal open on her lap and was making a sketch in pencil and watercolour of the bay and its traffic. They both listened to the harbour music: the screech of gulls overhead, the liquid slap of water against hull and pier, the ripple and snap of bellying canvas in the breeze, and the panting churn of the paddle-steamers.

Isobel broke their silence. 'Can I ask you something, Mama?'

'What is it, my darling?'

'I hope I am not prying but . . . why does Papa look so unhappy all the time?'

'Why, my dear . . .' Winnie was taken aback. She turned and studied her daughter's expression of sweet earnestness. On reflection, she realised she should not be so surprised by this question. In the last few months the Major's usual buoyant confidence seemed to be foundering. Of late, Isobel had encountered her father as he returned home from his offices on Macquarie Street, his face dark with despair. At dinner he would say little and drink too much, hurrying away to avoid the affectionate attentions of his family. On other occasions, friends and colleagues came rushing through the front hall, shoulders hunched, eyes averted, scurrying to the Major's study for what were evidently secret and weighty discussions. More than once Isobel heard voices behind that door raised in anger, her father's as clear and resonant as a bell.

Like any dutiful daughter, Isobel took a gratified interest in her father's accolades, basking in his reflected glory. He was always on the list of important guests for the Governor's grand levee held every year on the Queen's birthday. Winnie happily read aloud the plaudits in the Sydney papers and the *Government Gazette* to the enthusiastic applause of her children. In this way, Isobel formed a fragmentary understanding of Papa's public life. The male sphere of civic duty and achievement was closed to women, of course, and its secret business jealously guarded. Lately this had struck Isobel as unfair as the consequences of her father's troubles in that distant male world weighed heavily on his wife and children.

Isobel studied her mother's face in turn and could read her thoughts: was her daughter old enough to know the secrets of adult life? Isobel prayed to have that door pushed open, even if just a little. She was sick of being kept in the dark, of having to guess at what fears consumed her parents' minds. Like most children, she erred on the side of blaming herself for whatever upset them. In three years' time she would be ready to formally come out into society. Surely she was now old enough to start learning the ways of the world.

Winnie placed her glass of lavender lemonade on the stone seat and brushed macaroon crumbs from her lap. She had made up her mind. It was time to tell Isobel something of her father's troubles, and Winnie's own. What was the point of hiding the truth from her children forever?

'Are you sure you really want to know, my love?' she asked gently. Isobel nodded solemnly. 'Very well.' The story started with great promise. 'When your father took on the position of Surveyor-General all those years ago, the responsibility weighed heavily on him,' said Winnie. 'In his view, the prosperity of the whole colony lay in his hands.'

Her mother explained why. Not only was the Major expected to survey all the land grants that had been issued by the Governor (for which purpose he must prepare an accurate survey of the entire colony of New South Wales) but he was also responsible for the surveying and building of all roads and bridges. In a colony that was rapidly growing, both tasks were a huge undertaking that required urgent attention.

'And all this was to be done with a team of only sixteen men!' Winnie exclaimed incredulously. 'So your father had to do a lot of the surveying himself. For weeks at a time he camped out in the harshest of bushland and the most rugged of mountains. Against all odds, he and his men completed the map of the Nineteen Counties in only seven years.'

Already, Isobel was surprised at how little she actually knew of her father's life. This explanation accounted for her papa's long absences ever since Isobel had been a small child. She blushed to think how she could have spent all her young days in such blissful ignorance of what put supper on her table and clothes on her back.

Winnie's eyes sparkled with pride. The truth was the Major had an indefatigable passion for his work and, little by little, had grown to love the countryside that he mapped. The other compensation was that the Major's work came with handsome rewards. In a fit of magnanimity, Governor Darling decided to award members of his administration, including Major Macleod, generous grants of land on the peninsula east of Sydney Cove known as Woolloomooloo Hill and sometimes Woolloomooloo Heights. With a sweep of her hand, Winnie indicated the familiar craggy foreshore and vast bowl of silver water beyond—the world of Isobel's childhood. Unlike her explorer father, this dusty city and its luminous harbour was the full extent of the Australia that Isobel Macleod knew. Winnie narrowed her eyes a little as if trying to re-imagine the Hill as it had once been. 'Back then, this place didn't have much to recommend it. Except for its harbour views, and the windmills along the ridge that ground Sydney's daily bread.'

With its sandy soil and scrubby vegetation, Woolloomooloo Hill had largely been dismissed as 'sterile', prone to fierce outbreaks of fire and home to nothing but multitudes of snakes. The rough road from Sydney Town followed a native walking track through steep sand dunes that proved treacherous for wagons and carriages. Undaunted, Governor Darling conceived a 'vision splendid' for this sandstone promontory: an island of wealth and privilege for the colonial elite that would be, in his words, 'an example and chastisement to the debased populace of Sydney Town'.

'This was to be Governor Darling's great legacy,' explained Winnie. 'He required that each landowner build a villa within three years and at a cost of no less than a thousand pounds. Oh, and the villa had to face his Government House. Like a Mohammedan facing Mecca!' Winnie laughed, shaking her head at such hubris.

Folly or not, Darling's audacious 'vision splendid' soon became a reality. The windmills stayed but the ridge was renamed Darlinghurst Heights by the proud Governor. Within three short years, a manmade paradise had materialised on this barren stretch of sand and rock. Stately villas encircled by leafy gardens and broad carriageways transformed a wasteland into a cool, green idyll floating above the heat and filth of Sydney. Darling's second-in-command, Colonial Secretary Mr Alexander Macleay, was granted by far the largest lot, fifty-four acres around Elizabeth Bay. The Sydney papers were outraged at this shameless nepotism.

'We were given ten acres of land where your father built our first home, Grangemouth. That was before we moved here when you were ten.'

Isobel remembered that day very well; she had hated leaving her old home but soon realised she had been admitted to a paradise full of beautiful secrets. ('Oh my, we have our own forest!' she had exclaimed as she roamed the estate.) From the grotto, she looked back up the sloping lawn to the brilliant white splendour of Rosemount Hall itself. The estate was thickly wooded with eucalypts and casuarinas and, from the front gates, the coach road passed through low scrubland. Down here by the water, the cliffs and boulders showed the dry, ancient bones of the land. Isobel still struggled to imagine this peninsula stripped back to empty bushland, bare of all its villas and estates. These lush gardens and grand houses were the world she had been born into, as familiar and cherished as her parents' faces.

While Papa was often away, Isobel had some idea how hard he worked. But she knew very well how hard her mother worked. It had been left to Winnie to manage Grangemouth and raise her seven children while the Major made his name and fortune. She also served on the Ladies' Charity Committee of the Female School of Industry, whose patron was the Governor's wife. Unlike Major Macleod, she received no public accolades for these labours.

'Life had more challenges in store. Governor Darling turned out to be a meddler and a penny pincher. Worst of all, he questioned your father's judgement.' Winnie's face grew stern. Isobel felt that swooping lurch of foreboding in her stomach. This could not end well.

'One of your father's chief projects was looking after the road over the Blue Mountains, the main road west. He soon discovered there was a much safer way for carriages to descend the western slope than Mr Cox's original road. So he decided to pull the chain gangs off repairing that road and put them to work on his new route, which he named Victoria Pass. When he found out, the Governor refused to authorise the change of plan.' Winnie winced. It was plain that such memories pained her. 'Your father went over the Governor's head and wrote directly to the Colonial Office in London. Governor Darling was furious. He tried to have your father removed from office.'

'So what happened?'

'Fortunately, Darling's term as Governor was terminated and he was recalled to England. Your father was saved.'

Isobel was wide-eyed with amazement. She had not known any of this.

Winnie sighed. 'But that was just the beginning. The Major has now served under four different governors. And they have all, at one time or another, interfered in his work. They have even meddled in his expeditions, which have opened up thousands of acres of fertile land. Such is their gratitude for years of service.'

'Poor Papa.' Isobel shook her head in dismay. 'It sounds as if he has been treated very badly.'

'Yes, he has, my sweet. And now there is talk of yet another official inquiry into the conduct of his department. It seems the past never goes away. We are shackled to it like the wretched convict to his leg irons.' Winnie's face grew still and solemn. Her voice cracked as she spoke. 'That, my dear Isobel, is why your father looks so unhappy.'

Isobel may have been only thirteen and confined to the narrow world of domestic life at Rosemount, but she had been privy at times to what people thought of her father. That he did not suffer fools gladly. That he treated some of his staff arrogantly and unfairly. That he picked fights with his superiors and became involved in bitter, long-running public quarrels. That he was aloof, prickly, difficult. Isobel herself had witnessed only a few displays of his famous volcanic temper: a book tossed in anger, a voice raised in a moment of frustration. It seemed that at least Papa showed great forbearance with his own family if not the rest of the world.

'But enough of this gloomy talk,' said Winnie, producing two lollipops wrapped in bright paper from the picnic hamper. 'Your father is so immensely proud of his children and that makes him very happy. And tomorrow is your birthday, a day for celebration! I know he will be thinking of you.'

Isobel smiled. Strangely, this tale of woe had lifted her spirits. She felt fortunate to have such a father; there was nothing that daunted him, nothing that he refused to face with resolution and courage. For now, at least, she was grateful to still be a young woman safe in the bosom of her family, though lately she had sometimes felt the spur of boredom and impatience to step onto a wider stage. And, reluctant as she was to admit it, she was also relieved that father's moodiness had nothing to do with her. She had a horror of disappointing or upsetting him. It was the price she paid for being his favourite daughter.

Winnie asked to look at Isobel's harbour painting. With flecks of cream, chestnut and mustard yellow against a marbled wash of cobalt and aqua, the paper had mysteriously absorbed the restless caper of sunlight and shadow, the invisible heft of wind and wave that animated the harbour view before them. 'Oh my, you are so clever, my sweet. You have captured it perfectly!' cried Winnie.

Winnie was in no doubt that Isobel had inherited her father's artistic eye and aptitude. Angus was widely praised for his draughts-manship, not just his maps but also his sketches and watercolours. Winnie touched her daughter lightly on the hand. Her face was bright with gladness as she raised her glass of lavender lemonade. 'A toast! To my clever youngest daughter—may your future bring you all the happiness you deserve, Isobel, my love!'

'Thank you, Mama,' said Isobel, fighting a bittersweet urge to cry for joy. How fragile this moment of closeness seemed, so precious and so fleeting. Was that why her heart was so full, why tears pricked at her eyes? Looking back, Isobel wondered if, at that very moment, she had been given a glimpse of how it would all end. Was that even possible?

She hugged her mother tightly. How honoured she was to be trusted with her parents' trials and sorrows. Did any of her sisters know of these things? She looked on this new knowledge not as a burden but a gift. The gift of respect. It was the best gift a mother could give a daughter on the threshold of womanhood.

A fresh breeze sprang up off the harbour and fanned them both. Isobel took one of the lollipops and unwrapped it. It was cherry, her favourite. 'Even so, I still feel sorry for Papa,' she said, her final word on the matter before popping the birthday treat in her mouth.

Winnie kissed her on the brow. 'I know, my sweetness. He is a good man and should not have to bear such troubles. But we must not question God's wisdom in such matters. We are a family that is blessed in many ways.'

Isobel nodded. She understood the bounty of God's gifts. She smiled up at her mama, thankful for this cherished time together.

Her mother smiled back. 'Just be grateful, my dear,' she said, 'that you were not born a man.'

Chapter 6

GRANGEMOUTH

DECEMBER 1838

When it was finished, Rosemount Hall had been universally praised as the finest house in the colony. It had taken four years to build and cost its owner, the Colonial Secretary, Mr Macleay, a fortune, rumoured to be in excess of six thousand pounds. The funds had run dry before the Doric colonnade (envisioned by the architect, Mr Verge, to wrap around three-quarters of the house) could be built, leaving his Greek Revival 'temple' even more austere than planned.

With equally little thought for the capacity of his purse, Mr Macleay had also laid out a lavish design for his fifty-four acres. This included an extensive botanic garden stocked with exotics from every corner of the Empire, a forest, a vineyard, orchards and kitchen garden, and several follies including a maze, a Linnean spiral, two grottoes, and a series of ponds and waterfalls spanned by stone bridges. His money was all gone before completing the

Roman bathhouse on the foreshores of Elizabeth Bay. While most of the newspapers sneered at such hubris and excess, the *Sydney Gazette* had praised Mr Macleay for bringing order to the wilderness, showing *'how those hillocks of rock and sand might be rendered tributary to the taste and advantage of civilized man.'*

The house was almost an afterthought. Mr John Verge was engaged and soon became the architect of choice on Woolloomooloo Hill, designing villas and lodges for several wealthy clients. But Rosemount remained his masterpiece, even with its missing colonnade. Admired for its gleaming white façade, its elegant Regency proportions and unique elliptical dome and staircase, Rosemount Hall was the envy of every rich man in Sydney.

That included, of course, Major Angus Macleod, who rode past the estate's front gates every morning on his way to the Surveyor-General's office on Macquarie Street. The Colonial Secretary may have come by his piece of land through barefaced favouritism, but the Major had to agree that the house and its gardens reflected Mr Macleay's good taste and broad intellect. Little did the Major suspect that one day, thanks to the inexplicable twists and turns of fate, his admiring covetousness of Rosemount Hall would be richly rewarded.

Out of his habitual curiosity and stubbornness, Isobel's father had designed their family home all by himself, with some help from an architect's pattern book. The result was Grangemouth, a two-storey Italianate mansion featuring a grand ballroom and an imposing portico of Ionic columns in imitation of the Parthenon that earned the house its soubriquet of 'the Acropolis of Sydney'. There was no doubt it was worthy of Governor Darling's 'vision splendid' and the other impressive villas that appeared on Woolloomooloo Hill such as Goderich Lodge, Waratah House, Tusculum and Roslyn Hall.

For fourteen years this house served its purpose as a testament to the Major's wealth and status as well as a comfortable retreat for his family. It was here that Isobel was born in 1834, the youngest of Angus and Winnie's swelling brood. Winnie had endured the deaths of four babies in childbirth and the loss of a daughter, Margaret, as an infant; while Margaret's portrait hung in the morning room, her death and those of the four little ones were rarely, if ever, spoken of. Isobel was to be Winnie's last gift of a child to her husband.

It had taken Winnie the best part of two years to settle into her new life on the far side of the globe. She suffered terribly from homesickness and hated everything about Sydney. The dreadful heat and scorching winds. The clouds of mosquitos and flies. The extortionate prices. The venal convict servants who were invariably rude and lazy and stole the silver plate right out from under their noses. But worst of all was the suffocatingly tedious company of the Sydney society ladies, who talked of nothing but money and fashion. Eventually, the Major and his wife found kindred spirits among the more recent arrivals and became known for their excellent dinner parties and dances at Grangemouth.

For Isobel and her siblings, life was carefree. After their classes with the governess and the tutor, their days were filled with games and small adventures on the rolling sward in front of the house or among the trees along the coach loop. After lunch, Richard, William and Joseph would spin tops under the portico or play tag, Tom Tiddler's Ground and cricket on the green. Alice, Grace,

Anna and little Isobel took turns on the wooden swings hung from the tallowwoods or mucked around with mallets and hoops on the croquet lawn.

'Papa is holding an afternoon tea and a supper party tomorrow to celebrate his return,' Grace told the others during one such game. Their father had been absent for many months on an expedition, his third, into the uncharted hinterland of the colony. While they were not privy to all the details, the family were under no delusions about the dangers of exploring such savage country. They were always grateful to have Papa safely home again.

'He's inviting the Finches and Bradleys,' announced Grace. 'And Mrs Palmer is coming too!' She tapped her wooden ball lightly but it overshot and clanged on the outside of the iron hoop.

The news of the impending party was music to Isobel's sisters' ears. Nothing pleased the Macleod girls more than a lazy Sunday afternoon after church with Emily, Florence and Beatrice Finch and the Bradley girls, Emma, Hannah and Alexandra. If the day was cool, they would play battledore and shuttlecock or quoits out on the grass, or, if the sun was hot, hold tea parties with egg sandwiches and wedges of cake in the shade of the peppermint willow. And there was always tadpole and butterfly hunting down at the ponds or simply playing fetch with Livy, Tacitus, Dante and Petrarch, the Macleods' cocker spaniels.

Mrs Palmer was a most welcome guest too. She was the family's oldest friend. Widowed and childless, she had become very fond of the Macleod children and rarely visited without some homemade token of her affection. With no grandmothers to coddle them (they were both back in Scotland), the children looked on Mrs Palmer as a much-loved substitute.

'I hope we have dances after supper!' said Alice. At age fourteen, she was the eldest daughter and the undisputed beauty of the family ('Must be a changeling,' joked the Major, squinting self-critically in the mirror). She was beginning to take an interest in the male of the species and already had her eye out for a young gentleman of means. She insisted that he must also be of sterling stock (British born); her prejudice against currency gents, no matter how well-heeled, grieved the hearts of young native-born men in general and Aloysius, Dr Finch's eldest boy, in particular. She saw no future with such gentlemen—not a future she wanted to be a part of, anyway. Her destiny lay back in England.

While she still loved her sisters dearly, their childish world of dollhouses and tea sets, flower-pressing and decoupage, had begun to lose its appeal for grown-up Alice.

'Are you going to be cruel and haughty again with poor Aloysius?' teased Grace, adding insult to injury by knocking Alice's croquet ball sideways. 'You can't turn him down for *every* dance!'

Alice pretended to be outraged. 'I am never cruel, as you well know. I have made my feelings for him very clear. I have none.'

She swung her mallet. Clack! Grace's ball went spinning off towards the edge of the lawn while Alice's sailed through the next hoop. Anna and Isobel giggled.

'Upsy-daisy!' cried four-year-old Isobel, clapping her hands. 'My turn!'

'You know the mallet is too heavy for you!' admonished Alice. But Isobel was never one to be easily discouraged. She thrust her hands forward with a defiant jut of her jaw. 'Go on, let her have a go,' said Grace, her champion, winning a big smile from her little sister.

With both fists wrapped around the mallet handle, Isobel managed a good swing and sent her ball rolling across the grass at a respectable clip. It stopped less than an inch from the hoop. Anna threw her arms in the air in triumph. 'Knock 'em for six!' she screeched.

Her sisters had grown accustomed to Anna's oddness. Even so, they were in the habit of hushing her whenever she became over-excited in the company of others. She may have only been nine but Anna had an alarmingly loud voice; her expostulations had the force of pistol-shots and startled people with much the same effect.

With Alice spending more time with her head stuck in slim volumes of Romantic poetry and mooning over portraits of Lord Byron, twelve-year-old Grace had become the natural leader of the younger girls. It was she who organised shell-collecting and rock-pool expeditions along Coogee beach when the family ventured forth for a seaside picnic. It was she who decided who should play Guinevere or Miranda or Rosamund in one of their schoolroom costume pageants. It was she who taught both younger girls how to sit properly on Pegasus, their white pony, for a gentle trot along the coach road to Captain Bradley's house.

Anna and Isobel worshipped Grace, their stern but kind older sister who always knew exactly what needed to be done. While Alice's appearance was generally agreed to be angelic (milk-white skin, copper tresses, jade green eyes), the darker-hued Grace was not so blessed in profile and complexion but already had the cool and alluring hauteur of a young princess. Grace knew she would have to wait her turn until Alice was betrothed before she could even hope to draw the attention of any man who came to visit Grangemouth. And anyway, it was the natural order of things that the eldest should find a suitable match first.

Grangemouth's frequent parties were among its happiest and most memorable occasions. Though the Major's reputation in the wider world was for gruffness, pride and choler, anyone who knew him intimately thought such perceptions unfair. It was true he insisted on being the authority on many topics and had a low tolerance for stupidity, but that was far from the whole story. He also had a sense of humour, even making jokes at his own expense. He loved to paint and sketch, was an energetic dancer, could scrape out a tune or two on a fiddle, wrote and translated poetry in his spare time, and deeply loved his wife and children. All these qualities were on abundant display at his private parties, especially those he held to celebrate his homecoming after long absences.

'Welcome, welcome, one and all.' Angus was in a magnanimous mood the next day as he ushered his guests into the coolness of the sandstone portico, well-shaded at this hour of the mid-afternoon. While the worst of the midday glare had abated, the Major declared that 'Apollo's chariot still blazed fiercely, speeding westward'. The cold bottles of fizz and jugs of lemonade sweated while the blowflies turned their attention to the plates of jam tarts and cakes. Grangemouth's staff were on hand to shoo these intruders away and administer to the company's needs.

'It is good to see you, Angus,' said Dr Finch with a warm handshake. 'You appear remarkably well.' Months in the saddle on tight rations and in the unrelenting blast of desert sun had made Angus wiry and fit, his face and arms bronzed to a deep tan. Finch recognised that far-off look in the Major's eyes, habituated to focusing on the horizon when taking readings or keeping watch for early signs of trouble.

They were joined by Captain Bradley, who greeted Angus with a brotherly clap on the shoulder. 'Welcome home, Major. Good expedition?'

'I am pleased to report, gentlemen, that the Governor and the Executive Council regard my expedition as an unqualified success,' said Angus, allowing himself a moment of gratification. 'For good reason. As we pushed further south, we came into such fertile, well-watered grazing land, I called the region "*Australia Felix*". My bullock tracks have already left a path for thousands of pastoralists and farmers to follow.'

The three men retired to the study to inspect some fossils the Major had found on his adventures. Meanwhile the girls amused themselves with croquet and quoits followed by a concert in the gazebo. Winnie, who looked more serene than her children could ever remember, sat with Mrs Finch, Mrs Bradley and Mrs Palmer in the shade of the portico playing euchre and Black Lady and taking tea. The boys, James and Henry Bradley, Aloysius Finch, and Richard, Joseph and William Macleod, played several overs on the green followed by games of tag and hide-and-seek down near the ponds.

The shadows of the tallowwoods lengthened as 'Apollo's chariot' made its rapid descent into the west, tongues of fire licking the opalescent sky. The cocker spaniels, silly with the attention of so many children, never flagged in their excitable romping and barking. On the portico and in the drawing room, the lamps were lit with the usual fluttering of moth wings at the glass. A generous supper of cold cuts, jellies, fruit flans and mince pies was served indoors followed by dancing in the ballroom.

But the evening was so lovely that the guests drifted outdoors again to linger in the cool air and watch the stars winking into brightness in the gathering dusk. As the heat lifted, the garden breathed out its perfumes of gardenia and mock orange and pulsed with the insistent nocturne of cricket and frog music. In the gravelled square that enclosed the fountain the servants had built a small bonfire, well clear of the house, around which the adults and children now formed a circle, mesmerised by the spectacle of sparks leaping and vanishing in the dark.

It had been a perfect day, thought little Isobel. She grinned at her gaggle of friends as they sipped their steaming cups of cocoa and studied the sky for the five bright points of the Southern Cross. And then, to everyone's surprise, they heard a landau come clattering up the driveway.

'More guests?' asked Isobel, a little put out at having this lovely reverie interrupted.

The Major strode across the drive to greet the carriage as it pulled up near the front steps. It seemed these late arrivals were expected. Out stepped Dr Nicholson, another of Angus's most trusted friends, followed by the Assistant Surveyor, Mr Stapylton. Last of all alighted a little girl.

An Aborigine.

The Major welcomed the doctor and his assistant surveyor before bending down and shaking hands with the small black girl, who stood staring at the bonfire and the assembly of people. The Major seemed to know her and she him. He spoke a few words and she looked up into his face and smiled.

What on earth is going on, thought Isobel.

With his arm placed protectively around her shoulders, the Major gently ushered the girl into the circle of firelight, the whole company staring in bewilderment. Isobel could see flames dancing in her large brown eyes.

'Ladies and gentleman, may I introduce Ballandella.'

Chapter 7

BALLANDELLA

DECEMBER 1838 TO NOVEMBER 1839

Like the fossils he had shown his guests in the study, it turned out that Ballandella was another souvenir from the Major's expedition. By the light of the bonfire, Isobel and her brothers and sisters studied this exotic curiosity closely.

Ballandella was a good head taller than Isobel, though (as she was to find out later) the same age as herself. Her face was dark and glossy and, to Isobel's fancy, could have been carved from walnut. Her hair, as black as soot, sprung wildly in all directions, like wool that had just been carded and washed. Her eyes, dark-brown pupils in startling white irises, darted about like those of a frightened pup. She had full pink lips in contrast to her black face and her teeth flashed as white as chalk. Her legs were very long and skinny, as were her arms, but she appeared athletic and strong despite standing awkwardly, her right foot turned out at a strange angle. She had been dressed in a plain cotton frock with a shawl (no bonnet or stockings and no shoes!) and it was obvious she felt ill at ease in these unfamiliar vestments. To Isobel this remarkable specimen of the native race seemed as skittish as a lizard, overwhelmed by the sight of the gardens, the house and the company, all eyes fixed on her.

Who could blame her?

The Major called Winnie over. While everyone else was still speechless with shock, Winnie seemed perfectly at ease with this sudden appearance of an Aboriginal girl in their midst. It was clear the Major had informed his wife of the little girl's visit.

'Winnie, my dear, can you ask Mrs G. to take Ballandella upstairs and get her bathed and put to bed? She's had a long trip from Windsor.' He turned to the little girl again. 'I'll see you in the morning.' Winnie took the child by the hand and guided her indoors.

Stepping into the ring of firelight again and surrounded by a circle of eager faces, the Major began to tell his rapt audience the story of Ballandella. As the bonfire crackled and popped, releasing its stream of sparks towards the stars, the night felt enchanted as Isobel listened to her father speak of a world beyond her powers to imagine.

'It happened in the seventh week of my explorations along the Darling River down to the Murrumbidgee. Despite my usual precaution of taking a native interpreter to help negotiate our safe passage through unknown country, we encountered many threatening signs from the Barkindji tribe and feared for our safety.

'While I was resting at a friendly camp further south, I found time to make a sketch of a young native woman and her daughter, sitting on her shoulders. Their names were Turandurey, a widow, and her little girl, Ballandella. An old man sitting at the campfire with us persuaded the widow to join me as my guide. I was used to such offers as local tribesmen were often anxious to pass us onto the next tribal territory as quickly as possible.'

A few quiet chortles and nods from the adult men in the company acknowledged the common sense of such a strategy among the savages of the hinterland.

'It turned out that Turandurey, a Wiradjuri woman, knew the country well, especially where to find water, and spoke Jitajita, Wiradjuri and Muthi-Muthi. The party then pushed south again and made excellent progress, coming into such verdant and well-watered country that I declared it *"Australia Felix"*, a future boon for pastoralists and settlers.

'But luck was against us,' the Major continued. 'During a difficult river crossing, little Ballandella took a tumble from one of our drays and her right thigh was crushed by its heavy wheels. Riding up, I found her mother in great distress, wailing piteously with her head prostrate in the dust. I made Dr Drysdale set the thighbone immediately, but because it was broken very near the socket it was soon clear the girl would be permanently crippled. Every care was taken of the poor infant that circumstances would allow. She bore the pain with admirable patience though only four years old.'

Sighs of sympathy could be heard escaping the lips of those listening. In the firelight Isobel thought she saw a tear spill down the cheek of the soft-hearted Mrs Palmer. The Major acknowledged his audience's empathy with a nod and continued his story.

'This crippling injury was no doubt the reason that the girl's mother, upon the return of the expedition to her home country weeks later, asked me to take care of her daughter. I had certainly always been willing to take an Aboriginal child back with me to Sydney with the intention of seeing what might be the effect of education upon one of the race. I suspect Turandurey understood how much more her sex was respected by civilised men than savages. I believe that it was with such sentiments that she committed her child to my charge.'

The Major's voice swelled grandiloquently towards the conclusion of his narrative. 'My intention is that Ballandella will live here with us as one of my family and will be given every opportunity and benefit that a British education can afford a young woman. I hope in this way to be able to determine the natural capacity of the native to acquire the customs and values of our society, which may prove a salvation to the race in future.'

The Macleod girls looked at each other in amazement. An Aboriginal girl was coming to live with them! What an adventure, thought Isobel. At last, a part of her father's distant world, the lofty male domain of map-making, politics and exploration, had come floating down into their quiet domestic sphere. If Major Macleod had any doubts (which he rarely did) about how his scheme would be received by his family, they were quickly dismissed as his children crowded round to ask more questions. They had all been raised to have inquisitive minds, after all. Isobel went to bed that night excited and nervous about meeting the mysterious girl who slept (in the bed or on the floor?) in the room next door.

Within days it was clear that all the Macleod women were utterly entranced with the novel creature in their midst and glad to help Father with his 'experiment'. There were so few blacks around Sydney Town these days that this girl from an inland tribe was sure to remain a source of great curiosity to their neighbours for some time.

To Isobel's surprise, the child expressed little grief at the dramatic alteration in her circumstances. Instead, she showed a remarkable willingness to fit into this alien world of gardens, servants, family prayers and formal dinners. The Major had already noted in his expedition journal the alacrity with which Ballandella chose whitefella jam and bread over her usual fare of snake and goanna, and had mastered a handful of English words: 'dog', 'sun', 'eat', 'water', 'knife'. The Major had high hopes for his 'experiment'. He even talked of writing up the results as a short treatise on *The Education of the Native Tribes of the Colony of New South Wales for the Purposes of Their Improvement and Peaceful Integration* to be submitted (with a word in the right ear) to be read to the Royal Society in London.

Under the patient tuition of the governess (and, at different times, encouragement and guidance from Anna, Grace and Isobel), Ballandella soon acquired some social graces as well as an intimate acquaintance with the bath, the Bible and the embroidery needle. Within weeks she knew how to curtsy, smile graciously, tie a bonnet, put gloves on, and sit still for minutes at a time. With her frizzy locks combed straight, her shiny face scrubbed clean and her skinny limbs shrouded in stockings, crinoline, cotton and muslin, the native girl began to achieve a credible impersonation of a young Christian woman.

The Major noted with interest that her biggest strides forward were in the acquisition of English: spoken, written and even (to his great astonishment and even greater gratification) reading. In his view, this pointed to a God-given intelligence in the girl and not just a facile ability to ape the behaviour of her betters. Within three months, Ballandella was conducting short conversations. To mark this milestone, the Major asked her to join them at a dinner party with the Finches and Bradleys, at which she said grace perfectly and was praised for her table manners and skill with a knife and fork. Winnie and the Major were more than satisfied with Ballandella's progress and their daughters also rejoiced in her transformation.

And what did Ballandella think of it all?

No one ever asked. She appeared to enjoy the attention and the company of her new family, even if she was a bit intimidated by the governess at first. She saw very little of Alice and Winnie and spent most of her time in the nursery, schoolroom and gardens with Grace, Anna and Isobel. It soon became obvious that it was Isobel she liked most of all.

The Macleods' good friend Mrs Palmer dropped by regularly to learn how 'the little black girl' was faring. 'Does she not get lonely at times, poor thing?' she asked her hostess over tea and cakes one afternoon in early June. 'Surely she must pine for her own kind?'

'I don't believe so, Mrs P.,' said Winnie. 'She is such a sunny soul.'

Mrs Palmer had thoughtfully brought one of her delicious homemade plum cakes, a favourite with the Macleod girls. Ballandella's sweet tooth was a subject of affectionate teasing at Grangemouth and she, Isobel, Anna and Grace had swooped on Mrs Palmer's gift like a swarm of wasps on a gooseberry pot. They now sat about the drawing room, cups and plates delicately balanced on their knees. The adults continued their discussion, seemingly oblivious to Ballandella's presence. Isobel stole a quick glance at her new friend, absorbed in picking the plums out of Mrs Palmer's cake with her fork.

'Not that there are many natives left around here these days,' observed Mrs Palmer with a sad nod of her head. 'Most of the Sydney blacks died, of course, in the first year from the smallpox. Very sad business. You could hear men and women wailing for days on end.'

Winnie shot a quick look at her girls, worried that this topic was unsuitable for their young ears, but everyone was preoccupied with their cake and tea. Mrs Palmer liked to tell stories of her early years in the colony when she and her husband, John, the commissary-general under Governor Phillip, had started a farm in the valley beneath Woolloomooloo Hill. Sadly, John's overfondness for parties and luxury had driven him into bankruptcy and forced Mrs Palmer into more modest accommodation.

'Even so, one still saw blacks everywhere back then,' she said. 'They wandered the streets, half-naked, and turned up in our backyards and gardens to sell their fish in exchange for rum and tobacco. Up in the Domain you often saw the women fishing at dusk in Woolloomooloo Bay. And now and then tribes from far and wide gathered down in Hyde Park for their "revenge" spearings, a grisly spectacle that drew huge crowds.'

Mrs Palmer told them that Governor Macquarie had banned these vulgar 'entertainments' as unfit for his new civil order. Instead he tried to civilise the Aborigines of Sydney with a small fishing village and farm, called Elizabeth Town, near the beach at Elizabeth Bay. Here, under the guidance of an expert gardener, it was hoped the natives would learn the virtues of agricultural labour. 'I remember families took their carriages out to the bay on a Sunday afternoon to watch the black farmers at their honest toil.' The farm disappeared before Governor Darling granted the Rosemount estate to his Colonial Secretary.

'Now, of course, there are only a few small settlements left,' she said wistfully as Winnie refreshed her cup. 'Some gunyas in the Domain and around Woolloomooloo Bay. And the camps at Rushcutters, Rose Bay and Botany Bay. The last of a dying breed.'

Isobel had certainly seen blacks around these bays and even, now and then, on the Hill. There was that old crippled fellow Billy, 'Chief of the Rose Bay Tribe' and nicknamed 'Ricketty Dick' for his lame gait, who sat on the side of New South Head Road, wrapped in his blanket in all weathers, collecting the 'toll' as white folks' carriages rattled past on their way to Watsons Bay. In the evening, she sometimes saw the women in their fishing canoes out on Elizabeth Bay or heard the men walking along the beach, hawking their mussels and prawns.

Major Macleod had his own views on 'the dying breed'. Like Governor Macquarie, he had a strong faith in the blacks' adaptability to the white man's ways ('such nimbleness of mind, such sharpness of observation!'), which he hoped may yet prove their salvation. It was inevitable, if regrettable, that their customary existence would disappear. Their only future lay in the protection of British law. Thanks to his travels inland, the Major had seen first hand the natives' knowledge of country, and skills as fishermen, hunters, food-gatherers and trackers. Acknowledging this native expertise, the Surveyor-General made every effort to record indigenous names on his maps for mountains, valleys, creeks and waterholes.

He admired the natives in others ways too. It had become his habit on expeditions to sketch as he sat by the campfire after a long day in the saddle. These sketches included portraits of tribesmen and women, individuals and groups. He confessed his envy of these 'children of nature' for their state of grace. While some natives bore ritual scars or the disfiguring marks of smallpox, the Major was particularly struck by the muscular strength and beauty of their bodies, unencumbered by clothes and so eloquently fluid in dancing, running, tracking prey. He had personally witnessed two corroborees and wrote in his journal how he found these dances more enjoyable than anything he had witnessed at Covent Garden.

Some days when Isobel and her little friend were playing together on the lawn, she would look up and catch the Major staring at them from his study window with such a pensive expression that she wondered what her father was thinking.

Though slowed a little by her limp, Ballandella loved their rambles through the wooded estate at Grangemouth. She was transfixed by the insects, plants and birds so unlike those she knew at home and befriended the four cocker spaniels who soon became her hopelessly devoted companions. The two girls spent hours together, skipping stones across the ponds, searching for anthills, wombat burrows and echidna tracks, or digging for grubs and picking seeds off the wattle bushes and shoots from the she-oaks.

Isobel had started out assuming an air of haughty superiority as Ballandella's tutor, delighted to have someone lower in the family pecking order she could boss around. But this regime was short-lived. Not only did Ballandella put little Isobel to shame with how fast she learned English words and manners, she undertook to teach Isobel a thing or two about her own world. These *other* lessons were conducted in secret, out in the gardens or on the back stairs, well out of earshot of the governess. Isobel was an eager student.

'*Widyu-ndhu yuwin ngulung?*' Ballandella said at the start of each 'class', asking Isobel her name. '*Yoowingaddy Isobel,*' her pupil mumbled bashfully in response. Poor Ballandella. How she bit her lip to keep from laughing at Isobel's mangling of her mother tongue! Then, unable to control herself any longer, she fell about and howled until tears rolled down her cheeks. Isobel swallowed her pride and joined in.

Like a mirror image of the black girl's progress, Isobel slowly mastered a few words of Ballandella's language. She was now called '*Mingaan*' (older sister) while Ballandella became '*Minhi*' (younger sister). On their rambles through the estate, Isobel learned new names for horse (*Yarraman*), frog (*Gulaanga*), butterfly (*Budyabudya*) and snake (*Gadi*). She loved the feel of these strange words in her mouth.

Ballandella also drew pictures to show Isobel where she had once lived. Isobel thought these did not look so very different from the marks on her father's maps; in place of gridlines and compass points, meandering rivers and tear-drop lakes, there were dark dots, empty circles, spirals, crosses, arrows and wavy lines to represent the mountains, campsites, bird tracks, waterholes and stars.

Most of all Isobel looked forward to Ballendella's storytelling. After they had eaten supper, washed their faces, brushed their hair and said their prayers, the governess would sing the girls a lullaby and extinguish the lamps. It was then that the Aboriginal girl crept out of her bed and into Isobel's room. Here, under cover of night, she whispered tales of her ancestors who strode across the land and sky, fighting, hunting, seeking food, shelter or revenge.

One of Isobel's favourites was the story of the young Goanna woman who bravely went in search of the Goanna men's jealously guarded reservoir of sweet water. She prised open their secret rockhole in the mountains with her yam stick and released a mighty flood that became the Murrumbidya river. Ballandella warned her that, while some bush spirits were kind and helpful, Wahn the tricky Crow could never be trusted and was despised by most of the animal ancestors.

Against the odds (and, no doubt, against the unspoken rules), Isobel and Ballandella fumbled their way towards a friendship that they did their best to keep secret. But how else could this little girl become one of them if they did not become friends?

Everything appeared to be progressing according to the Major's fondest hopes, with the native girl's social and intellectual development thoroughly documented in his notebooks. That was until the day in July when Isobel, fiercely precocious for a girl of only five-and-a-half, had her 'very clever idea' and recruited two of her siblings to execute it.

Inspired by Mrs Palmer's talk of a settlement of blacks there, Isobel proposed to lead her two fellow explorers, Anna and Joseph, and her native guide, Ballandella, on an expedition to Rushcutters Bay. In the weeks following Mrs Palmer's visit she and her siblings began to draw up their plans. With the kind of courage and stealth that she hoped her father would admire (in retrospect, presumably) she and Joseph stole into Papa's study one afternoon and borrowed a local map and an old compass.

The night before their party was due to depart, the children secretly packed their supplies: two water bottles, a bag of apples and mandarins, five fish-paste sandwiches, two slices of fruitcake, candles, matches, pannikins, a picnic rug and a rucksack. Joseph and Anna would carry most of these provisions strapped to their shoulders. As the expeditionary leader, Isobel carried the compass and the map as well as several specimen bottles for anything unusual they encountered along the way. Ballandella was to be the tracker, decoding the prints of interesting fauna, and the interpreter once they reached the Rushcutters Bay 'tribe'. While Isobel suspected her brother and sister considered the whole thing a bit of a lark, she was determined to take it seriously.

The party slipped away shortly after lunch when the governess had retired for a short nap and the children were released into the gardens to play. They were all sworn to secrecy and made their excuses to their other siblings about their absences for the next hour or so. Joseph met the girls behind the tallowwood at the end of the drive and they set forth.

The expedition encountered few difficulties for the first stage of its journey as they cut through the scrub to avoid being spotted by anyone on the road. The wind got up about half past three and they sheltered for a while in a grove of red gums, eating their provisions and discussing their plans. The wind was strengthening and picking up a lot of dust but they decided to push on for another forty minutes or so before taking another rest, hidden from view in a hedge.

'Do you think they know we've gone by now?' asked Anna, her face puckered with anxiety.

Joseph reassured her it was still too early to worry. 'We'll be back before sunset. We can just say we were picking blackberries in the gully and lost track of time.'

'This way,' Isobel pointed. The brave explorers made sure there was no one coming and crossed the deep rutted stretch of Darlinghurst Road. On the far side, they climbed over a low drystone wall and walked into Mr Thomas West's thickly wooded Barcom Glen estate.

The party struggled on for at least another hour through the rough scrub and tightly packed trees as the sky grew dark with swollen grey clouds, the wind now rising to a new pitch and its cargo of dust growing thicker. Even dauntless Isobel began to lose heart as they thrashed through the prickly undergrowth in the failing light, the churning red dust caking their hair and plugging their ears and nostrils.

A sudden deafening crack brought rain descending in torrents. 'I want to go home now,' declared Anna, starting to sob.

Ballandella laughed at her. 'Big baby. Cry baby,' she hooted, tracing pretend tears down her own cheeks.

'Hey, that's not nice!' shouted Joseph. 'You bloody savage,' he added haughtily. Ballandella must have understood his tone if not his words and her nostrils flared.

'I go now. Leave you babies here. Bye-bye.'

'No, no, please don't go!' cried Isobel, genuinely frightened for the first time. She was not confident about her map-reading skills and, to be honest, had been relying on Ballandella's sense of direction. The black girl started to walk away. Joseph headed off in the other direction. Isobel's expedition was almost certainly lost and starting to split apart. She did not know what to do. 'Please, come back, Ballandella. Where are you going, Joseph?'

It was then that Isobel saw smoke rising in the distance between the trees and heard people chanting.

'Secret blackfella business. We gotta go!' yelled Ballandella.

Among the trees ahead they saw a face coming at them, fast. A black face with long, matted hair and features screwed into a scowl of such fury as to strike terror into the stoutest heart. Out of its mouth came a guttural flood of angry words accompanied by arms with clenched fists whirling like the blades of the windmills on the Hill.

'We not wanted here,' said Ballandella urgently.

'What's he saying?' asked Isobel.

The Aboriginal girl shrugged, looking at Isobel as if she was mad. 'Don't know. Just look at him face, willya?'

And then a pebble pinged through the air and struck Joseph on the arm. 'Black bastard!' he shouted. 'I'll get *him*.'

'You get head bashed, more like.' Ballandella grabbed his arm, pulling him away. 'This fella bad one.'

The children dropped most of their provisions including the old compass and the rucksack and ran as fast as their legs could manage. The screaming man followed for a few more yards and then stopped, but the brave explorers kept running until they reached Mr West's boundary wall. When the expedition finally found its way back to Grangemouth, the sun was long set and Ballandella was their leader. Isobel, Anna and Joseph tagged along in the dark, exhausted and miserable, dragging their blistered feet like dead weights. 'How do you know where to go?' asked Isobel humbly.

'The stars, Izzie,' Ballandella laughed. 'Up there, look. Stars, eh?'

Their reception back home was a cacophony of relieved weeping from the women and angry shouting from the Major. All kinds of punishments were promised. At last the tempest of emotions subsided and the explorers were bathed, made to pray for forgiveness of their sins and put to bed with no supper.

There were sulky, mutinous looks exchanged between the siblings when Papa asked, 'Whose idea was this escapade?' But they had all agreed to share the blame and not accuse Isobel alone; the fact that they had been talked into it by their baby sister was too embarrassing to confess! Isobel did her best not to cry, setting her face like stone in defiance of her father's temper, but in her heart she hid the true depths of her sorrow at having disappointed him. When the lamps were finally put out, Isobel filled the dark silence of her room with muffled sobs, her face buried in her pillows.

The following morning was a Saturday and she presented herself at her father's study door to apologise. She knocked and let herself in. His mood had settled overnight.

'Your idea, eh?' he said, once she had made her confession. 'An expedition. With Ballandella as your guide. I see. So, did you find what you were looking for?'

'Not really.'

'Often the way with expeditions,' said the Major, supressing a smile. He should know. Despite his reputed temper, he was exceptionally soft-hearted with his youngest daughter. Even at the age of four she had already shown an aptitude for drawing, and it pleased the Major to invite her into his study now and then to sit on his lap at his desk. He would bring out some of his treasures for her to admire and even sketch: fossil bones, reptile skeletons, a sea urchin (like a fragile pink pincushion), an emu egg the size of a small pumpkin and, from his mahogany specimen cabinets, trays of *lepidoptera*, wings pinned open in polychromatic splendour. These visits were cherished memories for father and daughter.

The Major leaned down and looked Isobel square in the eye.

'I understand why you did what you did, Miss Isobel Macleod. But your mother and I were frightened almost out of our wits yesterday. And poor Anna is still beside herself. You must promise me, right here and now, in the sight of Almighty God, you will never do anything like that ever again. Do you understand me, young lady?'

She nodded solemnly. To seal the promise, the Major made her swear an oath on the family Bible, which he kept on the shelf behind his desk. 'Now, off you go.'

That might have been the end of the whole matter had it not been for Winnie. When Isobel went in for breakfast, she was confronted with a petulant scowl from Anna (which was to be expected under the circumstances) and an angry frown from her sister Grace (which was not). What on earth had happened? It did not take long for Isobel to find out.

As they headed up the stairs to the schoolroom, Grace turned and hissed at her, 'I hate you! I saw you go into his study just now. *And* I saw you come out, with that little smirk on your face. Papa's little pet. His favourite!'

Isobel was at a loss for words. Grace's face was twisted into a mask of hate unlike anything she had seen before. What had provoked *this*?

'You get away with murder, you do! But not me! I'm to be punished thanks to you! Mama is furious with me for not keeping an eye on you stupid boobies. I don't expect the black girl to know right from wrong but you three should know better! And I blame you, Isobel Macleod, most of all. For dreaming up the whole thing!'

'I did not! Who told you that?' Isobel had only just made her confession to Papa. How could Grace possibly know this?

'Shan't tell!' said Grace, but her eyes flicked in Anna's direction. Anna blushed and whimpered a little. She had been easily intimidated by Winnie into surrendering the truth. Isobel later learned that

Joseph too had succumbed to threats of punishment and betrayed her. Even so, the burden of responsibility for Isobel and Anna's waywardness had fallen most heavily on their older sister Grace.

Isobel had only just turned five in January. It was absurd and unfair to accuse her of leading her two older siblings astray. 'She didn't have to come! None of them did!' Isobel snapped back as they stepped into the schoolroom where the governess was waiting, her face simmering with rage. She too had been chastised for Isobel's misadventure.

When Isobel looked back a few months later she realised that the failed expedition to Rushcutters Bay had been a turning point. Being so close in age, Anna and Isobel had always been firm companions and allies: Anna had admired her younger sister's spirit of daring while Isobel pushed Anna to be a little more courageous and a little less frightened. Isobel and Anna both looked up to Grace, who knew everything they needed to know about the world and their place in it. When it came to games, she was the rule-keeper; when it came to disputes, she was the peacemaker. And if the governess got cross with them, it was Grace who came to her siblings' rescue.

But from the day of the expedition, everything started to change.

Or had it started even before that? Isobel eventually came to understand that it was her friendship with the little black girl that had slowly but surely pushed Anna and Grace aside, making them into her enemies. Isobel had little time for her sisters now with a new, fascinating friend to play with. None of her sisters' stories or games could hold a candle to Ballandella's; hunting kangaroos along the 'Darling River' or digging up grubs for supper was a far more exciting game than playing at dressing-up and tea parties.

As Isobel and Ballandella spent more time together and grew ever closer, Anna's heart curdled with jealousy. She found solace for her hurt in the safekeeping of Grace, and it was in these circumstances that Anna and Grace became inseparable, their betrayal by Isobel a bond between them. How comforting to have someone to blame for life's disappointments!

And to make matters worse, Anna's outbursts started to become increasingly unpredictable and frightening. Most of the time she chose to ignore Isobel altogether but every now and then Anna would corner her in the nursery, spitting words of abuse under her breath, and even pinching and scratching. Grace would chastise her, of course, lest their governess overhear and report these transgressions to their mother. But Isobel could tell that Grace was only protecting herself from punishment. It was clear that over time she and Anna were becoming more firmly united in their hatred for their little sister.

Such was to be Isobel's fate.

Nearly a year had passed since the memorable day that Ballandella came to Grangemouth. Day by day, like an insect emerging from its pupa, she was growing into a well-mannered Christian woman. She attended church on Sundays, walked out with the Macleod women on weekdays or sat up in the family trap. Her reading progressed to short poems and hymns, and she played scales and simple pieces on the piano and could hold a tune with some help.

But it soon became clear that not everyone regarded the Major's experiment as a worthy one. A well-known squatter who served on the Legislative Council encountered Major Macleod one morning on Macquarie Street on his way to work.

'What's this I hear about you raising a gin as a Christian?'

'It is a scientific experiment, sir, designed to show that the native has the capacity to adapt to our civilised ways given the right persuasion and training.'

The squatter stared at the Major with an expression that left little doubt he thought the man insane. 'It is unnatural and absurd, sir. Everyone knows the blacks are little better than wild dogs who should be chained up or shot at every opportunity.'

'Do you really think so, sir?'

'I suppose you would have them own land and sit in parliament with us next? Is that the logical end to your experiment?' The squatter was red-faced with rage, his lips flecked with spittle. 'And I suppose you believe, sir, you can educate these brutes out of spearing our cattle, burning our crops, killing our farmers and raping our women? You are a menace, sir. Everyone says so. The gin should be sent back to her tribe where she belongs. Your so-called "experiment" is an obscenity.'

The Major did not reply and the squatter walked on. He was not surprised by such opinions—they were common enough in the colony—but taken aback at the white-knuckled, hot-blooded rage of its expression from a gentleman. It was not as if the Major did not know about the savagery of the natives; he knew more than most. But he refused to admit that the only solution was the complete extermination of the race.

Winnie had come to him the other night with her own concerns. 'I am deeply worried, Angus. Grace tells me that Isobel and Ballandella stay up all night talking. She even saw them creeping about in the grass yesterday with no shoes on. Carrying spears fashioned from grasstree spikes, no less! God forbid, I fear that our youngest is turning native.'

The Major looked at her, puzzled. 'You think so?'

'Did you really think that bringing a black girl into our house would change nothing?' asked Winnie. 'Isobel has always been impressionable. And adventurous. Is it so surprising that she, of all our daughters, would find an Aborigine an object of beguilement?'

Winnie was right. It was exactly Isobel's nature to be so curious. And bold.

While the Major congratulated himself on his experiment's success, Isobel knew better. She could tell that the transformation of Ballandella was neither permanent nor complete. Over time, there were more and more occasions when the homesick girl let the trappings of civilisation fall away. In the privacy of the nursery at night, it was Isobel who could hear her playmate singing low in her mother tongue. In the melancholy hours before sunrise, it was Isobel who had her heart pierced by the sound of wailing through the nursery wall. And then one morning, the gardener saw Ballandella wandering naked through the estate and alerted Mrs Macleod. Isobel grieved for her friend with good cause. She worried for her state of mind. She wondered how much she had changed.

And then one spring morning, only six weeks before Christmas, Isobel woke up and knocked on Ballandella's door. There was no answer. She pushed the door open and found Agnes, the maid, pulling sheets and pillowcases off the bed. The little bookshelf by the bedhead was empty, as was the wardrobe nearby.

'Where is she?' Isobel asked, feeling a tight fist of panic crushing her chest.

'She's gone, Miss,' the maid answered. 'Left by coach early this morning.'

Ballandella and Isobel had taken supper together the previous evening. Her friend had made her laugh with the greedy gusto of her consumption of jam and bread. They had brushed their hair, said their prayers and gone to bed as usual. Nothing different, nothing out of the ordinary. It had been a busy day and Isobel slept soundly. No dreams.

So where was Ballandella? Where was she now?

The Major explained it all to her over breakfast. Concerned about the native girl's increasing bouts of melancholy and restlessness, he thought she would prosper more in a rural setting. Something more akin to her home country. After careful consideration, he decided to consign her to the care of his good friend Dr Nicholson who owned a cottage on the Hawkesbury. There were some blacks who lived and worked in the district and she would soon find new friends. He promised that Isobel could write her letters.

'It is for the best,' the Major counselled.

Isobel cried for days after that, but only in private. She refused to give her sisters the satisfaction of seeing her heartbreak. Over the next few weeks and then months, Isobel wrote to her friend, desperate to hear some news and keep their friendship alive. But to her bitter disappointment she received no reply except for a short note from Dr Nicholson reassuring Isobel his charge was happy and well.

Isobel continued to write letters to Ballandella but fewer and fewer as time wore on and any hope of ever seeing her friend again sputtered and died. Even so, to herself Isobel made a solemn promise that she would never forget her 'Minhi'. Her little sister.

Chapter 8

THE LOVE TOKEN

MAY 1841 TO DECEMBER 1844

She may have been only seven but Isobel would always remember the night her father presented Winnie with his most lavish love token. He had decided to make a ceremony of it, announcing to the family during dinner that he had a surprise for them. And for his 'beloved Winnie' most of all.

At the conclusion of dessert, the Major instructed the servants to set up extra oil lamps and candelabras on the sideboard and mantel. 'I shall return shortly.' There was a delicious air of anticipation after he left the room. Alice, Grace and Anna swapped guesses in excited whispers as to what the surprise might be. Their brothers teased with ridiculous suggestions. An emu rampant stuffed by Mr John Hancock, perhaps? A Parian bust of Governor Darling to grace the mantelpiece?

The Major made his entrance with a stately slow march. His sons joined in the fun, drumming their fingers on the tabletop and humming 'The British Grenadiers'. The Major stopped, snapped to attention in front of his wife and bowed low. Isobel noticed he was wearing his white parade gloves and had something hidden behind his back. Cupping his wife's hand in his own, he gallantly pressed her fingertips to his lips. It was then he produced a crimson velvet jewellery case from behind his back and presented it to Winnie.

There was a hush as Winnie opened the lid. Her face changed to an expression of astonishment and tears dropped from her eyes. She looked at her husband with such sweet and tender affection that Alice and Grace too began to weep. Isobel did not really understand the cause of these tears of happiness but she felt her eyes begin to water.

'Oh my! Angus, my darling, it is so . . . *beautiful*.'

There was a slight quaver in her voice, the faintest note of discord that went unnoticed by her proud husband but did not escape the sensibility of her daughters. A fleeting exchange of glances, a flicker of recognition, made it clear that something was not quite right. Even little Isobel could feel it. Winnie lifted the object of her gaze from its velvet case for all to see. It was breathtaking. In the bright light of the candles its fluid play of colours hypnotised every eye.

It was an opal dragonfly.

The gift was to mark the Macleods' thirtieth wedding anniversary in two weeks' time. The Major explained that it had been fashioned by one of London's finest jewellers, whose skill had produced an artwork of more subtlety and refinement than anything Winnie or her daughters had ever seen.

A dragonfly made from opals—what a wonder! Isobel had always loved dragonflies. Unlike the aimless meanderings of butterflies or moths, dragonflies moved with absolute purpose, as swift as lightning bolts, to some fixed point in the air where they then hovered in perfect stillness. They were not gaudy like butterflies either. Except when they flashed rainbows in the sun, their wings were as transparent and pure as water.

Isobel stood next to her mother, studying the brooch closely. The insect's large compound eyes were two matched globes of black opal; its thorax and long segmented abdomen were also black opal, flashing sparks of red and blue, gold and green. The double pair of forewings and hindwings were outlined in silver and the mosaic of panels within each wing was also delineated in fine veins of silver, with delicate slivers of white opal imitating their pearlescent film. The entire masterpiece fitted neatly inside the palm of Winnie's hand.

Isobel had never seen anything so lovely. Within these gemstones there blazed liquid flames of blue, green, red, pink, gold and orange. Their unearthly fire reminded her of glow-worms, tiny methane-blue stars in the night blackness of a cave.

'Where on earth did you find these opal stones, my dear?' Winnie asked her husband.

'My third expedition. They are my little secret. Just for you, my love. Australian opals! Can you believe it? The jeweller in London was astonished to learn such stones existed. I don't believe anyone in the colony has seen stones like these.' The Major beamed at his wife almost boyishly. It was obvious he had been planning this night for a long time.

The happy occasion was shattered by a shriek. It was Anna. She had backed away from the table and now covered her eyes as if blinded by the sun. 'No, no, no,' she cried. 'Take it away, take it away! It will bring nothing but misery.'

Winnie looked at her husband, his face fixed in a rictus of shock. Trust Anna to blurt out the secret kept by every woman in the room. Except, perhaps, innocent little Isobel, her eyes as big as saucers. The others all knew what every woman knew: opals were *bad luck*.

The Major had read two short scholarly histories of the opal but neither had made any mention of their association with ill fortune. He had read how they had been used for adornment for centuries, how they were attributed special healing and spiritual powers. Arab folklore claimed they fell from heaven in lightning flashes and the early Greeks believed they conferred the gifts of foresight and prophecy.

What the poor Major did not know was that their reputation for bad luck in folklore and medieval superstition had only just resurfaced, as recently as 1829. It was all the fault of the author Sir Walter Scott and his lurid novel *Anne of Geierstein, or The Maiden of the Mist*. Therein an enchanted princess, Lady Hermione, wears an opal hair comb, which, when touched by holy water, has its ghostly fire extinguished. Hermione then falls into a faint and is borne unconscious to her bedchamber. The following morning, nothing of her can be found save a pile of cold ashes!

Thanks to Sir Walter, the opal's unholy 'curse' gripped the world's imagination. Within a year the sales of Hungarian opal had slumped to half their normal volume. These sensationalist associations were to haunt the lovely stones for years afterwards. How could the Major possibly know about this story? thought Winnie. Novels were frivolous distractions for the amusement of women. Winnie knew the superstition was preposterous but this did not change the fact that opals had fallen completely out of fashion.

Anna cowered in the corner. With the Major's moment of triumph ruined, his face began to redden with anger. Winnie hastened to reassure him. 'Silly girl, I don't know what gets into her head sometimes!'

Even Isobel could tell that her mother was lying for Papa's sake. 'It is the loveliest gift any woman could ask for, my love. I shall wear it always. Next to my heart.'

Winnie motioned for Grace to quickly escort her distraught sister from the room. Grace did so but let Mama know with a withering look that she was not fooled by this charade for one minute. Anna's impulsive outbursts were an open secret in the Macleod family, tolerated as much as was possible but never spoken about. Thankfully, on this occasion they had saved her father's pride and spared her mother acute embarrassment.

But the question remained: would Winifred tell her husband the truth or would she risk being seen in public wearing a brooch made of unlucky opal?

The answer came a fortnight later. To celebrate their wedding anniversary, the Macleods were hosting a ball at Grangemouth, intended to be a highlight of the season. The guest list boasted some of the colony's most distinguished public figures and their wives and offspring, including Lieutenant-General Maurice O'Connell, Commander of the Forces, and Major Thomas Bunbury of the 80th Regiment of Foot.

There was much excitement among the Macleod girls. In the upstairs drawing room Alice and Grace examined themselves in the mirror and finessed their hair and jewellery. Anna and Isobel had been recruited to stand by and admire. Alice's gown was rose pink with a broad sash to emphasise the smallness of her waist and a lacy *pelerine* was draped over her shoulders. The bell of her skirt brushed the boards as she twirled across the floor on satin-slippered feet. Grace's gown was lilac with blue irises and a sky-blue tippet. New feathered bonnets had thankfully arrived from Madame Ponder's millinery in George Street just in time that morning or there would have been drama and tears.

Oh, how splendid her sisters both looked, thought Isobel, a little jealously. It would be many years before she would be allowed to wear a gown as fine as these.

'Well, don't you look bang-up to the mark!' barked Anna. The others rolled their eyes and hushed her. She was in the habit of picking up all kinds of vulgar expressions from the convict servants and loved to upset everyone by dropping them into conversation.

'So who do you think will amuse you the most, tonight?' Grace asked her older sister. 'I believe that Lieutenant Ludlum will be here with other officers of the regiment. Such a fine figure of a man, don't you agree? And *so* charming.'

Alice snorted. 'I am not so in love with these redcoats as you, my dear sister. They have such a high opinion of themselves it hardly matters what I think. A few minutes of your lieutenant's bragging will drive me outdoors to hide in the garden!'

'What a terrible snob you are!' scoffed Grace. 'You have no respect for Papa's fellow officers.'

'I protest! I respect them deeply, I do. They just don't . . . suit my temperament. Give me a dull man with prospects in business or government any day of the week over a soldier. Or even better, a baronet with an annuity of ten thousand pounds.'

Isobel felt that giddy mix of nervousness and delight that often came over her around Alice and Grace. While there had been much bad blood between her and Grace in the past, some of its rancour had faded in the last year or so. Or at least that was what Isobel fervently hoped. Anna continued to make Isobel nervous with her sudden explosions of rage and cruel taunts but the family all conspired happily to disregard the seriousness of Anna's 'strange' behaviour. And so life at Grangemouth continued in its harmonious and well-regulated track with little to disturb its comfortable rhythms.

'Don't listen to *her*. She is utterly unromantic!' Grace cried, jabbing an accusatory finger at Alice. 'I swear your heart is an abacus. It clicks only when totting up a man's assets and income.'

'You should be pleased,' Alice teased back. 'I exit the field and leave you to win over your Adonis of the barracks. I wish you the happiest of futures as an officer's wife!'

'He will fall in love with *you*, Grace,' piped up Isobel, 'surely. In *that* dress!'

Alice and Grace fell into a fit of hysterics, their laughter so infectious, Isobel hiccupped with giggles. But whatever their hopes for potential suitors, tonight was not about the prospects of the Macleod girls.

Tonight was all about Mama and Papa. The front windows of the upstairs rooms had been covered with sheets of semi-transparent waxed linen featuring paintings of the Macleod family crest and portraits of Sir Angus and Winifred, backlit by pyramids of candles. These painted illuminations glowed so brilliantly they appeared to float in the night-time darkness, eliciting exclamations of delight as the first guests emerged from their carriages.

From the schoolroom window, Isobel watched with excitement as the great assembly arrived at Grangemouth. Coaches began queuing in the carriage loop outside the house at eight o'clock. The women descended first, chattering gaily and flocking up the portico steps like a bevy of swans with their long pale necks, snowy shoulders and puffed-up sleeves. The portico lamps shone on their braids and ringlets, adorned with hair combs, ribbons, tiaras, turbans and the bejewelled chains of *ferronières*. Behind them came the gentlemen, a clattering of currawongs, all silky black in high hats, frock coats and flapping cloaks, with a flash of white cravat at each throat. They swung their long black canes as playfully as dandies and doffed their hats to each other, the rumble of their voices sounding like far-off thunder.

Isobel and Anna were permitted to join in the opening of the festivities down in the ballroom. In their prettiest dresses, they hurried to the mezzanine balcony overlooking the entrance hall. Isobel heard the regimental band strike up a Scotch reel and her feet twitched. Next year she had been promised dance classes with Mrs Acutt now that Monsieur Girard, the watch thief turned dance master, had retired from giving quadrille lessons at his academy in Castlereagh Street. All the daughters of Sydney's best families were intent on perfecting the fiendishly difficult French dance.

Tonight would be a marathon of quadrilles, reels, polkas and waltzes. By way of another gift, the Major had commissioned Mr Ellard of Hunter Street, renowned for his set of Sydney quad-rilles (including Winnie's favourite, the lively 'La Woolloomooloo'). In honour of their anniversary, Ellard had composed a gay waltz titled 'Winifred's Pride'. The Major and his wife would lead the room to this tune later in the evening.

Anna and Isobel found a corner of the ballroom to watch the glamorous crowd pour in. The room blazed with light from a multitude of lamps and candelabras as well as the chandeliers overhead. The carpet had been rolled back to reveal the room's gleaming floorboards in the same way that the butler always removed the tablecloth and green baize for the dessert course to show off the French polish of the dining table. Frothy cascades of blossom tumbled from vases on tables and mantel, perfuming the ballroom. Servants passed through the throng bearing glasses of fizz. In the dining room next door, a supper awaited of lobster tails, cold cuts, jellies, soufflés and pastries, piled high in a glistening cornucopia.

The hubbub subsided as a bugle call announced the arrival of the hosts. Isobel beamed with pride at her father, so handsome in his evening tail coat and linen cravat, with his magnificent whiskers and black hair framing his noble face. He wore a tartan sash proclaiming the colours of the Macleod clan, secured to his vest with his medal of knighthood. And Mama! What a vision of elegance and dignity was she, her hair in silver ringlets, her Belgian lace cap fringed with flowers and ribbons, and her face so composed and happy. Her evening gown was simplicity itself, cut from brocade of the palest lemon trimmed with rosettes of ice blue. And there, pinned proudly to her bosom and catching the light of every candle in the room, was Papa's gift.

The opal dragonfly.

A muffled salute of gloved hands acknowledged Sir Angus and Winifred. But Isobel heard another sound: a sharp intake of breath and a low muttering that passed through the assembly like a rush of wind through grass. She looked up at the faces of the guests. Was it admiration she saw there or something else altogether? Shock, suspicion, jealousy? She was seven; what did she know about adults? But something was wrong. For a moment, she felt the room was filled with the stifling palpable heat of envy and the venomous glee of ill will.

This impression faded away as the band struck up a cheerful jig. A group of guests, all smiles and pleasantries, pressed forward for a closer look at the brooch.

'I have never seen anything to rival it!' exclaimed Mrs Palmer, clutching Winnie's arm in a spasm of affection. Mr Macleay, once the Colonial Secretary and Governor Darling's favourite, approached, his gait slow and painful, both legs swollen with gout. Why had her father invited him? Isobel wondered. He did not, as far as she knew, count Mr Macleay as a friend.

Never a handsome man, age had not dealt kindly with Mr Macleay. With Governor Darling recalled to England, he had been forced to resign his high office soon after Governor Bourke arrived. This sudden loss of salary had left him crushed by debt, most of it thanks to Rosemount. The talk in Sydney was that his eldest son, William, had bailed him out. A passionate naturalist (with an especial fondness for butterflies and moths), Mr Macleay possessed the largest private insect collection in the world. Forced to auction off his library of four thousand science books, he still clung desperately to his specimens.

The Major had no reason to love or pity this man. Isobel knew that the Colonial Secretary had in fact thwarted her father on more than one occasion. It was well known that while the Major was away on his first expedition, Mr Macleay had stepped in behind his back and changed the Surveyor-General's plans for a broad avenue from Sydney to Woolloomooloo Hill. Why? Because it had cut across a rich neighbour's estate. The steep narrow road that replaced the Major's was now cursed by coachmen and wagon drivers, whose blown horses staggered on its absurdly sharp ascent. The chance for a proper thoroughfare from Sydney Town to the east had been wasted. The Major never forgave Mr Macleay for his arrogant interference.

Isobel watched the wretched old man sidle up to her parents. 'Remarkable,' he croaked, his eyes wet with tears at the sight of the dragonfly. 'Truly remarkable.'

'Why, thank you, sir. You are most kind,' said Winnie, quite affected, if a little startled, at the depth of feeling in Mr Macleay's voice and countenance.

As the Major watched his old enemy bow his head to inspect the brooch, Isobel was shocked to see a look of the most repulsive gloating flash across her father's face. Did her mother not see it too? Or did she choose to ignore it out of love for Papa?

When Isobel looked back on this night years later, it was as if the whole affair was itself a painted illumination, a tableau of the wealthy families of Woolloomooloo Hill bathed in the golden light of nostalgia. In the ennobling glow of candlelight, her parents had appeared so young and happy as they waltzed across the ballroom to the lilt of 'Winifred's Pride'.

Isobel also saw something else clearly that night. The opal dragonfly was not just an innocent token of Papa's love for Mama. It was, whether by accident or design, a jewelled dagger aimed at the heart of his old enemy: the favourite who had once had the ear of the Governor and almost cost the Major his career but was now a broken man, teetering on bankruptcy. This lavish brooch perfectly captured the stark contrast in these men's fortunes. Isobel never forgot her father's expression that evening, so cruel and triumphant. She hoped it was not true but, in that instant, it seemed to her that the Major had rehearsed this scene of Mr Macleay's humiliation many times inside his head. Little could Isobel have suspected that her father already had plans in mind that would see the Macleods profit handsomely from Mr Macleay's downfall.

Later, Anna told Isobel all about Sir Walter Scott's 'opal curse'. Isobel in turn wondered if the real curse of the opal was that its very existence brought out the basest impulses in people, giving free rein to their greed, envy and hate. Whether the dragonfly was cursed or not, Isobel recalled that night as one of the last times she ever saw her family truly carefree.

For weeks after the Macleods' anniversary ball, Isobel nervously anticipated the arrival of bad news. She knew it was silly but the thought caught her off guard at dinner, while sketching or saying her nightly prayers. For some reason she could not dismiss the image in her head of her father's cruel face at the ball and the confronting glimpse it had given her into his soul. Her feelings of dread were confirmed barely two months later.

Attending a regimental dinner at the Military Barracks in Wynyard Square, the Major enjoyed the company of the young officers, who hung on his every word about his time as a soldier with the Iron Duke in Spain. Several rounds of port had followed dinner, which concluded around eleven o'clock when the Major shared a carriage with another guest up Brickfield Hill and along Campbell Street.

As it was a perfect moonlit night, the Major alighted near the junction of Old South Head Road, farewelled his fellow-diner and set out on a leisurely walk home to Grangemouth. At the corner of the newly opened Darlinghurst Gaol, the Major passed the hangman's hut near the prison's eastern wall. Without warning, two footpads came out of the shadows, both thickset ruffians brandishing steely blue knives in the moonlight.

'Let's have yer crabshells, yak and reader, gov'nor. Or we'll have to chiv ya proper.'

With no pistol on his person and his head cloudy with alcohol, the Major reluctantly surrendered his boots, watch and wallet, all the while composing an angry letter to Governor Gipps about his police officers hiding inside their watch houses. When he finally reached home (thanks to the assistance of a nearby tavern owner) the Major told his family all about the ambush, volubly expressing his low opinion of convicts: 'Scum, all of them, their hearts permanently closed to the promise of salvation!'

Isobel was simply relieved her father had returned unscathed. It was only later that she reflected on this misfortune as confirmation of her fears, and the straw in the wind of the mighty hurricane to come.

As the new year approached there were troubling signs for the colony's ruling class. Every morning the Major studied the papers for omens ('No need for worry, London will bail us out!') like a haruspex examining the entrails of sheep. The long drought had already made land and livestock hard to sell. It was when wool prices tumbled on the London market that the horsemen of the economic apocalypse could be heard galloping over the horizon.

The sacrifice of sheep soon became the order of the day: fat, healthy merinos, whose magnificent fleece once formed the bulk of exports to England, were now boiled down for tallow and candles. Those who had staked their fortunes on land speculation couldn't sell up or repay their mortgages. Stockhorses worth hundreds of pounds were flogged for a few guineas. The British banks tightened their credit and then completely pulled the rug out from under the colonies, withdrawing all investments. Cash dried up, shops closed, jobs vanished and goods piled up on the wharves. When the Savings Bank of New South Wales and the Bank of Australia crashed two years later, panic gripped every household. The boom years were well and truly over.

Nearly everyone on Woolloomooloo Hill had been granted or purchased land on the cheap and stocked it heavily to multiply their investments tenfold. For years they had grown fat and complacent on barrels of easy money. Now faced with falling markets and saddled with grand villas and country estates, they watched debt gnaw away at the foundations of their wealth like a giant swarm of white ants. Sir Angus sold off three parcels of land around Camden but, compared with the other residents of the Hill, he had few debts. When the Surveyor-General's department ran out of money, many staff fled into private practice. Sir Angus took a pay cut and Winnie oversaw belt-tightening at Grangemouth.

Down in Sydney Town, the mood grew ugly as the ranks of the poor and destitute swelled daily with as many as a third of the populace without employment. On several occasions the police watch houses were attacked and rioters rampaged through Sydney's streets so that the Governor was forced to call out the garrison troops to restore order with the threat of rifles with fixed bayonets.

One morning Sir Angus arrived at the sandstone fortress of the Surveyor-General's Office as usual, its empty corridors echoing to the tap-tap-tap of his lonely footsteps. Soon after, from his office window he saw, to his astonishment, the spectacle of Governor Gipps himself riding down Macquarie Street at the head of a cordon of mounted police. Stepping into the street, the Major could hear an angry commotion arising from Queen's Square opposite Hyde Park. It was here that he witnessed, to his even greater consternation, the Governor addressing a huge, boisterous throng gathered outside Hyde Park Barracks where the chanting of the convicts within was answered by the cheers of the crowd. Standing well back from this startling scene, the Major heard the Governor exhorting the citizenry to go home. There were catcalls and boos and someone shouted, 'What should we go to our homes for? We have nothing to eat!'

Then the voice of a lone Irishman, clinging to a lamppost to elevate himself above the crowd, rang out, 'You have cheered well and mustered in large numbers! But why do you wear this yoke of oppression so meekly? Rise up! Rise up, I say, like our brothers and sisters in Canada! Throw off the shackles of servitude and the heavy hand of our British overlords!' The crowd cheered lustily.

The Major felt a cold sweat break out on his neck and looked over to the Governor, whose own face seemed white with fear. On his sudden command the uniformed troopers surged forward, batons and rifle-butts flying, and the Irish agitator was seized and dragged away. The Major later read how the fellow was kept clapped in irons on Cockatoo Island for a year. The Government preferred to blame Chartists and Irish terrorists for the people's anger instead of starvation and despair.

By this time, the four horsemen of Debt, Ruin, Shame and Penury had come galloping up Woolloomooloo Hill. The owners of Tusculum, Goderich Lodge, Roslyn Hall and Waratah House auctioned off portions of their estates to stem the rising tide of debt but to no avail. One by one they began to sell their houses and move away. Poor Mr Macquoid, the sheriff of New South Wales, unable to bear the shame, took a pistol up to the attic of his villa and blew his brains out.

Sir Angus's old nemesis Mr Macleay was now encircled by creditors in New South Wales and London and sold off his rarest butterflies and most of his furniture. Finally his eldest son took on all his debts and moved into Rosemount Hall, auctioning off the family properties at Camden and a sizeable slice of the Rosemount estate, forty-four lots in all. Mr Macleay, his wife and daughters fled Sydney and sought refuge on their modest estate in the Hunter Valley.

Over a period of three years, Isobel watched, with a heavy heart, the great exodus from Woolloomooloo Hill, family by family. She was dizzy with guilt as many of her childhood friends were forced from their homes and she read the resentment in their eyes as they packed up and left: why should the Macleods stay while the rest of us are driven out? From her nursery window she saw the long funereal processions of wagons and carts pass by with their melancholy cargo. Clocks, pianos, chiffoniers and sideboards, chests of silverware from India and porcelain from China, and crates crammed with books, vases, Waterford crystal, Spode tea sets and Worcester dinner services.

And she waited and she prayed that her family might be saved from Judgement Day.

One evening, months later, as the Macleod women were sitting by the fire in the drawing room with their needlework in their laps, they heard a knock at the door. Richard poked his head around the frame. 'Come quickly. Papa has something important to announce!'

The whole family gathered in the breakfast room where a fire crackled merrily in the grate. It was here Papa liked to conduct the family's morning and evening devotionals, where the women played cards and the gentlemen chess and backgammon, and Anna entertained them all with Chopin polonaises on the Broadwood. This evening, the Major stood by the mantelpiece, stirring the fire with a poker as he waited for his family to settle into their usual seats. All eyes were fixed on him as he spoke, a smile twitching at the corner of his mouth.

'As you know, I designed this house with my own hands. I even carved the portico pillars myself. Everyone agrees it is a very fine house with a picturesque aspect and well-appointed gardens. However, I have been thinking for some time that our family could benefit from a change of situation.' The Major paused and his smile grew wider. 'I can now tell you that four days ago I made an offer on Rosemount Hall.'

Isobel noticed her mother's sly grin; she obviously knew something of these secret transactions. It was also clear that everyone else knew nothing and were astonished at the news, all talking at once with exclamations of surprise and disbelief. The Major motioned for them to sit down again and be silent. 'As we all know, Mr Macleay's eldest boy, William, has taken on all his father's debts and become the sole occupant and master of Rosemount. I believe he did this out of filial devotion, to protect his father from his numerous creditors.'

The Major took an envelope from the mantel and held it up for all to see. 'I am delighted to inform you that this evening I received young Mr Macleay's reply. He has gratefully accepted my offer and instructed his solicitors to draw up a contract of sale. As of next Friday, I will be the new owner of Rosemount Hall!'

Joseph jumped up from his chair with a shout of 'Hoorah!' and, turning to his older brother William, whispered, 'Well, at least now the house won't be shut up like a tomb!' Truth was that William Macleay had a reputation for being a miserly hermit, more interested in his shells and stuffed fish than in a good table and any civic duties or social obligations. Now Rosemount would be restored to its proper place as a beacon for civilised society and cultured conversation. Tears of happiness spilled from Winnie's eyes. The Major shook hands with his sons and embraced his daughters. Everyone was overjoyed at the prospect of living in 'the finest house in the colony'.

Except Isobel. Grangemouth was where she had been born. It was the only home she knew. Here she had explored the estate with Ballandella, her first true friend who she would never forget. She had played chasings with the cocker spaniels in the garden and croquet with her sisters. She knew every secret nook and subtle detail of this house and its grounds: the angle of the morning light on the tallowwood by her window, the sound of the magpies carolling in the driveway. Now she would have to leave all this behind for some other family to enjoy.

But there was something else that troubled her childish imagination. Isobel could not shake off the memory of old Mr Macleay's tearful face bent over her mother's opal dragonfly. Did he see, even then, his ruin reflected in its ghostly fire? Nor could she forget her father's face that night, so malicious and triumphant.

Did no one else see what she saw? Luck wore two faces: one man's victory meant another man's defeat. From Mr Macleay's ruin had sprung the Macleods' good fortune. It was the law of nature: the strong feasted on the carcasses of the weak. Isobel joined in the collective jubilation, but in her heart there lurked a terrible thought. When would the opal dragonfly turn its fateful, fiery eyes on them?

Chapter 9

A MOTHER'S LOVE

FEBRUARY 1849 TO AUGUST 1850

Since the family's move to Rosemount Hall four years ago, the Macleods' prospects had brightened considerably. Any misgivings Isobel held privately about the 'curse' of the opal brooch were soon forgotten amid the serious business of charity work and the ongoing demands of her education, not to mention society's ceaseless rounds of visits, parties and dances.

Father had undertaken a fourth expedition, this time to the north-west (in search of yet another great river), and was gone for a whole year. Winnie was stoic, as were the children. He returned in triumph with a handsome collection of fossils that he donated to form part of Sydney's first Australian Museum of Natural History. The publication of his expedition journals met with an enthusiastic response from credible quarters and the subsequent sales were heartening.

Despite the unrelenting pressure of his duties as Surveyor-General and the obstinate dim-wittedness of his superiors, the Major was gratified by the colony's burgeoning growth. He took considerable credit for this success as both explorer and surveyor, responsible for opening up hundreds of thousands of acres of productive land for settlement.

With these achievements, the Macleods' stocks rose, both materially and socially. The two older Macleod girls, Alice and Grace, were now eminently eligible and long overdue for courting. Interested male parties soon appeared in the offing of their social sphere and made steady headway in their direction. A prolonged preoccupation of the Macleod household (and subject of excited debate and speculation) became the intentions of two suitors.

The first was a cultured young aristocrat by the name of Lord Andrew Twyckenham, who (on his father's death) would one day in the not-too-distant future inherit the title of the 14th Baron Crawley of Gothamberly House, Hertfordshire. The young Baron— as Alice liked to call him for the sake of convenient (if premature) shorthand—had only recently arrived in the colony in pursuit of enriching experiences and even richer investments. The second gent was an officer, Captain Ralph Tranter of the 11th (North Devonshire) Regiment (dubbed the '*Bloody Eleventh*' for its service in the Napoleonic war), now posted at the new Victoria Barracks on Old South Head Road in Paddington.

Barely turned fifteen, Isobel was recruited as an intermediary between her sister Grace and the handsome Captain Tranter, bearing confidential messages (on gossamer-thin blue writing paper) and tokens of affection (flowers, gloves, a pretty charm bracelet) between the two parties as the need arose. It was all an innocent and amusing game at first and the Captain seemed appreciative of Isobel's assistance as a discreet Mercury.

While these tokens were received and responded to with alacrity in the first few weeks of their courtship, Grace began to grow strangely cool towards this young man's overtures. At this behaviour Isobel was deeply puzzled, especially given her sister's historic enthusiasm for redcoats. The only explanation that Isobel found plausible was fear. Was that possible? For all her hauteur and pride, it seemed that poor Grace, faced with the imminent reality of love (and no doubt marriage), was overcome with terror. Despite their strained relations, Isobel pitied her.

And then the rules of the game changed.

'Your sister does not seem pleased with my trinkets,' the Captain confessed sadly one glorious afternoon at a picnic lunch out at Lady Macquarie's Chair.

He and Isobel stood together at a distance from the main party, eating their cured English salmon sandwiches and admiring the harbour view. By the water's edge, Alice could be seen flirting with her well-dressed beau, the young Baron, as were Beatrice Finch and Emma Bradley with their respective suitors. Grace sat apart with the other single Finch and Bradley girls as if she did not have a young man to pay her court.

'They are certainly not trinkets, Captain Tranter!' said Isobel indignantly. 'I should think any woman given such gifts should consider herself deeply flattered. I know I would.'

Captain Tranter regarded her with a look of such intense curiosity as to make her blush. 'Would you, Miss Isobel?' he asked.

Oh my! thought Isobel. What have I said? She scrutinised the contents of her own heart to decide if she had spoken out of gallantry (to soothe his wounded feelings) or coquettishness (to arouse and distract them). For the sake of propriety she hoped it was the former but, if she was to be brutally honest, she was not at all sure.

Her face burned for shame. 'I should go and help Florence with her dogs,' she said, excusing herself and hurrying away to where Miss Finch sat on the rug with her pet foxhounds tumbling about noisily.

In the days following this scene, Isobel's heart was in a state of blissful confusion. The more she tried *not* to think about Captain Tranter, the more he wandered into her thoughts and then, one night, into her dreams. He had an undeniably fine visage, a good wit, winning manners, and, as far as she could tell, a kind and honest heart. With his officer's commission and rumours of a more than adequate income, it was a mystery why he had not already found a match.

On the occasion of the Captain's next visit to Grangemouth, Isobel could not help but notice the frequency of the handsome soldier's glances in her direction, glances of such unmistakeable warmth that they caused her cheeks to colour and her pulse to race. Isobel feared that her own eyes disclosed the warmth of her feelings no matter how hard she struggled to conceal them. Each subsequent visit only confirmed the persistence of this courteous gentleman's interest in her and between these visits she debated with herself as to whether her young, untutored heart was responding merely to the flattery of his attentions or was genuinely attracted to his fine qualities.

What should have brought a young woman like Isobel great delight was instead the cause for great alarm. She could tell that Captain Tranter was impatient to steal a moment alone with her and the idea filled her with a painful admixture of ecstasy and dread. For Isobel knew all too well the catastrophe that would ensue if she interfered in Grace's courtship. Anna and Grace found reasons to be disappointed in Isobel on an almost daily basis but she knew that a betrayal such as this would furnish them with a fierce and righteous anger she did not think she could bear to endure.

Isobel decided to find every excuse henceforth to be absent when the Captain called. The change in her sister's attitude was both prompt and remarkable. Isobel could not be sure if it was because Grace had become cognisant of her suitor's straying attentions or suspected the new target of his desires. Whatever the reason, Grace suddenly began to take a more active interest in the lover whom she had of late treated with a nonchalance bordering on disdain. 'Look what Captain Tranter brought me today,' she would boast at dinner, showing off the latest love token or billet-doux to her sisters while looking darkly in Isobel's direction (or so Isobel nervously imagined).

But Grace had let the young officer's ardour cool too long. Isobel tried to tamp down any excitement or hope she felt regarding what now looked like a fateful misfiring of Cupid's shaft. But why should she? she asked herself. How was she to blame? It was her sister, after all, who had played so recklessly with the young man's feelings. What could Grace expect?

The moment of truth was nigh. One afternoon, Captain Tranter rode over from the Barracks to Rosemount, arriving unannounced with a note for Isobel. The family were out that day but, thankfully, the note was taken by the maid, Agnes, and delivered directly into Isobel's hands. Inside was pressed a purple orchid, a floral symbol flagging a lover's ardent passion. With it the brave Captain declared his love without shame or reservation.

My dearest Isobel

The Poets know that when one has been blind'd by the brash & gaudy glitter of the Sun, one can fail to appreciate the pale & dignified Beauty of her sister, the Moon, she who seeks to hide her face modestly under cover of Night but still outshines even the stars.

As have I, dearest Isobel, at first distract'd by your Sister's undeniable and praiseworthy qualities, come to a deeper appreciation of your own peerless Beauty and good nature. Your loveliness of soul and figure, your fine intellect and tastes, your many virtues that declare themselves not vainly but discreetly through selfless deeds and considerate words, all these excellent qualities have taken my poor heart Prisoner. I entreat you, fair lady, to allow me the honour of courting you once you are of age. I am barely eight years your senior and shall happily await that blessed time.

The last thing I wish for is to cause a painful disruption to your sibling affections. Your sister has been kind enough to indulge my attentions but we both know that love does not

*flourish in her bosom or my own. I am sure she will be reliev'd
and glad to release me from our courtship and rejoice in the
fact that you and I (who wish her nothing but happiness) may
discover feelings of Mutual Tenderness.*

*One word from you and I shall seek your sister's and
parents' blessing to our courtship. Or, if my feelings find no
echo in your own, I swear I shall cease to importune you and
shall resign myself to my loveless fate with courage.*

Yours with respect and hope etc., etc.,
  Captain Ralph Tranter Esq.

Oh, how little it seemed that the Captain knew her sister! And
what a whirlwind of grief, Isobel feared, this would unleash. Her
heart was sorely tried. She did not really know what she felt; her
acquaintance with the young man had been very agreeable but
also very brief. What chance was there for them to come to know
each other better when their courtship would be overshadowed by
Grace's jealousy and hate?

She turned for help to the only person she felt she could
trust—Alice.

'How do you feel about him, Izzie?' Alice asked when she had
read the letter.

'I don't know. I . . . I think about him a great deal,' she confessed.

Alice smiled. 'And what do you think? Have you ever imagined
kissing him?'

'Oh, Alice!' Isobel blushed and stared into her lap. 'Well . . . yes.'

Alice laughed and clapped her hands. 'Well, that is a very good start! Now, tell me, my little sister, what is it about the man that you like so much? Apart from the fact he has the sense to see that Grace does not love him.'

To her own surprise, Isobel had quite a lot to say about Captain Tranter's good points. Alice promised she would talk to Mama. She was sure something could be worked out. It would be a tragedy to have a misunderstanding stand in the way of a good match and (who knows?) a loving marriage.

But Alice was wrong. Despite her best efforts, Winnie would not be moved. 'Isobel is too young and it is not her turn,' she insisted. 'Everyone on the Hill knows the gentleman is courting Grace. Imagine her humiliation to be replaced by her little sister! It would be a scandal! I will not have it.'

'But, Mama, Grace does not love him!' Alice insisted. 'Surely Isobel should at least be given a chance to find out what is in her heart. God moves in mysterious ways.'

'God has nothing to do with it!'

At Winnie's insistence, the letter was returned with a curt note from Isobel terminating all relations with Captain Tranter. The Captain graciously made his exit, proffering his deepest apologies to Isobel and to Grace in separate notes. His rapid exit may have averted gossip and saved Grace's pride but there was no hiding the truth. Grace had eyes to see what had occurred, and the smouldering fire of her resentment against her little sister (who had always been her parents' favourite and was now the preferred choice of her first suitor) blazed even hotter than before.

And Isobel? She too resented Grace, who had flirted coldly and cruelly with such a fine young man and thrown away a chance at love. And, in defiance of her deep and instinctual affection and respect for her mother, Isobel harboured a kernel of resentment against Winnie, who had forced Isobel to surrender her first love to save her sister's pride.

Thankfully Alice's courtship was more happily resolved with the acceptance of a proposal from the Baron and the fulfilment of her long-held ambition to marry a dull man with a handsome annuity. The wedding at St James' was a splendid affair, with Alice's sisters and friends (two Finches and two Bradleys) making up a party of seven bridesmaids in white muslin trimmed with blue bows, while the bride shone in white silk with a tulle veil and orange blossom wreath. Sydney society turned out in force and all its finery to pay tribute to the eldest daughter of Major Macleod. 'What a truly excellent match!' Mrs Palmer declared tearfully to anyone who would listen amid general agreement that the Baron would provide Alice and her family with many reasons for joy and honour.

Among all the happy faces in the church that day, Isobel was struck by her mother's strained expression, at variance with the overall mood of celebration. With a look of the most intense scrutiny, Winnie stared at the groom as if she might lay bare the inner secrets of his soul. What on earth was going on? Isobel wondered. Why this sudden air of suspicion? The Baron had been a frequent guest at Rosemount over the last year and the object of much admiration and affection within the household and beyond. In all that time, Winnie had remained one of the most enthusiastic advocates of this match. What had changed?

Isobel dismissed this strange behaviour as no more than a mother's natural *tristesse* at bidding her daughter farewell. After the awkward matter of Captain Tranter, Isobel had noticed that her mother was more temperamental than usual, even short-tempered. It was understandable, of course; finding suitable husbands for one's daughters (and wives for one's sons) was known to be an exhausting, often drawn-out rite of passage for every mother.

For Isobel, tears of joy were alloyed with heartache at the departure of her dear sister Alice with her new husband to England. The only balm was the prospect of frequent letters and the knowledge that Alice had found happiness. Isobel herself found refuge from sadness in her sketching and painting, with a renewed focus on and dedication to her art lessons with their art master, Mr Vasey.

Life at Rosemount resumed its normal rhythms, albeit without Alice. Grace, Anna and Isobel attended their weekly rounds of music, dance and language lessons, and their social calendar was never empty for more than a day or so before their attendance was required at a supper, dance or picnic.

With Papa so often away, Isobel had grown accustomed to this busy female sphere. But she did miss her brothers. It felt only like yesterday that the three boys had played cricket on the lawn and hide-and-seek under the tallowwoods late into the long summer afternoons at Grangemouth. Her fondest memories of childhood at Rosemount were of winter evenings in the morning room, where she played draughts with Joseph, listened to Richard reading poetry or to William singing a duet with Grace or Alice, accompanied by Anna on piano, while her parents read or dozed by the roaring fire.

Now all three of her brothers were men, embarked on their own adventures in the wide world beyond Rosemount. How she envied them. Enlarging the Major's paternal pride, William was serving as an officer with the frigate HMS *Iris* on anti-slaving patrols off West Africa. The youngest, Joseph, was finishing law studies at university and hoping to be articled to a firm in the city. The middle son, Richard, had put his plans to study classics at Oxford on hold at their father's request that he manage the family property at Camden.

Studious and gifted, Richard possessed a scholarly rather than agricultural disposition but took on this heavy responsibility out of filial love. He had proved a most intelligent and conscientious manager and had made a success of the venture, despite his initial self-doubt. His duty almost done, Richard looked forward to his release early in the new year.

And then catastrophe struck with the unexpectedness of lightning from a clear sky.

Afterwards, Isobel would be haunted by the argument she had overheard between her parents in the breakfast room a few weeks before. She had hung back, unseen, in the doorway and noted every word of their exchange. It was a rare occurrence for her mother to question Papa's judgement, especially within earshot of others, so Isobel had paid close attention. Winnie had implored her husband to appoint a new manager for the Camden estate as soon as possible and bring Richard home before Christmas. She had urged this course of action vehemently, saying the 'dear boy' deserved a rest over the summer before leaving for Oxford. The Major had dismissed her concerns and insisted Richard stay on into the new year.

In the second week of the following January, Richard rode out with the head stockman to inspect a broken fence in the northern paddock. Startled by a red-bellied black snake in the long grass, Richard's horse threw him violently from the saddle. He broke his neck and died instantly. Within a twelvemonth of Alice's splendid wedding, the Macleod family gathered again at St James' for the funeral of one of its sons.

In her grieving mother's shrouds, Winnie wore a mourning brooch woven from strands of Richard's hair. But Isobel could not stop thinking of the opal dragonfly; it hovered in her mind, a malignant shadow over this unforeseen calamity. When only six months later Winnie was laid low with severe dysentery, Isobel heard the ominous thrum of the dragonfly again, its wings reverberating like a tocsin inside her head.

The room was still darkened when Isobel entered. She carried a bowl, a jug of warm water and a flannel. In the bed, Winifred lay half-dozing, clutching the coverlet. On the bedside chair was Isobel's journal, splayed cover up. Isobel had sat here all night keeping vigil by the light of an oil lamp. In the bottom corner of some pages she had sketched her mother's face in sweet repose. Thankfully her mama's sleep had been peaceful. But the odour of sickness and memory of pain still clung to the room that had been her prison for the last three weeks.

Winnie's eyes fluttered open. 'Open the curtains a little, please.'

She was too ashamed for any of the servants to see her in this state. The Major visited regularly but had no stomach for the indignities of the sickroom, so it had fallen to her daughters to nurse her. It was no easy task. In the depths of delirium, she wept freely, confessing her fears for her family if she died and begging her husband (in his absence) to 'be patient with the children and protect them from worry'.

Isobel parted the drapes. A shaft of sunlight relieved the chamber's gloom. She also opened the window a touch to let in a waft of spring air and the familiar sounds of the garden and distant harbour. Isobel hoped these comforting reminders of the everyday world would revive her mother's spirits. She refused to countenance the possibility of her mother's death. She knew it was wrong but last night she had used her prayers to bargain with God that he may judge the Macleods worthy of more good fortune. Whatever her father's or siblings' sins may be (as well as her own), surely her mother's goodness cancelled all the others out?

She poured warm water into the basin and washed her mother's face and hands. Winnie flinched as Isobel offered her a sip of cool water from a tumbler, her lips parched and cracked. 'Try to take some,' Isobel murmured. Over the last week the abdominal pains had worsened. Winnie had lost more weight and her face was sharpened by hunger and anguish.

Dr Finch had visited again yesterday and prescribed an increased dose of Logwood Decoction with a few raspberry leaves and drops of laudanum. 'The bloody flux has her in its grip,' he had told the Major, 'but she is strong. I am confident she will make a full recovery.'

'You slept soundly,' chirped Isobel as cheerily as she could manage.

Winnie beckoned her to come closer. 'Close the door,' she whispered, as though someone might overhear them. 'I have something I want to give you.'

Isobel hoped her mother was not delirious again. 'What is it, Mama?'

'I have something . . . I have . . . *something.*' Winnie became insistent and a little agitated. She tried to pull back the coverlet and sit up but the effort defeated her. She appeared weaker, overcome with exhaustion.

'Please rest, Mama,' Isobel insisted gently. 'I'll get it.'

Winnie pointed to the cedar dresser. 'The green box.'

Isobel did her mother's bidding, closing the bedroom door and fetching Winnie's favourite jewellery box from the dresser. It was embossed silver inlaid with malachite. Her mother caressed its lid for a moment, which seemed to calm her. She motioned for Isobel to sit beside her. 'Listen, there is something very important I have to tell you. But you must promise me something first.'

'What is it, Mama?'

'You must promise me not to cry.'

Isobel nodded. Her face was still but her spirit was greatly vexed.

'Last night I had a dream. A beautiful dream. You and I were having our picnic in the grotto down by the harbour. For your thirteenth birthday, remember?'

Isobel nodded again. She could feel her chest tighten and tears spring into her eyes. But she had promised. She would not cry.

'Such a clear sky. And so many boats. And you with your cherry lollipops. And then across the bay I saw a light coming towards us. As bright as the sun. Brighter. And in this light I saw the most beautiful thing of all. An angel.'

A sob broke from Isobel's mouth. 'Oh, Mama, no.'

'Please don't be sad, my sweet. I know this is hard. But don't you see? This is a sign of God's mercy. And His love. He is preparing me for what is to come.'

Isobel could not speak. She looked down, two tears dropping into her lap. Winnie stroked her daughter's solemn face. She then opened the lid of her jewellery box and closed her hand around something hidden inside. Then Winnie opened her hand. There in her palm lay the opal dragonfly. 'I want to give this to you, my love. As a memento. A reminder of a mother's love. So you will think of me when I am gone.' Isobel could contain her tears no longer. She clasped her mother's hands and sobbed like a child. 'There, there, my little Izzie. You will not be alone. You have your sisters and brothers, and your father to protect you. And you will have me to watch over you. Listen.'

Isobel wiped the tears from her face and looked at her mother.

'I want to give you this but . . . I am afraid to do so. There is something . . . I have such strange dreams,' she said, looking through Isobel as if at a phantom hovering just past her shoulder. 'Terrible dreams, some of them. Unimaginable. And then there are others of such beauty that you would weep to see them. They show me . . . I do not understand what they show me. Or where they come from. They began when your father gave me this gift.'

Winnie sighed deeply, her face in a spasm of doubt.

'I wish I knew what to do. I believe this . . .' She held the dragonfly up to the sunlight that poured in at the window. Its effulgence fixed Isobel's eye—so beautiful, so mysterious. 'I believe it is a special gift, you see,' said Winnie, 'A powerful gift. But only for one who has a pure heart. It would be fatal for a heart filled with bitterness or anger . . .'

Winnie's eyes closed for a moment as if to shut out a vision of horror. She opened them again and smiled at her daughter, but bravely now as if fighting against a surge of pain, a torment. She spoke with a desperate urgency. 'But you must promise me something, Isobel. This is to be kept safe by you. No one else. Not your father. Not your sisters. Grace, especially. I know how much she has her heart set on it. She must never have it.'

What was the terrible secret of this brooch that Winnie could not name? Isobel noticed her mother's attention wander and her face and hands become agitated. Had the delirium returned or had it never left?

'If this powerful gift should ever cause you—or anyone you love—pain or suffering, then throw it away! Promise me you will do this. Cast it into the sea, bury it somewhere secret. Promise me that.'

Winnie's eyes darted about in bewilderment, her breathing now sharp and rapid. She seemed gripped by a terrible panic, her thoughts increasingly addled and distressful to her. 'Maybe this is what I should have done. Maybe I should do it now. Oh, please, Isobel my love, destroy it, do what I could not do . . .'

'Please don't upset yourself, Mama,' said Isobel, having no idea what it was she should promise to assuage her mother's fears. 'Please calm yourself.'

Winnie closed her eyes again and slipped back into her half-sleeping, half-waking limbo. Isobel held the opal dragonfly in her hand. Was it her mother's love token to Isobel as it had been the Major's to his wife? If it did possess some strange power, how would she ever know? Her mother seemed torn between two convictions: that the opal dragonfly was a gift that would help her daughter and a curse that might bring her harm.

Isobel kissed her mother's face.

'I will do as you ask,' she said, hoping that when the time came she would know the right path to choose. 'Sleep, now, Mama. Sleep.'

ISOBEL

SEPTEMBER 1851 TO JULY 1853

Chapter 10

A MATTER OF HONOUR

27 SEPTEMBER 1851 TO OCTOBER 1851

A carriage bore Papa's inert body back to Rosemount. Dr Finch had staunched the wound in his neck but the Major had still lost a great deal of blood. The doctor stayed for several hours, administering leeches and poultices, grinding powders to assuage the Major's pain and the onset of his fever. He was laid out in a camp bed made up in the library as Dr Finch advised against taking him upstairs. 'He is too weak. Best keep him down here.'

Isobel returned from the duel with Lieutenant Manning. When she had run onto the duelling ground between the Major and his adversary, the group of men all about had exploded with rage, screaming a torrent of the vilest abuse at her: 'What is the meaning of this outrage?' 'The girl is plainly a lunatic!' 'Brazen hussy!' 'She-devil!' The cruel words rained down like physical blows until

Lieutenant Manning stepped in and wrapped his cloak about the shivering, weeping young woman who lay prostrate in the mud.

'Gentlemen, gentlemen, please! This is Sir Angus's youngest daughter,' implored the young officer. 'She is obviously quite overcome.'

Dr Finch knelt at the Major's side, urgently attending to his wounds. 'The girl is in shock,' he told the lieutenant. 'Give her these salts and take her back to Rosemount at once. We will follow shortly.'

Mr Davidson, his head now bandaged by his own physician, came forward. 'I hope this concludes the matter. Can I assume that honour has been satisfied?'

'I think you can,' replied Lieutenant Manning.

Mr Davidson turned to leave. He looked back at Isobel, still on the ground, her clothes spattered, her hair in disarray, her face red raw with weeping. 'Miss Macleod, I don't care what any of these gentlemen may think,' he said pointing at the circle of onlookers. 'I believe what you did today was courageous. I apologise that you had to witness this. And I wish your father a speedy recovery.' With that, he doffed his damaged bell-topper and walked away with his seconds and other associates towards the paperbark grove.

Isobel's reception at the house was as unpleasant as she might have feared. She had hurried upstairs on her return and changed into her normal clothes, but not before Grace had seen her in the driveway alighting from a carriage with Lieutenant Manning. Meanwhile the officer explained to Grace and Anna the circumstances of their unexpected arrival. When the lieutenant had withdrawn and while Dr Finch attended their father in the library,

Grace and Anna summoned Isobel to speak with them in the drawing room.

'You will no doubt be gratified to learn that I have dismissed James this morning for the part he has played in the humiliation of our family,' Grace began. 'He is packing his bags as we speak. I understand that Sarah was complicit in this travesty and chooses to go with him. They shall have no references from me or Papa.'

Isobel's face flushed red. She knew Grace had done this to wound her but she did not feel any guilt on this score. Yes, she had ordered James to prepare her a horse but he had volunteered to accompany her to the duelling ground. And she also knew that he and Sarah had no need of references as they sought their fortune at Bathurst. She wished them well.

'As for your part in this disgraceful affair, I am at a loss for words,' Grace continued. 'The lieutenant has described your behaviour to me in some detail. I cannot imagine what our dear mother would have made of such a performance! She would be astonished that she had raised a daughter with so little modesty, propriety and respect for her betters.'

Isobel's face burned with shame but also anger at her sister's calculated unkindness. To speculate about her mother's disappointment in her: that was low, exceedingly low.

'Is Father so childish, in your view, that he cannot conduct his own affairs?' cried Anna, pacing in front of the mantelpiece. 'You've made him the laughing stock of the colony. And us.'

Isobel stared at her feet. She tightened her jaw in defiance. She had endured so much these last few years. She would surely endure this. Her sisters were such hypocrites. They did not love her father as she did. How could they begin to understand?

'And dressed in your brother's clothes! What were you thinking?' Grace looked up at the ceiling as though beseeching God to bear witness to her suffering, 'As if this family did not have enough troubles, you heap dishonour on our heads with your unnatural . . . your impious wilfulness! To make such a display of yourself is . . . is . . .' Grace struggled for the right words. 'It is perverse and fanatical.'

'Perverse and fanatical!' echoed Anna, still pacing like a nervous cat.

Grace's face was now bright red. She had abandoned her usual superior hectoring tone and was clearly in the throes of a rage. 'Do you regard the privileges of your family's position and of your own education and prospects as worthless? Is that why you are happy to throw them away so lightly?'

Isobel said nothing.

'And what about us, your siblings?' Grace continued. 'Do you give tuppence for our position in the world? Did you stop for one moment to consider the damage your preposterous pantomime would inflict on us? Our name will be mocked in every drawing room, in every house, in every important family in the colony.'

Isobel still said nothing.

'What did you hope to achieve?' Grace shouted. 'To *save* your father? Is that what you imagined? When in fact it appears that you have achieved exactly the opposite!'

Isobel looked up. What on earth did Grace mean by that?

'Charging like a bedlam inmate into the middle of a gentlemen's duel. No wonder Papa was distracted. No wonder he turned to look at you and made himself an easy target. No wonder he misfired and did not strike his opponent. You did not *save* Papa with your foolishness, Isobel. No, it is thanks to your foolishness that you may well have *killed* him!'

Isobel cried out as if struck. 'That is a lie. And you are wicked for saying so!'

She ran from the drawing room and up the staircase to her room where she lay on her bed and wept copiously, angry at her sisters' cruelty but also fearful that there could be some truth to their accusations. Was she really to blame for what had happened? She did not know. She prayed with all her heart that Papa would not die and leave her alone in the world.

That night the Major fell into a coma. Dr Finch was summoned again and he, in turn, called on a colleague, Dr Marsden. There seemed little they could do apart from examine the patient every few hours, checking his pupils, pulse, reflexes and breathing, and attending to his dressings. Dr Marsden was overheard speaking low to his fellow physician: 'If all functions of sense disappear, he may only have four or five days left. But we must not despair until the pupils cease to contract. With any return of sensibility our hopes rise.'

On this occasion, Sir Angus cheated death. But he still took three nights and much of a fourth day to recover his wits sufficiently to sit up in bed and ask for a lamb chop. His full rehabilitation would take at least another three weeks of bed rest and gentle exercise.

His right hand shook for some time after that, possibly from nerve damage or as a residue of the shock. Dr Finch came by daily to provide soothing medications and words of encouragement.

Grace did her best to quarantine her father from any enervating stimuli. Unfortunately, it took less than a week before the Major received a letter of outrage on his behalf at the puffed-up indignation and satirical barbs of the newspapermen. *The Empire* scoffed at 'the fiery old soldier and frothing senator popping at each other with a barbarism unutterably grotesque', chastising them both for setting a bad example to the lower orders. 'If our lawmakers get their hats bored by pistol balls in such encounters, who shall chastise the brutish pugilist for putting himself in the way of black eyes and bloody nose?' A satirist at *Bell's Life* even wrote a poem about the contest of arms:

A MATTER OF HONOUR
They met!—'twas in the bush,
And each thought—Heaven knows what;
And each cheek wore a flush—
For each one was a slow shot.
One wore an Albert hat
His rival wore a helmet
They both were somewhat fat
And as such, they were well met.
They raised their murd'rous tools
The signal then was given,
To see which of the fools
Sent t'other fool to heaven.

Behold! A queer 'youth' dashed
To interrupt the slaughter
'Old Blazes' was abashed
The 'lad' was his own daughter!
The world may think them right,
For neither killed their brother
But, surely, they'll ne'er fight
Such daring duel another!

The Major did not see the humour of this doggerel. Nor did Isobel. To have her father so publicly lampooned as a doddering coward and fool was intolerable. She struggled to forgive Papa for exposing himself—and her—to such ridicule. Grace and Anna's scorn was also roused to a new pitch, largely directed at 'the devils of the press' but also finding a nearer target in their 'reckless' sister. They adopted a brave public face of laughing off the journalists' mockery but in their hearts the shame smouldered for a long time. 'Once fallen, forever socially dead' was the well-worn phrase that haunted Isobel and her sisters.

On the third day of her ordeal of wondering if father would be taken from her, Isobel received a letter. Grace was still advertising for new help (in the absence of Sarah and James) so it was left to the scullery maid, Jane, to fetch the two o'clock mail and bring it to her mistress. It was close to dusk when Grace summoned Isobel to the drawing room.

'There is a letter here from William. Addressed to you,' she said frostily, holding the envelope between thumb and forefinger. 'I assume you have written him about the duel.' Isobel nodded almost imperceptibly, unsure whether she was obliged to betray such a confidence. 'Given your recent history, I would be justified in exercising extreme vigilance over your communications.' Grace's eyes glittered, relishing her authority.

Heavens above! Was Grace proposing to read Isobel's private correspondence? Was this a taste of the new regime at Rosemount? Isobel imagined herself as a prisoner in a domestic version of Mr Bentham's Panopticon, her every movement and thought scrutinised by her sister-gaoler. She was momentarily overcome by a suffocating dizziness.

'But out of my love for you, dear sister, and in the interests of your proper rehabilitation, I shall not insist on such oversight,' Grace informed Isobel with an unpleasant smile. 'I only ask that you share any news of our brother William's whereabouts and plans. If—Heaven forfend!—anything should happen to poor Papa, it will be necessary to notify Alice, William and Joseph and arrange for their speedy return home.'

Isobel agreed to share any pertinent news and withdrew. William had last written her from Melbourne where he had been seeking business opportunities. She fervently hoped he was already on his way back to Sydney. She opened the letter and read:

Dearest Isobel,

I received your alarming note two days ago when to my astonishment I discover'd The Argus *report of 29th Sept, entitled 'Absurd Test of Arms in Swamp'. I regret I could not provide timely counsel to prevent this unseemly Farce and this injury to our family name. In the circumstances, I would have admonish'd you not pursue your perilous stratagem. While I have no illusions about your Courage, dear sister, I am fiercely protective of your personal safety—and Reputation! If that is a fault, I plead fraternal love as my defence. I was surpris'd that you felt unable to consult your sister Grace about such 'desperate measures'. I have taken the liberty of writing to Dr Finch to learn about Father's prospects for recovery.*

I wish to share some Important News: Joseph and I have both been offered promising situations with a trading company in Madras. I hope this will furnish an ideal resolution to the ongoing conflict with Father over Joseph's (rumoured) authorship of the scandalous pamphlet that upset Mr Macleay and his son, William. With luck, tempers will cool over time and Joseph's new prospects will win him favour again with Papa. We have already book'd our passage from Sydney to Madras in three weeks' time. There are many urgent matters to orchestrate before then but I shall make every effort to visit Rosemount Hall. My prayers are with Father and, of course, with you, my brave but impetuous, headstrong sister.

With a brother's affectionate concern & love etc., etc.,
    William E. Macleod

Isobel had sought reassurances of William's sympathy but this response left her bewildered. The chiding tone of her brother's letter stung. It appeared to blame her as much as it did Papa for 'this injury to our family name'. How unfair! *She* had not challenged

Mr Davidson to a duel. Even *he*—her father's enemy—had praised Isobel's courage. And in public too. And the suggestion that Isobel should have conferred with Grace! This betrayed William's total ignorance of the chasm that had grown between the sisters and was a measure of her brother's remoteness from the world of Rosemount. And there were even more unpleasant surprises. The shock of learning about both her brothers' departure for India (for how long, she wondered) only confirmed Isobel's sense of loneliness and isolation. What help would her brothers be to her in Madras? She would be lucky to be favoured with a letter every twelvemonth or so.

Isobel felt tears on her cheeks. She could no longer deny the truth that she was utterly alone. There was nobody to be her confidante or champion, nobody to hear her sorrows and fears or take her part. On all sides, she was subjected to censure and reproach.

And she suspected there was worse to come.

Chapter 11

THE INTERVIEW

1 OCTOBER 1851

The afternoon after her father's resurrection and request for a lamb chop, the Major asked to see Isobel. Too weak yet to ascend the staircase to his bedchamber, he was content to stay in his camp bed in the company of his books. Despite telling herself she had no reason to fear him, Isobel knocked on the study door with trepidation.

'Come in,' came the familiar reply.

Isobel entered the dim room, all its wooden shutters closed but one. A stream of sunlight poured in behind her father's bed, crowning his head in a bright aureole and casting his face in shadow. She could barely credit that it was here, only five days earlier, she had spied her father cleaning his French pistols and resolved to save his life. The Major sat, propped upright with pillows and bolsters, a pile of books at his bedside. 'How are you feeling, Papa?' Isobel asked as she approached the bed.

'I am much improved. As you can see,' her father replied.

A silence followed that lengthened uncomfortably as Isobel stood, staring at her feet, trying not to fidget. She felt like a little girl again, summoned to her father's study to be scolded. The Major cleared his throat. 'Here, sit down. I can't see you standing there in the dark.'

Isobel pulled a chair up close to the bed. There was a second awkward pause.

'I expect you think I am angry with you,' said the Major at last. This remark hovered uncertainly between an assertion and a question.

'Yes,' said Isobel in a small voice, choosing the latter.

'I expect I should be,' the Major said gruffly. 'It is regrettable that you had to witness . . . events,' he struggled for the right words, 'events that no young woman, in fact no woman of *any* age, should witness. It is most regrettable.'

'Yes, Father.' Isobel looked at her hands, folded in her lap. Without much conscious thought, she dug her fingernails into the flesh of her palms, a small act of penance. The pain was a reminder of her sin and would keep her focused on her obligation to be contrite. She was still unsure how angry Papa was but his stern face and tone of voice did not bode well.

'It is also regrettable that regarding a private matter to be settled between two gentlemen, some people see fit to judge. And to mock.' The Major began to cough, a spasm that threatened to overwhelm him. Isobel reached for the jug and tumbler on the side table. Her father took a gulp of water and regained his composure.

'This *disgraceful* trial by press is hardly your fault, of course,' he conceded. 'I attribute no bad motives to you, Isobel, believe me. What you did was foolish but not malicious. You intended no harm.'

'Oh, Papa, quite the reverse!' Isobel protested, a sob shaking her breast.

The Major patted the air soothingly with both hands and shushed her as one would a small child. 'Now, now. Calm yourself. I understand that you only wanted to help.'

Isobel's face was ashen. She leaned forward, clutching her father's left hand and speaking low to make her confession. 'I was *so* frightened, Papa.'

'Of course.' Her father patted her on the wrist. 'Of course you were.'

If the Major had any intentions to chastise Isobel, he had lost all momentum and enthusiasm for that course. His own countenance softened and he squeezed his daughter's hand. 'I only wish your mother was here to counsel you. She would know what to say.'

Isobel smiled at him through her tears. 'I miss her so much.'

'So do I,' her father murmured, his voice hoarse with emotion. Papa had borne Winnie's death with the usual public stoicism expected of a gentleman but Isobel knew that, in private, the loss of his wife had overwhelmed him with sadness. The Major wiped his face and cleared this throat as if to shrug off this upwelling of grief. He spoke now in a brisker tone, suddenly mindful of his weighty responsibilities as a parent. 'I fear that your moral and spiritual welfare have been sorely neglected since your mother left us, Isobel.'

Isobel looked puzzled. What did he mean by this?

'I blame myself, of course, for not taking a more direct interest. I assumed—or I hoped at least—that your sisters would prove exemplars in your mother's absence. Perhaps that was a mistake.'

Isobel did not know how to respond. This seemed a much less charitable view of her conduct; neglect of her 'moral and spiritual welfare' sounded like a failure of her own character. She was disappointed by Papa's change of heart. For one precious moment, Isobel had felt protected and exonerated by her father's open-heartedness. And their shared grief. But now she was confused. Had her father forgiven her or not?

'I promised your mother I would take good care of all of you,' the Major sighed, his focus turned inwards. 'I have done everything in my power to ensure your happiness and good character. I have also made provisions in my will to secure your future when I am gone. What more can a father do?' A shadow of sorrow passed across his brow. 'I wonder sometimes if it is enough.'

'Please do not reproach yourself,' Isobel said softly. 'You have done so much.'

There was another silence. Isobel could tell that Papa had more that he wanted to say. She waited patiently, trying to stay calm.

'I have been giving your situation a great deal of thought.' The Major spoke but his voice sounded distant and he did not meet her gaze. 'A young woman, all alone in this big house with no mother to look out for her. And with her sisters preoccupied with their own concerns. It is not a situation conducive to happiness or propriety.'

'But Papa, I beg you . . .' The words tumbled urgently from Isobel's lips before she had time to check herself. Her father's face flashed with anger. He was not used to being interrupted.

'Do me the courtesy, please,' he insisted sharply. 'This is not a trifling matter.'

Isobel kept her counsel and listened. The Major continued. 'I have written this morning to your Aunt Louisa and proposed that it could be an arrangement beneficial to all parties if you were to live with her for a while.'

Isobel was in shock, unable to comprehend what Papa had just said.

'Your aunt has lacked for company ever since her poor George passed on and her youngest, Mary, married. As you know, my sister is a good-hearted woman, esteemed for her charity work and excellent common sense. She has raised three fine daughters of her own. I believe you would thrive under her care.'

Isobel was crying now, head bowed and tears slipping down her face. Banishment! What had she done to deserve this? This was a much worse fate than she had imagined. She expected harsh words and punishment but certainly not this. Never this.

Aunt Louisa was no monster. But the prospect of any period as her companion filled Isobel with dread. The widow lived in an elegant villa in Paddington, not far from Grangemouth, the Macleods' old home. She was well advanced in years but, much like her brother Angus, tireless in all her good works. Her husband had been a successful solicitor and had left her a handsome pension. Isobel had made many visits with her mother and sisters to pay their respects to Aunt Louisa as well as her three daughters, now all happily settled in advantageous marriages. Isobel regarded her aunt as not an unkind soul but one who managed a tidy, austere household and had no tolerance for frivolity or pleasure.

Isobel feared she had little hope of swaying her father's heart. This was surely her sisters' cruel victory. It was entirely possible that Anna and Grace had suggested such a plan, conspiring to overthrow their father's fondness for Isobel, his favourite. Who knew? Maybe they had even hatched a crueller future for Isobel and Papa had offered this as a compromise. With the deaths of Winifred and Richard, the news of William and Joseph going abroad and now this new calamity, there seemed no firm ground left for Isobel to stand on safely. Everything was permanently changed and ever changing.

'You will, of course, still attend all your lessons as before and be welcome here as our guest whenever you wish,' her father continued. 'You will enjoy all the advantages of your aunt's wise counsel and tender attentions and lose none of the pleasures and benefits of the society of family and friends.' He was still speaking but his voice was far away, drowned out by the galloping thud of Isobel's heart and the loud surf of blood in her ears.

Isobel nodded in obedience to his wishes. As soon as he finished, she fled the room, unable to speak or look him in the eye. The study door swung shut with a loud bang and she was quite certain, as she hurried across the saloon and up the stairs, that she could hear her sisters whispering in the breakfast room, no doubt eager to learn the outcome of the meeting.

Back in the shelter of her room, Isobel recalled the chill that had come over her the morning of the duel as she rode out with James and looked over her shoulder at Rosemount. She had wondered then if the vision of her home bathed in morning fire was a beacon of hope or an apocalyptic warning. It seemed she now had her answer.

Chapter 12

A LAST WALK IN
THE GARDEN

OCTOBER 1851

Aunt Louisa acceded to her brother's proposal, glad to have a young woman to share in her busy schedule of charity work. Preparations were begun for Isobel's room at Faulconstone, her aunt's sombre villa on Old South Head Road. The house had a fine piano that only wanted retuning and a quiet aspect despite its location near the tollgate on one of Sydney's busiest thoroughfares east, the main road to the signal station and the lovely beaches on South Head. A large frangipani tree in its front garden and a high stone wall protected the house from the din of passing coach traffic. Isobel's only consolation was that the house was within walking distance of Victoria Barracks, a proximity that promised glimpses into (and maybe even encounters with) a world beyond the dreary isolation of Faulconstone.

Isobel waited anxiously for the day of departure. She mourned the loss of her beloved Rosemount each morning on waking as she stood by the window trying to absorb every detail of the harbour view she loved so well, hoping to fix it in her mind. In the same spirit of anticipated loss, she memorised the exact curve of the staircase banisters, the play of afternoon light on the walls of the saloon, the composition of Mr Conrad Martens' oil painting *A Distant View of Rosemount over Elizabeth Bay* that hung above the specimen cabinets in the study. Like one of Mr Freeman's photographic plates, her mind recorded the waterleaf motif of the ceiling rose in the morning room, the red and buff pattern of the wallpaper in the breakfast room, the tapering architraves of the cedar doors to the study and the bulging perspective of the gilt-framed mirror in the dining room, in whose convex surface Grace checked that the servants didn't purloin the cutlery or spill the gravy.

Nearly three weeks after the Major had pronounced her banishment from Rosemount, Isobel took up her artist's satchel and went for a long walk in the gardens in search of some peace of mind. It was a warm spring afternoon with a light breeze off the harbour to cool her. She crossed the emerald expanse of the front lawn. Scattered profusely through the grass like the floral tapestry of a meadow were massed blooms of ixias, freesias and harlequin flowers, setting the lawn ablaze in pinks, peaches, corals and mauves. This was the scene of many a picnic lunch under a cloudless blue sky and country dances beneath starry summer nights, filled with music and fireworks. Isobel sighed at the unexpected rush of so many memories.

She strolled past the sun-speckled orchard with its orderly brigades of orange and lemon trees, their lovely blossom scenting the air. The immense guavas by the stone wall promised a harvest of plump, creamy fruit in many shades of green and yellow, apple red and olive grey. Isobel was especially fond of the pineapple guava blooms with their festive sprays of bright red, yellow-tipped stamens and shell-like white petals flushed with purple. The pomegranate trees boasted a carnival of large flowers with their orange and white frilled petals like the ruffled skirts of Spanish dancers.

Isobel followed the labyrinthine paths that wound through Rosemount's botanic garden, all its exotic shrubs and flowerbeds now in bloom. The rose garden alone was a revelation, with every variety known to botany competing for one's admiration. Visitors marvelled at this embarrassment of riches, so many botanical curiosities collected from every continent and corner of the Empire and miraculously raised out of Sydney's poor, sandy soil.

Isobel descended through the three terraces, each with a curving stone wall ending in lovely ornamental scrollwork. Away to her left, bordering the shining arc of Elizabeth Bay itself, grew Rosemount's extraordinary curated forest: colossal Moreton Bay figs and lofty Norfolk Island pines, umbrella-canopied Chilean monkey-puzzle trees and ancient Mauritian banyans, their roots hanging down like the ruined rigging of ghost ships.

Isobel came out near the chain of carp ponds. This lovely oasis was encircled by man-made rockeries plush with mosses and silvered by waterfalls. Beneath a glossy archipelago of waterlily pads and velvet-tipped bulrushes, the stillness of the dark water was broken only by the occasional splash of a frog leaping or a fat white koi lazily coming to the surface.

Isobel lingered a while. This was one of her favourite childhood spots. How much she wished she could have shared its secret pleasures with her playmate Ballandella. They had spent hours in the gardens at Grangemouth in search of small everyday miracles: a newly built bird's nest, a lizard skull picked clean by ants, the footprints of bush rats and wallabies. Ballandella would have loved Rosemount and its endless trove of wonders.

Over the years, Isobel had written letters to her little sister care of Dr Nicholson but the only news she had ever received was that Ballandella was now married to an Aboriginal named Barber and they lived at Wisemans Ferry. Ballandella herself never replied. She had vanished from Isobel's life so completely and so long ago that it took an effort of will for Isobel to recall the finer details of her face. But Isobel still had dreams and memories of her friend in which Ballandella's spirit was as vivid as ever.

Isobel listened for the familiar thrum of insect wings. There it was; her patience was rewarded. A dragonfly, its wings broader than her hand, alighted on a clump of reeds. Could it be? She smiled. *Petalura gigantea*. A south-eastern petaltail or giant dragonfly, one of the largest species in the world. It must be a female, her five-inch wingspan wider than the male's. The dragonfly's huge glassy eyes resembled the domed paperweights on her father's desk while the insect's body, long and skinny as a penny whistle, was segmented into bronze and black stripes, notched like a shaft of bamboo. And her wings! Oh, such delicate, gauzy wings! The tracery of their veins reminded Isobel of the leading in St Mark's stained-glass windows, casting kaleidoscopic patterns on stone and wood.

Memories burst upon Isobel like sunlight breaking through clouds. As if it was only yesterday, she recalled her first day at Rosemount as a child of ten. Her family's coach and retinue of wagons were pulled up in the carriageway outside the house. As their trunks and furniture were unloaded, her parents prepared to enter their new home. Little Isobel headed off in the direction of the garden. 'Don't get lost!' Winnie cried after her.

'All the paths are signposted, Mama!' she called back, though in fact she rather hoped to get lost, at least for a little while, in this vast Edenic garden. As she wandered in solitary and happy contemplation along its many forking pathways, Isobel arrived at last, just as she had today, at the quiet oasis of the carp ponds. Only to find she was not alone.

A woman in a blue sashed muslin dress and ribboned bonnet stood with her back to Isobel, facing the harbour. She started when she heard the girl behind her and turned to look at the intruder. This woman was at least twenty years Isobel's senior, her face plain but thoughtful and intelligent. 'I'm sorry. I didn't know you'd be here so soon,' said the stranger, picking up a basket of flowers she had been collecting from the garden, and making to leave.

'Please don't hurry away,' said Isobel.

Before they had time to make introductions, Isobel heard a deep drone, oddly mechanical and much louder than the low buzzing of a bee or wasp. A huge insect appeared out of nowhere and hung in the air only inches from her face. It was a dragonfly, bigger than any she had yet seen. She flinched involuntarily, startled by its size and noise.

'Don't worry, she won't hurt you,' said the woman.

As if it recognised the stranger, or so Isobel fancied, the dragon-fly zigzagged across the green mirror of the pond and landed on the woman's left sleeve. It hung there sparkling in the sun, an exotic jewelled pendant. 'Isn't she beautiful?' the woman said, beckoning to Isobel. 'Come, take a closer look.'

Isobel approached a little nervously.

'She's a Giant Dragonfly. First described and named by the zoologist William Leach from a specimen my father presented to the Linnean Society in London.' The woman smiled at Isobel.

So this was one of Mr Macleay's daughters! Probably Fanny, who was known as a talented botanical artist. Isobel had seen and admired one of her Dutch still-life paintings of Australian natives and exotics mingled in a stone amphora; the work had been exhib-ited at the Female School of Industry just that year. Fanny was said to be a great help to her father, preparing and cataloguing his large collections and preserving and packing specimens to be shipped to naturalists in England.

Thinking back on the meeting now, years later, Isobel felt a pang of guilt at the thought that she had disturbed Fanny on her last walk through her father's gardens, no doubt to imprint all its riches on her mind as well as gather a few cuttings to be pressed as mementos.

The little girl and the older woman fell unselfconsciously into conversation, dispensing with the formalities of introductions. Fanny told Isobel the proper name for the jewelled insect that clung to her dress: *Petalura gigantea*, named for the petal-shaped appendage at the tip of the male's abdomen. She told Isobel about the insect's life journey from underwater egg to larva to nymph. She described how the ungainly nymph emerged from its murky pond water, clambering up a reed or rock and bursting from its casing into a full-grown adult. At this point of transformation into a creature of breathtaking agility and beauty, the insect was also at its most vulnerable.

'Waiting for her wings to dry, a female dragonfly sits on her slender reed or exposed rock, trapped, a tempting meal for every bird or frog,' said Fanny, her eyes glittering with an amused menace. 'It is not so different for us human females, is it? As young women, we come out into society, ready to spread our wings, and we are instantly prey to every suitor who fancies he is eligible, waiting to pounce and gobble us up in the jaws of matrimony.'

Isobel could not help giggling and Fanny's face lit up with laughter. Only later did Isobel learn that Fanny's mother had, years before, insisted she turn down a proposal from a much older man, a noted English naturalist. Fanny had refused all offers since; the gossips of Sydney had labelled Mr Macleay's bookish daughter 'forward' and 'queer'.

She was certainly 'different', thought Isobel, and so wonderfully frank. With no hint of shame or apology, Fanny described the mating ritual of the dragonfly and his female, locked together in tandem flight, their bodies arched in coitus in the shape of a heart. 'Ah, the romance of dragonfly sex! It is far too little appreciated,' she observed with a grin.

Isobel felt her cheek burning and hoped she was not blushing. Why, this was no more than scientific knowledge. What reason had she, or any woman, to feel ashamed?

'Do you know Mr Tennyson's poem about a dragonfly?' asked Fanny. Isobel shook her head. 'It is written about a male—*of course!*—but I shall change it to a female in honour of our beautiful friend.' Fanny cleared her throat.

> 'Today I saw the dragon-fly
> Come from the wells where she did lie.
> An inner impulse rent the veil
> Of her old husk: from head to tail
> Came out clear plates of sapphire mail.
> She dried her wings: like gauze they grew;
> Thro' crofts and pastures wet with dew
> A living flash of light she flew.'

Isobel sighed. 'How lovely!'

Fanny nodded. 'Yes, isn't it? The poem teaches us how we must be prepared to lose our old selves—our husks—to undergo change, no matter how risky or dangerous, so we can discover our true natures. And fly like a "living flash of light"!'

Fanny's eyes sparkled as if in sympathy with this thought. Her gaze lingered tenderly a moment on Isobel's face. What was she thinking? Isobel wondered. Did Isobel remind her of a younger, more innocent version of herself whom she had discarded? And what had this cost her? What would it cost Isobel to discover her 'true nature' when the time came?

They both heard voices nearby. 'Isobel! Lunchtime!' The dragonfly's wings became a shiny blur and the giant insect took to the air and vanished in a blink. Fanny's smile evaporated instantly. She touched Isobel lightly on the arm by way of farewell.

'I must go. My brother is expecting me. I wish you every happiness here at Rosemount. It has enough wonders to satisfy even the most restless curiosity.'

Fanny ducked her head, grabbed her basket of flowers and, without another word, disappeared into the bushes. This abrupt cessation of the women's discourse left Isobel feeling bereft. And guilty. There was no escaping the fact that the new, exciting life promised for her at Rosemount was only made possible with the termination of Fanny's life here.

And now, seven years later, here Isobel was, about to become an exile herself from this paradise just like Fanny before her. This strange parallel even included her encounter with a dragonfly that came into the garden to bid them both farewell. Isobel's heart was filled with poignant melancholy. It was as if the insect acknowledged her as a fellow inhabitant of the gardens, her stay here as transitory as its own, too soon to depart.

And, of course, Isobel could not help thinking of her mother's gift, Isobel's mysterious inheritance. She recalled Fanny's father, poor Mr Macleay, stooped under the weight of his ill fortune, his face etched with self-pity at the sight of Winnie's opal brooch. That same night of her parents' anniversary ball and her own cruel father's triumph, little Isobel had understood, if only fleetingly, the two-faced nature of fate. *One man's victory meant another*

man's defeat. From Mr Macleay's ruin had sprung the Macleods'
good fortune.

She was not ready to return to the house just yet.

Her father had gone back to work at the Surveyor-General's
office in Sydney a few days ago, ignoring the muttering behind
his back about the 'disgraceful' duel. Isobel's only company now
was Grace and Anna, both unashamedly cheerful at the prospect
of her departure. Her sisters could now enjoy absolute rule over
Rosemount, though Isobel could not imagine what would give them
as much pleasure as finding fault with their little sister.

Father had reassured Isobel that she would not miss out on the
society of her friends. But she feared that Aunt Louisa would keep
her too busy with good works to attend parties or balls, assuming
any such invitation penetrated the citadel of Faulconstone. With
her mother's death just over a year ago, Isobel, now seventeen, had
not yet had the opportunity to formally come out at a ball. The
official twelvemonth of mourning had precluded such gaiety and
her mother's absence now meant she had no one to present her.

The season was not quite over so Isobel had reason still to hope
that she would be welcomed at one of the later spring debutante
balls. But these hopes were dashed again and again as the weeks
passed by and the awful truth dawned on the Macleod women
that they were being spurned by their friends and acquaintances.
No calling cards were left in the hall, no invitations arrived by
mail. Grace and Anna called on the Dickersons and the Bradleys
but nobody was ever home to receive them and their cards elicited
notes of apology. Dr Finch was their only guest in his capacity as
their father's doctor and he did not stay long.

Grace and Anna were mortified by this chilly ostracism and took every opportunity to remind poor Isobel that it was all her doing. The only explanation, in their view, was that no family would risk their respectability by letting such a headstrong and ill-behaved woman as Isobel into their midst. The lacerating sting of wounded pride deepened to anger and resentment as the third week rolled by.

And then something unexpected happened. Invitations arrived for all three Macleod women to attend a ball to be hosted by Mr and Mrs Robert Cooper at Juniper Hall, the fine Georgian mansion on the high point of the ridgeline in Paddington. It was to be a debutante ball for their eldest daughter, Catherine, and would include among its guests many of the officers of the 11th Regiment just down the road at Victoria Barracks. The invitation made clear that it could provide Isobel with the perfect opportunity for her formal entrée into society, if she so wished. This was a generous offer. But it was also tricky territory.

The problem, as Isobel knew all too well, was that Mr Cooper was an *emancipist*. Unlike the usual run of poor, brutish convicts transported to New South Wales, Mr Cooper had been a well-off owner of two gin distilleries in London, convicted for receiving three thousand pounds' worth of stolen silk and ostrich feathers. Having served his time and now a free man once more in the colony, Mr Cooper had amassed a substantial fortune with investments in a gin and beer distillery at Blackwattle Bay, a timber mill, a textile mill and a gunpowder factory.

Affectionately known as 'Robert the Large', this stout, affable gent had sired twenty-eight children and jokingly called himself 'a founding father of the colony'. He courted his third (much younger) wife, Jane, with a promise of building her the 'finest house' in Sydney. For some years, Juniper Hall easily retained that title, with its elegant cedar-floored rooms, its entrance surmounted by a large fanlight and flanked by Ionic columns, and its upper-storey balcony commanding views over Rushcutters Bay, Botany Bay and as far west as the Blue Mountains. Isobel's father had remarked (a touch acidly) on Mr Cooper's ambitions, 'which knew no bounds'. Standing for the first election to the Legislative Council in 1843, Mr Cooper had upset the colony's ruling class by promising to champion the rights of the discontented workers and unemployed of Sydney. He even gave land grants to forty of his distillery workers and built them cottages so they were qualified to vote for him. His political ambitions were roundly flouted at the elections but he had endeared himself to the exploited masses of Sydney.

Sir Angus had always made clear his unflattering view of emancipists; he had even chosen to pay a hefty fine rather than serve on a jury alongside one of them. He was ready to praise the best of the convicts he recruited for his expeditions and rewarded them with tickets of leave or pardons and certificates of freedom. But, with few exceptions, the Major viewed convicts and ex-convicts as depraved, sinful creatures, permanently stained by their moral failings and criminal history. On the other hand, his contempt for the nepotism and self-interest of the landed gentry (the Macarthurs, Icelys, Marshes and their ilk) inclined him to look favourably on the honest ambition of free settlers and, yes, even emancipists who sought to make themselves men of consequence through dint of hard work and intelligence.

The Major conceded Robert Cooper was such a man.

Maybe it was because the Major was furious at the petty snob-bishness of his family's ostracism and viewed this invitation as an opportunity to express his displeasure; whatever his motivation, he gave permission for his daughters to attend Mr Cooper's ball. Isobel was so excited. Her debut was to be at a fancy-dress ball attended by garrison officers and (it was rumoured) by Governor FitzRoy himself, despite his unpopularity with everyone in the colony, squatters and city men alike. Aunt Louisa agreed to chap-erone and the hostess, Mrs Cooper, agreed to introduce Isobel into society in her mother's absence.

With these novel thoughts drifting through her mind, Isobel wandered from the carp ponds, past the kitchen gardens, past the glasshouses, past the vineyard all decked in its best spring livery, and past the potting sheds and poultry yards. The path took her upwards into the wood on the northern side of the estate that bordered the serpentine carriageway to the front gates. Isobel strolled beneath the silver-green canopy of the native trees—euca-lypts, turpentines, tallowwoods and feathery she-oaks—smothered in blossoms of white, pink, red and yellow. Elkhorn, bird's nest and staghorn ferns adorned tree trunks with their vivid green vegetable antlers, while fiddleheads and maidenhairs caught the sunlight in the baroque lacework of their leaves. Flights of rosellas, crested pigeons and blue wrens went chinking, whirring and fluttering overhead, causing branches to nod at their passing and let loose snowfalls of blossom. The air was heavy with a syrup of fragrances, so sweet and strong and intoxicating that Isobel tarried, sitting on a nearby rustic bench to savour it all.

All about her the undergrowth was dotted with orchids, each with their fleshy star of petals and their engorged tongues in such bright throats. These shameless displays of stigmata, labellum and cap were so lurid that Isobel blushed with forbidden pleasure. Like all cultured young women, she had read Mr Henry Phillips' *Floral Emblems* among other floral dictionaries. She understood very well the wordless poetry of orchids. In men they inspired an obsessive lust for rarity and status, both the ruthless orchid hunter who risked his life in remote jungles and the avaricious collector who paid huge bounties. For women they were Nature's own sonnets to female beauty and erotic allure, *sotto voce* confessions of passionate and irresistible desire.

With a violent flutter in her breast, Isobel recalled her young suitor, Captain Tranter, and the single purple orchid pressed between the pages of his love letter to her, tantamount to a marriage proposal. As dusk embronzed the drawing room at Rosemount, she had sat with Alice and shared the secrets of her heart. Brave Alice had championed the captain's love suit to their mother in vain. Winifred had brought the affair to a swift end before it had begun. Isobel sighed as she recalled her captain's sweet face.

Now, here she was, seventeen years old and about to be exiled to her aunt's like a scarlet woman being shut up in a nunnery to smother her shame. Was she so fallen, so beyond redemption? Surely not. Like Mr Cooper and his fellow emancipists, Isobel hoped that she deserved a second chance. Was her crime so great as to exclude that possibility? No.

And where was Captain Tranter now? she wondered. He had vanished from her life and her family's social sphere faster than a dragonfly in flight, never to be seen again. There had been one last clandestine note delivered from the Captain to Isobel as a postscript to their romance, expressing his deep regret at how the episode had ended but giving his word as a gentleman to withdraw discreetly. Isobel's heart had been crushed by this kind officer's brave surrender to her family's demands; he would never know the depths of her affections and she would never have the opportunity to express them.

She looked at the carpet of orchids all about her. Would she ever find such a love again? Or would she become a spinster like her heartless sister Grace and her mad sister Anna whom no man with any sense would ever take for a wife?

She had heard that dear Fanny Macleay, now approaching forty, was still unwed, leaving her plenty of time to sketch and paint when she was not attending to her aged parents and the demands of her sisters' children.

Was this to be Isobel's fate?

Chapter 13

UNEXPECTED VISITORS

Isobel sat in the dappled shade and worked at her easel. The sun slid westward and she noted how the lacework of bright rays and purple shadows shifted across the lovely scene. Her attention was absorbed in the graceful individuality of each orchid she painted, trying to let her mind quieten its busy treadmill of thoughts and soak up colour and light like a sponge. As she worked, something snagged at the corner of her field of vision. A darker shadow, moving between the trees. Was it a visitor, someone lost?

'Hello? Anyone there?' she called out, feeling a little foolish.

She was sure she heard footsteps in the undergrowth, saw an indistinct shape slipping away into the forest. Perhaps it was a wallaby, a wombat, not a person at all. Or was her mind playing tricks on her?

She started at the sudden thunder of carriage wheels in the drive and the clatter of hooves on gravel as a vehicle rattled past, heading down the carriage loop to the house. A carriage at this time of day? Papa was not due home until at least six o'clock. No cards had been left at the house and no guests were expected. Isobel wanted to remain here, unseen in the peaceful sanctuary of the woodland, but her curiosity impelled her to investigate. As she quickly retraced her steps through the forest and across the lawn, she could see a trap pulled up in the driveway near the house and two gentlemen, already alighted, taking in views of the estate. As she crested the slope and drew closer, she recognised her brothers. What sweet joy flooded her heart then, what tender affection! It had been an age since she had laid eyes on either of these beloved souls.

'William, dear brother! And Joseph! You are a sight for sore eyes!' cried Isobel, wiping away tears as she raced towards them. The two men greeted their little sister effusively and complimented her on her obvious good health.

'You are a good head taller than when I saw you last!' said William.

'And fairer than I remembered. But then I have a terrible memory,' Joseph laughed.

Isobel returned their compliments, noting the fine cut of their clothes, which they confirmed had been freshly tailored for their travels. Relishing this happy reunion and the sight of her brothers' smiling faces, she wished she could monopolise them for longer but knew the staff would have already hurried to alert Grace and Anna to their arrival.

Isobel had written a reply to William's letter over three weeks ago, telling him of her banishment from Rosemount, but she had had no reply. What did he know of her situation? It was entirely possible he had left Melbourne before the letter arrived. Grace had at least informed Isobel that Papa now knew of his sons' plans for India and William's intention to visit Rosemount. She did not know if Joseph, the 'black sheep' in Father's view, was expected or not.

'Father won't be home until this evening,' she told them.

'Yes, we suspected as much,' confessed William. 'Which is one reason why we decided to come earlier, unannounced. We wanted to spend some time with our dear sisters before meeting with Father. We have rooms in town; our ship leaves first thing tomorrow morning.'

Before Isobel could speak another word there were exclamations of delight from the portico. In their best bonnets and shawls, Anna and Grace rushed out, arms outstretched and faces lit up with smiles. Another round of embraces and compliments followed.

'We were not expecting you so early,' chided Grace. 'Thankfully, Cook has a few treats stored in the pantry and I have set us up in the drawing room for tea.'

The siblings made themselves comfortable on the chaise longue and the sofas while the butler tended to the fire. Grace unlocked the tea caddy on its rosewood poy and offered her brothers a choice of gunpowder or pekoe. Once that critical issue was settled, the tray arrived with Winifred's most prized Spode tea service, taken down from the dining room cabinet for the auspicious homecoming of the two Macleod brothers.

Cook had managed to rustle up two dozen lemon cheesecakes, generous slabs of plum cake and gingerbread tea loaf, and two plates of rout cakes. Grace officiated at the urn while Anna and Isobel passed plates, forks, spoons, milk jug, sugar box and tongs. The usual pleasantries (how beautiful the garden looked; how clement was the spring weather; what progress the sisters had made in music and drawing; praise for their new lace doilies) were soon exhausted. There was an awkward pause as everyone present realised it was time to embark on more challenging topics.

William went first. He explained how he and Joseph had met up in Melbourne last year to pursue some business opportunities. Their successful trading in hemp and tea had brought them to the attention of a well-known exporter who offered them both positions in his company's Madras offices. The brothers seized on this chance to learn more about the flourishing Indian market, especially now the East India Company's monopolies had ended. Grace expressed her devout hope that they would thrive in India while Anna prayed they would not die from the bite of a cobra.

'I am sure that two such clever fellows as yourselves will do very well.' Isobel smiled at her brothers, hiding her grief that they were going so far away. 'Of course, once you have made your fortune, you will make Australia home again?'

'Yes, of course. We plan to be away for three or four years at most,' said William, avoiding his youngest sister's gaze. 'But I promise we will regularly write you of our progress.'

Always the good son, William had resigned his commission with the Royal Navy to run the Camden farm after Richard died. Released from these duties by the Major, with the appointment of a manager, he had then taken off to Melbourne to form a business partnership with an old friend.

Having finished his law studies, Joseph had been articled to a Sydney firm but soon drifted into political circles and journalism, much to his father's displeasure. The Major had threatened to disinherit him if he did not return to the law and eventually made good this threat (and his son's banishment) when Joseph's insolence and rebelliousness became intolerable. In the throes of a heated argument between father and son nine months ago, Joseph had shamelessly admitted – nay, boasted – to his father about writing a slanderous poem attacking Mr Macleay's son, William. This cruel portrait of the former penny-pinching, antisocial occupant of Rosemount Hall had been published anonymously over a year ago and had provoked a minor scandal.

> Bleak house blears blindly o'er Eliza's Bay
> Chill as the owner's hospitality
> No music here save weeping willows sigh
> And wavelets ripple murm'ring lullaby
> Chance picnic pilgrim, seeking scallop shell
> Draws down in dudgeon this high Admiral
> Too puffy, selfish, greedy and effete
> For Council's squabbles or the world's debate.

With rumours rife about the poem's authorship, the Major came under intense pressure from his superiors to reveal the poet's name. Though he had his suspicions, the Major decided to protect his son's honour and said nothing. Joseph's ingratitude for this kindness as well as his stubborn refusal to return to the law left the Major with little choice.

Unconstrained by gentility or diplomacy, Anna asked the obvious question. 'So, has Father agreed to see Joseph again?' William confessed that their father had neither agreed nor disagreed to see Joseph. 'We will see what he says when he returns today. It is a matter for his own conscience. We are resigned to his stubborn refusal but we are also hopeful that our plans may meet with his approval. And even blessing.'

'I think you will find Father a little changed since . . .' Grace hesitated to name the event that had caused everyone so much distress, allowing the absent word to hang in the air unsaid. By a happy coincidence all parties had independently decided to avoid the subject of the duel; there was nothing to be gained by risking upset in this all too brief reunion. For the sake of family harmony, Isobel had also promised Grace to say nothing of her banishment when William visited; her sister had no knowledge, of course, of the letter Isobel had already written him.

'Papa is almost fully recovered except for a small tremor of the right hand,' said Grace. 'His spirits are still troubled but Dr Finch said that is to be expected.'

'He has always had an exceptionally strong constitution and a mind of such clarity and discipline that there are few to equal it,' said Joseph.

With almost visible relief at having negotiated this perilous terrain, the siblings moved on to other subjects, including their sister Alice's news from England that she was expecting and the glowing reports from Dr Finch's son about the Great Exhibition.

Despite her promise to Grace to say nothing, Isobel still brooded on the injustice of her impending banishment. She planned to steal a few moments alone with her brother to tell him of her horrid fate (assuming that he had not received her last letter). She even hoped that William, the favourite son, might agree to intercede with Papa on her behalf. As it turned out, this opportunity never presented itself.

Isobel reflected later on how cleverly Grace had managed to keep Isobel and William apart. When the business of serving tea and cakes was concluded, the brothers admired Anna's performance of four Chopin polonaises. Joseph then joined Anna on the piano stool for a robust duet performing a pastorale he enjoyed by Willam Byrd. Isobel also liked this song well enough but was always amused at how the powerful and rich were presumed to be so dreadfully jealous of the honest and humble virtues of the poor.

Several sentimental ballads ensued, then the improvised concert was followed by an invitation for Joseph and William to make up a four for a game of euchre. Isobel insisted she was content to watch her siblings at play while she did her mending by the fire. Despite her anxiety to speak alone with her brother, she was enchanted by the familiar scene before her, reminiscent of happier times when Alice and Richard were still here and their sweet mother, Winifred, presided over such domestic felicity.

This heartwarming gathering was rudely interrupted by the drumroll of carriage wheels in the drive. They all hurried to the windows. To their collective dismay they discovered that the Major had returned from his office two hours earlier than anticipated.

'Quick, quick, take Joseph into the breakfast room. And lock the door,' Grace urged Isobel. 'I will greet Father and break the news.' Isobel stayed with Joseph who stood pale and trembling by the mantel, with more reason than anyone to fear the old man's temper.

Meanwhile William and Anna waited in the drawing room while Grace hurried out to the vestibule. As her father entered,

Grace welcomed him and inquired as to what had brought him home at such an early hour.

Standing behind the locked door of the breakfast room, Isobel could hear only the timbre of this conversation, not its content. The exchange sounded troubled and then shifted suddenly to a more alarming register when her father exclaimed, 'Why all this mystery?' She did not hear Grace's answer but heard her father's response: 'Very well, send him in.' The study door opened and closed again. Now William's voice could be heard joined with Grace's in the vestibule and their urgent dialogue concluded with Grace bidding him 'good luck' as he knocked on his father's door. On Grace's signal, Isobel unlocked the door to the breakfast room and admitted her and Anna, both in a state of agitation.

'What is the matter? Why has Father come home so early?' she asked.

'The timing of this visit could hardly be less propitious,' said Grace. 'Father tells me that the Governor has this very day informed him that he is about to appoint a commission of inquiry into the Major's conduct of his department.'

The colour drained from Joseph's cheeks. The Major would be in no mood for a reconciliation today. Isobel recalled all too clearly her mother's distress some three years ago that her husband's loyal service was to be rewarded with the threat of official sanction. 'There has been talk of an inquiry for some time,' said Grace. 'But I wonder if more recent history has given encouragement to our father's enemies. I bet that Mr Davidson had a hand in this.'

In the late afternoon light, the four siblings sat in miserable silence with no fire in the grate and no candles lit on the mantel.

Huddled in the gathering cold and gloom, they were like a group of school children playing hide-and-seek who dared not breathe too loudly for fear of revealing their presence. The meeting between William and the Major felt interminable. Only the sluggish pendulum of the mantel clock and slow advancement of its hands gave any sign of time passing.

At last there was a rap at the breakfast room door. 'It's me,' said William, and was admitted by Grace. Isobel was saddened to see how much her brother's spirits had altered. His face was now sombre and his demeanour subdued.

'I am glad to see that Father's strength of mind has returned,' he observed. 'But luck is against us, dear brother. It seems there is to be a government inquiry into our father's career. It may well affect the future of his employment, and even his entitlements and pension. I am sorry to see him treated so wretchedly. His mood is very dark.'

'He refuses to see me then?' Joseph asked bitterly.

'He does,' answered William. A sob broke from Isobel's mouth. Banished! She and Joseph were both exiles from their father's love. It was insupportable. She felt dizzy with despair. The Macleod family, once so assured of their social position, was now divided and faced with ruin and disgrace. Isobel realised that the sacrifice of her good name had not saved her family; at worst, it had contributed to their downfall.

'I thought it unwise to press the point, given the circumstances,' said William. He could not meet his sisters' gaze or acknowledge their expressions of fear. 'Even so, I am reassured that Father looks forward to hearing how our ventures abroad shall prosper.'

Joseph, his eyes downcast and his deportment one of utter defeat, was unconvinced. Spurned by his father and unwelcome in his own home, he was anxious to leave. 'There is nothing to detain us here, William. We must bid our sisters adieu.'

The group reassembled in the drawing room. The two gentlemen called for the butler to fetch their hats and outer garments. Poor Isobel had failed to consult privately with William and it was now clear that she would not get the chance. Unwilling to burden Joseph with her woes, she had scratched a quick note while they both waited in the breakfast room.

Dearest W—

Supposedly for the sake of my own welfare, Papa has banish'd me to Aunt Louisa's. For how long? I do not know. I hold grave fears for my future at Rosemount as Grace & Anna cannot be trusted. I wish I could alter Papa's mind and win back the Love and Esteem I once enjoy'd. Please write to me soonest. I wish you and Joseph every blessing with all my Heart and will pray for your safety, good health and Success.

Your doting & foolish sister,
   Isobel C. Macleod

The solemn party made their way out onto the gravel driveway. Rain clouds had gathered on the horizon and a fresh gust off the harbour played havoc with bonnets and hats. The sisters made their farewells, wishing their brothers 'bon voyage' and 'good fortune' with tears of sorrow brimming at their eyes. Just before they climbed aboard the trap, Isobel hugged William, pressing her letter into his hand with a whisper in his ear. 'Please read my note, dear William, I beg you. And send me your good counsel.'

The women watched the trap pull away with its two occupants bidding them loud farewells, hats raised high. The three sisters waved their final goodbyes until the trap bearing their brothers vanished beneath the trees, leaving the forlorn trio alone in the lengthening shadows of the house. The scene struck Isobel as momentous. And ill-omened.

Here, standing centrestage in the grand amphitheatre formed naturally by Rosemount's sloping lawn, lush gardens, wild forest and harbour prospect, the women's private grief assumed the epic quality of Greek drama. Under the darkening, windswept sky, she and her sisters were tragic heroines in a play by Sophocles, lamenting their dear brothers' departure for foreign shores and contemplating their family's inevitable doom.

What Isobel did not see was her father's face at an upstairs window. An awful gravity resided in that grief-stricken countenance, for it was the Major's sorrowful conviction that he would never see either of his two sons alive again.

Chapter 14

SYDNEY TOWN

There was only one week left until the ball at Juniper Hall. To her immense surprise, Isobel found herself happily preoccupied with her fittings at the premises of the Misses Burnill, dressmakers of Riley Street. These accomplished ladies had been busy with their expert needles creating a debutante's evening dress of white silk, trimmed with lace and bouquets of violets. It was close to completion, needing only minor adjustments to cuffs and neckline.

Isobel's companion was none other than dear Mrs Palmer, who had loved Winnie greatly and was now strenuously protective of her daughters. Too poor to host even an afternoon tea for Isobel to come out, Mrs Palmer said she would do whatever else she could to assist Isobel's entrée to society.

'The dress will be delivered to Rosemount on Friday as promised,' reassured the younger Miss Burnill. 'It should be quite the occasion if our orders are anything to go by.'

'So why is this the last ball that Mr and Mrs Cooper are hosting at the Hall, do you know?' asked Mrs Palmer, hoping not to cause any offence. Neither she nor Isobel's family mixed in the same circles as Mr Cooper so they were not privy to the gossip.

'Well, they are leaving Juniper Hall, I believe,' said the dressmaker. She lowered her voice. 'The rumour is that Mr C. is in extreme financial distress and has had to give up the house. Not altogether surprising given the number of his offspring and their taste for luxury. This ball is the Coopers' final farewell.'

Isobel and Mrs Palmer nodded. Miss Burnill continued: 'I've been told that the Hall is to be turned into an Asylum for the Relief of Destitute Children. They say that Mr Robert's son, Augustus, who has done very well for himself, offered to buy him out, but the young Mr C. already has a house in town and a country estate. He was advised not to over-extend.'

'I see.' Mrs Palmer smiled. For reasons not that hard to understand, she found that dressmakers were excellent sources of gossip. Isobel was intrigued to hear about 'the young Mr C.' and sorely tempted to ask if he was attached or not. But she thought better of it. 'Thank you both. The dress is perfection.'

'And you, Mademoiselle, shall look perfection in it.'

The two Misses Burnill waved goodbye as Isobel and Mrs Palmer took their leave. Now that the session at the dressmakers was concluded, they caught another omnibus into town where they could amble along George Street to consider the purchase of new gloves and maybe even a shawl and a reticule to complement the evening gown.

Seated atop the omnibus, Isobel and Mrs Palmer hung on tightly to their bonnets. The hot, boisterous winds whipped at the hems of their skirts despite the omnibus's ankle boards (intended to protect female modesty from straying eyes as well as stiff breezes). Isobel enjoyed these trips into Sydney in daylight hours, especially when the weather was this fine and the streets filled with so many gentlefolk. Days like these afforded her a closer acquaintance with the broad river of humanity in all its variety and colour. As the omnibus passed along Old South Head, Isobel saw Sydney spread out grandly before her under a royal blue sky, like one of Mr Augustus Earle's celebrated panoramas.

The two women alighted on George Street two blocks from Hyde Park, which pulsed with the shrill chirruping of cicadas in the summer heat. The thoroughfare resounded with the cheery racket of cabs, jaunting cars, phaetons and, further down towards the warehouses of Circular Quay, the slower traffic of bullock-drawn drays laden with wool. With amused curiosity, Isobel and Mrs Palmer watched the young bucks and Brummells in their felt toppers and silk vests, parading along George Street. At the Café Français, a favourite haunt of these swells and sprigs, smartly turned-out gents lounged at little marble tables, copies of *Punch* and *The Times* in their laps, playing chess or dominoes and sipping sherry cobblers and strawberry ices. The place was always busy and the atmosphere lively and gay.

On such days, Isobel's estimation of her hometown rose considerably. There was much to admire. In her father's study she had found a handsome book entitled *Sydney in 1848,* a gift to acknowledge the Major's contributions to this proud maritime city. Dedicated to

His Excellency, the Governor, Sir Charles Augustus FitzRoy, and with copperplate engravings by Mr Joseph Fowles, its stated object was 'to remove the erroneous and discreditable notions current in England concerning this City by exhibiting its spacious Gas-lit Streets, its Public Edifices, and its sumptuous Shops, which boldly claim a comparison with those of London itself.' As she wandered down George Street with its bustling, awning-shaded emporia and taverns, its well-heeled throng of splendidly and soberly dressed citizens, and its distant glimpses of blue harbour, Isobel felt her heart lifted by such lofty sentiments. While she still longed to one day make her pilgrimage to majestic, golden London, that bright spinning governor regulating the engine of Empire, she could also feel pride in her hometown.

There was no denying that Sydney's architects had furnished their city with many imposing and beautiful buildings. These were the *sine qua nons* of a civilised society, sandstone monuments to its prosperity and testaments to its faith in a future far-removed from its origins. With its elevated position commanding views of Sydney Cove stood the city's crown jewel, Government House; this Gothic Revival spectacle of castellated towers and tall chimneys was the keystone in Sydney's vaulting ambition to be an antipodean version of London. Stately houses graced Burdekin's Terraces on Hyde Park and Horbury Terrace on Macquarie Street, each one as fine a row of dwellings as anything one could see in Mayfair or Kensington. On summer evenings, piano music drifted from the opulent drawing rooms and the laughter of white-gowned society women from the ironwork verandas.

Isobel truly admired all these architectural gems. But she also loved the open spaces of the city: the grassy expanse of Hyde Park, once a racecourse and cricket ground, now enjoyed by families for recreations from walking dogs to flying a kite; the shady, verdant Domain and Botanic Gardens, where people picnicked while entertained by bands or strolled by the seawall, lulled by the spell of the harbour itself; and the headlands of Port Jackson, with bays and beaches where one could ramble over rocks, collect shells and chase seagulls. Most of all she loved the grandeur of the harbour itself, the hypnotic dazzle of its water light and ever-changing colours, the tonic of its salt air, the enchanting Kyrie of its tidal music.

Sydney's main streets were now largely denuded of trees, replaced by an iron grove of gaslights. Anyone who had seen the town in its infancy would gasp at how the bush had been razed around Port Jackson. But for all its pretensions, Sydney was still hemmed in by the wildness of nature, thought Isobel; landscape still dominated every view, swallowed up every prospect. The Colonial Secretary, Mr Macleay, and her father as Surveyor-General had each in their own way tried to bring balance and order to this savage green chaos through their curating and collecting, and their surveying and mapping.

But, as Isobel knew, nature pushed back.

When drought sucked riverbeds dry and killed livestock and crops, as it had without mercy for the last ten years, there followed the dreaded scourge of fire. Terrifying conflagrations would erupt without warning on Woolloomooloo Hill, or charge up gullies near Glebe, or lay siege to the small township of St Leonards on the harbour's north side. At times like these, Sydney felt very small and vulnerable. Summer also brought the 'brickfielders', those hot, dry winds out of the south and west that drove towering dust storms across the city, choking everything in its fine reddish powder. There were the sudden downpours of rain, monsoonal and deafening, that overwhelmed gutters and drains, turning streets and lanes into quagmires.

And then there was always the unpitying violence of the ocean that broke ships on reefs and rocks, like the hapless merchantman *Edward Lombe* at Middle Head or the schooner *Governor Hunter* off Port Stephens. These were reminders of the city's isolation, of the fragility of its umbilical link to the Mother Country. There were other deadly threats from outside as well. An outbreak of typhus and scarlet fever from passengers on the *Lady Macnaghten* had led to the building of a quarantine station on North Head in the hope of stemming contamination from abroad. Poised between the vast hostile hinterland and the vaster hostile ocean, it sometimes seemed to Isobel that Sydney's foothold on the eastern lip of the continent was more tentative than anyone liked to admit.

Apart from these cataclysmic dramas, there were subtler, more persistent corruptions eating away at the city's foundations. The slow, quiet corrosion of iron and stone by salt water. The rising damp and blossoming rot molesting plaster and wood. The fetid stench of mangrove swamps and puke of overripe Moreton Bay figs splashed on pavements. The ammonia fume of seagull guano dissolving sandstone. Every household braced itself for seasonal invasions of mosquitos, spiders, crickets, cockroaches, beetles, possums and bogong moths. Despite the daily exertions of dung boys and street sweepers, horse excrement perfumed every avenue with its sweetish stink, while the city's dusty squares and backstreets ran with dogs, chooks, foraging pigs and goats.

And there were other sharper discordant strains in this city's triumphal symphony. While its good citizens liked to imagine themselves living in a shining New Jerusalem, sustained by faith in God, law and the market, Sydney had not yet wiped clean the convict stain of its past. Two years earlier, the Female Factory had been closed at Parramatta. A huge public rally protesting the arrival of the convict ship *Hashemy* had put a final stop to the Colonial Office's efforts at restarting transportation. Or so people hoped. But Hyde Park Barracks still disgorged its cargo of human misery every day to labour on public works. And the good citizens still quaked whenever there was a murder in the Rocks or a drunken gang broke windows in Wynyard Square or a bushranger attacked the gold escort from Bathurst.

And, much as it tried, Sydney could not turn a completely deaf ear to the echoes from the frontier, stories of theft, rape, murder and war. When Isobel was only three, a troop of mounted police had murdered hundreds of natives at Waterloo Creek in northern New South Wales on the same day that Sydneysiders flocked to watch a regatta on the harbour to celebrate Foundation Day. Six months later, the massacre of twenty-eight unarmed natives (men, women and children) at Myall Creek had resulted in a scandalous trial and storm of outrage against Governor Gipps, who was accused of failing to protect settlers from '*filthy, brutal cannibals*'. Despite this, seven men were charged with murder, convicted and hanged. Little Isobel and Ballandella were spared these nightmares as they rambled in the gardens at Grangemouth but they were well known to Ballandella's mother and the tribes along the Darling, the Murray and the Murrumbidgee.

On this perfect sunny, blue-sky day, however, Sydney appeared to Isobel as a city brimming with confidence and contentment. The voters had just elected a new Legislative Council made up of city folk who dared to imagine a brighter future for the colony, weaned off its fatal dependence on wool and convict labour. These men resented the rich squatters' boast that Sydney owed all its prosperity to them alone and that, without their wise leadership and steady hand, the city would explode into a hell pit of violence and bloodshed.

Isobel's mind was unclouded by worry as she and Mrs Palmer wandered among the happy crowd near the band pavilion in the Botanic Gardens. Men sweated a little in their bell-toppers and cravats and women shimmered under their parasols and lace collars and gloves. But all was merriment and fun! The band of the 77th played airs with a brisk, cheerful tempo that never failed to elevate the spirits and made the world seem a carefree carnival.

Isobel's heart was so boosted by the gaiety of the music, the liveliness of the throng and loveliness of the sun-brightened park that she imagined she knew some of the friendly faces in the crowd, smiling sweetly even at strangers. Today she exulted in the gaze of this multitude, their eyes gleaming with love and kindness, pride and gladness. She had a new gown, new gloves and new ribbons in her hair. Why should she not be looked at?

There were other reasons she was determined to be happy. Life was not nearly so grim as Isobel had feared ten days ago when her dear brothers left them. She had the fancy-dress ball to look forward to at Juniper Hall and the thrilling anticipation of her coming out. And there had been other news to lift her spirits. Only yesterday the Finches had sent an invitation to Rosemount for Isobel and her sisters to join them and the Bradleys at the weekend for a picnic at Watsons Bay. They would also be joined by officers from the visiting vessel HMS *Neptune,* anchored in Darling Harbour. At last it seemed the drought of social isolation was broken. Their confidence in their friends, while greatly tested, had ultimately been justified.

It was also possible, Isobel hoped, that her sins, if not forgotten, had been forgiven.

Chapter 15

THE LETTER FROM ALICE

There was still no word from Faulconstone of Aunt Louisa's plans but Isobel was calmly resigned to her fate. In more optimistic moments she had even decided that her exile from Rosemount was tolerable, if neither lengthy nor permanent, and would afford her time to consider her future. She had the ball to look forward to as well and a brave new world to explore once she was out in society. How could she not be excited and hopeful?

But the Major's peace of mind was still greatly perturbed. He had just spent most of a trying week filling out the questionnaire sent to him by the Governor, scrutinising his conduct of the Surveyor-General's department and management of its budget down to the last draughting pencil. The Governor would forward this report to the Executive Council and the Major now waited to see if the matter would proceed to an official investigation.

That evening the Major entered the dining room at half eight. At Grace's insistence, a formal dinner was served at least twice a week with a full table setting, including the family's crystal epergne piled high with quinces, grapes, pomegranates, custard apples, clusters of aster, boronia and maidenhair, and, at its apex, that most highly prized rarity, an unripened pineapple with its explosive green crown. The silverware and crockery appeared liturgical in the glow of eight virginal candles and the hushed, well-rehearsed ritual of the eight-course dinner took on the air of a sacrament. 'Why should we be deprived of pleasure just because our friends desert us?' Grace had argued, turning dinner into an act of protest against the family's social disgrace. They all hoped that the Finches' invite to Watsons Bay that weekend spelled the end of this sentence and that soon their friends would return to the Major's table.

'Sydney looked so beautiful today,' ventured Isobel, wanting to break the silence that had persisted to the second course. 'I have never seen so many ships at the quay. A flotilla! It must be the gold bringing them here in such numbers. Mrs Palmer and I had a lovely walk along the wharves counting all the vessels and identifying their flags.'

'Did your fitting go well?' asked Grace. 'Have you picked out your new gloves?'

The Major looked up from his meal. 'You do realise that if this inquiry goes against me we will be reduced to surviving on half pay? If we are lucky.' He dabbed at his chin with his napkin and tossed it onto the table. 'I find the calls on my purse are endless.'

'What is the matter, Papa?' asked Anna. 'You seem exceptionally out of sorts.'

The Major wrung his hands, as if debating with himself and then seemed to come to a decision. 'I have had a letter from Alice,' he announced. 'I can share with you the good news that she has a healthy baby boy, Xavier John Angus.'

'But that is wonderful!' exclaimed Isobel. How overjoyed Winnie would have been to hear such news, she thought. A baby boy. The sisters clasped each other and got up to embrace their father with tears of joy. The Major had a grandson and an heir. But how could this be an occasion for her father's moodiness? Isobel soon had her answer.

The Major motioned for them to resume their seats. 'Yes, yes, this is wonderful news, I agree. But my joy is diminished by the far greater and more sombre part of her letter.' The Major sighed and wiped his face. 'Alice's letter reveals that the Baron and his family are not the rich aristocrats they pretended to be when he was here in Australia, telling the world of his fortune and grand plans.' Isobel had been privy to much of the Baron's confident talk as a man of great ambition and abilities.

'Yes, the Twyckenhams may have a country seat in Hertfordshire and townhouses in London and Bath. But it turns out that, over the last few years, the Twyckenhams, father and son, have made many poor—some would say reckless—investments, a disaster that has been compounded with ill-considered loans and usurious letters of credit.'

The three Macleod sisters stared at their father, dumbstruck. The Major's face was drained to a frightful whiteness. 'The Baron and his father have now been dragged to court by their creditors. The manor and townhouses are swallowed up in an abyss of debt and this distinguished family does not have two pennies to rub together.' The Major's voice faltered. 'Which leaves the young would-be-Baron facing a long stretch in debtors' prison. And Alice and her new baby facing penury and destitution.'

A sob broke from Grace's throat. Anna began rocking back and forth, whimpering. Isobel watched her poor father struggle against tears. 'What will happen now?' she asked.

'Nothing will happen unless I send them the five thousand pounds they ask for to settle a fraction of their debts and keep her feckless husband out of Newgate,' said the Major. A muscle twitched in his cheek. 'He is no gentleman to make his wife write to her father begging—*begging!*—for money. We have all been grossly deceived. The man is no better than a liar and a thief. My daughter's honour has been traduced and our trust betrayed.'

'Dear God, this cannot be true,' mumbled Grace.

'Your dear mother had her suspicions,' the Major cried. 'If only I had listened. She wanted to delay the wedding until she could find out more about this so-called Baron Crawley and his family. But she knew how much Alice would be humiliated. And she did not want to interfere again in an affair of this kind, especially after the matter with that young captain.'

Grace and Isobel exchanged looks. To think that Winnie might have saved Alice had it not been for the tangled affair of Captain Tranter. That was too bitter an irony! Isobel recalled her mother's face the day of Alice's wedding, her eyes scrutinising the groom with the intensity of an inquisitor. *What* had she known to make her so worried?

'Well, I'll be damned if I bail that blackguard out of prison,' the Major shouted, slamming his fist on the table. 'The man has made a mockery of everything sacred: your sister's devotion, his marriage, his duty. And now there is a child that bears his name and face and shall also bear his ignominy!'

'But what about Alice?' implored Grace. 'You cannot abandon her.'

'I will do no such thing. I shall pay for her passage back to Australia. She is a victim of fraud and desertion. He has no hold over her. Let him rot in Newgate for all I care!'

'Oh, this is beyond endurance,' wailed Anna, 'Our sister will come back a deserted mother. Imagine the scorn and calumny! Imagine the disgrace! As if we have not suffered enough these last few weeks.'

'Silence!' roared the Major. 'Enough of your endless self-pity.' He stood up, his face bright red. His right hand shook uncontrollably. 'Is the esteem of rich families all you hold dear? I am ashamed to be your father, all of you. My foolish, selfish daughters!'

Papa appeared on the point of collapse. Isobel was frightened. She bowed her head, her heart full with unbearable shame and sadness.

The Major stumbled from the room, leaving his daughters to their weeping.

Chapter 16

WATSONS BAY

NOVEMBER 1851

Saturday morning dawned hot and bright, with gusting winds that rattled Isobel's windowpanes in their sills. The original plans for a picnic had been greatly improved with the offer of luncheon at the Marine Hotel at Watsons Bay. Everyone prayed that the wind would die down to a cooling zephyr. Isobel was excited but also nervous about her first appearance in society since the disgrace of the duel. Her rehabilitation now lay in the hands of the Misses Finch and Bradley but she was confident of their historic love for her and felt no shame.

Five cabs arrived at eight o'clock. Isobel travelled with Emily and Florence Finch while their sister Beatrice accompanied Anna and Grace. They were to be joined en route by the Bradleys, Emma, Hannah and Alexandra. Mothers and assorted aunts were in attendance as chaperones, Mrs Palmer acting as Isobel's. Their special guests, six officers from HMS *Neptune*, were to meet them at the hotel.

The Finch girls were in excellent spirits. They complimented Isobel on her new ribbons and gloves, all ordered from Madame Ponder's in honour of the first day of the new month. Isobel felt overjoyed to fall so easily back into the company of her old friends.

'Is it true you are to come out at Mr Cooper's fancy-dress ball next Tuesday?' asked Beatrice.

'Yes,' said Isobel. 'Mrs C. has kindly agreed to introduce me to her guests.'

'Well, who has all the luck?' exclaimed Florence. 'Mr Cooper's fancy balls are a highlight of the season. No expense spared. And you will meet such interesting people!'

Isobel was sensitive to any note of mockery in Florence's voice; it was more than likely that the Finches did not have a high opinion of the rich emancipist and his family. But Florence smiled sweetly with no hint of snobbery. 'I must confess to being quite jealous.'

Isobel felt a heady bout of joy as their carriage raced over the crest of the ridge. Laid out before her was the panorama of South Head, the lovely narrow peninsula that bent like a crooked finger to beckon ships into the world's largest and most beautiful harbour. Looking across the low heathland and sparse forest of eucalypts, native oaks and myrtles, Isobel could see two golden arcs of sand: the long crescent of beach at Watsons Bay and the smaller scoop further south of Camp Cove. Across the mouth of the great harbour, the magnificent sandstone bluff of North Head floated in a blue haze.

There was only a smattering of dwellings on the peninsula: cottages for the Portuguese pilots who boarded every vessel entering the port; the buildings and flagstaff of the signal station that sent news back to Observatory Hill; and a handful of stately marine villas that took advantage of the views. At the far end of Watsons Bay a long jetty jutted into the harbour, a drop-off and collection point for pleasure steamers. Close by stood the Marine Hotel where they were to have lunch. As their coach drew closer, Isobel could see a group of men dressed in white breeches and blue frock coats, milling about near the beach. Isobel felt her pulse quicken and smiled at her own habitual weakness for men in uniform.

Lunch was a raucous affair consisting of a delicious collation of vegetable and fish curries with side dishes of chutney and sambol, all prepared by the black Ceylonese cook, Samuel. The meal was accompanied by much laughter, wine and good-natured flirting, which continued as the party of young men and women spilled out onto the beach. One of the officer's stewards came out after them with a champagne bottle and several glasses. A round of toasts followed. Isobel did not conceal her pleasure at the attentiveness of the young naval men who demanded to be introduced properly.

'Has Miss Macleod ever entertained the prospect of becoming a Royal Navy officer's bride?' asked Lieutenant Matthews, proffering a second glass of fizz. Isobel laughed but did not answer his question. Some of these men were only six years her senior and yet they were already commissioned officers who had seen service in India and China. Isobel was jealous.

'Miss Macleod does not look favourably on the Royal Navy. Her father is a Major and a veteran of the Peninsular War,' teased Beatrice Finch. 'She is much more at home in a barracks than a barquentine.'

'That is simply untrue,' protested Isobel light-heartedly, anxious to steer clear of any discussion of her father; the shame of the duel hung like a shadow in her mind. 'My brother William served on HMS *Iris* off West Africa. No one could be more proud than I.'

'Is he still in Her Majesty's navy?' asked Lieutenant Matthews.

'He grew tired of weevils and seasickness and cashed in his commission for the richer fields of commerce,' intervened Emma Bradley. 'He is in Madras, I'm told. Seeking his fortune. Is that right, Izzie?'

Isobel nodded, a little alarmed how quickly news travelled in their small circle. Two more rounds of fizz were downed and the party broke up into smaller groups. Isobel joined Florence, Emma and Beatrice with Lieutenants Dunnock, Matthews and Brown. They strolled up an inviting green sward fringed by she-oaks and came out onto a plain strewn with native flowers and sweet-smelling clover. In the distance a freshwater lagoon sparkled between the branches of myrtle trees on its banks. The lagoon was busy with flocks of wild ducks alighting on its bright surface, wings outspread, or diving underwater for food.

To their right loomed the intimidating cliffs of The Gap. Isobel had heard of this place but this was the first time she had seen it for herself. She was awed by its dramatic sandstone, banded honey-brown and caramel, that had been hammered for millennia by the sea into giant shards and boulders. From the cliff top she looked down onto turquoise waters crashing over slabs of tessellated basalt. She breathed in the salt spray and ozone from each monstrous wave that heaved itself against this raw, serrated edge of the continent. One could easily imagine God (or perhaps one of Ballandella's spirit warriors) wielding a giant axe to crack this peninsula open and allow the sea to tear away at its innards. As far as the eye could see, the ceaseless ocean stretched to the horizon, changing colour from foam-flecked aquamarine to its bleak and lovely grey-green depths.

The party clambered over rocks and headed towards Camp Cove. Some local fishermen had drawn their boats up on the beach and were cooking freshly caught fish over a fire. The aroma made Isobel hungry again even after their substantial lunch. Lieutenant Matthews larked about on the sand, offering to pay the men for a piece of fish for 'the famished young lady' despite Isobel's protestations.

As she attempted to cross one of the rock platforms near a tidal pool, Isobel slipped and her horrid muslin petticoat snagged in a crack, anchoring her tight. She would have to tear it to come free. Her 'distress' elicited swift gallantry from all three officers, who ran to her aid with penknives drawn. Lieutenant Brown was the swiftest. 'Command and I shall obey!' He knelt before Isobel to perform the surgery and then gallantly withdrew.

Poor Isobel. As soon as she began to walk across the sand, her petticoat, already badly torn, came apart and fell to her ankles. She almost toppled over as she caught her heel in the crumpled hemline. The shrieks of seagulls overhead sounded like mocking laughter. Mercifully, Emma snatched up the damaged petticoat and she and Isobel dug a quick hole in the sand and buried it.

Lieutenants Brown and Matthews were preoccupied, running races along the beach to compete for Isobel's favour. Meanwhile Isobel and the other young women took turns to spy on North Head through Lieutenant Dunnock's spy-glass. Dunnock brandished a small flask of rum and offered it to Beatrice, entreating her to sit beside him. While Isobel had enjoyed the lunch and was flattered by male attention, she was starting to tire of all this banter and horseplay. Perhaps she had drunk too much fizz. Her head ached.

And then behind her there erupted a chorus of laughter. Not seagulls this time. She turned to see Lieutenant Brown sashaying up the beach with her ruined petticoat draped around his waist; he must have spied them burying it. If the truth be told she was amused at this charade, but she blushed even so. They were all fine fellows, these naval officers, with their gallantry and silly antics, but she suspected this was all no more than a game. Should she be annoyed or upset? She tried not to be either. What harm was there in a little teasing?

As Lieutenant Brown trotted up, he stepped clumsily out of the petticoat and handed it over. 'I hope you are not offended, dear lady!'

Lieutenant Matthews, rather flushed in the face from drink, was close behind and cried out so that everyone within earshot could hear. 'Do not fear. Miss Macleod is quite the devotee of swapping sex!'

There was another raucous explosion of laughter from the whole party. Isobel's soul withered. How did Lieutenant Matthews, a visiting naval officer whose ship had been in port for only a week, know of her disgrace? Either the Finches or Bradleys—or both—had gossiped about Isobel in front of these men. Once fallen, forever socially dead. That was the common wisdom.

Thank God neither Grace nor Anna were present. Isobel lowered her face to hide her shame. She refused to give anyone the satisfaction of seeing how hurt she felt. When she looked up again she saw a conspiratorial trio of Finch and Bradley girls, barely able to conceal their mocking grins, studying her. Isobel met their curious scrutiny with a cold stare. She felt deeply betrayed and utterly alone. Even her so-called friends would not spare her the lash of public humiliation.

It was unfair. Grossly unfair. What have I done that was so terrible? she argued with herself. Why did she deserve to be treated with such contempt? It seemed to Isobel that her crime of impersonating a man had become more scandalous than the fact of two gentlemen shooting at each other in a swamp. Her father had once described to Isobel the breathtaking sight of a giant swarm of wild budgerigars in their tens of thousands, a bright green whirlwind of flashing wings, swooping above the spinifex near the Darling River. 'This cloud of birds moved as if with the will of a single creature,' the Major told her, 'a vast multitude acting as one.' Isobel was beginning to think human society showed the same flocking instincts when it came to gossip, swooping in mindless unison on whatever juicy morsels of scandal came its way.

Whatever their motivation, her friends had betrayed her. In exchange for Isobel's desperate act of love intended to save her father's life, she had traded away what she held most dear: her reputation, her closest friends and her faith in the essential goodness of others.

Chapter 17

SINKING

That night Isobel had a bad dream.

In the wee hours, she was woken by a slight tremor. She felt it at first as no more than a jiggling of her bed so that the four posts swayed a little and creaked. The jiggling grew more insistent accompanied by a tinkling as the jug and basin on her washstand jostled against each other. She sat up upright in bed then and looked out the window to see if a storm was coming. But there was no sign of rain or lightning.

Without warning, the house gave a shudder from roof to basement and emitted a loud groan. What in the name of God was happening? The groan kept growing louder and deeper. Isobel felt the house lurch and her bedroom pitched sideways—slowly at first, like the deck of a ship in a high sea. Her stomach lurched too as she watched the ceiling roll over her head, its plaster rose tilting off-centre and its lamp swinging askew.

Isobel uttered a sob and clung to the bedpost. Against the windows she heard the patter of raindrops and saw silver shadows coursing down the wall opposite. Outside, a storm had now arrived in full force. The darkness all about her was transformed with each lightning burst to blinding whiteness, and she could hear the other furniture in her bedroom begin to move.

The majolica jug and basin hurtled from the washstand and exploded against the wall close by Isobel's head. The stand itself then tipped over with a crash and the cheval glass followed suit. The wardrobe took off next, squealing as it juddered down the tilted floor, caroming off her chest of drawers and slamming into the corner of the room, doors flung open in total surrender. Last of all, Isobel's four-poster bed lost its footing and began to slither across the floorboards, rucking the rug up under its castors as it slid. With a deafening crack it careered into the mantel, its canopy collapsing on Isobel like a broken mast.

The room continued to roll drunkenly. The house protested this absurdity with its own screams of splintering wood and rending brick, underscored by explosive volleys of heavy objects falling and smashing. 'Save me!' Isobel shouted, her voice puny against the storm. At her windows, the gale hurled all the windblown litter it could gather up in fistfuls of debris. Panes shattered and the wind came rushing in, screeching and clawing at Isobel's hair and face as she cowered on her bed.

The whole house was wallowing dangerously now, accompanied by calamitous noises in every room. Downstairs, the piano and hall clock tumbled to their deaths with a chaotic jangle. The dining table lumbered towards the doorway, crushing chairs in its path, and dragging the Chinese carpet, the chiffonier and the china cabinet in its wake. In the study, the Major's desk charged bull-like at the fireplace. The cabinets and bookshelves disgorged their contents. So many beautiful, rare and delicate things obliterated in the blink of an eye.

Like a ship keeled over for careening, the house leaned at such an angle that the light in her room was splayed against the ceiling and the wrack of the room's contents piled up against the walls. Isobel's thoughts mirrored the chaos around her. Was this the End of Days? Or was it a singular punishment for Isobel and her family alone, Rosemount razed by an earthquake or some other cataclysm?

And then the house's subsidence suddenly stopped and the racket of the gale died away. In this merciful silence, Isobel could hear her own breathing, short and ragged, like the panting of a terrified animal. She had never known terror like this before in all her life, except perhaps the sense of self-annihilation when her mother had died and all meaning had vanished from the world. Or when she had watched her papa face death on a duelling ground.

The lull was only brief, a quiet reprieve before the even more unimaginable horror to come. As the storm resumed its fury overhead, Isobel felt the ground begin to shake beneath her feet, joggling the house and all its trinkets like dice in a box. Then there came a deep rumbling, a tremendous sound, drowning out even the cacophony of the storm. Isobel struggled up from the wreckage of her bed and raised her head above the windowsill.

She saw a wall of water advancing on the house. A giant grey-green wave.

She closed her eyes. 'Forgive me my sins,' she prayed and awaited certain death.

The wave wiped away all the splendours of the estate in an instant: the forest, the gardens, the orchards and ponds. It broke on Rosemount Hall with such force that her ceilings buckled and floorboards sprang from their beams. Already listed over, the house now began to sink in earnest as seawater gushed in at every window and doorway, cascading into the cellars and filling up the ground floor.

Finding that by some miracle she had not been killed in the first onslaught, Isobel decided to save her own life. She could hear seawater rising rapidly, grinding up the broken treasures of Rosemount like gravel in a slurry. Where could she go?

There was only one choice.

Clambering down the floor of her bedroom in the near-darkness, Isobel found her way to the wardrobe lying on its back. Thankfully, none of the drawers had spilled open. She slid out the bottom drawer and, from beneath layers of old fabric, extracted a small tin box. Groping desperately through its contents, at last she found what she was looking for.

A key. A tiny brass key that promised her salvation.

And then *it* caught her eye, half-buried in this miscellany of coins, bracelets, necklaces and curios: the opal dragonfly. It glinted at her, challenging her to save it, her mother's gift. She scooped it up and put it in the pocket of her bedjacket as she turned to go.

With her bedroom door torn off its hinges, it was easy for Isobel to climb out onto the mezzanine where she heard the furious rush and gurgle of water as the saloon filled up like a giant bathtub. When she looked down, she could see the spiral staircase was more than half submerged. Holding fast to the cedar railing, Isobel pulled herself to the far side of the mezzanine and found the entrance to the servants' backstairs. She ducked her head, passing through this low portal, and mounted a short flight of stairs to her left. Here, she found a locked door that led to Rosemount's dome and rooftop, access for the servants tasked with keeping the dome and skylights cleaned. Isobel had discovered this secret passage as a child and made it her mission to 'borrow' one of the housekeeper's keys; it had been tricky (it involved bribing a maidservant with one of her jade hair combs) but it had been worth it.

The house lurched again and threw Isobel against the wall of the stairwell; it was only luck that saved her from dropping the key. She peered over her shoulder and saw dark green water lapping at the bottom of the stairs. She heard flotsam banging against the saloon walls and there were more loud pops and crashes as water poured into the upstairs rooms.

'Go, go, go,' Isobel exhorted herself as she unlocked the door and began to climb. The narrow stairwell curved steeply, winding upwards to the topmost floor of the house under the roofline. Isobel shouldered open the rusted door at the head of the stairs and tumbled out onto the rooftop courtyard surrounding the dome. As far as the eye could see there stretched water, black-green and fathomless, and, above her, an unbroken fogbound sky suffused with the melancholy glow of the moon.

Isobel was alive—for now. But she was utterly alone.

Isobel woke from the nightmare, bathed in sweat. Her room was stiflingly hot and close. Outside her window, a waxing gibbous moon hung in a clear sky. There was no sound of wind or rain. Her dream had been so vivid and terrifying, blood still fizzed in her ears and she felt fear pounding at the cage of her chest.

The house was silent.

There was no doubt in Isobel's mind that this was one of the dreams her mother had spoken of before she died. *I have such strange dreams. Terrible dreams, some of them. Unimaginable . . . They show me . . . I do not understand what they show me.'*

Since Winnie's death, Isobel had done just as she had promised: kept the opal dragonfly, her secret inheritance, hidden away. This had been the cause of bitter arguments and heartache when the brooch—Father's love token to his wife—could not be found among her belongings. Grace was distraught and remained convinced that it had been stolen. 'Why would Mother lose such a beautiful thing? I simply don't believe it!' she shouted when her sisters tried to calm her. She had made no secret of her fond hopes for inheriting the brooch (jewellery, after all, was Grace's great passion) and felt betrayed that somehow this gorgeous object had slipped through her fingers. When Grace directly accused Isobel of being a thief, she had flatly denied any knowledge of the dragonfly's whereabouts. But she knew Grace did not believe her. In the habit of blaming Isobel for most of the disappointments in her life, Grace added the missing brooch as another betrayal to this list.

Isobel rose from her bed and went to the wardrobe. From the bottom drawer, she pulled out her tin box of secrets and plucked out a tiny key. And there—just as she had seen it in her dream—lay the dragonfly. She spoke to the darkness. 'What do the dreams mean, Mama? Such strange and terrible dreams.' There had been the one of the drowning man, the night before her father fought a duel. And other dreams too, both frightening and wonderful. But she could only guess at their meanings, assuming they meant anything at all.

Her room was so stifling she could barely breathe. A frisson of terror still lingered when she looked at her washstand and cheval glass, easily able to recall their destruction. She had to escape. To find fresh air, take a deep breath. She would steal away to her favourite hiding place as a child when the household slept. Isobel took the key and tiptoed across the mezzanine to the servants' stairs. She half expected to see water sloshing about in the saloon below but all was normal and calm. Unlocking the same secret door as in her dream, she climbed the winding stairs and, at last, came out onto Rosemount's rooftop.

The night was still warm after such a hot day. Even the waist-high wall around the courtyard radiated a little heat. Isobel went over to the dome and lay sprawled, arms outstretched, on its warm slate-tiled mound, just as she loved to do as a child. It felt daring to let herself be suspended over this great drop, her feet lifted into the air and the dome bearing her full weight. Between her legs she could see to the marble floor of the saloon below. She knew it was safe but even so it challenged her mental defences.

Now Isobel sat on the courtyard wall, looking out to the bay beyond. The cloudless sky was a luminous blue wash with the brilliance of the moonlight igniting the harbour in rills of white fire. Clark and Shark islands slept, mere shadows against the glossy water. Away on the horizon there was a thin ribbon of paler light—the glow of Sydney's gaslights perhaps?—and, above it, a long, leaden cloud hanging over the city. She wondered why such a cloud always seemed to hang there at night. Perhaps it was a pall of smoke mixed with other fumes. And yet, strangely, she never saw it in daylight.

A voice penetrated the dark. 'Prawns, fresh prawns!' a man cried out in a surly tone, as if angered that no one could be bothered to purchase his catch at this late hour. It was one of Sydney's blacks walking along the beach. One of the last of his people.

Isobel thought of Ballandella then, the girl she had sworn to never forget. When she first moved to Rosemount, Isobel had crept up here regularly to sit on this wall under the stars, trying to remember Ballandella's night-time stories. Stories of the Goanna woman who used her yam stick to release the waters of the Murrumbidgee. Stories of Baiame, the Creator, hanging upside down with his shield and boomerang on the horizon, and Maliyan, the Wedge-tailed Eagle with a diamond-bright star for an eye. Ballandella had shown Isobel these starpatterns in the night sky, used by the storytellers to recall the story-songs. She may have only been four when she was taken from her mother but she had learned how the great wheel of stars helped you find your way at night, and to keep track of the season and the time of year. *'The stars, Izzie. Up there, look. Stars, eh?'*

Ballandella, her playmate, her friend. Why had she not replied to any of Isobel's letters when she was taken away? Isobel had written again and again care of Dr Nicholson, asking him to forward her letters to wherever Ballandella was living. Much later, Dr Nicholson wrote to Isobel to say he had heard that Ballandella had found a husband and started a family near Wisemans Ferry. Was she happy? Had she found a good life? Did she ever think about Grangemouth and Isobel? These were questions that Isobel asked in her letters. But none of them were ever answered.

It was only as she grew older that Isobel began to realise that, perhaps, Ballandella simply did not want to answer the letters. Maybe she had good reasons to resent (even to *hate*) Major Macleod and his family. Did she blame them for taking her away from her mother, for turning her into a spectacle, a plaything for their amusement and curiosity? Did her grief as a little girl darken all her memories of her days at Grangemouth?

Now that she herself faced exile from Rosemount, Isobel found that easy to understand. She had the merest inkling of how help-less Ballandella must have felt, so far from home and her loved ones. Isobel had flattered herself that she was Ballandella's loving companion. In her arrogance, she had never considered the black girl's profound loneliness. Mrs Palmer was the only one who had taken that seriously. *'Does she not get lonely at times, poor thing? Surely she must pine for her own kind?'* Winnie had been dismissive. *'I don't believe so. She is such a sunny soul.'* But it was Isobel who would never forget the plaintive sound of her friend singing to herself in her mother's tongue and crying for her country.

Now it was Isobel's turn to feel lonely.

Winnie and Richard were gone. William and Joseph were headed for India. Her brave sister Alice was on the other side of world. Grace and Anna were glad to be rid of her. She felt more estranged from her father than she would have thought possible. While Mrs Palmer was sweet and loyal, it felt wrong to burden her. Aunt Louisa was well meaning but her high principles did not invite confidentiality. And her childhood friends, the Bradleys and Finches, had shown they could not be trusted.

It would soon be time for Isobel to leave Rosemount. Perhaps that was the portent of her terrifying dream: that Rosemount and everything it had meant to her and her family was now lost. Its time had passed. The Macleod family's prestige was dissipated. If she stayed to help Father and her sisters try to reclaim the glory days, she too would be marooned.

As she sat contemplating the night sky, Isobel felt something inside the pocket of her bed jacket. Had she placed it there in her dream or when she had awoken? She could not be sure. Her hand closed on the brooch. She held it up and the lovely fire of its stones was kindled by the moonlight. 'Oh, Mama,' she sighed. 'What is it I am supposed to do?'

Papa was right about one thing. She had been without proper guidance since her mother's death. She felt more unsure about her future than at any other time in her short life. But wasn't that story already written for her, the daughter of an exalted colonial official? To be wooed and wed by a gentleman of respectable station and means, to bear him children, raise his family and be the mistress of his house? Surely this was her destiny.

Was that story changed now that she had stepped outside the boundaries of social decorum? Because she was perverse and fanatical as her sisters had insisted? Or was it because she wanted something else, something that she hardly dared put into words? She thought about the little girl whose father took her into his study to draw emu eggs and fossil bones. Who befriended Ballandella and listened to her stories. Who dared to impersonate Papa as an explorer on her 'expedition' to Rushcutters Bay. The young woman at work with her paint set and easel, enraptured by the harbour and forest through her window. The artist with a restless heart, yearning foolishly for the talents of Mr Martens or Mr Earle, marvelling at her own breathtaking conceit. The woman dressed as her brother who dashed into the middle of a duel to save her father's life. The woman who crept out of her bedroom at night and sat on the roof to stare at the stars. Who had inherited her mother's ambivalent gift and her dreams of sublime terror.

Who was *this* woman? How did she fit into the story of Isobel Macleod? There came to her then the poem that Fanny told her that first day in Rosemount's gardens:

> Today I saw the dragon-fly
> Come from the wells where she did lie.
> An inner impulse rent the veil
> Of her old husk: from head to tail.

What had Fanny, that high-spirited 'queer' woman, said to her? *'We must lose our old selves so we can discover our true natures.'* Isobel prayed she might still have the chance to do just that. It was time for her to change. To shed her past. To find a place where she would be cherished for who she truly was. She sensed that time and place were near.

Chapter 18

JUNIPER HALL

The evergreen magnolias were hung with lamps that cast pools of honeyed light about them, illuminating their silver trunks, their stooping branches laden with greenery and blossom, and the perfect bright circles of emerald-green buffalo grass at their feet. In Isobel's eyes these pools had the enchanted air of faery rings, enticing but also menacing, tempting her to leave the narrow pathway.

The gardens at Juniper Hall were one of its chief splendours. This front garden, through which guests were arriving under a filigreed iron arch, was dominated by a colossal Moreton Bay fig. As Isobel made her way to the house, she saw that the paved pathway was flanked by beds of Nile lilies, foxgloves, pinks, daisies and field poppies, while along the perimeter walls, flowering shrubs of mock orange, jasmine and gardenia perfumed the evening air. It was a charming, modest garden compared with the encyclopaedic profusion of Rosemount but pleasing to the eye nonetheless.

Isobel's white silk evening gown matched the simple loveliness of this setting. The dress was cut to flatter the slope of her pretty neck and shoulders, unadorned but for her necklet. Father had called Isobel into the study the night before and presented this lovely gift, made in India and taken from Winnie's private collection, in honour of Isobel's debut. 'Your mother would have wanted you to wear this,' he said. Isobel kissed him tenderly on the cheek. Little did he know that she had an even lovelier gift from her mother but one she could never wear proudly in public.

The Major's ill temper had not abated completely since the receipt of Alice's bad news. But he reassured his daughters that his solicitor had written a long letter to the Baron's family and another to Alice, instructing her to prepare for her return to Australia with her baby son. Uncle Fergus would go to London to make the arrangements. In the meantime, the Governor had informed the Major that the Executive Council was appointing a commission of inquiry to investigate his conduct of his department and would submit a report by early next year. The commission would consist of four gentlemen including his old nemesis, Mr Macleay, the former Colonial Secretary. Naturally, Isobel fretted over her father's state of mind.

It had been only three days since her ambush at Watsons Bay. Isobel had wept for the loss of both her innocence and the childhood love she had once borne her friends, the Misses Finch and Bradley. But she deliberately put aside all these worries as best she could, determined to make the most of this happy occasion.

As she neared the house, Isobel pulled on her new cream gloves and her silk hat trimmed with three ostrich feathers, a concession to the whimsy of a fancy-dress ball. Isobel hoped that her debutante's dress would not disappoint. The costumes she had seen so far were exceptionally sumptuous including three Greek goddesses, a maudlin Hamlet, two Cavaliers, a Highland warrior, a Roman centurion and a haughty Catherine the Great.

At her side there walked Aunt Louisa in a simple brown dress and knitted shawl. She was a short, plain, sensible woman and a devout Methodist who did not approve of frivolities such as balls or beverages stronger than tea. But she had decided to turn a blind eye as tonight's festivities were to raise funds for the establishment of a Society for the Relief of Destitute Children.

As they approached, Aunt Louisa pointed out Mrs Jane Cooper, their hostess, in the doorway, dressed in a medieval gown of sky-blue silk with long, trumpet-shaped sleeves and a linen wimple that left visible only the lovely white oval of her face. 'So you must be Isobel,' she smiled, taking her guest's hand. 'You look charming, my dear.'

'Why, thank you. I love your costume. Who are you, if I may ask?'

'I am Queen Adeliza of Louvaine, wife to King Henry I of England. A great patroness of writers.' Mrs Cooper laughed self-mockingly as she was a well-known dilettante, famous for hiring a posse of art, literature and music tutors to work on her own education and that of her huge brood. 'And my warmest welcome to you, Mrs Blunt.'

Aunt Louisa nodded gravely, discombobulated by all the finery, the champagne and the loud merriment within. 'Very good, very good,' was all she managed to say, fumbling with her fan. Recognising Louisa's discomfiture, Jane called over a woman of comparable vintage and dedication to charity work. 'Mrs Meredith, Mrs Blunt.' The two women fell to talking about the fancy bazaar to be held in the Botanic Gardens on New Year's Day.

'Come, stand next to me and I shall introduce you to my guests,' said Jane.

She and Isobel were joined by Catherine, the family's thirteenth daughter and the other debutante of the evening. Dressed in a heavily embroidered red brocade gown with an extravagant lace ruff and trimmings of cloth of gold and pearls, Catherine's outfit was a startling impersonation of Elizabeth I. Isobel complimented her costume but privately thought that the Virgin Queen was an odd choice for a young woman's 'coming out' into society.

The ball was quite different from those her parents held at Rosemount. For a start, the guests were altogether louder and more boisterous than her parents' guests. Juniper Hall was different too. Not as theatrically grand as Mr Verge's Rosemount, it was a fine Georgian mansion, nonetheless, with strong, clean lines, pleasingly proportioned rooms, an air of rationality and restrained good taste, and polished cedar floors that shone like amber.

Isobel stood at the door for two hours or more with her hostess, being introduced to a multitude of ladies and gentlemen. The guests were wealthy businessmen and women: proprietors of hotels, taverns, warehouses, tanneries, shipyards, brickworks, timber and textile mills, as well as lawyers, doctors, engineers, architects and bureaucrats. Most of them were probably emancipists, thought Isobel, though she also recognised a few familiar faces from families she was surprised had condescended to enjoy the hospitality of the wealthy Mr Cooper. There were also the officers of the 11th Regiment, who had swapped their redcoats and shakos for mail and plumage as Richard the Lion Heart, Sir Lancelot and King Arthur.

At one point, 'Robert the Large' himself came into the reception hall to speak with his wife. He was a big man in every sense, tall and exceedingly round. He had capitalised on his rotundity by transforming himself into Holbein's portrait of Henry VIII. When he spoke, Isobel could hear the squashed East End vowels of this son of Stepney. 'Well, well, so this is the remarkable young woman I've heard so much about. Quite the freethinker and firebrand, I'm told. I only wish my own daughters had half your spunk.'

Isobel's face reddened. She did not know whether to be appalled or delighted.

Among the later arrivals were her sisters, Anna and Grace, no doubt delayed by one of Anna's tantrums. Isobel smiled sweetly at them both. Despite their snobbish disdain, they seemed impressed by Juniper Hall's simple grandeur and even excited to be out in public again. Mrs C. introduced them both to her eldest son, Augustus, who escorted them to the ballroom.

At ten o'clock, His Excellency, Governor Sir Charles FitzRoy arrived by coach. He was a handsome man but tonight looked careworn and exhausted. The last few years had taken a toll on the once-popular governor. There had been the widely mourned death of his wife, Lady Mary, in a carriage accident in the grounds of Government House, with Sir Charles at the reins of the runaway vehicle. There had also been a furious public row over the Colonial Office's orders to restart convict transportation. And now there was the challenge of keeping law and order on the goldfields where tens of thousands arrived each week.

Isobel curtsied as she received His Excellency's congratulations. She felt as if her 'coming out' was now formally sealed, not quite the customary presentation in the Queen's drawing room at St James's Palace but the best equivalent available in the colony, short of a ball at Government House. 'Pass on my compliments to your father,' the Governor added, before turning away to join the festivities. Isobel was flummoxed by this condescension from the very man who was about to authorise the destruction of her father's career.

'You have performed your duties with exemplary manners, my dears,' said Mrs Cooper to Catherine and Isobel. 'Now let all three of us go and enjoy ourselves.'

Dance music, courtesy of the regimental band, flowed mellifluously from room to room, animating the spirits of everyone present as did the contents of Mr and Mrs Cooper's large Chinese punchbowls with their panoramas of old Sydney Town. Aunt Louisa had found refuge in the company of three other eminent charity women and was able to relax her moral guardianship over Isobel for a short while, confident in Mrs Cooper's vigilance.

At one point, Isobel spied Anna at the supper table in conversation with a young lady who seemed to be enjoying her company. Miracles were possible. Even more intriguing was the sight of her sister Grace talking to Mr Augustus Cooper, a tolerably good-looking gentleman with a rumoured fortune to his name that did much to improve his attractiveness. It was obvious Grace was enjoying herself. For her part, Isobel's confidence waxed as the evening progressed. To her delight, she was soon engaged for four dances with four different gentlemen. All her cares melted away in the arms of these charming and considerate men on the dance floor and in witty conversation on the veranda.

It was outside that Isobel encountered the last person she ever hoped to see again. With a start, she heard his voice before she laid eyes on him. The only report she had had of his whereabouts, a year or so ago, was with the 65th Regiment of Foot in New Zealand. Out in the garden, she saw him, a fair-haired gent dressed in Greek helmet and bronzed breastplate to resemble the all-conquering Macedonian.

Captain Ralph Tranter.

Isobel felt her cheeks burn and her heart begin to race. Oh, good heavens, no! The last thing she wanted was to revisit that awkward episode. At that very moment the captain turned and looked in her direction. He took a second or two to recognise her, then struggled to hide his shock.

'Why, Miss Macleod—it *is* you! How well you look!' he said.

'Thank you. You are well too, I trust?' she said, anxious to avoid any remarks that would lead down paths she dare not tread.

'Tolerably well,' replied the handsome captain, equally at a loss as to how to steer the conversation safely. 'I was saddened to hear of your loss. Your dear brother and mother.'

Isobel wondered what else he knew of the Macleods' recent troubled history. Despite her nervousness, she could not help studying his face for any signs of affection that lingered there. But what she feared most of all was that *she* might still harbour affections. She recalled the scene at the picnic at Lady Macquarie's Chair that had been the prelude to their intimacy, his courtship rushing swiftly to a love letter and the ardent declaration of a purple orchid. She also recalled Alice's fierce but failed advocacy for the match and felt a pang of great love for her older sister.

So what was the state of her heart now? Isobel knew an old pain resided there, lodged like a thorn. She was shocked at how sharply it ached, such sweet anguish. From one heartbeat to the next, Isobel realised she still longed for Captain Tranter.

'I thank you for your kindness, sir,' said Isobel, looking away to hide her emotion. She hoped that the catch in her throat would be interpreted as a sign of grief for her family members and not something else. A shadow passed across the captain's face and then Isobel heard a voice calling out from across the faery-ringed garden.

'Darling, please come. I want you to meet Mr Probius. He's a very clever artist.'

A woman stepped into the light. Her hair was elaborately coiffed, dyed violet ash-grey, and crowned with a turban of ribbons and feathers. Her bustled blue satin dress gleamed lustrously in the lamplights, and in her left hand she held a single pink rose. Isobel recognised at once Marie Antoinette, the Dauphine and later Queen of France, from a painting by the celebrated portraitist Madame Vigée Le Brun.

The woman's cheeks were highly rouged and her eyes an icy blue. Older than Isobel by several years, she was very striking: slim-waisted, poised, with a china-like complexion and a slender, soft-throated neck. But there was nothing fragile about this woman's character, that much was obvious at once. In keeping with her regal impersonation, there was a haughty self-possession that Isobel knew to be the mark of an aristocrat, as well as that cool, honeyed insistence in the voice that spoke of unshakeable entitlement.

'Come on, Ralph, my dear, I do insist.'

'I—I'm—so . . . sorry . . .' Ralph stuttered to Isobel, either repeating his last sentiment or apologising for this new intrusion. The woman crossed the lawn and approached the veranda. Isobel felt trapped like an insect in amber, unable to escape.

'Aren't you going to introduce me, darling? I don't believe I have had the pleasure,' she said, turning her ice-blue eyes on Isobel.

'Of course. May I present Miss Isobel Macleod. An old friend,' said Ralph. There was an odd pause between the utterance of Isobel's name and 'an old friend' as Ralph decided how best to describe the woman he had once wanted to marry.

'One of tonight's debutantes. Congratulations,' Marie Antoinette took Isobel's hand warmly in hers, before adding: 'I have heard so many interesting things about you.'

Isobel curtsied politely and with a playful, slightly tart smile replied, *'Je suis honoré Votre Majesté!'* She then looked inquisitively at Ralph.

'Ah yes, of course,' he stammered, his face reddening a little. 'Let me have the pleasure of introducing—my wife.'

Isobel's heart bolted. His wife. Of course, how could she have been so foolish? Men do not hang around when an investment in love fails. They move on to new opportunities. Judging by everything about this woman, Ralph had reinvested wisely.

'The Lady Charlotte Bathurst, before we were wed,' continued Ralph. Yes, there was no argument. Isobel's erstwhile suitor had invested his love very handsomely indeed. He had married a niece of the 3rd Earl Bathurst, Secretary of State for War and the Colonies. It seemed that Mr Cooper was forgiven his past sins by some of the loftiest social ranks, who were happy to drink his fizz, toast his health and support his charitable works.

'The pleasure is all mine,' said Isobel with a small curtsy, her head bowed in part to hide her astonishment. She must exit at once. 'I'm sorry to rush away, but our hostess is expecting me. It was good to meet you again after all this time, Captain Tranter.'

'*Major* Tranter now,' prompted Charlotte, beaming with uxorial pride.

'Indeed!' Nothing like friends—or even better, family—in high office to ensure preferment, thought Isobel. 'It has been an honour to meet you both.'

Isobel hurried inside. She refused to shed a tear for this man's sake. But she choked on the bitterness of his betrayal and was enraged, knowing full well that her rage was wholly immoderate and unreasonable. Major Tranter owed her nothing; her own mother had seen to that. Even so, she felt the liberating force of her anger, felt its molten heat course through her body. This white-hot rage had been building in her for weeks, ever since the duel. Rage at all the people who sat in judgement on her.

As she re-entered the ballroom, she glanced over her shoulder one last time. Marie Antoinette had tucked her arm through that of her husband's and led him away.

Chapter 19

THE ARTIST

Back inside the house, Isobel was overcome with dizziness. She made her way to a chair in the corner and sat down. The room and the people and the music whirled about her, indifferent to her panic. She closed her eyes, letting her heart settle and her breathing calm. The last thing she wanted was to make a scene. She sat here for what seemed a long time, ten minutes or more, she could not be sure. To dissuade anyone from approaching, she closed her eyes and fanned herself vigorously as if overwhelmed by the closeness of the room.

'Can I help you, mademoiselle?'

A male voice, not one she recognised. She opened her eyes again and looked up in surprise. What kind of man addressed a woman to whom he had not been introduced?

'Forgive my impertinence but you appear to be unwell.'

A tall gent stood before her. His face was striking: finely boned and aristocratic with full lips and a high forehead. There was an ennobling air of defiance and resolve evident in the set of his brows and the searching gaze of his dark eyes. 'My name is Probius. Charles Probius.'

'I am Miss Isobel Macleod,' she replied.

'Yes, I know. I have had the pleasure of meeting your father once or twice.'

'I apologise for alarming you. I was feeling a little faint.'

'Well, if I may be so bold, fresh air may help. Can I escort you to the veranda?'

'Why, thank you,' she replied a little hesitantly. No doubt this was the same Mr Probius to whom Lady Bathurst wanted to introduce her husband a little while ago. With luck Major Tranter and his wife had withdrawn indoors and she would not have to suffer the indignity of another conversation with them. But then again, if he was still in the garden it was perhaps no tragedy that he should see her with this solicitous man.

Out on the veranda, the air was sweetly scented by the flowering shrubs along the perimeter wall. It was now past midnight and the full moon was high in the sky, its milky light draining from the garden like a thawing sea of blue ice.

'You are an artist, I believe, sir.'

Mr Probius wore a wide-collared brown frock coat with a large, loosely tied linen cravat high at his throat over a white calico shirt. The outfit was of antique fashion and had the well-used roughness of working clothes. 'I am dressed as Monsieur Jacques-Louis David, if that is what you are asking. Don't tell anyone, though, or they would be outraged!'

Probius smiled. Isobel laughed.

This was indeed provocative! David—the heroic painter and chronicler of the French Revolution and later of the tyrant Napoleon himself. Not a figure much admired in British or for that matter colonial circles. Her own father, like so many veterans, hated all things French. Part of the Major's pride in map-making and surveying was based on his conviction that Britain must, at all costs, claim and occupy the entire continent to ensure the prosperity and stability of the Australian colonies. This was the best defence against French adventurists like La Perouse, Freycinet and d'Urville, sniffing about for somewhere France could gain a foothold. His daughter had inherited her father's distrust of the French despite the fact she admired aspects of French culture—painting, science, music, dancing—and had a respectable grasp of the language.

'But you are an artist *now*, I mean,' Isobel hastened to clarify. 'That is to say, it is your *real* profession, not your *assumed* one.'

'Yes, I have been known to dabble in that field,' he replied. 'I am the drawing master for Mrs Cooper and her tribe of children.'

'I know your fine work, Mr Probius,' said Isobel. 'It is an honour to meet you.'

It was indeed. Mr Probius was an accomplished painter in great demand as a portraitist, especially of prominent society ladies and gentlemen, and his commissioned works hung in many of the finest houses in the colony. Like his distinguished colleagues

Messrs Martens, Earle and Prout, Mr Probius was adaptable as to subject, producing picturesque landscapes of Sydney, its harbour and its elegant villas, as well as many popular images of her exotic fauna, flora and natives. But his portraits remained his best-selling work and included some of Sydney's most famous and notorious figures: fire-breathing radical the Reverend Dr John Dunmore Lang; the libertarian newspaperman Edward Smith Hall; the doomed German explorer Ludwig Leichhardt; and the convicted murderer John Knatchbull. Isobel had also seen a set of his lithographs entitled *The Natives of New South Wales*, which Father kept in his study. These were some of the most sympathetic portraits of the indigenes she had ever seen, capturing not just their dignified humanity but their individual personalities. Her father had also shown her Probius's fetching portrait of old Ricketty Dick, the cripple who sat by New South Head Road and begged for 'tolls'. Isobel was unapologetically envious of his sensitivity and skills.

'Well, I am very flattered that you think so, Miss Macleod,' said the artist with a small bow of his head, acknowledging her compliment. 'But I have a confession to make.'

Isobel looked at him with even keener interest. 'Yes?'

'First you must solemnly swear that you will not take offence'— he put his right hand over his heart—'for *I* swear that none is intended.' Her interlocutor had an air of such sincerity that Isobel tried not to be alarmed by the prospect of a 'confession'. There was a smile of wry, self-deprecating humour on this man's face that punctured any suggestion of arrogance or impertinence.

'I am intrigued, sir'—Isobel placed her hand on *her* heart—'and swear as you ask.'

'Well, the truth is I have been interested to meet you, Miss Isobel Macleod, ever since I first heard your name. Is that very forward of me?'

'I am sure there are those who would say it is. But I am prepared to reserve judgement. What have you heard that you find so interesting?'

Isobel was surprised at her own equanimity, even though she felt a pronounced and not unpleasant flutter in her breast. The artist studied her with warm curiosity. 'I am given to understand that you are a most unusual young woman, Miss Macleod. People whom I trust inform me that you have a passionate interest in natural history.'

His eyes lingered on the necklet at her throat, her mother's gift that featured a row of small silver scarabs, their horns and legs interlocked. She had already noted the carved handle of his elegant cane fashioned into the beak and head of a brightly coloured parrot.

'I am also reliably informed that you possess an excellent eye and hand for sketching. I am familiar with your father's fine work, of course. Such a superb draughtsman. Has he encouraged your talent in this direction?'

Isobel remembered now that Mr Probius had worked for a while as a draughtsman in the Department of Public Works, preparing plans for some of Sydney's loveliest buildings. It was probable that was where he had become acquainted with the Major's maps and drawings.

'I do sketch, sir, and am fond of natural subjects. Father has been very indulgent of my hobby,' said Isobel. 'But I am a most unaccomplished artist, I'm afraid, and have no hope or ambition for advancement.'

'Because you are a woman?' asked Probius with startling candour.

'Yes,' Isobel blushed. 'Of course.'

'Maybe you would allow me to see some of your sketches one day?'

Isobel laughed and her blush deepened. 'Oh, sir, now you *are* in danger of embarrassing me. I do not think . . .'

'That they are good enough, Miss Macleod? Pish,' chided the artist gently, 'I would be honoured if you were to let *me* be the judge of that.'

No man had ever asked to see her work. She was at a loss for words.

'Dear Miss Macleod, I hope you do not think me flippant. I fully acknowledge that there are no easy paths for a woman artist. Indeed not. The common prejudice is dead against them. It is held that drawing and painting are merely *ornamental* skills for women.'

Mr Probius sighed. Isobel nodded, acknowledging the bitter truth of this view.

'But you and I both know there are exceptions. Some women, with *uncommon* strength of character and will, as well as *prodigious* talent, have managed against all the odds to become artists. Mentors can help too, of course.'

'So I believe.'

'At the risk of presumption, Miss Macleod, I have a feeling that you could be one of those women. Could I be right?'

Isobel was astonished at this disarming frankness. On such a short acquaintance, this man had tugged at the veil hiding her most forbidden passion. 'Why would you say that, sir?'

'When I was teaching and studying in Paris many years ago, I had the good fortune to meet an artist by the name of Rosa Bonheur. Her father was a painter and had nurtured her precocious talent from adolescence.'

Isobel had heard about Mr Probius spending time in Paris; there were even rumours of his being associated with radicals in the uprising there in 1830, but they were probably no more than hearsay. He continued, 'Rosa's chief subject was animals, which she painted exquisitely: horses, cattle, dogs, lions, elk. She was so determined to learn more about animal anatomy that she even disguised herself as a man to gain admittance to the Paris abattoirs.'

Isobel blushed. 'Is that why you are telling me her story, Mr Probius? Because you know what I did at the duel?' She looked defiantly into the artist's face for any trace of mockery or contempt. There was none. Instead she saw a steady gaze of what she could only hope was respect. It was not a look she was very familiar with from men.

Charles Probius smiled. 'Let me digress a moment. As you may have guessed, Probius is not my birth name. I was born Charles Ludiger, but I took my assumed surname from a Latin word, *probus,* meaning honest and good. Pretentious, perhaps, but I wanted people to know that I took these values seriously.'

Isobel had never heard anything like this; she was transfixed. He was so strange, this man, so different from most men she had met. 'I tell you this because I hope you will take what I say seriously. I mention Rosa Bonheur's dressing as a man because, just like you, it shows that she was willing to take great risks for something she loved.'

Isobel felt tears of happiness spring to her eyes. Here was the first person to see clearly what she had tried to do for her father.

'Rosa also painted a large canvas of a wild horse fair held just outside Paris. No women were ever allowed at this event. So again, she disguised herself in male clothes to attend the market twice a week to make sketches. She did this for nearly eighteen months.' Isobel was enchanted by the spark of genuine admiration for Rosa that she saw in Mr Probius's eyes. 'I believe you may have the same kind of courage and independent spirit that is needed to become a professional artist. If you would indulge me one visit to see your work, I could tell you more.'

At this point they were interrupted by Mrs Cooper, who tapped Isobel lightly on the shoulder. 'I see you have met our brilliant drawing master. He has promised to do my portrait soon, isn't that right, Mr Probius?'

'Indeed, I have,' assented the artist.

'I'm sorry to call you away, Miss Macleod, but your aunt is quite tired. Her coachman is standing by to take you both home. I believe your sisters have already departed.'

'I must hurry then.' Isobel took Mrs Cooper's hand and pressed it warmly. 'I cannot thank you enough for such a wonderful evening. You have been so kind and thoughtful. And please thank Catherine and Mr Cooper as well.'

She turned to the drawing master. 'It has been good to meet you, Mr Probius. I hope we may have the opportunity to continue our discussion at some future date.'

Isobel hurried across the garden, through the enchanted circles of light and out into the street where her aunt's coach waited to take her back to Rosemount.

Chapter 20

GOOD WORKS

DECEMBER 1851

Little happened to improve the general mood at Rosemount. There had been no letters from abroad in the last mail, and with the next ship not due until February, the sisters were left to ponder the fate of Alice and her child now the Baron was presumably imprisoned. Nor would they have any word from their brothers, as their journey to India would take at least six months. A silence seemed to engulf all three but Isobel resolved to remain optimistic.

At last the day arrived for Isobel's transfer to her new home at Faulconstone. Her farewell was a hurried and tearful affair, at least on Isobel's part, and somewhat strained on the part of her sisters and exhausted father. A wagon had been sent ahead to collect all Isobel's belongings, followed by Aunt Louisa's brougham to collect Isobel herself. In less than an hour, the deed was done.

The frangipani in the front garden at Faulconstone was in full bloom. In the bright sunshine, this lovely tree with its profusion of waxy ornate flowers and peachy scent lent the grim façade of the house an air of gaiety. Aunt Louisa welcomed her niece in the front hall and took her on an inspection of the property, starting in the drawing room. Faulconstone was a solid Regency villa, built by Louisa's late husband, George. Its stuccoed walls, French windows and ironwork balconies were pleasing to the eye, but overall the design favoured a minimum of classical detailing and a sparseness of decoration. In Isobel's unspoken view, the elegance of the interiors was spoiled by the gloomy Jacobean furniture.

Aunt Louisa had been preoccupied for the last month or so. As the president of the Benevolent Asylum's committee for the annual fancy bazaar to be held on New Year's Day in the Botanic Gardens, she had recently hosted an important high tea at Faulconstone for the members of the ladies' fundraising committee. This had necessitated days of work for her gardener and handyman to make the house fit for such distinguished company, and, as no decision big or small could be undertaken without Mrs Blunt's close attention, the work progressed slowly. This in turn had delayed the replastering and whitewashing of Isobel's attic room. 'You have gone to so much trouble, Aunt Louisa,' said Isobel when they finally finished the tour on the landing outside her new bedroom. With its sloping roof and dormer window, the room was narrow and plainly furnished, but sufficiently light and private to be a comfortable retreat from the cares of the world.

'Dinner is served at half past seven as I like to retire no later than half nine,' said her aunt, enumerating the rules of the house for Isobel's benefit. 'Morning devotionals are at six thirty with my staff in the breakfast room and again at half six in the evening. I choose a passage of scripture or read from the *Book of Common Prayer*. I attend church on Saturdays and Sundays and at least one other day a week.' Aunt Louisa had converted to Methodism some years ago but did not, of course, require that Isobel attend the same church, unless she was curious. Isobel would continue to join her family for services at St James' or St Mark's as previously. She would also still attend her art, language and dance lessons in Woolloomooloo and Surry Hills when she could be spared from helping Aunt Louisa with her charity work.

Isobel was familiar with such work. Her mother Winnie had served on the Married Ladies' Committee for the Female School of Industry. This charitable institution had been founded with a grant from Governor Darling and with his wife, Lady Eliza, as its first patron. With one in three babies in the colony born out of wedlock, the school had declared its mission to rescue the daughters of convicts from destitution, brutality and 'utter ruin', otherwise known as prostitution. The school provided these neglected girls with the moral guidance that their parents had failed to give. Their mothers—'fallen women'—had either been deserted by their husbands, rendered unfit by their attachment to vice, or, if employed as live-in servants, were unable to care properly for their offspring. There were sceptics who feared that the education given by the school to such humble girls would inspire ideas above their station and fill them with social discontent. Isobel somehow doubted that classes in scripture, housework, knitting, needlework, reading, writing and arithmetic were a breeding ground for revolution.

Isobel's chief exposure to the rigours of charity work was her mother's efforts towards the school's famous fancy bazaar. The Macleod women had already sharpened their needlework skills to fill the 'Mission-basket' or 'Jew-basket', passed each month from household to household in their congregation at St James' to raise funds for the conversion of Jews and enlightenment of savages. Exhorted by Winnie, Isobel and her sisters then worked their fingers to the bone for the monumental undertaking of the annual fundraising bazaar. Despite her sacrifice, Isobel had never been to this grand day and was curious to see the bazaar for herself.

Whereas Winnie's evangelical zeal for fancywork and fundraising was constrained by her other duties as mother and wife, the widow had no such limitations. Louisa was a generous subscriber and indefatigable worker for the Benevolent Society of New South Wales whose handsome asylum on Devonshire Street provided succour for the aged poor, and indigent mothers and their children. It had expanded considerably during the hard times of the 1840s depression, to meet the ever-growing influx of deserving poor.

Isobel soon discovered that she barely had a moment to herself at Faulconstone. With less than six weeks to go until the grand bazaar, she and Aunt Louisa spent most afternoons and evenings seated by the fire, busy at their needlework and crocheting. The parlour quickly filled with patterns, fabric patches and scraps of flannel and brown holland; despite all attempts to keep everything orderly, their wicker work baskets overflowed with a tumult of needle books, cotton reels, ribbons and elastic, scissors, thimbles, pincushions and bales of Berlin wool. The results of these prolonged labours accumulated in admirable profusion in Mrs Blunt's trunk in the morning room, especially reserved for bazaar fancywork.

Some days they were joined by dear Mrs Palmer and other society ladies whom Isobel had never met before. The cast of this fancywork group variously included Mrs Cornwall, Mrs Burdekin, Mrs Thierry, Mrs Forbes, Mrs Herriott, Mrs Smart, Mrs Long, and Mrs Drummond. To her surprise, Isobel enjoyed these working circles with their lively conversation and frequent outbursts of laughter. It was obvious these women respected Isobel's aunt greatly, and, as Louisa's niece, Isobel was accorded great kindness and consideration. For the first time in an age, she felt protected, by the camaraderie of these older women, from the relentless assault of censure and gossip. What's more, Aunt Louisa, a consummate mistress of fancywork, and her expert comrades were generous with their knowledge, happy to teach Isobel new skills.

Truth was, Isobel had begun to realise that ever since Alice had left home and her mother died, she had often felt lonely at Rosemount. Her companionship with Grace and Anna had been poisoned years ago, and while she had good reasons to pine for her lovely harbourside home, Isobel welcomed the easy intimacy and enjoyment of these gatherings.

During one morning's work circle, two weeks after the ball at Juniper Hall, the conversation turned to Mr and Mrs Cooper and their family's future. 'I hear that they have plans to return to England with Mrs Cooper's relatives and put five of the children into boarding school. Even more expense. And with money still owing to creditors!' So said Mrs Forbes, whose husband had once partnered with Mr Cooper in business but had split acrimoniously soon after.

'Can their son not help them out at all?' asked Mrs Cornwall.

'I believe Augustus has taken on some of his father's debts,' said Mrs Herriott. 'Children must do their duty, of course, but they must also think of their own futures.'

'On that subject, have you heard the rumour that a particular young lady has set her cap at Mr Augustus? With some certainty of success, so I hear!' exclaimed Mrs Drummond.

'Who is it, do you know?' asked Isobel. She disliked the commonplace phrase 'setting a cap' but her curiosity was piqued.

'Well, my dear, I am surprised *you* have to ask,' said Mrs Drummond with a smile.

Isobel stared at her blankly and then her cheeks coloured. She recalled the scene at the ball of her sister Grace and the scion of Juniper Hall talking closely. Was it possible this had progressed so quickly to courtship? And with the prospect of marriage, that Holy Grail for which Grace had prayed and pined but despaired of ever finding?

'Oh, Isobel, you look so shocked. I did not mean to embarrass you, my dear!' said Mrs Drummond, patting her on the arm. 'It will be news to be celebrated if your sister Grace does indeed make a successful match with Mr Cooper. He is a wealthy and honourable gentleman and she would be well looked after, I can reassure you.'

'Were you aware of this, Aunt?' asked Isobel.

'I have only heard what the ladies here have told me today, my dear,' said her aunt, looking a tad annoyed at her friend's indiscretion but not enough to be upset. 'Neither your father nor Grace has mentioned it to me. Yet. I am sure we will learn more soon enough.'

'Well, I'm very happy for Grace, of course,' said Isobel warmly, not wishing to appear peevish. 'It's just unexpected news! I think I should pay Rosemount a visit soon.'

Isobel's greatest hope arising from this intelligence was the possibility that she and her sister would finally be reconciled. For too long she had been shut out from the love that Grace had borne her when they were children. Grace still blamed Isobel for many of her life's disappointments, most painfully her betrayal by the erstwhile Captain Tranter. This wound had festered into such a chronic condition of distrust between them that it seemed only the hope of matrimony could remedy it. There was the not insignificant hurdle to clear of securing the Major's acceptance of an emancipist's son in the family. But if anyone could sway her father's opinion, it was Grace.

Whenever Isobel's mind dwelt on the awkward meeting at the ball with Ralph Tranter, her former suitor, she found that the sting of that remembrance was growing duller. This was especially the case when her thoughts alighted on the face of the drawing master, Mr Probius, whom she associated with feelings of the greatest satisfaction and curiosity. There had been no further communication from this gentleman since the night of the ball but she thought of their intimate dialogue often.

'When Mr and Mrs Cooper leave Juniper Hall, I suppose you have not heard what their intentions are for their staff? I met their drawing master, Mr Probius, at the ball and Mrs Cooper seemed well pleased with his service to the family.'

'I am sure she is,' smiled Mrs Cornwall, and there were grins all around the work table. 'I suspect Mr Probius may have to seek new employment. I would guess that he is a luxury Mr Cooper cannot afford in the straitened circumstances in which he finds himself.'

'I do not think Mr Cooper shall weep too many tears at the loss of his drawing master,' rejoined Mrs Forbes. There were more meaningful glances and chuckles.

'More tea, my dears?' asked Aunt Louisa, bringing that topic to a close.

Eighteen days after the ball at Juniper Hall and only three since his name was mentioned in the ladies' fancywork circle, Mr Probius paid a visit to Faulconstone. Aunt Louisa and Isobel were engaged at their writing desks in the morning room. Isobel was composing a letter to her sister Alice, expressing her concern for her welfare and that of her little boy ('you are in my thoughts and prayers every day, my sweet sister') and her hope that she would see them both soon. She had already penned another long letter to her brothers ('I pray that your sea passage has been a safe and not too tedious one, my dearest William') addressed to the offices of the company in Madras where they were to be employed.

The butler knocked on the door and presented Mr Probius's card. 'The gentleman says he has the honour to be an acquaintance of Miss Macleod's. He is anxious to meet her esteemed guardian, an opportunity denied him at Juniper Hall a fortnight heretofore.'

'An acquaintance of yours?' Aunt Louisa turned the card over. 'Do I know him?'

'He is the drawing master at Juniper Hall,' explained Isobel, struggling to disguise her true feelings about the man. 'We were introduced at the ball. He was kind to me when I was feeling unwell.' It was a small and harmless lie.

'The drawing master?' Louisa had evidently forgotten all about the sewing circle's discussion a few days ago. 'And why, pray, does he wish to see you?'

Isobel coughed. 'He is an admirer of the Major's sketches and has heard favourable things about my modest efforts,' she said. At this point she became a little more inventive with the truth. 'I asked him if he would be so kind as to look at my work to see if I might benefit from some tutoring. He is a highly accomplished artist.'

Aunt Louisa looked sceptical. 'Well, I think this is a matter for your father to adjudicate. A man calling on a young lady is no paltry matter.'

'But, Aunt, Mr Probius has no intentions of *that* kind!' protested Isobel, who, to be perfectly honest, was not at all sure what his intentions were. 'I am hopeful that he may agree to take me on as his student. I'm sure Father would have no problem with that.'

'Well, be that as it may, I feel a little fatigued this morning and am not fit to have company.' She turned to the butler. 'Please thank Mr Probius for his courtesy and inform him we are not at home for visitors today.'

Isobel was surprised at how bitter was her resentment at her aunt's interference. Her leash of moral guardianship was beginning to chafe. Isobel feared that Charles Probius would read this rebuff as a final rejection. He was a man held in high esteem in Sydney's loftiest social circles and had no shortage of people to take an interest in. His brief infatuation with Miss Macleod's case would soon pass and be forgotten.

She could not deny the tender stirrings of her heart when she pictured his face or recalled the timbre of his voice. She did not want to anticipate the course of their friendship too hastily for fear of driving it away like a startled deer, chanced upon in the forest. Even so, she could not help wondering if her father could possibly approve of such a man as Charles Probius. If the Major might be willing to accept Augustus Cooper, son of an ostrich feather thief and gin distiller, then why should he have any objections to a famous artist?

She calculated the points for and against Charles in her father's estimation. He had lived in Paris (a definite liability given her father's Francophobia) but as he also had the Germanic-sounding birth name of Ludiger, she had reasons to hope otherwise. While there were rumours to the contrary, his politics might be liberal and reformist (overlapping with some of her father's views) rather than tend towards the radical or revolutionary. He had something about him of the dandy in dress and bearing, if the parrot-headed cane and the way he wielded it were anything to go by. Even if it was just a costume for a fancy-dress ball, there was no disputing that the cut, shade and accoutrements of Charles Probius's outfit were exquisitely tasteful and eccentrically individual. What her sensible father would make of this élan and stylishness in a gentleman was anyone's guess! There was the fact that Probius was a widely acclaimed artist, at least in the colony, with a wealthy clientele and steady income, possessing skills her father had always admired and aspired to with some degree of success and recognition himself. On the other hand, Major Macleod might not regard the profession of artist as a calling fit for a gentleman or as a secure basis for his daughter's future as a gentleman's wife.

No, no, no, stop this folly! she scolded herself. What was she thinking? The man had simply taken a kindly interest in her as an artist and asked to see her work. And here she was, inflating this pleasant if accidental encounter into a romantic tryst! What madness, Isobel! she heard her mother's scolding voice. You must not fret away your heart like this in such foolish, idle speculation. I must not, she told herself.

Even so, how was she ever to see him again?

As she returned to writing her letter to Alice (who had been so grievously deceived and punished in love), Isobel tried to heed her own inner voice of caution: silly girl, do not, do *not*, I tell you, give away your heart too easily!

Chapter 21

THE ROCKS

The fancywork circle continued in their arduous labours, spinning and stitching, sewing and knitting, with the tireless dedication of Odysseus's Penelope. Even so, Aunt Louisa found time in her busy schedule to fulfil her other charitable obligations. As a volunteer visitor, she had been asked to call on a poor woman and her children who lived in The Rocks. The deserted mother had made a claim for assistance from the Benevolent Asylum and now had to be inspected to be eligible for relief.

'It will be instructive for you to see why our hard work is so worthwhile,' Louisa told her young companion. 'I am sure it will inspire you to even greater efforts, my dear.'

In all her young days, Isobel had never visited The Rocks. It was the name given to the crowded area of dwellings and dockside buildings on the peninsula separating Sydney Cove and Cockle

Bay (renamed Darling Harbour by the self-same governor). From the first days of settlement it had remained the domain of convicts and, later, ex-convicts. A few fancy villas had been built on the high ridgeline to the north for the harbour views. On the eastern side was the ghetto where poor convict families lived and worked in a riot of tumbledown cottages, terraces, shops and small businesses, cheek by jowl with the government's bond stores and merchants' warehouses facing Circular Quay. Clinging to the peninsula's craggy flanks like fleas to a dog, The Rocks presented the visitor with a labyrinth of crooked streets, narrow laneways and steep flights of stairs.

Isobel was too ashamed to admit to her aunt, who had paid many visits there, that she was afraid. If you gave any credit to the lurid accounts in *The Sydney Morning Herald*, The Rocks was a place to be feared and reviled. With its reputation for crime, drunkenness, prostitution and violence, it was the chief site of the city's moral pestilence, detested by the good citizenry of Sydney for spoiling their enlightened self-image.

Isobel may have been tempted to dismiss much of this talk as melodramatic had she not heard about two famous murders in The Rocks the year she turned nine. The first was the cold-blooded killing by Norfolk Island convict John Knatchbull, who clove the skull of a poor widow with a tomahawk while being served in her shop. But it was the second sensational murder that year that made the deepest impression on Isobel: that of Mr Thomas Warne, a debt collector, by his French valet and ex-convict Mr Videlle. This atrocity had done nothing to improve the Major's opinion of convicts or Frenchmen.

In a nasty, mischievous mood, her brother Joseph had tormented his sisters by reading aloud every grisly detail of the case: how Warne and Videlle argued; how the servant struck him in the head with an axe; how the dead man's blood stained the ceiling of the house; how the murderer dismembered the body and tried to burn it in the fireplace; how the melted fat of the corpse caused the fire to roar out of control and had to be put out; how the charred body parts were then conveyed in a chest to Cadman's Cottage; how a waterman was hired to throw it into the harbour; how the alarm was raised with a constable and the gruesome contents discovered. Isobel had nightmares for weeks afterwards.

The Rocks were permanently fixed in her mind as the setting for acts of horror and depravity and violent death. It was common wisdom that no respectable person, and certainly no woman, should venture near the place after dark. She risked being attacked, robbed, drugged, even kidnapped and forced into slavery in one of the brothels or opium dens. Isobel could not imagine how anyone survived, least of all women and children, in such a hell.

Thankfully, it was still daylight hours when Aunt Louisa and Isobel alighted from their coach on lower George Street. From there they made their way on foot to the house on Gloucester Street. Through the cramped passage of Brown Bear Lane, past the rowdy pub of the same name on the corner, they walked up to Harrington Street, turned right and ascended again by a set of stone steps to Cumberland Place. These thoroughfares were little more than dirt tracks, being scarcely traversable by vehicles, and destitute of all signs of metalling, guttering or drainage. On this hot, sunny day, the air was filled with clouds of fine dust, kicked up by their shoes as they walked. Isobel could imagine these same 'streets' quickly turning to mud in a heavy rain.

She was grateful that her aunt had advised her to wear a pair of sturdy boots, though the real reason became clear as soon as they entered the first side street. Isobel's nostrils were assailed by the most noisome stench she had ever encountered. When she saw human excrement washed up against one of the houses in a stream of brown muck, she gagged in disgust. In one dead-end lane where several houses backed onto a high wall of rock, she could see a line of privies—crude outdoor huts of brick and iron—for the use of the next higher row of houses. Channels and chutes, carved into the rock wall to discharge sewage, were vividly stained where the moist filth had been baked hard by the sun.

Whatever attempts at drainage she could see were in such a state of disrepair as to be useless. Aunt Louisa passed her a handkerchief soaked in lavender water and indicated she hold it to her nose. 'This will help.'

Some of the dwellings were ancient stone cottages, so unevenly and irregularly built that the doorstep of one residence some-times approximated to the eaves of another. Whitewashed walls stretched like the ruptured skin of a smallpox victim, blotchy and cracked with disease. Slate-shingled roofs were inevitably broken and patched.

The brick terrace houses were impossibly narrow, with gaunt façades and small hollow-eyed windows. Everything appeared poorly built and in urgent need of repair, rickety and askew: weathered wooden backstairs or slumped guttering and rusting downpipes, or weed-infested backyards surrounded by humpbacked walls. It was a scene nothing short of shocking for a tender soul like Isobel's. Not even the bleakest passages of Mr Dickens' novels could prepare her for the reality of such squalor.

And yet there was something else that struck Isobel with equal force. As they turned the corner into Gloucester Street, she could hear children singing. On the doorstep of a nearby house, a woman sat, smoking a clay pipe. Her skin was sallow and lined and her face hollow-cheeked but she flashed a smile, through dirty yellow teeth, at the two visitors as they passed. 'Good mornin', ladies. Wouldn't be dead for quids, wouldya? On a day like today.' Aunt Louisa murmured something gracious in reply.

They passed side alleys where children could be heard whooping and shouting in games of street cricket, leapfrog and horseshoes, and women in aprons swept the stoop or pegged out clothes in narrow backyards. Isobel saw window boxes of hydrangeas, morning glories, pigface. The shutters on the corner store were freshly painted bright green and the sign on the top floor reading 'CHEAP CASH GROCER' had been retouched within living memory.

Through the open window of the nearest house, Isobel caught a glimpse of the parlour inside: translucent printed cotton curtains; a rude table; teapot and cups set out on a patterned tablecloth; two wooden chairs and a stool; a single seashell and one polished brass candlestick on the wooden mantel; a black kettle on the hob. The back wall was spoiled by a large patch of damp and its paint had flaked, but overall this domestic scene was one of familiar cosiness and order, even if the furnishings were sparse and the chamber dingy.

As Isobel and her aunt walked on, several inquisitive dogs followed and in their wake came a growing pack of three, four, five, six curious but silent children of differing heights and ages. Isobel wondered if they were drawn to the two strangers for the novelty of their appearance or in the hope of a spare farthing. They were all dressed far too warmly for such a hot day, though two of the boys were barefoot. To Isobel's surprise, while their clothes were crude and worn, they were quite clean, as were the children's hands and faces. At this hour of the morning, it was clear they were not in school.

Once the initial shock of entering this new world began to wear off, Isobel had eyes to notice such things: happy children, busy housewives, tidy households, well-stocked shops, flowers in pots and window boxes, clean bedsheets flapping in the sunshine. The Rocks was not all crime and vice and horror. People lived here and made a fist of a normal life.

Aunt Louisa knocked at number 52. The door opened and a woman stood blinking into the sunlight. Mrs Pittman ushered them into her humble front room and seated them at a deal table. Isobel noticed that on the bench opposite sat a work basket and a pile of material; the room evidently doubled as a parlour and workshop.

Mrs Pittman had already been recommended for assistance by Mrs Edwards, a former employer and a subscriber to the Benevolent Society. Two weeks ago, Mrs Pittman had attended the asylum on Devonshire Street for an interview where her 'particulars'—including health, religion, employment history and family circumstances—were recorded. She had also presented all her children's birth certificates as proof of their legitimacy and their fathers' names. Aunt Louisa told Isobel she would be shocked how often these documents were forged or women simply made up the existence of marriages and husbands, pretending to be abandoned or widowed. The purpose of this visit today was to verify Mrs Pittman's claims, inspect the property and ask her a few more questions.

The woman was clearly nervous as there was a great deal at stake in the impression she made on the two strangers. While the Benevolent Asylum had grown dramatically in size, the demands for its services from a swelling population of desperate poor far outstripped its capacity to help. Isobel was quick to realise that the true purpose of this visit was to find excuses to declare Mrs Pittman ineligible.

There was no denying the house was in a terrible, dilapidated condition. Mrs Pittman was months behind on her rent and without some assistance almost certainly faced eviction. But it did not seem that the landlord wasted a penny on keeping the shabby six-room dwelling in more than a barely habitable state. The floorboards in this front room were unpainted and riddled with white-ant damage, only a threadbare rug covering their shame. In the corner near the fireplace, black earth erupted through a hole in the floor. The walls had not been painted or replastered in many years and showed a pitiful mosaic of stains and fissures. While Mrs Pittman prepared tea for her guests down in the tiny basement kitchen,

Isobel and Aunt Louisa mounted the narrow staircase to inspect the two upstairs bedrooms.

Mrs Pittman had seven children, four by her first husband who had died in a boiler accident and three by her second husband who had deserted her. Or so she claimed. The bedrooms facing the street had windows so begrimed as to admit only a sickly, sepia-toned light. Two iron-framed beds hid in the shadows, thin blankets pulled up over bare mattresses. An odour of must and damp fouled the room. Isobel saw mouse droppings along the wainscoting. In her usual brisk, no-nonsense manner, Aunt Louisa pulled back the blankets, looked under the beds, rummaged through the trunk that served as a wardrobe, opened the drawers of a forlorn bedside table.

'What are you looking for?' asked Isobel.

'Any evidence of a man staying here,' said her aunt. She held up a collarless, tobacco-stained shirt. 'Mmm.'

'How old are her sons?' asked Isobel, hoping to dispel her aunt's suspicions.

She knew the reason her aunt was hunting down such clues: as Mrs Pittman was claiming desertion, she would be disqualified for cohabiting with a man. Or even worse, consorting with several men or selling sexual favours. The Benevolent Society looked dimly on 'fallen' women engaged in prostitution or bearing children by different fathers—at least, that was its official charter, even if blind eyes were sometimes turned in compassion. But these fallen women were usually segregated from other single mothers inside the asylum as if they might contaminate them with their sin. Simple arithmetic says that more than one person sleeps in each of these beds, thought Isobel, looking around the room. It was likely that at least two of the younger ones shared with their mother. So how could Mrs Pittman possibly conduct intimate relations with any degree of privacy? The thought made Isobel shudder.

Back downstairs, they were introduced to four of the offspring, two boys and two girls, all snotty-nosed and dull-eyed. Mrs Pittman was clearly not managing her affairs as she might have wished. The children were putrid, their faces and hands black with dirt, which she made pathetic attempts to clean with a rag and spittle. After a few dabs, she handed them chunks of bread coated with dripping—a late breakfast or early lunch?

'Been playing down the docks again, have ya?' she whined, and turned apologetically to her guests. 'They get so dirty 'round the docks.' She shooed them off like chooks. 'Now run along.'

It was the plight of the children even more than that of the mothers that inspired Aunt Louisa in her endless labours, she had explained to Isobel. If the children were not rescued from the moral laxness and viciousness of their parents, they would almost certainly end up tainted. The boys usually turned to drink and petty crime, either out of anger and despair or to 'help' their family. They sometimes ran away from home, ending up as vagrants or beggars and were often sent to prison, the first leg of their lifelong journey as professional criminals. The girls, who were in greater moral peril, were arrested for drunkenness and profanity or 'public acts of indecency'. Rates of prostitution were on the rise, especially over in the industrial district of Chippendale where casual workers came and went. And with the alarming increase in unmarried mothers, more and more weak and sickly illegitimate babies were born and perished soon after from starvation.

Mrs Pittman had laid out things for tea. She handed over the milk in a fancy jug. Isobel could not help noticing her own teacup was greasy. She reluctantly took a sip out of politeness but declined the offer of an arrowroot biscuit. This woman could barely put food in the mouths of her children and here she was trying to impress Aunt Louisa with her hospitality and good manners. This absurd ceremony made Isobel feel sick.

'Now remind me, please, which church you attend regularly, Mrs Pittman?' asked Louisa, taking out a pencil and Mrs Pittman's report card from the asylum. The nervous woman answered a battery of questions: about her church attendance, who was her priest, had she relied on charity before now, had she ever used contraception or had an abortion, the history of her relationships with both husbands, had she been beaten, did she drink, did he drink, how much, did she drink at home or out with friends, who were her friends, did she believe in the forgiveness of sins and her salvation through the love of Christ our Saviour, and why had her husband deserted her.

'Gold!' Mrs Pittman spat the word out. 'That's why!' Her face was ashen; she looked exhausted from the relentless interrogation. 'Gold. Him and his mates talked of nothing else these last few months.' She sighed and pressed her hand to her forehead as if to mollify a persistent ache there.

Isobel wondered if, by this simple gesture, Mrs Pittman had betrayed herself. Was that a bruise blossoming under that hairline? Was that why she clutched at her head so often, because of

234

the pain of an injury? Aunt Louisa had boasted that she had a nose for 'weak or troublesome' women who had been hit by their husbands, and was an expert in telling when a woman brushed her hair a certain way or used a bonnet or scarf or heavier make-up to disguise bruises. Her aunt admitted it was not always the woman's fault. Men gambled, drank, committed crimes and were caught, then returned from prison more violent and unpredictable than when they went in. These were circumstances in which men were more likely to harm their wives. The depression had led to many ugly scenes and tragic consequences. It was frightening all the things that Aunt Louisa knew about the lives of the underclass.

'We've been fighting a fair bit since he lost his job,' confessed Mrs Pittman, pathetically grateful, thought Isobel, to be unburdening herself of her woes. 'I bin doin' some shifts at the bottlin' factory. On top of my sewing work. But we were pretty skint, if you know what I mean. So when the gold rush come, Peter is like a man converted. He has a new religion. It will save us all: me, him, the children. Praise to almighty gold, our saviour.'

Mrs Pittman sipped her tea. She smiled bitterly.

'*I* was not so easy to convert. Refused to join in the hymn to almighty gold! So he left me. Cleans out our bank account and takes off. Where? To Bathurst probably, or Ballarat. Who will ever find him out there on the diggings? Tens of thousands out there. And I'm not alone. This neighbourhood has plenty of gold rush widows.'

The visit had almost finished. 'The kitchen, Mrs Pittman, if you would be so kind?'

This was an absurd piece of gentility. In a six-room house it was not hard to find the kitchen. Even so, Mrs Pittman pointed down the stairs to the basement below street level. Isobel and Aunt Louisa could barely both fit in the tiny room with its black stove, skillet, pot and kettle on the hob, stained ceramic sink, wooden sideboard, and table made from a packing case on which to prepare food and take a meal. A small curtained alcove served as a pantry, and Isobel watched with shocked disbelief as Aunt Louisa took down bottles, uncorked them and sniffed the contents. 'You find a lot of cheap and home-made alcohol masquerading in vinegar bottles,' she told Isobel. 'Did you smell a whiff of something on her breath? I did.'

The visit concluded with an inspection of the backyard, so small that Isobel counted only twelve steps from the back door to the corrugated iron fence, wrapped in the sinuous stranglehold of a choko vine and laden with prickly gourds. Here they made the acquaintance of a trough, a copper, mangle and washboard, a clothesline drooping on a prop, and, down the back next to the alley, the brick shed of the privy.

'Thank you, Mrs Pittman. You have been most helpful,' said Aunt Louisa, remembering to smile. 'The society will notify you very soon about your claim.'

Mrs Pittman's head hung down. She made an abject figure for contemplation. Her voice was hoarse as she whispered, 'Can you tell me what you will recommend?'

Aunt Louisa grimaced with alarm. 'I'm afraid that would contravene our rules.'

Mrs Pittman nodded. She knew that would be the answer. And now she had time to repent her question and wonder if her impertinence would count against her.

Isobel and Aunt Louisa walked back down Gloucester Street. Between the grubby, ramshackle cottages and the handsome brick warehouses, Isobel could see the blue-green waters sparkling in the noontime sun. It struck her how strange it was that this place of so much suffering, disease and pollution was within sight and sound of the harbour's improbable beauty. A southerly buster would come through here later in the afternoon and stir up the backstreets into a yellow dust cloud but it would not be enough to drive away the stink.

As they walked down Argyle Street and came out near the quay, they could see the forest of ships' masts above the roofline of the government bond store. Sounds of the working harbour—the ringing of bells, the drumroll of wagon wheels, the shouts of navvies loading and unloading, the shrieking of gulls—drifted up to them.

'Will Mrs Pittman and her children be accommodated at the asylum, do you think, Aunt?' asked Isobel in as respectful a voice as she could manage, earnest and eager to learn.

'I doubt it, my dear,' replied her aunt, 'She has the means to support herself but lacks the discipline and will. I suspect she drinks and has more than one male "friend" visit. But she may be willing to put some of the younger ones into our care—for their own good—while she looks for work.'

The coachman approached and directed them to where he had tied up at the Black Dog tavern further down the road. They were soon encoached and, with one backward glance at the busy streetscape, Isobel bid The Rocks a silent farewell.

Chapter 22

CHRISTMAS

Isobel had returned from her visit to The Rocks in a state of moral bewilderment, haunted by what she had seen. Wrestling with feelings of guilt and shame, she worked secretly by candlelight in the privacy of her room trying to hold onto her impressions with sketches in her journal: the street children in their raggedy clothes, the sorry rows of houses, the pitiful rooms at number 52 Gloucester Street and poor Mrs Pittman's anxious, downcast countenance.

If Mr Probius ever deigned to pay a visit to Faulconstone again, she would show him these. Loath as she was to praise her own work or to give in to the sinful impulse of pride, she could not help feeling pleased with these sketches, which seemed to her enlivened by a heightened sensitivity to the suffering of her fellow creatures. Was this just vanity? She hoped not. She found the stark fact of human suffering so confronting that she sometimes struggled to see it as God's gift, intended to bring us to the love of Christ and our own salvation. Was Aunt Louisa an instrument of God's love when she denied succour to Mrs Pittman and her children? Was that woman's suffering not sufficient in God's eyes?

Isobel's soul was troubled by such thoughts.

Last week she had visited the Benevolent Asylum with her aunt. An impressive two-storeyed brick edifice designed in a mock Classical style with a grand gable and pillared portico, it was situated on a grant of land on the seedy outskirts of the city, opposite the tollgate at the start of the Parramatta Road and next door to Carters Barracks, which housed convicts, and the Devonshire Street cemetery, which housed the dead.

Inside was less impressive. Isobel was shown the dormitories, their beds so tightly packed it was barely possible to pass between them. She visited the chapel where the women inmates prayed for atonement; the kitchen, laundry, vegetable garden and bakery where they toiled to keep the asylum running; and the work-rooms where they sorted hair and wool, and unpicked rope for oakum. In exchange for all this free labour they were clothed and fed (bread and tea three times a day, meat and potatoes twice a week). The overcrowding and poor hygiene had led to terrible outbreaks of disease and the asylum had been shamed by the press for the high death toll of children within its walls. Even with all these faults, it was still a merciful alternative to destitution, starvation and the living hell of Darlinghurst Gaol.

Having proved her devotion to the good cause, Isobel was still keen to go to the Benevolent Society's bazaar in the Botanic Gardens on New Year's Day. She was aware of the unsavoury insinuations that were sometimes attached to a young woman's appearance at such public affairs. Mr Dickens himself was not above lampooning women at charity bazaars. In a fit of pique, Aunt Louisa had taken down from the library shelf her copy of *Sketches by Boz* and read aloud to Isobel the offending passage, in which the author mocked a woman who *'made "an exhibition" of herself . . . behind a counter at a fancy fair, to all and every of Her Majesty's liege subjects who were disposed to pay a shilling each for the privilege of seeing some four dozen girls flirting with strangers, and playing at shop'.*

That was unkind and unworthy, thought Isobel. Why did men use every opportunity to belittle and make fun of women's work? Did they take nothing women did seriously? Even so, Isobel hoped that her aunt would favour her request to work at a stall at the upcoming fancy fair. But such hope was in vain.

'I cannot influence the way men think, my dear, but I can protect your reputation,' admonished her aunt. 'Young women at fairs are exposed to the danger of scandal.' Aunt Louisa did not have to say aloud the inevitable corollary, 'And this family has had enough of that to deal with lately!'

'Oh please, Aunt, I have worked so hard,' pleaded Isobel. Louisa Blunt could not reproach her niece on that score. 'I want to help out at the fair to ensure we have the success that all our efforts deserve.' Isobel thought she saw her aunt's stern expression soften a little.

'We shall see,' was her only concession.

'Thank you, Aunt,' she said, and even planted a small kiss on the dowager's forehead. With still over a fortnight to go before the bazaar, she had had an idea that might tip the odds in her favour.

That afternoon's mail brought a note from Rosemount addressed to Aunt Louisa. It was an invitation for her and Isobel to come for dinner at the hall on Christmas Eve and stay as their guests for Christmas Day. Isobel wondered what had bought on this gregarious impulse, this sudden surge of familial love in Grace. Or was this at the Major's insistence? Following the example set by Queen Victoria and the Prince Consort three years ago (and as portrayed in the 1848 Christmas edition of *The Illustrated London News*), the Macleods were adopting the novel custom of erecting a Christmas tree. It promised to be a splendid occasion.

Isobel had been so busy that she'd barely had time to give Christmas a second thought. The fancywork circle was still meeting every day as the bazaar loomed ever closer, convening regularly at Faulconstone but also now and then in the homes of its other members. This was a perfect treat as far as Isobel was concerned as she gained entry to magnificent houses she had never heard of before, much less seen. She relished the thought of how jealous Grace would be of her visits to these fine houses: the gorgeous villa Mona on Darling Point, the elegant Burdekin House on Macquarie Street and the lovely gem of Tusculum on the Hill, also designed by Mr Verge and recently acquired by the emancipist Mr William Alexander Long for his wife, Isabella, and their three daughters. With the fancywork circle, Isobel visited and venerated them all. She recorded in her journal: *To think that before I came to Faulconstone I had nursed a real horror of social isolation and loneliness! It has all turned out rather differently—to my great satisfaction.*

She may have been ostracised by one social set but Isobel had been welcomed into another. The composition of the colony's ruling class was like that: a series of families, each their own tribe connected through their social sphere, their church, profession, charities, industries and enterprises. Substantial wealth was the price of admission to all these Sydney tribes but one had to possess something else. In some circles it was a title, breeding, connections in London and the Colonial Office. In others it was commercial canniness, a hunger for profit and invention, a vision of a better future. All the tribes had political ambitions: they either cultivated friends or pursued careers in the colonial parliament or started newspapers and wrote muckraking pamphlets.

Isobel did not know who the other guests were going to be at Christmas dinner ('plain bad manners on Grace's part,' huffed Aunt Louisa) but she was hopeful it would be anyone but the Finches and the Bradleys, her treacherous former friends. Was it conceivable that Mr Augustus Cooper, Grace's suitor, would be there with his parents? Had Grace's courtship already progressed that far? Now that would be a scene worth the seeing, thought Isobel: the meeting of her father, the old soldier, and Mr Cooper, the emancipist businessman.

She wished she could invite Mr Probius as she was sure he would make an excellent dinner party guest. She had read in the *Herald* that the artist had dined last week with the firebrand champion of liberty, the Reverend Lang, whose portrait he had painted to such a nicety. Faced with bankruptcy, Mr Lang had recently resigned from the Legislative Council and it was now rumoured he had plans to flee his creditors on the next ship out of Sydney.

Despite all her efforts at sangfroid, Isobel could not stop thinking about Mr Probius. It was an undeniable case of absence and a heart that daily grew fonder. Last thing at night before closing her eyes, she would speak his name aloud as a benison in the absurd hope that he would not forget her, all the while scolding herself for her adolescent foolishness. She reasoned that he must be busy with portraits for clients, especially at this time of year. There was no evidence that her feelings were in any way reciprocated and that his interest was anything more than professional or platonic so she refused to shed tears or break her heart for him.

No matter how weary at day's end, Isobel sat in her room every evening, finishing off sketches she had started that morning in the bright wedge of sunlight that sloped in through her dormer window. She no longer had time for her art classes in Surry Hills. She had discovered instead a new impulse that drove her to draw religiously, day in, day out. Was it to gain Mr Probius's flattering attention or to please him if he came to look at her work? Or was it merely the power of his suggestion that she was a woman 'with *uncommon* strength of character and will, as well as *prodigious* talent' that impelled her to work so assiduously? Sometimes, as she was putting the finishing touches to a piece, she would even murmur to herself, 'So what do you think of that, Mr Probius?' and then laugh.

Her subjects were many and varied: faces in the street, architectural details, plants, trees, birds, cats and dogs. Vignettes of Sydney life: two lovers walking in the Botanic Gardens, a woman on horseback in Hyde Park, the gaily dressed theatre crowd outside the Royal Victoria, the raggedy children on the backstreets of The Rocks.

She was never happier than when her mind glided like wind across water and the sketches came from her hand with barely a conscious thought. Snatches of her conversation with Mr Probius at the ball haunted her, talk of Rosa Bonheur and his question: *'I have a feeling that you could be one of those women. Could I be right?'* She did not know. How could she possibly know? All she knew for certain was that she had to see him again. She believed that Mr Probius was the only way she would find an answer to that question.

Christmas Eve arrived at last. Sydney had sweltered all day in a heat-wave. Birds dropped dead on lawns, grass browned, leaves curled, flesh oozed and prickled, women squirmed and men scratched. Everyone waited for the southerly buster like crazed sailors in the doldrums with their parched prayers, 'Please, oh, Lord, release us!'

How strange it was to arrive back at Rosemount as a guest, thought Isobel, as they came down the long drive in Aunt Louisa's carriage, turning out of the forest to see the fiery disc of the sun dipping mercifully at last into the sea. It had been seven weeks since Isobel had left this beloved house but it felt like an age. Nothing much had changed as far as she could see. She knew the place so well it was as if she gazed fondly upon the face of a parent or lover in which the slightest alteration of mood could immediately be apprehended. As the coach drew up in the carriage loop, Isobel thought the house appeared watchful, expectant.

The spectacular novelty of the Christmas tree, a tall, dark-green conifer, stood at the far end of the drawing room. Its branches had wilted somewhat in the heat but it was still an imposing sight. 'My, oh my!' exulted Isobel, her eyes glistening with childish glee.

'Is it not the most beautiful thing you have ever seen?' cried Anna, clapping her hands with equally childish zeal. 'I helped Grace with all the decorations!'

'It is, without argument, a wonder to behold!' boomed the Major, catching Grace and Anna in a warm embrace as he stood between them, his eyes shining with pride in the tree's lovely glow. 'And a credit to you both!' Bathed in the light of thirty candles, there hung from every thickly needled branch of the Christmas tree colourful paper streamers, clusters of gilded walnuts, garlands of threaded raisins and pecans, and sweet baskets carved from oranges. Painted cameos of children and angels and a tiny chimneysweep doll for good luck completed the decorative embarrassment of riches.

It turned out that the Christmas Eve dinner was only for the immediate family with the singular exception of Mrs Palmer, their long-time friend and confidante. It was an intimate gathering, but no less formal and extravagant for that. The epergne was fully stocked with its tower of quinces, melons, pawpaws, grapes and unripened pineapple, and the silverware gleamed smugly in the radiance of ten candles.

The twelve-course feast consisted of every conceivable meat, roasted, broiled, smoked and preserved, but, in chief, a gargantuan chestnut-stuffed turkey. There were side dishes of sweetbread pâté, oyster soup, rice croquettes, potato pie, quail with truffles and fried smelts in tartare sauce. The Christmas puddings, each crowned with a sprig of holly and with a lucky farthing hidden in its moist fruity depths, arrived at the table, ringed with a pretty blue fire of flaming brandy. With considerable foresight, Uncle Fergus had sent them a hamper of treats months ago. 'Look at these!' exclaimed the Major with a boyish grin. 'A box of lemon cheese Puff Cracknels!' These had been mailed direct from the new Jacob's biscuit factory in Ireland. Encouraged by the seasonal spirit of excess, Cook had also served up plates of brandied cherries, shortbread, rum balls, sugar cookies and gingerbread men.

As she contemplated the glossy surface of Rosemount's dining table, revealed as was customary for the profligate freight of the dessert course, Isobel saw a faint image reflected there, a trick of her imagination. It was the face of Mrs Pittman. What would she be feeding her children this Christmas? a voice whispered inside Isobel's head. Bread and dripping?

The dinner conversation was mostly amusing and inconsequential. Everyone present deliberately avoided any reference to the heated political debate that had recently erupted in Sydney since news arrived that, thanks to the Colonial Office, the rebellious colony of Canada had been rewarded with the precious gift of representative government while the undyingly loyal subjects of New South Wales were still denied this rightful inheritance.

There was much well-informed banter about the triumphal debut of Mr Dion Boucicault's five-act comedy *Love in a Maze* staged by Charles Kean at the Princess's Theatre in London and the sold-out premiere of Mr Verdi's new opera *Rigoletto* for the La Fenice opera house in Venice. On a more solemn note, they discussed the sinister news of the *coup d'état* by Louis-Napoleon, elected President of the French Second Republic, who had dissolved the National Assembly and introduced a new constitution to extend his term of office. 'Another dictator just like his uncle, you mark my words!' muttered the Major darkly.

The dinner reminded Isobel of the best evenings they had enjoyed together as a family around this table. It was odd to now be a guest at Rosemount, a spectator to a drama that she had always watched from the other side of the stage. Her father looked pale and a little tired, but he was in good spirits tonight and his face full of cheer. She could not recall the last time she had seen her sister Grace so animated and carefree, except perhaps at the ball. And when Grace was happy it invariably followed that Anna was happy too.

'So how are things over at Faulconstone, dear sister?' the Major asked at last, draining a second tumbler of hot brandy and rum punch. Aunt Louisa was generous in her praise of her niece's endeavours for the fancy fair. Mrs Palmer concurred heartily. The Major beamed at Isobel, nodding his head as if to say, *'I knew I made the right decision.'*

'Well, well, I shall look forward to seeing the fruits of your considerable labours,' said the Major. 'I propose a toast to the New Year's Day fair and its success!' Aunt Louisa raised her glass of ginger beer in unison with her fellow diners' goblets of punch and wine.

It was at this point that a bottle of French champagne arrived at the table, cradled in a bed of shaved ice inside a spectacular campagna urn–shaped pail. With its gilded, twisted handles and lovely painted studies of China roses and passionflowers, the aqua-glazed cooler was the ostentatious showpiece of Rosemount's dessert service.

'French champagne?' Isobel looked curious. 'In honour of something special?' She had already guessed the 'something special'. No one could miss the palpable air of excitement in Grace and Anna's demeanour, quivering like foxhounds on the scent. Even so, Isobel feigned ignorance.

'Tell her, Grace,' said the Major, almost languidly.

'I am *engaged*! I am to be married to Mr Augustus Cooper in the autumn! It is all arranged!' Grace flung her arms about Isobel's neck, crying for joy. Anna joined in.

'Oh, my dear Grace.' Isobel was so overcome by her sister's happiness that she could not find the words to express her true feelings. She too wept. In this blessed announcement, Isobel found hope that the wounds that had divided the family and sent her into exile could now be healed. Grace had no reason to be bitter now. She had everything she could possibly want: a doting wealthy husband, her father's blessing, generous in-laws and a bright future.

Aunt Louisa and Mrs Palmer had known of this event's likelihood for some time but they were no less affected. 'Look at you all!' laughed the Major. 'So many tears and for such happy tidings!' The glasses were all charged with the expensive fizz—even Mrs Blunt agreed to a few sinful drops in honour of the occasion—and the Major stood to make a speech.

'I am the happiest of men, and the most fortunate of fathers, to see my daughter make this excellent match!' he began, his face lit up with unapologetic pride. 'I have had the pleasure of several meetings with my future son-in-law. I find him to be a man of great intelligence, gentlemanly courtesy and consideration, good taste and judgement. All of this evident, of course, from how wisely he has chosen his wife!'

'Oh, Papa!' Grace's face shone with her father's approbation.

'Some may say that the alliance of the Macleods with such a family is totally unexpected and surprising. I say to them, "Not so!" That is exactly what the Macleods have always been famous for. For striking out, without fear or prejudice, into new territory.' Applause met this observation.

'I pride myself on possessing one virtue above all others. The humility to know that I still have much to learn. And so, thanks to my daughter Grace, wise beyond her years, I have learned a most important lesson, a lesson about my fellow human beings. That there is always forgiveness and hope for redemption. Was this not the lesson of the two thieves taught by Christ our Saviour on the Cross?'

The Major raised his glass. 'And so I embrace Mr and Mrs Cooper and their esteemed son with a glad and full heart. I wish Grace and Augustus every happiness and good fortune in their nuptials. And I look forward to this time next year when they will sit here with us at this table as members of one strong, united and blessed family! To Grace and Augustus!'

'To Grace and Augustus!' the rest of the company echoed as they all stood and clinked glasses.

And then came the moment that, for Isobel at least, would later seem pregnant with foreboding. As the butler stepped away from the table with the campagna urn ice pail in his hands, his left foot slipped on a grape that had escaped the epergne and rolled onto the carpet.

With a shout, the butler crashed to the floor. Before anyone could move or even speak, the magnificent Worcester urn, a cherished family heirloom, flew from his grip and exploded against the wall into an unsolvable jigsaw of shattered fragments.

Chapter 23

THE BAZAAR

DECEMBER 1851 TO 1 JANUARY 1852

The portentous accident on Christmas Eve resurfaced in Isobel's dream later that night in the form of a giant mirror shattering into tiny pieces. But it did not dent Grace's confidence in her future. Plans continued apace for her wedding day. Isobel was surprised at first at the warmth of her father's endorsement of this match, given his previous views on emancipists. Had the trials of life and the cares of age finally worn down the Major's famous stubbornness? Maybe it was the tragic debacle of Alice's marriage to a blue-blooded wastrel that made this match with an emancipist's hard-working son even more attractive by contrast.

In the week following Christmas, Isobel concentrated on her own private project that she hoped would change her aunt's mind about the fancy fair. With three days left to the 'big day', Aunt Louisa returned from an interminable meeting at the asylum of the Benevolent Society's fancy bazaar committee. Fancywork from subscribers and supporters across Sydney had been arriving in vast quantities all day long. There had been discussions with officials from the city council about preparations: the layout and pitching of the tents; the order of events for the opening ceremony; and the seating arrangements for the official party including the Governor, the Colonial Secretary, the Attorney-General, the Lord Mayor, the society's patron, Mr George Allen, and their respective wives.

Aunt Louisa was tired when she arrived home but generally satisfied that all was properly in train. On her retirement to the drawing room, she found Isobel waiting with a smile on her face and the tea trolley ready with a selection of pastries and pot of freshly brewed pekoe. 'Please take a seat, Aunt, and let me pour you a cup,' offered Isobel.

'That's very obliging of you, my dear. Oh, macaroons, my favourite,' enthused Aunt Louisa, sampling one of the delicacies on the trolley.

'I have something I want to show you that I hope you will find agreeable,' said Isobel, 'But it is a surprise so you have to close your eyes.'

Louisa was in a good mood and prepared to indulge Isobel's whims. She took a sip of tea, a bite from a macaroon and then closed her eyes.

'Very well. Now you can take a look.'

When Louisa opened her eyes again she saw a large ink and watercolour sketch propped up on the chiffonier in her direct line of sight. It was a landscape study of the Botanic Gardens in all its civic grandeur and fecund loveliness. There was the wide sweep of the newly constructed seawall scooping out a dark glitter of harbour. And there, with its carousel-roofed bandstand, was the sunlit, pea-green Band Lawn, laid out like a welcome mat before the garden's young forest of native and exotic trees. Thickly dotted across this bright rectangle were tiny figures in white and black, a happy congregation of men, women and children at leisure in their Sunday best.

'Did you do this?' Louisa gasped, wiping macaroon crumbs from her chin.

'Yes, Aunt,' said Isobel. She tried to sound modest but was secretly thrilled at her aunt's undisguised admiration.

'Why, this is remarkable! With no word of exaggeration, it is worthy of a Lycett or a Martens,' said her aunt, looking at her niece with wide-eyed astonishment. 'I had no idea you were so talented, my dear!'

Isobel laughed. 'Thank you, Aunt. I painted it for the fancy fair. It can be auctioned if you like. I would hope it may fetch a pound or two.'

'I am sure it will fetch more than a pound or two!' scoffed Aunt Louisa. And then the penny dropped. The dowager grinned slowly. Her niece was seducing her with this gift. 'Of course, it would only be right that the artist be present at the auction. So that she can see the appreciation of the crowd.'

'Oh, Aunt, would you let me?' cried Isobel.

'Yes, my dear, of course. I shall be there as your guardian as will the other ladies of the committee. So I shall have no fear for your safety.'

'Thank you, Aunt! I promise to be as useful and hard-working as I can.'

'I know you will, my dear,' nodded her aunt, and even tilted her face a fraction in anticipation of a grateful kiss, which was cheerfully bestowed by her niece.

And so it was settled. Isobel Macleod was to attend her first fancy fair.

New Year's Day arrived, hot and windy. There had been no reprieve from the heatwave at Christmas and the winds blew stronger, drier and warmer every day thereafter. Thirteen white marquees were arrayed around the Band Lawn close to the seawall, their sides billowing as wildly as the sheets of a tea clipper in a gale. Isobel admired the swarms of white sparks that shimmered on the harbour in the blazing sun, dancing across its azure waters like fireflies. When the wind got up, those waters stiffened to white-capped peaks, dashing themselves against the seawall in an ecstasy of sea spray. But the wind brought no relief, only gusts of hot air, which, at their most fierce, blinded eyes and filled mouths with dust and grit.

Despite this unrelenting hot weather, the opening ceremony went off punctually at nine o'clock with the official party seated on a festooned dais and the regimental band of the 11th providing the required accompaniment of patriotic pomp. Clutching his cocked hat firmly and extemporising in place of notes that refused to sit flat on the lectern, the Governor praised the work of the Benevolent Society in general and the Fancy Fair Committee in particular, finally declaring the bazaar open. The audience, some three hundred by Isobel's estimate, applauded as best they could while being buffeted by the hot winds. At the conclusion of formalities, the crowd gratefully sought refuge inside the marquees. The number of visitors that day (calculated later by takings at the gate of one shilling for adults and sixpence for children) swelled to well over two thousand.

Isobel had never seen anything quite like the ambitious scale and rich variety of the bazaar. Each billowing white marquee had been decorated with wreaths of flowers, branches of evergreen and fronds of rainforest fern. Suffused in the green light from these decorations and from the overarching trees, the interior of these tents resembled cool, welcoming sylvan glades. The walls were bedecked in a plethora of national flags and the entire exhibition inside each marquee made to seem even more spacious and luxurious with the strategic placement of large mirrors to reflect the riotous treasures of the stalls and gay apparel of vendors and visitors.

Each of the marquees specialised in goods of one kind or another. The first was dedicated to toys and was, unsurprisingly, the favourite of families. Here, Master Charles pestered his parents for a sailboat or a wooden redcoat while his sister, Miss Sophie, pined after a composition doll in a cotton dress or a velveteen donkey with a red collar and silver bell. A zoological garden's worth of plump fabric elephants, zebras, lions, rhinoceroses and tigers demanded to be cuddled by little hands. There was the usual offering of adorable puppies, kittens, hedgehogs and mice, and farmyard boxes of bright wooden cows, pigs, chickens, sheep and shepherds with crooks.

A second marquee was devoted to baby clothes and accoutrements. A third was given over to small fancywork items including crochet and needlework, cross-stitch and embroidery—pincushions, work baskets, purses, reticules, tea cosies, slippers, snuffboxes, card holders—arranged tastefully in glass exhibition cases, some of them so high they eclipsed the stall vendors themselves. A fourth marquee was dedicated to quilts in myriad patterns, styles and materials, and a fifth to larger fancywork items: ottomans, chair-coverings, rugs, cushions, bolsters, firescreens, and card racks. A sixth marquee was solely the province of knitting and beadwork. The seventh was a 'wonders of nature' tent with a veritable florilegium handcrafted in paper, silk, wool and satin, in cross-stitch and embroidery. Its specimens included the ghostly blanched filigrees of skeleton leaf work, and the desiccated remains of flowers and seaweed pressed into mock-leather bound albums to resemble a kaleidoscope of inkblots. The eighth marquee was reserved for painted and sculpted items: ladies' fans and mirrors, writing pads and blotters, diaries and albums, and diverse paraphernalia modelled out of wood, leather and wax. Cordoned off in self-important isolation was a gallery of landscapes and portraits executed by the multitudinous schools of Sunday lady painters.

A ninth marquee featured metal and rustic work such as brass peacock-tail fireplace screens, miniature wheelbarrows to hold jewellery and all manner of objects beautified with pinecones, pebbles, leaves, moss, shells, fish scales and feathers. A tenth was the intriguing domain of pokerwork (both pyrographed wood and leather) with lovingly detailed jewellery boxes, trunks and chests, mirror frames, cameos, statuary, furniture, even musical instruments. Two tents, dominated by giant tea urns and battalions of teacups and saucers, had been allocated for the serving of finger food: scones, sandwiches, bran pies, cakes, jellies, toffee, lollipops and popcorn. Patrons were accommodated at marble-top tables and in wicker chairs where they took tea and were entertained by singers, magicians and jugglers.

The thirteenth tent was for the auctions, raffles, lotteries and wheels of fortune, where either specially selected, cheap and inconsequential, or simply unsold goods were disposed of through harmless games of chance. These included a lucky dip with a fishpond, bamboo rods and dangling paper fish on hooks. All this Isobel had anticipated except perhaps the impressive scale of the enterprise and the heady carnival air of excitement that she inhaled in greedy gulps. Nor did she expect the thrill and pride she secretly felt to be part of this astonishing public demonstration of the genius and tireless energy of women.

She also did not anticipate the variety of other amusements and sideshows that gave the bazaar the atmosphere of a funfair. Apart from the regimental band with its program of bright, brassy marches and mazurkas, there were musicians on gypsy violin, xylophones and bagpipes. Madame Vadoma waited in her fortune teller's tent with the promise of readings from palms, tea-leaves and a crystal ball. Gentlemen tried their luck at quoits, a coconut-shy and a small shooting gallery. Families watched gymnastic displays and acrobatic tumblers, pony jumping and a maypole pageant, and later that evening they would be entertained by tambourine and fan dancing and a pyrotechnic display. There was even a live chess match, with men dressed in mock-medieval cardboard costumes to resemble black and white pieces, who were then directed to move about a board the size of a croquet lawn.

Isobel spent much of her time in the third tent assisting Mrs Long and Mrs Smart. She wished she had been old enough to help Winnie at the fancy fairs for the Female School of Industry. She felt close to her mother today. She told nobody but she had taken her mother's opal dragonfly from its secret hiding place and wore it pinned to her pinafore underneath her blouse. How she wished she could wear it proudly in public but she dared not break her promise. Even hidden away, the dragonfly served as a constant reminder of Winnie's love and protection and, in a way she could not explain, a comforting talisman that evoked her presence. She hoped her mother would be proud of her today, following in her footsteps and helping her sister-in-law.

Whatever misgivings about charity work for the deserving poor she had harboured following her visit to The Rocks were dispelled today by the prevailing sentiments of altruism and goodwill. What she found most heartening was the convivial attitude of all the ladies and gentlemen attending the fair. Despite the scepticism of Mr Dickens, the male customers were, to a man, civil and courteous. They doffed their hats, paid charming compliments and parted with their sovereigns and shillings with no hint of condescension, reluctance or grumbling. Nor did Isobel feel troubled or oppressed by any unwarranted attention or unpleasant innuendo.

A general agreement as to the worthiness of the cause informed the whole proceedings, thought Isobel, and, thus liberated from doubt or worry, everyone seemed determined to have a good time. Not that Isobel had a spare moment for reflection as she was kept furiously busy all morning, answering questions, wrapping up goods and calculating change. Even after her short lunch break, the pace of sales never slackened as long queues of customers swarmed around the stall tables, waving their currency about with gay abandon.

At one point she thought she saw Major Tranter and his wife in the distance and even felt his eyes trained on her. Under this scrutiny, her heart trembled painfully with shame. The same occurred when she spotted the Misses Finch approaching her stall but she was spared that horribly awkward encounter when they were waylaid by friends. Familiar faces did appear in the crowd including those of Grace and Anna, whom she welcomed warmly and sold two pincushions and a beaded reticule. All in all, Isobel felt nothing but serene happiness and gratitude to be a useful pair of hands.

At three o'clock, Aunt Louisa bustled over to Mrs Smart's stall and took Isobel aside. 'It is time for your painting to be auctioned, my dear. Come with me.'

Isobel felt a thrill of anticipation pulse through her, a giddy childish joy that she had not experienced for as long as she could remember. As they entered the auction tent, she even squeezed her aunt's hand like a small girl does when overcome with strong feeling.

There was a large audience seated for the three o'clock session. The public auctioneer, Mr Steven Archer, was in his box and had already started the bidding on a peacock-tail firescreen. 'I have two shillings from the gentleman in the red vest over here. Do I hear three shillings? Her Majesty herself would envy you this fine piece! Three shillings? Three? Thank you, sir. I have three shillings down here! Do I hear four?'

Isobel watched the rowdy pantomime with pleasure. It reminded her of the music hall master of ceremonies at the Royal Victoria Theatre when she'd been taken there by William and Joseph a couple of years ago. This high-energy performance had the same cheeky brashness, parading as gentility, with sly winks and jokey grins as an aside to the crowd.

'And now, ladies and gentlemen, I have the great pleasure of introducing to you an as yet unknown young artist of prodigious and precocious talent!'

Aunt Louisa looked at Isobel with an air of barely suppressed excitement. 'You!' she mouthed in exaggerated dumb show, in case Isobel had missed the point. Isobel nodded vigorously to indicate she understood.

'Here is a lovely piece that perfectly captures the setting of our bazaar today. What an ideal souvenir of your time here, ladies and gents. The Botanic Gardens, superbly executed in ink and water-colour. And what a rare chance for the art collectors among you to discover the gifted artist, Miss Isobel Macleod.'

Isobel's *Botanic Gardens* was unveiled on the easel close by Mr Archer's auction box; it had been substituted for one of Louisa's paintings inside a very fine gilt hardwood frame. Loud muttering bubbled up in the crowd, heads twisted sideways, eyes narrowed, some people raised their opera glasses. Isobel blushed deeply. She would have preferred that Mr Archer not mention her by name.

She was certainly not so proud as to seek such publicity, which, she knew, would appear immodest and unseemly in a young woman.

But it was too late now. And then Isobel was seized by a twinge of panic. What if nobody likes it? What if it sells for only a few shillings—or doesn't sell at all? She had seen several exceptionally ugly items pass in without bids. Dear heavens! She had walked, eyes wide open, into yet another ambush, another opportunity for public humiliation. How could she be so conceited? She blushed to think of her own arrogance, all puffed up by her aunt's well-meaning flattery, that she had not stopped to consider such a disastrous possibility.

'I start the bidding at half a crown. Half a crown. Who will offer me half a crown?'

The silence that followed stretched out for an agonising eternity. At least that was how Isobel experienced it, a yawning abyss of degradation opening up at her feet. But she was mistaken. It was a pause of merely a few seconds. 'Over here!' shouted a man in the front row.

'I have half a crown from this gentleman. Do I have a crown?'

A hand shot up from another man seated six rows back. 'And I have a crown!' Mr Archer rose onto his toes and pointed his auctioneer's hammer at the second man. The bidding then bounced around four different men in the audience and climbed smartly to three pounds, at which point the auction for Isobel's painting settled into a tense back-and-forth volley between only two gentlemen. Isobel observed all this from her position alongside her aunt at the back of the tent, so all she could see were the backs of people's heads: a sea of men's fur collars and dark jackets and ladies' elegant shawls and coats.

'I have three pounds from the gent in the front row. The bidding is against you, sir,' Mr Archer informed the second man, six rows behind. The auctioneer, normally a sober, sensible fellow despite his histrionic manner, was emboldened to proceed in leaps of one pound. 'Do I hear four?'

The current bidder turned his head a fraction to see his competitor and Isobel gasped. His profile was unmistakeable. It was Major Tranter. She then recognised the slope of the shoulders of his wife, once Lady Charlotte Bathurst, seated at his side. Major Tranter was bidding for her painting! What could this mean? And who was the other gent?

'The bid now stands at six pounds! *Six* pounds. Do I hear seven?'

The crowd was abuzz with exclamations of surprise. Aunt Louisa herself was growing quite red in the face and her short, ample frame was aquiver with nervous agitation. This was already much more than anyone had ever paid for a piece by an amateur lady painter that she could remember. She kept looking significantly at her niece as if to say, *You see, I knew I was right about more than one or two pounds! Silly girl!* Isobel smiled back at her but her heart was galloping far too fast. She could not decide if this was a good experience or a terrible one, to be so publicly and explicitly judged right down to the last pound, shilling and pence of one's worth! How did professional artists tolerate such scrutiny?

That was when the proverbial penny dropped. She stared hard at the nape and shoulders of the man in the sixth row, the other bidder. She studied the back of his head closely, his mop of golden tousled hair touching the collar of a mint green frock coat. There was a languorous ease with which he sat in the midst of this dramatic bidding battle. She had never seen him from this angle but there was no doubt in her mind who it was.

Mr Probius. Of course it was, who else? Charles Probius.

'I have ten pounds! And now fifteen! Twenty! Twenty pounds!'

The audience were thoroughly enjoying the duel of the two bidders, which had turned into a full-pitched tournament. The excited murmuring grew louder and the audience became more aroused and amused by this overheated contest. There were even outbursts of laughter. Isobel's face burned hotly. In a fanciful, almost delirious moment, she saw herself exhibited in place of her painting, standing up there next to Mr Archer's auction box, the object of all eyes. Before her these two men, the one who had loved her ardently once and the one her heart suspected she may love now, were locked in metaphorical combat, wallets brandished like duelling pistols, to claim her as the property of the highest bidder.

Isobel had heard of the barbaric practice of wife selling at country fairs in England, a custom observed last century by the poorest classes to dissolve unhappy marriages by mutual agreement but now largely outmoded by modern divorce laws. Depending on one's view, reflected Isobel, was not marriage itself always a transaction in the marketplace? Was this not the way of the world even in the best society? Suitors bid for young brides with adequate dowries and young women hoped to ensnare husbands with substantial property and income. Every family of any reputation was on the hunt for a suitable match that would make a sound alliance of wealth and privilege.

Instead of the pride and exhilaration she should have felt at this moment, Isobel was in a state of spiritual queasiness. Her face reddened with shame. No lady of any worth put herself on display in such a vulgar manner. What was she thinking? She had persuaded her aunt to relax her moral guardianship and this farce was the result.

'Twenty-five pounds!' Mr Archer's voice had risen to an incredulous bellow. The crowd were very stirred up now, breathless with amazement. Isobel could read the discomfiture in the erstwhile Lady Charlotte Bathurst, the way her shoulders tensed and her head bowed as if she wished to shun the glare of public attention. What on earth did Major Tranter think he was doing? Could this be passed off as a magnanimous gesture of public charity or the extravagance of an art lover's intemperate passion? Or would people suspect something else? Isobel hoped that neither Grace nor Anna was present to witness this scene.

Charlotte had so far stared straight ahead as if deaf to the whole proceedings, but at this point she turned and looked directly at her husband. 'The bid is against you, sir,' said Mr Archer looking down from his lofty box. Major Tranter lowered his head in resignation. Whatever his motives, he had decided to withdraw. In the sixth row, the golden-haired artist leaned sideways a little and threw his arm over the back of his chair in an attitude of languid, victorious repose. 'Twenty-five pounds! Going once! Going twice! Going three times! Congratulations, sir, the painting is yours!'

There was a polite round of applause and a fellow gentleman patted Mr Probius on the shoulder by way of approbation. Out of the corner of her eye, Isobel saw Major Tranter steal a surreptitious look in her direction as he and his wife quietly slunk away to the nearest exit. His expression was difficult to read at this distance but there was an unmistakeable air of injury and regret, possibly even humiliation. There will be an interesting conversation between those two, thought Isobel, with some sympathy for her ex-suitor.

The auction moved on to the next item. Aunt Louisa flung her arms about her niece in genuine affection. 'Twenty-five pounds, my dear! What a very clever girl you are!' She seemed untroubled by any scruples about this rather profligate display.

Isobel smiled. 'Why, thank you, Aunt. I hope people did not think it too brazen for my name to be announced like that. I promise you I did not seek any publicity of that sort!'

'Oh tosh, it does no harm at all,' reassured Louisa Blunt, who seemed to have abandoned all notions of modesty in the pursuit of commercial profit as three committee members—Mrs Cornwall, Mrs Thierry and Mrs Drummond—appeared with beaming faces. They formed an enthusiastic circle of admirers around Miss Macleod, singing her praises.

'Please excuse the intrusion, ladies,' said a deep voice behind them, 'but I thought you may like to meet the new owner of the painting in question. May I introduce our drawing master, Mr Charles Probius.'

The voice belonged to none other than the lumbering figure of Mr Cooper, the much-loved Robert the Large, hero of the working class. Next to him stood Mr Probius in the glorious mint green frock coat, dark crimson vest, lilac gloves, mustard topper and black breeches. He inclined his head to acknowledge the chorus of universal gratitude and approval from the ladies of the Fancy Fair

Committee. Both gentlemen regarded Isobel with a look of benign esteem. But in Mr Probius's dark brown eyes Isobel could see that a particularly incandescent spark had been ignited. She dropped her own eyes modestly under his warm gaze.

'I hope my extravagance did not alarm you in any way, Miss Macleod,' he said quietly, with a sensitivity that she noted with gratitude. 'I hasten to reassure you—and the ladies of the committee—that my persistence was motivated not only by charity. It was intended as a gesture of public appreciation of the work itself. It is indeed a very fine piece.'

'I am deeply flattered, sir,' said Isobel, still feeling confused and a little exposed.

'I am no expert in such matters but, for what my opinion is worth, Miss Macleod, it does the gardens proud,' echoed Mr Cooper, in a surprisingly expansive mood, given that art was a province he generally claimed was best left to the formally educated and those who professed to have 'taste'. 'I would be honoured if you were to accept a commission on behalf of my wife and myself. We leave Juniper Hall in April and we wish to have something to remember her by.'

Isobel was stunned. Surely Mr Probius would be the obvious choice for such an undertaking? He knew the house intimately and must have hours to spare in which to sketch it. She suspected the truth of the matter: Mr Probius had put the idea in his employer's head.

'Why, sir, I would have thought Mr Probius could . . .' she began to protest.

'Dear me, no,' objected the artist. 'I am far too busy with Mrs Cooper's portrait.'

266

'Well, then I—I—would love to,' she replied. 'I am deeply flattered, thank you.'

'Very good, very good,' said Robert with a clap of his hands. 'It is all agreed.'

'And so begins an illustrious career,' Charles chimed in with a gentle smile. He addressed himself to her aunt. 'Mrs Blunt, it is a privilege to meet the chief organiser of this magnificent affair. Please accept my congratulations.'

Louisa's cheeks flushed pink and she giggled almost girlishly. Isobel was amused at how easily the artist charmed the dowager. In what amounted to a small epiphany, Isobel realised she had not properly evaluated Mr Probius's charismatic good looks. Only now did she see his handsomeness reflected in the eyes of the women around her.

'You are too kind, sir,' Aunt Louisa said.

'I regret I have not been able to revisit Faulconstone these last few weeks as my work has kept me occupied,' he continued. 'But with your consent, I would be flattered if there was an opportunity for such a meeting to take place at some future date.'

'Of course, of course,' said Isobel's aunt. 'I shall be free for such social arrangements now this bazaar is over. As Isobel will testify, it has taken up all our time.'

Isobel nodded. 'So it has.'

'Well, that is all settled then,' smiled Mr Probius. 'I shall look forward to it. And to acquainting myself with some more of your work, Miss Macleod, if I may be so bold. Now that I am fortunate to count myself as your first patron.'

Isobel looked at him from under her eyelids. He was flirting with her, right here in front of the Benevolent Society matrons and her aunt and the redoubtable Mr Cooper. But doing it with such finesse that his lovemaking was expertly disguised as gentlemanly wit and Christian charity. Both men doffed their hats and took leave of the committee ladies.

She watched the two gentlemen retreat, accompanied by Mrs Cornwall, who obliged Mr Probius by taking him to the cashier for payment of the twenty-five pounds. In one afternoon, Isobel fancied, she had managed to find not only her artistic metier but also, all being well with the world, her first true love.

The day was almost concluded with the sun low on the horizon and Venus gleaming as bright as a diamond in the twilight gloom. There would be fireworks in half an hour. Oil lamps were lit in every marquee so that they resembled the flickering spheres of giant hot air balloons.

Isobel was very tired. She could only marvel at the ceaseless energy of the charity workers like her aunt and her committee ladies, who were many years her senior. She envied them the certainty of their faith and zeal. The crowd had thinned a little in the mid-afternoon but, with the hot winds dropping in the early evening and the prospect of fireworks that night, families had begun to gather again near the seawall.

The harbour looked majestic in the gloaming, its waters as dense and dark as ink and just starting to catch the scattered fluorescence of the city's gaslights. Sunset had arrived suddenly and the clouds in the western sky had combusted into their habitual fiery glory. Above them, trails of blue and acid green drifted uncertain as smoke. Isobel watched as the sky burned like hot coals, imperceptibly yielding, orange to ochre to umber, to velvet darkness.

Isobel had loved the night as a child; a time for family closeness at the fireside and for sleep after long days in the gardens at Grangemouth and Rosemount. But ever since her mother had died, night had amplified her feelings of loss and loneliness. The empty blackness made her think heretical thoughts: of life's finiteness, of the endless sleep of death with no consolation of angels or God's eternal love. And after the death of her mother, the night had also brought her such vivid dreams, frightening, sublime, strange and unsettling.

But tonight she did not feel any fear, only a sense of intense anticipation. She no longer stood on tiptoe like a child to stare out her bedroom window and look at a black harbour and an incomprehensible sky of stars. Ballandella had given her stories from the sky. And while they were not Isobel's stories they had helped her believe, and hope, that the world was rich in meaning. One just had to be ready to read the signs. Today the signs had been shown to her. She faced the dark night as a young woman, no longer a girl. She now stood tiptoe on the threshold of her womanhood. She had read the signs and knew what they signified. For better or worse, she was an artist. For better or worse, the slender golden thread of her destiny had snagged on this man Charles Probius. For what purpose? What else but love. Or was love only a pretext for a greater intention? Time would tell. Time always did.

Aunt Louisa was busy with the cashier, and Isobel had finished helping box up the few unsold trinkets and treasures from Mrs Long and Mrs Smart's stall. 'Enjoy the fireworks. I'll be another half hour or so,' her aunt instructed, leaving her in the company of Mrs Palmer, who had spent all day in the food tent dispensing a Niagara of tea.

'Can I?' asked Isobel, nodding towards Madame Vadoma's tent. 'Just for fun?'

'Of course, dear,' smiled Mrs Palmer indulgently.

Isobel passed through a crimson silk curtain and came into the inner chamber of the fortune teller's tent. In the half-light of a bronze lantern overhead and the pearlescent glow of a large glass ball sat a woman. Her hair was long and white in untidy tresses, dressed with brass ornaments like coins, and her head was encased in a blood red scarf. About her shoulders clung a purple shawl run through with silver threads and printed with many obscure motifs, possibly birds or animals.

Isobel had idly imagined that, for the purposes of the fair, the Benevolent Society of New South Wales, a pious Christian charity, would have hired a young actress to dress up as a Romany sooth-sayer. As she contemplated the swarthy face of the old woman seated in front of her, Isobel was sure that this was not the case. This woman was clearly no actress. Isobel surmised she was from India, having seen pictures of the natives of the subcontinent. The woman motioned for her to be seated and asked for sixpence, which was quickly spirited away into a bag in her lap. 'What kind of reading do you seek?' she asked with half-closed eyes, whether from fatigue or to give an air of mystery it was hard to tell.

'What choices do I have?' Isobel asked a little nervously.

The woman sighed. It had been a long day. 'The future can be foretold in many ways,' she said, 'The Egyptians and Greeks taught us to read it in fire, in water, in numbers, in the entrails and flights of birds, in the spirits of the dead, in the map of the human hand. The diviner Artemidorus says that the future speaks to us through our dreams if we have but the wit to understand.'

'I have many strange dreams,' whispered Isobel, almost to herself.

There was a moment's silence. Isobel realised the woman was studying her closely. 'What do you have there, hidden beneath your blouse? I can feel its presence,' she said, leaning into the circle of light beneath the lantern, a new note of intrigue, even eagerness, in her voice. Isobel smelled a syrupy musk on the air. The woman's face was ageless. Her forehead was unlined but there were pronounced creases about her eyes, a youthful bloom on her cheeks but a fleshy heaviness about the jaw. The woman's hand reached out towards Isobel. 'A gift. From your mother.'

Isobel gasped. How on earth could this woman know that?

'Please, let me see it. If you wish to know your future.'

Isobel turned away and unpinned the opal dragonfly from beneath her blouse. She then held it out into the light for the old woman to see. The fortune teller's eyes glistened.

'Scrying stones. Opals. But I have not seen the likes of these before. A strange gift.'

The woman looked pained for a moment as if wrestling with a difficult decision. She breathed heavily and a little too fast. 'How long ago did your mother die?'

Isobel's eyes met the woman's. Almond green. Still as pond water. 'Just over one year.'

'And why do you still wear her brooch?'

It was a good question. Why did she? Because she missed her mother, loved her. That was the simple answer. Isobel felt irritated now. She had come into Madame Vadoma's tent for a lark, an idle moment of fun at the end of a long day's work. This was no fun.

'Please don't worry about it. I'll go.' She rose from her chair and turned to leave.

'You don't wish to know what the opals have to tell you?' asked the woman.

There was something about the way she phrased the question that commanded Isobel's attention. She was half-convinced, despite her initial resistance, that the dragonfly was the source of her dreams. Dreams she barely understood.

She resumed her seat.

'Put the brooch on the table,' the old woman instructed. Isobel did as she was told.

'Silence.' The woman laid her hands either side of the brooch and stared at the opal dragonfly with a steady gaze. Isobel sat back in the shadows on her side of the table. Aunt had said she would be half an hour. There was time. Her own breathing deepened into a slower rhythm, as she was anxious not to break the woman's concentration.

The long silence that seemed unnatural and awkward at first in this close chamber became little by little a delicate bubble of shared silence that deepened and deepened. Outside were the wild screeches and pops of the fireworks overhead and the cheers of the onlookers. But all that belonged to a remote world, almost unreal, fantastical. The real world was in here, in the sepia glow of the bronze lantern, in the intense gaze of the almond-green eyes of an old woman. She began to speak in a continuous, flowing stream of words.

Time shifted into another rhythm, another river, another flow, an eternity. *'Water. You live by water. A house by water. And a garden. A garden you love. A garden that is a whole world. A garden that is all your world. But you must leave. You must leave now. You must go. To another place. So many you have loved. They have all left. Your mother. Your brother. Gone. And now two more brothers. Over water. And a sister. Over water. They are lost to you.'*

The words were intoned as if in prayer, as if chanted, toneless but crystal clear. They fell from the woman's mouth like drips from a tap, each one splashing into the silence. Isobel wanted to speak but dared not. The woman was in a trance now, her eyes, both still, green pools, unblinking, her face softened like wax, unmoving. *'You are lost to them and they to you. This is what appears. I speak of the past. I speak of now. Your father is now lost to you. His love is lost to you. His protection is lost to you. There is a woman. There are women. In a circle. They protect you. They protect you now. They are your sisters. Your new sisters.'*

Isobel closed her eyes. The words fell, crashing into the silence, each phrase deafening, crushing, so painful to hear. They could not possibly be true. How could they be true? There came a loud buzzing in her ears. Was she going to faint? Was her blood deserting her, rushing away, filling her skull and body with air, with light, with nothing at all? Please, let me faint, let this stop, she said to herself. Please stop this, it is unbearable.

The woman's voice droned on, as if bereft of sense, as if abandoning any purpose in speaking, as if just dropping these words like droplets into a well, like pebbles on a path for Isobel to follow, but only if she wishes, it is not important, it is so important, it is meaningless, it means everything. Only she can choose. The buzzing grows louder.

'*I speak of the future. The future not set in stone, not carved in marble. Of what will come if nothing is changed. Of a man that you love who sees you clearly. And the man that you love who does not see you clearly. And of the man that you never loved who watches and waits. There will always be water. So much water. Your life flows like water. Its current is strong.*' The woman's voice began to waver, to become her own again. Isobel could feel a struggle inside the trance, see a restlessness behind the eyes, a tic in the woman's waxen face, as if she was willing herself to break free, to stop the flow of words, as if she suddenly heard them and grasped their sense and understood how they were striking the young woman. Like stones.

'*Your life is long. Your life must change. Your life will change. You will endure. You will find peace. You will find love. You will find what you are looking for. But everyone. Everyone you love. Everyone you love will . . .*' The voice stopped. There was silence.

Isobel opened her eyes. Her voice was a hoarse whisper. 'Will what?'

'*Will be gone.*'

Chapter 24

WEDDING PLANS

JANUARY TO FEBRUARY 1852

Isobel had returned to Faulconstone on the night of the bazaar in a state of high anxiety bordering on terror. By a supreme effort of will she managed to keep these feelings hidden from her aunt, who was still in a triumphal mood. Aunt Louisa had calculated that the funds taken for the Benevolent Society bazaar were in excess of a hundred and fifty pounds, a small fortune, of which Isobel's painting alone accounted for a sixth.

This generosity was remarkable at a time when Sydney was still reeling from the madness of the gold rush and the exodus of thousands of people like floodwaters down a giant drain: servants walking away from masters, crews abandoning ships in the harbour, husbands deserting wives, businesses closing their doors for lack of staff and custom. Charities were never busier rescuing the flotsam of this flood tide: broken families, bankrupts and beggars and, flowing back to Sydney in an ebb tide of bitter disillusionment, the failed diggers who had gambled and lost everything on the promise of easy fortune.

In the privacy of her room, Isobel sat on the bed contemplating her mother's brooch, the old woman's prognostications sounding in her ears. Much of what she had said touched on Isobel's life with a startling degree of accuracy (how could she know so much?) but there was also a great deal that simply made no sense. She sketched the old woman's face, the sinister play of light and shadows that had made the scene so menacing.

In the daylight hours of the following day, Isobel's feelings of horror seemed less credible and potent than they had in the fortune teller's tent at twilight. Her initial fear began to yield to anger as she suspected she was the victim of some low trick. Was it possible that this woman was acquainted with someone Isobel knew? Was this a conspiracy bent on giving her a nasty fright? And if so, why? She had lost faith in the Misses Finch and Bradley but could not imagine why anyone would want to scare her. She told herself that the only alternative explanation—that the opal dragonfly had, by some mystic means, revealed the truth of Isobel's future—was too preposterous to be taken seriously.

Grace's wedding plans preoccupied Isobel's two sisters for the next four weeks. The service was to be held at St James' followed by a wedding breakfast at Rosemount. While Isobel now had time to resume her lessons, she was also engaged in her new commission for Mr and Mrs Cooper, preparing sketches for an ink and watercolour study of their beloved Juniper Hall. As the hall was only a short distance from Faulconstone, Isobel could walk there by herself. The summer heat remained oppressive and the winds blew strongly over the ridge in Paddington. Isobel carried her parasol like a shield against the blast and sought refuge from the sun under the jacaranda trees near the sandstone walls of Victoria Barracks.

It was here, on her first excursion to the hall a week after the bazaar, that she encountered Mr Probius, walking in the opposite direction. He was on his way to the barracks to paint a portrait of Lieutenant Colonel Bloomfield, commanding officer of the 11th Regiment, commissioned by Sydney's mayor. The city still owed this fine gentleman a debt of gratitude for the way he had kept the peace back in 1845. At the request of the Governor, he had sailed with his regiment from Hobart, disembarked his troops at Circular Quay and marched them smartly up George Street with bayonets fixed to put a stop to a mutiny of the garrison soldiers of the 96th Manchester Regiment. One of the officers serving under Bloomfield that day had been none other than Captain Ralph Tranter.

'Why, it is Miss Macleod, the renowned artist. What an unexpected pleasure!' cried Mr Probius as he drew near. Such a splendid sight he made! Isobel took in the ensemble of his elegantly tailored outfit: his deep blue claw-hammer morning coat and matching blue silk waistcoat, the broad linen cravat, the striped dove grey trousers, the black Chelsea boots and the lemon chamois gloves. In his right hand he sported a mahogany walking cane, its ivory handle worked into the profile of a mallard duck.

'The pleasure is mutual, Mr Probius,' said Isobel warmly. 'I was hoping I might find you at Juniper Hall this morning. I am about to begin my sketches for Mr Cooper.'

'Yes, so he told me. I do apologise I am not free to welcome you there properly. I am engaged this morning at the barracks. The lieutenant colonel has made time for a sitting.'

'He should make a handsome subject for a portrait.'

'By the time I have finished he will,' quipped the artist. Isobel laughed. She could not begin to imagine what a fraught business a portrait commission must be.

Without warning, the wind renewed its vigour with a hot, dry gust. Isobel's pretty cream parasol was torn from her hands and wheeled along the street like a child's hoop. Mr Probius gallantly gave chase and returned the fugitive parasol to its owner. As she took it from him, his fingers brushed lightly against hers. She felt her heart race at this touch and discovered that she wished they had lingered there a moment longer. Thoughts that could only be described as wicked came unbidden to her mind and she hoped that her face did not betray her desire. 'This infernal wind!' she exclaimed and blushed at her own blasphemy.

'I quite agree,' concurred Mr Probius. 'This wind is definitely hot enough to be infernal. Let me escort you to the hall. The commander will indulge me a small delay.'

'Oh, you are too kind,' protested Isobel. 'I do not want to make you late for your appointment. I shall be perfectly fine now you have rescued my parasol, thank you.'

'As you wish,' he replied with a courteous nod. 'With your blessing, I hope to call on you and your guardian as soon as my duties allow. I suspect we will have much to discuss after your preliminary sketches today.'

'I shall very much look forward to that, Mr Probius.'

Isobel made no effort to disguise her warm interest in his impending visit. This man had won over her aunt with his charm and gallantry and, propitiously, her own sister was about to marry into the family that regarded him with pride and affection. There seemed no obstacles to furthering her friendship with Mr Probius. And many reasons to be hopeful.

With great reluctance Isobel bade him farewell and proceeded on her walk. Less than ten yards along the street, she could feel that almost imperceptible weight of someone's attention trained on her. She paused and glanced over her shoulder, hoping to steal a glimpse of her handsome friend and patron.

To her astonishment, Mr Probius had also stopped at precisely the same moment. He was standing in the shade of a jacaranda tree to observe her retreat along Old South Head Road. They looked directly at each other. A wide smile spread across Mr Probius's face and he waved. Isobel did the same. And, her heart giddy with happiness, she kept walking.

Now that the bazaar was all done and Isobel had more than proved her devotion to good works, she was free to resume her lessons in Surry Hills and Woolloomooloo. And so it came to pass that at Mrs Arnold's German class two days later Isobel first heard the unexpected glad tidings. 'Fanny Macleay is to be married!' her classmate Philomena informed her breathlessly. The banns had just been promulgated at St Mark's and the wedding day was fixed three weeks hence. Isobel was surprised at how moved she felt on hearing this news.

'I am so happy for her!' she exclaimed, supressing tears of joy. She pictured her only meeting with Fanny by the ponds at Rosemount when she was a girl of ten. She clearly recalled Fanny's facetious comparison of a dragonfly as it emerges from its pupa to a young woman's 'coming out' into society, when she falls prey to the attention of suitors pouncing to 'gobble us up in the jaws of matrimony'. Who was the gentleman who had 'gobbled up' the bookish botanical artist, just turned forty years of age? His name, reported confidently by Philomena, was Mr Thomas Carlton Hungerford. He had once worked as an assistant to Mr Macleay when he was Colonial Secretary.

Isobel was greatly heartened by this intelligence, which she took as a sign of encouragement in matters of the heart. She had heard the gossip that Fanny had rejected several proposals in the past so she had presumably agreed to this match with good reason. Isobel was in no doubt that Fanny valued her own liberty and interests too highly to give them up for the sake of pleasing society or saving her 'reputation'. She must love Mr Hungerford. Or at least they must have interests in common and souls in sympathy sufficient to sustain a marriage. At least that is what Isobel hoped.

If the Major had heard this news it would be unlikely to have produced the same warm feelings of approbation. The Governor had informed him only two days ago that the Major's old enemy, Mr Macleay, Fanny's father and the chair of the inquiry into the Surveyor-General's department, would submit the panel's report to the Governor by September. As part of his already heavy workload, the Major was engaged in writing a report on the state of the roads across the colony, which he now regarded as a defence of his career as Surveyor-General. These roads were his proudest legacy, the main arteries of trade and traffic that pumped goods and people into the burgeoning settlements at Newcastle in the north, Bathurst and Orange out west, as well as his Great South Road to Goulburn and the city of Melbourne, the capital of the newly created colony of Victoria.

Meanwhile, the Major had made a momentous decision, which Aunt Louisa conveyed to Isobel that evening in the front parlour at Faulconstone. "'As soon as Grace's nuptials are concluded, I intend to book my passage to England,'" she read aloud from her brother's letter.

Isobel gasped. This was astonishing news! But why?

"'As there has been no word about Alice and her little boy, Xavier, either from the Twyckenham family or from my brother, Fergus, I have applied to the Governor for a leave of absence on urgent family matters.'" Isobel had no doubt that Uncle Fergus, as conscientious and resolute as his brother, had done everything within his power to contact Alice. The lack of communication did not encourage hope and had weighed heavily on her father's conscience. Isobel knew Papa would not rest until he had rescued his eldest daughter and his newborn grandson from whatever disaster had enveloped them.

His letter also detailed how, while he was abroad, he would conduct more trials of his patented 'boomerang' ship's screw and oversee the printing of the journal of his fourth expedition. His labours, physical and intellectual, were indefatigable.

Aunt Louisa continued: "'I shall be abroad when the commission's report is released in September and can only hope that my absence may make some people more appreciative of the value of my leadership and hard work.'" Isobel could not shake a sense of foreboding on hearing this news and the old soothsayer's words came unbidden into her mind: '*Your father is now lost to you. His love is lost to you. His protection is lost to you.*'

'Of course you will be welcome to stay here while he is away,' reassured her aunt. 'I see no reason for you to hasten back to Rosemount. You have your commission over at Juniper Hall and can still attend church and your lessons as before. The ladies of our charity committee value your contributions highly, as you know. And, to speak plainly, I have grown quite fond of your company myself, dear Isobel.' Aunt Louisa was not given to professions of sentiment of any kind, so this admission took Isobel off guard.

'Why, thank you, Aunt. I feel the same.'

But even as she said this, she felt a chill enclose her heart. Her brief exile from Rosemount had just become a longer sentence. That very same morning she had at last received a short letter from her brother William, penned quickly and posted from the small settlement at Moreton Bay where his ship had put in months ago to pick up passengers and drop off mail and supplies. William had responded to her plea for 'good counsel' regarding her exile from Rosemount:

Dearest Sister,

As one who feels exil'd himself from the warmth and comfort of my family Home, I sympathise with your unhappy situation.

I can only advise you to bear your new circumstances with your habitual courage and be reassur'd that, harsh as Father's regime may sometimes strike us, I sincerely believe he acts out of Love for his children and in the belief he serves our best interests. I will write you again as soon as we make Madras.

With greatest affection etc.,
   William

Post-script: When I refer to your 'habitual courage' I cannot help thinking of the time you and Joseph and that little black girl went on 'an expedition' to Rushcutters Bay! Do you remember? Joseph certainly does! Father was quite forgiving of his little 'explorer'.

Isobel smiled to think that both her brothers recalled this episode. She was flattered, of course, by William's faith in her courage but still yearned to return to her proper home. Faced with her extended exile, Isobel empathised for the first time with the profound homesickness that a convict must feel, far from the country and family he or she loved. She had only one reservation about the prospect of going home. While Grace had been kinder to her of late in her newfound happiness, Isobel was reluctant to put this fragile peace to the test in her father's absence. And anyway, presumably Grace would move into her own house with her new husband after the wedding. What then would become of Anna? Surely she could not stay all alone at Rosemount.

It was true that Isobel's time at Faulconstone had been more tolerable than she had anticipated and even enjoyable thanks to the fancywork ladies of the Benevolent Society, but even this could not completely displace the longing she felt for Rosemount. Again, the words of the soothsayer came to her: 'There are women. In a circle. They protect you. They protect you now. They are your sisters. Your new sisters.' Isobel shivered every time she thought of the old woman and her prophetic riddles. Try as she might to dismiss them as nonsense, her words resurfaced repeatedly in Isobel's mind. She dared not share them with anyone lest they think she had become as mad as her sister.

Poor Anna. She was to be pitied, thought Isobel, though she could be so cruel and unreasonable at times. While Anna had joined in the general chorus of jubilation that greeted the news of Grace's nuptials, it did not take much imagination to see that Grace's marriage spelled the end of her and Anna's close (one could even say conspiratorial) sisterhood, which over many years had grown fast and intertwined like ivy and stone. Anna's bond with Grace went beyond conventional sibling love. It had become a dependency and the prospect of its ending threatened Anna's very existence.

Cocooned in premarital bliss, Grace seemed deaf and blind to the torment endured by her sister. Anna had begun to unravel in ways that were all too familiar. Temper tantrums, bullying the servants, opening and closing curtains for no reason, rearranging furniture, pacing back and forth furiously in the drawing room, the hall, the carriage drive, talking to herself, sleepwalking and, of course, finding fault with Isobel. Her outbursts of abuse directed at Isobel had grown ever more vile and threatening.

On one of her rare visits to Rosemount, in the second week after the bazaar, Isobel had offered to help with any aspect of the wedding plans that Grace cared to assign her.

'She's just trying to interfere,' Anna accused in a venomous, hurt voice. Isobel felt the slap of this rebuke as if her sister had struck her. She chose not to respond.

'You're just trying to be nice so Grace can't tell how jealous you are about her wedding,' hissed Anna, her eyes narrowed to hateful slits, her hands clenched as if ready to claw at Isobel's eyes or squeeze her throat. Isobel knew how Anna looked when the madness took hold of her. Like a rabid dog, a creature in the grip of a blind, violent fury.

Grace tried to calm her. 'Now, now, sister dear. Do not be so unkind,' she soothed, stroking Anna's hair and speaking low. 'She means no harm, I assure you.'

Usually when Grace intervened in this manner to keep the peace, these pats and strokes and calming words would suffice to restrain Anna's fit of temper. But not on this day. Anna looked entrapped, cornered by both sisters: the one she purely hated and the one she professed to love but now hated for betraying her.

'You are taking her side again,' she screeched, tears running down her cheeks. 'You told me you wanted *me* to help! Not *her*. You can't trust *her*, you said so yourself.'

Grace rolled her eyes and shot a look at Isobel to reassure her that this was not true, that this was poor Anna's affliction talking. 'Of course, you are the one I rely on the most. Nothing changes that, Anna, dear.'

'Oh, *everything* changes that, Grace. You do not love me anymore!' Anna sobbed, and ran from the room in a flood of tears, her hair falling down and her face blotchy and red.

Grace looked shaken. Maybe her cocoon of bridal bliss had finally been punctured by the realisation of how her marriage appeared to her grieving sister. For how long could she delay the hard decision about Anna's fate?

One of the few bright points in this dismal sequence of events was how much Isobel was looking forward to Mr Probius's visit to Faulconstone. New Year's Day had provided clear proof of his interest in her and he had also won the dowager's favour that day so that Aunt Louisa equally looked forward to the gentleman paying her a visit. Ten days after the accidental meeting outside the Victoria Barracks, Mr Probius dropped his card onto the butler's tray at Faulconstone and it was conveyed to the morning room.

'Please ask Mr Probius to join us in the drawing room for tea, Emmet,' ordered Aunt Louisa. The two women hastened to their respective bedrooms to adjust their hair and clothes, don a more colourful shawl and a suitable ring or bracelet. Once installed in the drawing room with their tea and scones, the party enjoyed a lively conversation. Mr Probius was in excellent spirits and had come bearing a gift.

'I hope you do not find this presumptuous, Mrs Blunt, but as I have been walking about this district a fair deal of late I took the opportunity to do a small sketch of Faulconstone. A mere trifle, I'm afraid, but I hope it may amuse you.'

The artist unwrapped a rectangle of board with a handsome sketch of Faulconstone behind its flowering frangipani tree. Mr Probius had presumably made some quick notational sketches from the front garden during his previous visit back in December and worked it up into a more detailed work during his local perambulations.

'This is a very fine likeness, Mr Probius, and a generous gift, sir,' exclaimed Mrs Blunt as she held the picture in her hands.

'It is by way of a small thank you for the opportunity to pay my respects to you both,' said Mr Probius, a master of courtesy and good manners. 'If it pleases you, madam, I will have it properly prepared as a lithograph to add to your excellent collection.' The artist's gaze made a sweeping appraisal of the artworks on the drawing room walls.

'Well, I don't know what to say! Please accept my deepest gratitude,' replied Mrs Blunt, quite abashed. 'You are welcome in this house whenever you can spare the time.'

'Thank you. As you probably know, Mr and Mrs Cooper are vacating Juniper Hall and plan to return to England. They have asked me to join them.'

Mr Probius's dark eyes met Isobel's for what seemed a long moment. Isobel felt her heart lurch in her chest. She had struggled to hold any strong sentiments concerning Mr Probius at arm's length to safeguard her heart. The vertigo of darkness that threatened to overcome her at the notion of him leaving proved that she had failed.

'But I have declined their offer.'

Isobel felt her heart resume its normal rhythm. She hoped that her cheeks were not too flushed from her seizure of panic but her face betrayed her untrammelled relief with a broad smile. The smile was returned by the gentleman with such a look of tenderness that it was a fresh spring to Isobel's wilted soul. 'The colony has changed so much for the better in the last few years. I feel, as so many others do, that this strange, infuriating and yet lovely land is my permanent home. I have hopes of making a bright future here.'

'Well, that is good news, Mr Probius,' said her aunt, seemingly oblivious to the dramatic exchange that had just passed between Isobel and the artist. 'But what of your employment, sir, if you do not mind my asking?'

'Ah, yes. It is true that I will no longer have my post as drawing master. But I am confident of securing such a position, or something similar, with another family.'

'I am greatly pleased to hear that,' said Isobel for more reasons than she could name publicly. 'I am sure you will be much missed by Mr and Mrs Cooper and their children.'

Mr Probius asked if he might look at some of Isobel's work, including the sketches she was currently doing for Juniper Hall. Isobel excused herself and hurried to her room to fetch her sketch-books. Her heart was full, agitated by a mix of fear and joy and she could not say what. She had never been so delightfully confused. The looks she exchanged with Mr Probius were as eloquent as the most heartfelt declarations of passion. She prayed that these sentiments were felt equally on both sides.

Mrs Blunt looked on as Mr Probius and her niece sat side by side on the chaise longue with Isobel's sketchbooks in their laps. 'You show a good grasp of perspective here,' said Mr Probius as he studied the first page closely. 'And I like the way you have filled in the shadows under the eaves. That provides a nice sense of weight to the roofline. But you must keep in mind the position of the sun in relation to the building. Shadows must be consistent.'

With careful deliberation, Mr Probius turned the pages. His observations were all expressed with a respectful frankness and sincerity that disclosed no hint of aiming to please. Isobel understood that his criticisms paid her the honour of taking her work as seriously as he would those of an assistant or acolyte. As their talk grew increasingly animated and obscurely technical, with references to charcoal and penmanship and chiaroscuro, Aunt Louisa excused herself. 'Please don't get up. I have one or two matters to attend to. Emmet will refresh the tea tray. I shall be back soon.'

Aunt Louisa shut the drawing room door behind her. This lapse in her aunt's moral vigilance as her chaperone was totally unexpected, if welcomed as evidence of her trust in Mr Probius's honour as a gentleman. Even so, Isobel was taken aback. Was it possible that Aunt Louisa had no idea how she felt about this man? Or did she completely discount the possibility that Mr Probius may have an interest in her? It was then that the novel and alarming thought flashed across Isobel's mind that while Aunt Louisa was undeniably charmed by this handsome and dashing gent, she regarded him as no more than a fop, a dandified drawing master, clever and sweet-natured and stylish but in no sense a hot-blooded man who posed any threat to her niece's morals. Was that even possible?

Left alone, an awkward silence sprang up briefly between the couple seated on the lounge. Isobel spoke first, her heart brimming with feeling. 'My father is going to England after my sister Grace's wedding in two weeks. He will be gone for most of a year.'

She knew exactly why her heart had alighted on this topic as the most urgent to convey in the short time they had alone. If Mr Probius had any honourable intentions regarding her future then he would not be able to seek her father's permission in person for a whole year if he did not act soon. There, she had laid her cards upon the table.

'Miss Macleod.' Charles Probius spoke softly. 'May I call you Isobel?'

'Please do.'

'You know I believe in plain speaking, Isobel.'

She nodded. He prized honesty so greatly he had even taken it as his name.

'I have something to tell you that I cannot in good faith keep secret. I would not wish you to discover this other than directly from my own lips. If—by any good fortune—you should regard me with favour, I would like to take this opportunity to tell you what is in my heart.' Isobel could barely speak. Why did she feel so nervous? Did she have reasons to be afraid? Please let it not be some great obstacle to their love.

'Dearest Isobel. I told you at the ball how I had been curious to meet you from the first time I heard about you. That curiosity has grown quickly, even on so short an acquaintance, into nothing short of fascination. And admiration. And dare I say it, affection.'

'Oh, Mr Probius. Charles,' said Isobel who could not stop a tear or two spilling from her eyes. 'My tears are happy ones. Relief that my own feelings are so perfectly mirrored.'

'Do I dare hope that you regard me with favour?' the artist asked, taking both her hands in his and looking into her eyes with such fervour that she felt consumed by their fire.

'I do.' Neither had spoken the word 'love' but Isobel knew how much she yearned to explore the landscape of that unknown territory with this man.

'Then I must tell you something before either of us takes another step. To not tell you would be deceitful and would put everything at risk. It is the only honourable path.'

Dear God! What was this secret that Mr Probius must confess, so very dreadful that not to confess to it could imperil their courtship, even their love? And in the instant before he opened his mouth, Isobel knew exactly what it was. What else could it be? Her heart stopped.

'You are to going tell me that you were once a convict,' she said.

'So you knew?'

'No, but I have guessed. This is the colony of New South Wales after all.'

'Are you shocked?' the artist asked.

'Surprised. But not shocked,' she lied.

'I want us to have no secrets that could be an impediment to our happiness,' said Charles Probius. He kept one eye on the door in case Aunt Louisa suddenly entered but his voice stayed steady and calm. 'If you can bear to hear the details, I will tell you.'

'Please,' Isobel nodded, barely able to speak.

'In 1832 I was living in London, a poor artist. There were many times I could not find work. I went hungry and homeless. One evening I stole the contents of a rich woman's purse right outside the Royal Opera House at Covent Garden. To this day, I cannot tell you my motive beyond simple desperation. One could imagine a much less public and better-planned theft. But I was no seasoned highwayman; I acted on impulse. I say none of this to excuse my behaviour. I was convicted, sentenced to be hanged and had my sentence transmuted to transportation. After seven years in New South Wales, I was exempted from government service and have plied my trade as a painter ever since.'

Isobel looked at him closely. She knew he told her the truth. It must have cost him dearly. But there was nothing abject in this confession. He told his story with a quiet dignity.

'I do not ask you to tell me now if this alters your view of me,' he continued. 'I want you to have time to think about what I have told you. If you find it in your heart to still look on me with favour, then, of course, I will be the happiest man alive. But you must decide this freely and without consideration for my feelings. You must instead consider your own situation. Including the opinions of your family and friends.'

Isobel was grateful that she had not been pressed to declare her intentions right away. Charles probably knew about her father's views on emancipists, even though the Major had given his blessing for Grace to marry into an emancipist family. 'I thank you for your honesty,' said Isobel. 'I shall do exactly as you ask and you shall have my answer soon.'

The door to the drawing room opened and Aunt Louisa came bustling in. 'Has Emmet not been in to refresh the tea? I shall summon him at once!'

'That is fine, Mrs Blunt, please do not disturb yourself,' said Mr Probius as he stood up from the chaise longue. 'I am expected at Juniper Hall soon and must reluctantly take my leave. Your niece and I have had a most instructive time together. With your permission, I hope I may continue to help with her art tuition in future. I believe she has a fine talent.'

'I think you are right, Mr Probius,' agreed Isobel's proud aunt, still basking in the glow of her niece's New Year's Day triumph. 'I am more than happy for you to come here as often as you think fit to instruct my niece. In fact, I am happy to meet whatever costs are involved from my own purse.'

'Oh, Aunt, that is so generous!' Isobel flung her arms about her aunt's neck. Did Aunt Louisa feel sorry for her niece, forced to stay even longer at Faulconstone? Was this her gift to compensate for Isobel's homesickness? Whatever the reason, it was warmly received.

'Now, now. Dear me, no need for fuss. I believe that a young woman should be accomplished in whatever way she is gifted but never proud. And I have no doubt that the Lord Himself takes pleasure in artistic work that pays tribute to the wonders of His Creation.'

Emmet was ordered to bring in Mr Probius's coat, hat and cane. 'Thank you both for your hospitality,' said Mr Probius as he stood on the threshold of the drawing room door. 'I shall see you soon for our next lesson, Miss Macleod. I bid you both adieu!'

'What a very well-bred gent he is. And so talented,' said Aunt Louisa after the artist took his leave, admiring again the sketch of Faulconstone that sat on her chiffonier. As if in a trance, Isobel nodded her agreement. Her heart was in a state of turmoil, as delight and alarm, passion and fear contested for the upper hand in her emotions.

'Yes, Aunt. Yes, he certainly is.'

Despite Anna's persistent hostility towards her, Isobel accepted the invitation to join her aunt, sisters and father for luncheon at Rosemount the following week to discuss Grace's wedding, which was only six days away, as well as the family's arrangements while the Major was abroad. His plan was to board his ship for England the morning after the wedding feast.

Papa had recently spent two days in bed after a trip away survey-ing an improved detour to the Great South Road and catching a nasty chill, but was up again as soon as he felt fit. Even so, Isobel was shocked to see how much her father's health and state of mind had deteriorated since she had last seen him at Christmas. He appeared paler than she remembered, his skin waxy and grey. Isobel wondered if this was a projection of her own distracted mind but she saw the same concern reflected in her aunt's face.

Her father recharged his glass with claret several times during luncheon and his speech grew more agitated and voluble. He was fighting again with the Governor over his leave pay, expressing in a recent letter his outrage at the 'insult of being put on half pay given my tireless service to Your Excellency and the Executive Council.' He had even written to the Colonial Office challenging the authority of Mr Macleay's commission of inquiry, with the claim that, because of the nature of his appointment as Surveyor-General, the Major reported directly to the sovereign and her ministers and not to the Governor and his Executive Council.

The Major's most immediate cause of grievance was an insulting satirical poem that had recently begun circulating in Sydney. It made cruel fun of the Surveyor-General's quixotic tilts at multiple windmills in pursuit of wealth and fame. While conceding praise for his map-making and road-building, it echoed strident public criticism of the land titles system where surveying work had ground to a standstill in large part due to the Major's distractions and long absences on expeditions and trips abroad. The Major insisted on reading the offensive verse aloud to his family:

> See him of aspect dire and haughty gait,
> As though one man t'were a triumvirate!
> Who dreams of honours, forges Boomerang screws
> And does Ambition with High Dudgeon confuse;
> High roads Colossus once was yours the power
> To move each bullock team as coach and four;
> Go grave your maps, in survey you succeed
> Where praise is worthy, let me grant the meed:
> Thousands of men and money shout for land,
> But here as elsewhere work is at a stand.

'Damn the cowardly scoundrel who wrote this! He should be publicly horsewhipped!' the Major shouted, his face bright red, flushed with anger and wine.

'Please calm yourself, Papa,' said Grace soothingly. 'Nobody takes these silly poems seriously. You have the respect of everyone on the Legislative Council and the most intelligent men of consequence in the colony. Do not trouble yourself with this nonsense.'

But the Major was in no mood to be mollified. There had been renewed speculation that the author was in fact his own son, Joseph, who had already been publicly accused of scurrilous versifying against the young Mr Macleay. Could Joseph possibly have written this before he embarked for India, a parting shot at a father who refused to see him? It seemed inconceivable to Isobel.

'If that ungrateful boy of mine has penned these lines . . .' The Major was too overcome with grief to finish the sentence.

'Shame on the people who have suggested such a thing!' cried Aunt Louisa. 'I do not believe for one moment that Joseph is behind this. He is headstrong, yes, but not a viper.'

Isobel was grieved to see Papa so embittered and besieged on all fronts. She had hoped for a moment alone with him to raise the delicate subject of Mr Charles Probius. She now questioned the wisdom of speaking with him at all when he was in such a disturbed state of mind. But when else would she have the chance before his departure? Certainly not on Grace's wedding day. If she did not broach the subject now, she would have to raise it in a letter, which would take months, and was not her preference as she believed her persuasive powers were greater in person. And so she decided to take her chances.

Her father's mood was much improved by the conclusion of lunch, with the discussion of Grace's forthcoming nuptials and his own plans for London. Grace wished to consult her aunt about the table settings for the wedding breakfast for which Louisa had kindly volunteered that she and Isobel would make fancywork card holders and table ornaments. Anna had drifted upstairs in a funk, leaving Isobel with an opportunity to talk with her father.

'Papa, it looks like the wind has dropped. I would love you to join me for a walk in the gardens.' Her father readily agreed. He was a man who preferred the outdoors, having spent much of his life in the saddle or by a campfire. Nothing gave him more pleasure than the sight of the morning sun breaching the dark ramparts of mountains to the east or the immense starry firewheel in the southern sky circling over his head at night.

They donned their hats and outdoor vestments and set out, the Major seeming rejuvenated by the fresh air and the opportunity to survey his domain. For a while they walked arm in arm in companionable silence, broken only by observations about the garden, the weather and the maritime traffic on the harbour, bristling with masts like the bare trunks of a wintry pine forest. In three days her father would board one of these vessels and be gone.

The Major breathed in a lungful of salty air. 'I hear that the P&O Steam Navigation Company have built a new steamship, the *Chusan*, for the mail service between here and England. She makes her maiden voyage to Sydney very soon. People say she will be able do the entire voyage in only sixty days! Not four to five months as we're used to now. With a bit of luck, my dear, you will have letters from me sooner than you think.'

'I will miss you, Papa,' she said. 'I *have* missed you these last few months.'

'Of course,' said her father, patting her arm with affection. 'But your aunt tells me you have thrived at Faulconstone. You are greatly treasured in her circle of friends and acquaintances. I hope you feel the benefit of your time there.'

'I do,' replied Isobel. 'It has turned out better than I could have hoped.'

They strolled on a little further into the wood walk that had been thickly dotted with orchids when Isobel last wandered here in the spring. The Major rested on the same rustic seat where she had sat sketching when her brothers' carriage arrived all those months before. Isobel sat beside him.

'Your aunt has told me about your commission for a study of Juniper Hall,' said her father. 'Congratulations! Maybe you should do Rosemount next? I flatter myself I had a hand in encouraging your talents for drawing when you were younger.'

Isobel kissed him on the cheek. 'Dear Papa, you know you did! And I was encouraged by your example too. Your lovely drawings. You showed me some of your sketchbooks from when you were a young lieutenant in Spain, do you remember?'

The Major nodded, pleased that Isobel recalled him sharing these juvenile scribblings with her in a moment of unguarded intimacy between father and daughter.

'I loved that drawing you did of a soldier lying on the grass, propped up on his elbow reading a book. Still wearing his helmet. Such a telling picture! Snatching a few moments alone from the blood and smoke of battle. No one ever looked so glad to be lost in a book.'

The Major smiled ruefully. 'That seems a very long time ago now. But drawing has always given me the greatest pleasure, even if my achievements are meagre.'

'You are far too modest, Papa. But I know exactly what you mean,' said Isobel. 'Which brings me to a subject on which I seek your counsel. In my own modest artistic efforts, I have been favoured with a mentor. You may know him.'

'Indeed! Who is he?'

'Mr Charles Probius, the artist.'

'Yes, I remember that name. I think he was engaged as a draughtsman at the colonial architect's office for a while. Taught sketching to some of the younger civil and military officers,' recalled her father. 'Talented fellow. I have a copy of his lithographs *Natives of New South Wales*—portraits of native men and women. Quite beautiful.'

'It was Mr Probius who introduced me to Mr Cooper and praised my work to him,' said Isobel, a little encouraged by her father's good opinion of her suitor. 'He also purchased my sketch of the Botanic Gardens at the bazaar on New Year's Day. Did Aunt Louisa tell you?'

'She told me it had sold for a handsome sum, and highly praised your work.'

'Has Aunt told you anything about him, Papa?' inquired Isobel, her cheeks growing warm and her hands moist in nervous anticipation.

The Major looked his daughter full in the face, his own expression kindly but curious. 'No, she has not. Is there something *you* wish to tell me about this gentleman, Isobel?'

Isobel could not hide her feelings. She blushed and a coy smile spread across her face. 'How can I describe him, Papa? He is so courteous and kind, so attentive and sympathetic. I have good reasons to believe he admires me a great deal. And respects my talent.'

'Has he told you as much?'

'Yes. Yes, he has.'

'And do you know what his intentions are? Has he proposed?'

'No, not yet. But I think it is possible.'

'Well, well,' smiled the Major. 'That is good news. I believe he is highly regarded and makes a good living as a portraitist, is that right?'

'I imagine so. He has been the drawing master to Mrs Cooper and her children these last few years. He intends to seek a new position when they return to England.'

'I see. So, tell me, Isobel, do you have feelings for this fellow?'

'Oh, Papa!' Tears welled in her eyes. Her emotions had crept up on her, taken her by surprise. 'I do. We have not known each other long. But there is much I admire in him.'

'Well, my dear, that is a very good start. But you seem . . . troubled.'

'He has told me something that he believes should not—in fact cannot—be kept hidden.' She took a deep breath. There was no retreating now. She must tell her father Mr Probius's shameful secret. 'He came to the colony as a convict. But he is now a free man.'

'Ah, I see.' The Major nodded. His face darkened. He sighed. It was obvious his mood had changed as suddenly as when a cloud passes in front of the sun. Isobel continued, flustered, but determined to make her case. 'He knows what it means to bear shame. But he has served his sentence and been reprieved. I believe that he has truly repented for his past and redeemed himself in the eyes of the world. He—I—we both wish to have your blessing before our courtship goes any further. If that is possible.'

She realised how breathless she sounded. She studied her father's face for signs of hope. 'Do you know the nature of his crime?' asked the Major.

'When he was a young man, he stole the contents of a woman's purse.'

The Major nodded again, taking in this information. 'Did he say why?'

'He was poor. Homeless and hungry. But he does not believe that excuses him.'

The Major thought in silence for a minute. He seemed pained, his face set in a grim scowl, his shoulders hunched as if a terrible weight oppressed them. He sighed several times and wrung his hands nervously. It seemed that there were too many burdens for him to bear all at once: Alice and her son, Grace's wedding, his fight with the Governor. And now this.

He spoke at last. 'I have already embraced the *son* of an emancipist as my future son-in-law. And so, I suppose you think it is only fair I should do the same for an emancipist.' The Major took his daughter's hand in his. He looked at her intently for a moment and then let his gaze settle on the middle distance, somewhere in the dappled shade of the forest.

'I wish I could give you my blessing, Isobel. But I cannot.'

Isobel whimpered in shock. Tears spilled from her eyes.

'Please, hear me out, I entreat you. Our family has endured such unrelenting public humiliation these last few months. I wear some responsibility for this, of course. I am happy to admit it. The duel was ill-advised and has given rise to vile gossip. People we thought of as friends have deserted us. And it has done nothing to help your prospects, Isobel. I fear for your future. To make matters worse, your poor sister, Alice, has been appallingly deceived and as good as abandoned by her husband. You can hardly blame me for being protective of you, my dear. Men—some unscrupulous men—will tell lies to convince women of their fitness as husbands and to steal their family names. If only I had listened to your mother.'

The Major's face was ashen. His right hand shook. Isobel could hardly bear to see her father in such torment. As a little girl, she had been in the habit of looking up at his tall, immovable frame, and standing in the shadow of his broad chest and square shoulders. He was a colossus then, untroubled by doubt or fear, impregnable, supremely confident in himself and the future. Now he appeared more diminished than ever, a tremulous old man.

'I swore to Winnie that I would look after you all. But what am I to do? I have no idea what will happen to Anna now that Grace is to be married. Who will care for her? I can only hope that Joseph will come to his senses under William's influence and stop behaving so scandalously. And you, my youngest, my sweet but headstrong daughter, how am I to take care of you?'

'Oh, Papa,' Isobel moaned, her heart breaking.

'You deserve a husband who commands the respect of all society. Only in that assurance can you feel protected. Only in that can you know that your children are safe. A reputation is a fragile thing, easily broken, almost impossible to repair. This man, Probius, may feel he has repaid his debt. He may be a good man, a kind man, a well-meaning man. But how do others view him? I do not know. He may be a very fine artist, even a successful one, but is this enough to save his reputation, to make him a worthy husband and father?' He looked at Isobel and spread his hands. 'I do not know.'

The Major then took a handkerchief from his jacket pocket and mopped his brow. The sun came dappled through the trees but still his forehead glistened with perspiration.

'That is why I cannot risk my daughter's future in his hands unless I am reassured that he is a respectable man. Do you think I am being unfair? Why should I let Grace marry into Robert Cooper's family, you ask, but not approve this possible union with Mr Probius? Grace's betrothed is the *son* of an emancipist, don't you see? He does not bear any blame for his father's crimes. Augustus was born innocent, washed clean of his father's sin. He has remained virtuous, hard-working, respected all his life. Yes, there will be those who shun him, tar him with his father's crimes, insist on an inherited shame. But no one can justifiably point an accusing finger at Augustus for anything he has done, suspect him of any vice, distrust his character or have doubts about his own past. He is not and never was a convict. That, my dear, is the difference.'

Isobel stared into her lap where her hands were folded. She whispered, 'I . . . I think . . . I love him, Papa.'

The Major's face softened. He placed a hand on Isobel's shoulder. 'And I love you, my dear. I do not wish to be cruel or tyrannical. I only want to protect you.'

Isobel could not look at her father. 'Please, Papa. Give him a chance. I beg you. Meet him, talk to him. You have much in common. You will like him. I am sure of it.'

'I leave for England in four days. There is much I have to do before I go. And there is your sister's wedding to attend to. I would need to know more about this man before I could give you my blessing. There is no time now. Our family has been the subject of so much vicious scrutiny and gossip of late, how can I risk your reputation any further?'

'Perhaps you could meet with him when you return? And you could inquire about his reputation with anyone—even when you are abroad—to find the reassurance that you need. Aunt Louisa and the ladies of the Benevolent Society hold him in very high esteem.' Poor Isobel was clutching at straws. If she could just keep the door of fear and prejudice in her father's mind chinked open long enough, perhaps there was some hope of saving Mr Probius.

'Very well, I promise to meet him on my return. But until then, I cannot give my blessing. You will both have to wait, do you understand? If he does love you and wants to do what is best for you both, he will understand the reasons why.'

Isobel smiled at her father through her tears. She felt there was a small shred of hope for her to hang on to. 'I will tell him this. I promise.' She felt like the little girl who, following her failed 'expedition' to Rushcutters Bay, had stood in the Major's study and sworn an oath on the family Bible to 'never do anything like that ever again'.

The Major nodded. A change of mood came over him then and he spoke in a low, hushed voice, almost as if making a confession.

'I admit that we can all make mistakes. What man can honestly look back on his life and say he is blameless? That would be an act of supreme arrogance. We are sometimes a victim of circumstances or the plaything of low and base impulses. We commit sins and wish to only be given the chance to atone for them.'

The Major looked again at his daughter. 'All my life I have tried to do what I thought was right. But I too am not without regrets. I too have made mistakes. Terrible mistakes.' He held his daughter's hand with a touching paternal tenderness. His right hand still trembled.

'I miss you, Papa. Please write to me often. I will count the days until you are home safely again.' She knew there was nothing more she could say to change her father's mind. It was enough for now that he might meet Charles when he returned. Father and daughter sat for a while, her hand in his, watching a flock of rosellas tumble overhead as if in celebration of the ever-present possibility that life is full of promise and joy, despite all the odds.

The wedding day arrived. Grace was radiant in her white silk gown with scalloped flounces, a blue sash and a tulle veil with a coronet of bluebells. Her bridesmaids wore white muslin sashed in blue silk, with bonnets trimmed in blue velvet ribbons and posies of lily of the valley. The bridal party included three of the Misses Finch and Bradley but Isobel could not begrudge Grace that. St James' was filled to capacity with friends and family. Aunt Louisa and Mrs Palmer sat in the front pew, alternately smiling and crying, while Anna sat two places along, her face a thundercloud at not having been chosen as the matron of honour, that position having gone to one of Augustus's sisters.

Augustus wore a fine yellow silk waistcoat and a well-cut dark green frock coat. His moonish face glowed with contentment. On the few occasions that Isobel had met him she found Augustus to be a dry, punctilious fellow despite the sybaritic cast of his face and fleshiness of his form. But it was obvious Grace was in a rapture that looked very much like love. She had never appeared more animated or carefree, having shed the carapace of pain and disappointment that had grown around her soul as protection against life's inevitable blows.

Isobel had suffered a great deal under Grace's tyranny but today she was disposed to forgive her a little. She knew that Grace had for a long time felt taken for granted by both her parents: the neglected middle sister, living in the shadow of the accomplished and beautiful Alice, eclipsed by the novelty of talented Isobel, made the guardian of her troubled sister Anna and even held responsible for her imperfections. Her failure to inherit the opal dragonfly from her mother perfectly symbolised the cause of Grace's self-pity. Everyone knew how much Grace loved jewellery, took an expert pleasure in it, knew the names of the most famous cutters, designers and houses and had made no secret of her passion for her mother's brooch. At Winnie's funeral, Grace stood dry-eyed, her body clenched in rage against her dead mother. This was proof again of life's unfairness: even though it was Grace who took Winnie's place and kept Rosemount running smoothly, it was Isobel who was the favoured object of her mother's affections and her father's indulgence. But for today, at least, all this acrimonious history was put aside.

Even so, little did Grace know that on her wedding day, Isobel stood in the front pew of the church with Winnie's opal dragonfly hanging like a pendant on a fine silver chain beneath her blouse. Isobel could feel the weight of it close to her heart and the stone cold against her bare skin. She had her own reasons for this subterfuge.

After the doleful scene with her father in the forest at Rosemount, it had taken a supreme act of will for Isobel to conceal her distress. But as soon as she found refuge in the privacy of her room back at Faulconstone, she had poured out all the bitter heartache and rage her father's betrayal had stirred up in her. Her screams of anguish and the cataract of her weeping, though muffled by pillows, had continued unabated for a long time.

How could Papa be so heartless? She could not believe it possible. She had even confessed her love for Charles Probius and her father had withheld his consent. The unfairness of her situation was unbearable. Grace was to be married to the son of a vulgar, uneducated gin distiller from Stepney, grown rich from peddling 'mother's ruin', the curse of the working class, while posing as a hero of the same, and convicted for receiving three thousand pounds' worth of stolen goods to be sold, no doubt, on the black market. Whereas Isobel had declared *her* love for a refined, cultured and talented man, an artist highly esteemed by the colony's richest families. His crime had been born out of hunger and despair, not greed, and he had been convicted for purloining the contents of a woman's purse worth—at Isobel's best guess—fifty pounds. Where was the justice in that? What nice distinctions Father had made between the permanently stained ex-convict and the blameless, untainted son of a convict!

Feeling more alone now than ever before, Isobel had taken the opal dragonfly from its secret place and held it in her hands. She spoke, as if in prayer, to her dead mother. 'Oh, Mama, what have I done to deserve this? I have always been obedient, always respectful of your guidance, never questioned your judgement, even when it broke my young heart. But *this*! From my father who plunged me and this family into disgrace with his French pistols and wounded pride! Oh, Mama, you would have been scared to death and so ashamed! Please, Mama, show me what to do. Let the dragonfly open my eyes to my future!'

She stopped then, realising she was speaking utter nonsense. Had she been driven insane? She did not know. But clasping the brooch in her hand, she felt comforted nonetheless, as if her mother had heard her plea. Whatever the truth, she decided then and there to wear the dragonfly at Grace's wedding. It seemed fitting: an act of brazen defiance against her father and sister, a silent protest against Papa's approval of Grace's marriage and Grace's selfish joy in it. Who was the favoured daughter now? Isobel thought bitterly.

She had not yet given her answer to Charles as she had promised at their meeting at Faulconstone. She was so afraid that if she told him the truth, it would spell the end of their friendship before it had barely had a chance to take root. Whether out of forlorn hope or injured dignity, it was probable that Charles would make a quick and gracious exit—just as Major Tranter had before him. And where would that leave disgraced Isobel then? Condemned to a life as a lonely spinster, as unloved and unhinged as her wretched sister Anna. So for now, she resolved to say nothing to Charles. Nothing at all.

Over the last two days, Isobel had kept her counsel and did her best to appear happy for Grace and to help with the nuptials. It was a painful pantomime, as it no doubt also was for miserable Anna. Aunt Louisa helped Grace prepare her trousseau of linen and plate while Father bestowed a generous dowry, a vote of confidence in the couple's bright future. Isobel was not familiar with the terms of her father's will but she assumed that with the death of her brother Richard, the banishment of Joseph and even possibly the new crisis with Alice, Father had made adjustments. The fate of Rosemount was a matter for conjecture among the siblings as Father had not yet made public how he intended to dispose of it on his death.

Isobel felt sick at heart as she watched the wedding ceremony. That could be her at the altar, veiled and serene, by Charles Probius's side if only her father would relent. She glanced along the pew to where the Major sat, dressed in his most expensive blue frock coat and lilac waistcoat. He appeared to be in a state of unassailable bliss. No doubt, in his eyes these nuptials were a triumph and godsend. In this hallowed marital contract he had found a haven for Grace and was about to rescue dear Alice from her desecrated one.

The wedding breakfast was a sumptuous banquet, laid out on tables on the lawn at Rosemount in defiance of the summer winds. The speeches were mercifully short and heartwarmingly affectionate and the whole company cheered and raised their glasses many times to wish the happy couple a propitious, fertile and prosperous future. The day was blessed in every way. There was still laughter and music and dancing on the lawn when the first star appeared in the evening sky over the harbour.

Chapter 25

SECRETS

FEBRUARY 1852

That night Isobel had another bad dream.

Again, she awoke in her old bedroom at Rosemount to the sound of the great house creaking and listing like a stricken ship. When Isobel sat up she found her room had already keeled over, its furniture like so much driftwood piled up against the wall. She dragged herself to the window and looked out. No tempest raged, no screaming wind or high water, but lightning flickered in the dark cloudbanks on the horizon and the muffled timpani of thunder could be heard in the distance. As far as the eye could see stretched the ocean under a fog-white sky, as still as a mirror and the colour of tin. The sun shone on this dead calm sea with a dull sheen. Far and wide, flotsam was scattered, stuck fast as if in treacle. This was the aftermath of Isobel's first dream, once the violent storm and the great wave had passed.

Isobel crawled across the sloped floor as before, finding the tiny key and pocketing her dragonfly brooch before climbing the spiral staircase to the roof. From here Isobel surveyed the bleak ocean in all directions. And there in the middle distance she saw a rowboat with a hunched figure busy at the oars. This was unmistakeably her Charles. Isobel could hear the dip and splash of each stroke but she could not be sure if the boat was travelling towards or away from her. She could see Charles's handsome face as he looked hopefully in her direction but his strenuous efforts seemed to gain him no progress. The oars struck against the proliferation of objects all about, suspended like vegetables in thick soup. She recognised the wreckage of Rosemount's furniture, the Broadwood piano, the chiffonier, a wooden globe with its upper half stove in, glass cases of butterflies, her father's precious leatherbound books circling lazily like a fever of stingrays, Conrad Martens' painting, face up.

Isobel heard water lapping at the courtyard wall that surrounded Rosemount's dome and rooftop. She realised that the ocean, though flat and unruffled in appearance, was imperceptibly creeping higher and higher. With a bright burbling, a gush of water rushed over the lip of the wall and pooled around her ankles. The house was still sinking.

'Charles! Charles!' she screamed. Dear God! Charles was her only escape. If she stayed here on this rooftop she would drown. As if her dream could not become any stranger, she heard a young voice behind her, giggling. *The stars, Izzie. Up there, look. Stars, eh?*'

There stood Ballandella, still a girl of only four dressed in the guise of a well-bred young lady, pointing towards the horizon. The clouds overhead had fled, revealing a blue-black sky peppered thickly with stars. Despite her desperate situation, Isobel could not help feeling a mantle of deep peace settle over her. She smiled at her childhood playmate and hurried to embrace her. But Ballandella had already stripped off her muslin dress and discarded her shoes, gloves and hat. She stood on the edge of the courtyard wall in nothing but her petticoats. 'Time to go, Izzie,' she said, and with a shout launched herself into the sea.

Isobel woke in a state of disquiet. How strange it was to have dreamed so vividly about Rosemount and to wake instead in her attic bedroom in Faulconstone, still a refugee from her beloved home. It was the morning of her father's departure so it was understandable she should be preoccupied. Her rational daylight mind dismissed her dream as nothing more than a maudlin fancy, fashioned out of her anger against Father and anxiety about Charles. She dressed, now almost out of habit secreting under her blouse the dragonfly brooch on its chain, her constant companion and confidante, and went down for breakfast with Aunt Louisa. As she descended the main stairs, a sense of profound unease lingered.

That unease was not dispelled when she was greeted in the breakfast room by her aunt. 'Good morning, my dear. There is something your father has asked me talk to you about.' Her aunt cracked the top off her soft-boiled egg, ready to receive its strips of buttered toast.

Isobel fetched a plate of kippers from the sideboard and poured a cup of tea. She apologised for not attending morning devotionals at half past six as she had suffered a bad night's sleep and could not be woken by the housemaid. 'What is it you have to tell me, Aunt?'

'As you know, your father leaves for England this morning. And in the next day or two Grace will join her husband at their splendid home at Hunters Hill to start their new life there.' Aunt Louisa had each hand splayed, fingertips pressed together in a mirror image, mimicking the shape of a pyramid. The two index fingers of this pyramid rested against her upper lip, a gesture implying careful consideration. 'Your father has decided to close up Rosemount while he is away. The staff will be dismissed and a caretaker and gardener left in residence.' Isobel looked thunderstruck that Papa had not communicated such momentous news in person. Her voice cracked as she asked, 'But why?'

'The Major has been struggling with this decision for some time,' said her aunt, recognising Isobel's shocked look of hurt. 'As you can imagine, Rosemount costs a considerable sum of money to maintain. With Grace no longer there to manage the house, your father will have to hire a head housekeeper. Depending on the outcome of the Governor's report, he may no longer have the income to sustain these costs.' Aunt Louisa tapped her fingers against her top lip. She seemed to be debating with herself whether to go on. 'I think it is possible, Isobel, that he may wish to sell the house when he returns. Especially if the government's report means he will be forced to retire.'

'Sell Rosemount?'

This was more than momentous news; this was earth-shattering. Rosemount was Isobel's and her siblings' inheritance. She had always imagined that it would stay in the family and that one of them would end up living and raising their own children there as Winnie and Angus had done. It was impossible to contemplate it in the hands of another family. 'I am not saying that is what *will* happen,' warned her aunt. 'It is just a possibility.'

'And what will happen to Anna?'

'Ah, now that is what I have to tell you,' said Aunt Louisa. 'There was a discussion about her going to live as a companion to Mrs Palmer. But the dear woman is eighty-two and has been suffering from a terrible bout of nerves of late. It was felt that . . . well, it was considered not fair to burden Mrs Palmer with any extra responsibility.' Anna had no friends as such. Isobel could not imagine the Finches or Bradleys taking her in. Nor could she live at Rosemount all by herself, taking on Grace's role of looking after the house and Father. She had neither the wit nor surety of mind to be trusted in that capacity.

'Until we arrive at a better arrangement, I have agreed that she can stay here,' announced Aunt Louisa. The hall clock struck a quarter past seven, its chimes splitting the silence like the tolling of a church bell. Isobel stopped breathing for several seconds. She heard a loud buzzing in her ears as if she was about to faint.

'Isobel, my dearest, you look terrible!' Her aunt was suitably alarmed as her niece spilled her tea and her face drained of all colour. How could Isobel even begin to explain to her aunt the secret history of Anna's troubled mind? This was an unforeseen catastrophe: Rosemount to be sold and Anna to live in the same house as Isobel with no Grace to umpire her temper tantrums. Charles! thought Isobel, with an absolute conviction that her only route to survival was escape into the arms of her lover. The dismal prospect of being trapped at Faulconstone with Anna for the rest of her days was now an even greater spur to Isobel's love and determination to be married, as if she needed any greater incentive.

'What does Anna feel about this arrangement?' she asked.

'Your father hasn't told her yet. He plans to explain it all to her this morning.' Isobel did not like to think about how Anna would receive the news that she was to be expelled from Rosemount and forced into exile at Faulconstone with Isobel.

'Come, it is time for us to repair to Circular Quay for your father's departure,' said Aunt Louisa briskly, rising from her soft-boiled eggs and toast, seemingly unaware of the trauma her announcement had inflicted.

Isobel, Grace, Anna, Aunt Louisa, and Mrs Palmer made a tearful chorus at the dock where the brigantine *Johnstone* was taking on its last few passengers. Accompanying this honour guard of female tenderness was the stoic figure of Augustus. The whole company was gathered at the quay to bid farewell to the Major on this cool summer morning, a strong wind whipping off the harbour. The trunks had been loaded earlier and the Major now stood by the gangplank in his smartest bell-topper, swathed in his greatcoat against the wind and carrying only a leather portmanteau. In consultation with the petty officer, he had learned that among his fellow travellers were a Dr and Mrs Poet, Mr Lethridge, a retired solicitor, and Mr Lang and Mr Cummins, two business-men. 'I sincerely hope some of these characters will furnish me with diverting conversation for the next four months,' said the Major. 'Otherwise I shall have to content myself with redrafting my speeches.'

With favourable weather, the ship was expected to arrive at Gravesend in late June. The Major was excited about the engagements he had secured in London and in the counties to address marine engineering institutes about the prototype of his 'boomerang' screw. Over the last few years the Admiralty had been busy converting their warships from paddlewheel to propeller-screw propulsion, and the Major saw a very profitable market opportunity for his innovation. He also hoped to speak with one of his patrons, Lord Sherbourne, a former Under-Secretary in the Colonial Office, who might intercede with his superiors on the Major's behalf when the Governor delivered the commission's report. He had already written to arrange a meeting with his brother Fergus shortly after his arrival and had promised to send any news regarding Alice as soon as he was able. 'I will write to you at Faulconstone, Louisa my dear. The caretaker at Rosemount will send on any other mail that arrives there.'

With all practical talk exhausted, the time came for embarkation. The pangs of longing that usually attended such scenes of farewell were also underwritten by fear. Only three days ago *The Sydney Morning Herald* had reported the horrifying tragedy of the HMS *Birkenhead* lost off the South African coast with 643 soldiers and civilians on board. She had hit an uncharted rock and sank rapidly. All the soldiers stood aside to let the women and children board the available lifeboats. Only 193 passengers survived. At every breakfast table across the Empire, people caught their breath at such proof of British pluck and chivalry but also the mortal danger that stalked every sea traveller.

The party on the dock waved at the dark shape of the *Johnstone*, growing ever smaller until she shrank into an indistinguishable dot, swallowed up in the blue vastness beyond the Heads. 'I hope Papa has a safe passage,' murmured Isobel, reluctantly breaking off her intense surveillance of the departing ship and her tenuous connection with her father.

Isobel was now faced with two challenges.

The first was to accept the fact that Anna was coming to live with her and that she must negotiate a *modus vivendi* to make life bearable for them both. When Anna arrived with all her belongings, she was in a dark, subdued mood, as was to be expected from anyone who had just bade farewell to her sister, father and home all in a matter of twenty-four hours and whose prospects were, at best, unclear. While she had her periodic bouts of delusion and anger, in her more lucid moments she was cunning and fearful enough to realise her fate now hung in the balance, and so she had made a resolution to be as well behaved as her demons would allow her. She understood the need to settle amicably into her new life at Faulconstone as the possible alternatives were much more unpleasant and intimidating. Isobel's heart was pierced with a strange pity to see Anna so unnaturally quiet.

For the first month or so Anna did her best. She continued to attend music classes with Madame Bertheau, German classes with Mrs Arnold and dance classes with Mrs Acutt, although at times even she wondered what point there was in an ornamental education with no prospects of marriage in the offing. Music was Anna's truest passion, the one that she expressed daily for no other purpose than to lose herself in its perfectible beauty. Aunt Louisa agreed that Anna could bring the family's Broadwood with her from Rosemount as it was as familiar to her touch as her own face. It was her refuge, her shrine, her intimate.

Aunt Louisa's Methodist tastes tended towards heart-stirring hymns like 'Guide Me, Oh Thou Great Redeemer' and 'O'er the Gloomy Hills of Darkness', the second verse of which she would sing with exceptionally pious gusto, thinking of the good work of missionaries among the pagan natives of the Australian wilderness:

> Let the Indian, let the Negro,
> Let the rude Barbarian see
> That divine and glorious Conquest
> Once obtain'd on Calvary;
> Let the Gospel
> Loud resound from Pole to Pole.

Anna condescended to play these hymns for Aunt Louisa at her twice-daily devotionals. By way of exchange, the widow agreed to indulge a guilty pleasure in the sacred music of Mozart and Bach and the secular delights of Chopin's études, nocturnes, preludes, polonaises and mazurkas. Morning and evening, Anna could be found at the Broadwood in the drawing room in rapturous execution of her beloved Chopin. Ever since the Polish composer's death two and a half years earlier, Anna had become obsessed with his music and religiously paid tribute to him twice daily, her own version of matins and evensong. Isobel suspected that Chopin had come to occupy a place in Anna's heart akin to an unrequited love. What objections could anyone have to this harmless devotion if it kept Anna's inner turmoil pacified?

The second challenge that Isobel faced—and perhaps the greater one—was what to tell Charles. The previous week he had sent Isobel a short note to ask if the following Monday was suitable for their next art lesson at Faulconstone. She had already written him a brief apology for being so busy with her sister's wedding and father's departure and he had accepted her explanation gracefully with no hint of anxiety or annoyance. But now the day approached when Charles Probius would expect an answer to his question.

Isobel had been raised to believe that honesty was always the best policy in the knowledge that nothing escaped the attention of God. But there were some exceptions. As a child, she had tested God's alertness when she bribed a maid and hid a key for her solitary vigils under the stars beside Rosemount's dome. By good fortune she had never been discovered or asked to explain the missing key. And then her mother had begged her to keep the opal dragonfly hidden from her own family. Surely she must not break that promise! She now wore it secretly every day next to her heart as a talisman of her mother's love and faith.

It was alarming how easy the habit of lying could become.

Was there any reason she should tell Charles the truth now her father had left for a year? If she chose not to, would she not be inevitably found out? She decided she would face those consequences when the time came but right now her chief object was not to lose Charles. To Isobel's surprise, Aunt Louisa seemed unaware of the Major's injunction against her courtship with the ex-convict and of Isobel's promise to obey her father. Had the Major left it solely to his daughter to comply with his solemn request or had he raised it with his sister before he departed? The only evidence that anything had been said was Aunt Louisa's remark in passing that Isobel's father had asked for her 'to keep a close eye on you'.

'Why would he say that?' asked Isobel over supper the night after the Major's departure, a lump rising in her throat as she feared what would come next.

'Well, my dear, I assume it means no more than that he loves you and wants to protect you,' her aunt observed. 'Poor Alice has paid such a heavy price for her husband's deception. Which is why your father has become so wary of the flattering attentions of young suitors! That is all.'

Isobel held her breath in anticipation of Mr Probius's banishment. And then in the very next sentence, Aunt Louisa put her mind at rest. 'So when is your next drawing lesson, my dear?' Her aunt's change of tone implied she had switched to a new topic. By some preordained miracle (awkwardly unflattering to Mr Probius, perhaps), her aunt made no connection between the elegant art master and the threat of predatory male suitors.

'He asked if next Monday was convenient,' said Isobel. 'Oh, and he is also bringing that lithograph he promised you. Done by Mr Austin, one of the finest printers in the colony, so he tells me.'

'He is such a charming gentleman, that Mr Probius,' mused Aunt Louisa, already imagining where the picture would be hung on her drawing room wall. 'I think it is important you keep busy with your lessons. It will keep your mind off your father's absence.'

Out of compassion or by mistake, God had given Isobel her aunt's misunderstanding as a gift. But God never made mistakes so she was happy to receive it as a sign of His love: a blessing. There was too much at stake to do otherwise. Of course, Isobel deeply trusted that Charles loved her, but she could see no reason to put that love at risk when—all in good time—her father may very well change his mind. Why throw away her only chance at happiness on an absurd principle? She would not let this unusual, sympathetic and considerate man slip through her fingers. She simply would not.

So it came to pass that Isobel Clara Macleod took her destiny into her own hands with her characteristic impulsiveness and courage. She sat in her room late one night, staring into the bright firelight of the opal dragonfly, and spoke to her mother, seeking reassurance. 'You would like him, Mama, I know you would,' she whispered. 'Such a clever and unusual man. He wants to nurture my talent, teach me new ways of seeing the world.'

Charles Probius arrived the following Monday with the lithograph of Faulconstone tucked under his arm as he had promised. Aunt Louisa was seduced by its expressive beauty. He was crafty, thought Isobel, when she saw how effortlessly he charmed her aunt. To be honest, it did the dowager no harm to have her heart animated again by gentlemanly courtesy and attention. No one could blame her for being flattered.

The art master and the student soon retired to the morning room, where Isobel's easel and paint set had already been assembled.

Charles took off his apricot suede gloves and his cherry-coloured frock coat and the lesson began. Perspective. After ten minutes or so, Isobel put down her charcoal. 'I promised to give you my answer,' she said.

'You have spoken to your father then? I did not want to burden you, but the matter has been pressing on my mind,' Charles confessed. 'Has your father left for England yet?'

'I have spoken to him. And yes, he has left for England, I'm afraid.'

'And?'

'He is in favour of the match!' she said, her face breaking into a broad smile. Charles beamed at her with a look of almost indescribable relief and gratitude. And then he frowned a little. He had detected a note of reservation in Isobel's voice.

'Is there something wrong?'

'No, no, not at all,' lied Isobel. 'My father has no objection to our courtship. In principle. He would still like to meet you in person and discuss your proposal for my hand in marriage.' Isobel blushed at her own boldness and hastened to add, 'If that should be what you seek, of course. He is old-fashioned that way. He apologises for not being able to meet you before he had to hurry away to England.' Isobel briefly explained her sister Alice's heartbreaking dilemma and explained how urgent it was that Father attempt to find and rescue her and his grandson.

'That is a truly terrible situation. Of course I understand.' Charles looked genuinely shocked to hear of the young Baron's deceit and Alice's abandonment. 'I hope Alice and Xavier will be able to return safely to Australia as soon as possible. You must miss her.'

'I do.' Isobel nodded. 'There is one other important matter to consider.' She sighed and her breathing became a little shallow and rapid. 'I hope you will not think our family history is nothing but an imbroglio of scandals and emotional dramas. My mother died a few years ago, as did my poor brother Richard. It has affected our family deeply.'

'I know something of your sorrows, Isobel. Mrs Cooper told me a little of your family's trials. Both deaths must have been a shocking blow to you and your siblings. Not to mention your poor father.'

'Yes. Yes, they were. And this has made everyone very—how can I put it fairly?—fearful . . . wary of the future. The first good news we have had in a long time was my sister Grace's betrothal. To be honest, I think Grace had given up all hope of finding a husband.'

'It is a great blessing to find someone to share your life with,' Charles said with an appreciative smile as he studied Isobel's face tenderly.

'My father is very protective of both my sisters, who have suffered severely since my mother's death. He does not want to disturb their peace of mind. Grace can be seized with the most unreasonable fits of jealousy, as can Anna. Both have often regarded me as Father's favourite.' Isobel grinned guiltily. 'Not without good reason.'

'I see.'

'Father has asked a great favour of me. And you. That we conduct our courtship in private and with the greatest discretion. He is worried that both Anna and Grace will become jealous of our . . .'—Isobel blushed a little—'. . . of our fervent friendship. He hopes that you will be patient and caring enough to give them both time. Time for Grace to grow in confidence in her marriage. And for Anna to make peace with her new situation.'

'I hope to prove myself both patient and caring enough to be worthy of your love, Miss Isobel Macleod.'

Isobel's eyes sparkled. 'I knew you would understand! Less than a twelvemonth from now Father will give his formal consent to our engagement. This will afford us time to grow closer in spirit and in mind, unhindered by my siblings' resentment or any vicious talk abroad about our family. I have endured enough of that!'

'So it shall be. Time heals all wounds, they say. Your aunt seems happy for me to be your art tutor and pay you regular visits.'

Isobel laughed. 'Dear Aunt. I do not think she has yet understood the nature of our friendship. I see no reason to disabuse her!'

Mr Probius laughed, with a mischievous spark in his eyes. 'Dear, oh dear, you are asking me to dissemble? To traduce my name and my sacred vow to honesty? You are more wicked than I thought, Isobel Macleod.'

Isobel was taken by surprise when Mr Probius sealed their lover's covenant with a sly wink and a gallant press of his lips to the fingers of her right hand. 'It shall be our secret then, my sweet. Until your father returns.'

Isobel sighed dreamily at the bliss of her lover's first kiss, albeit so light and delicate a one. But she also sighed from relief at Charles's willingness to believe her, and her own exhaustion from such a sustained burst of duplicitous and creative invention. 'I will write to Father tonight and reassure him he has nothing to fear, my dear Charles.'

And so, under cover of being Isobel Macleod's drawing master who visited Faulconstone weekly and assisted with her commission at Juniper Hall as often as required, Mr Charles Probius had the perfect pretext to covertly make love to his young bride-in-waiting for the best part of the coming year. To be honest, it appealed to his sense of theatre and daring, very much in the spirit of a true bohemian.

Chapter 26

LOVE

MARCH TO AUGUST 1852

What followed were some of the happiest months of Isobel's life. In the weeks and months after the Major's departure and Grace's wedding, Charles and Isobel spent many blissful hours together, either in art classes in the morning room at Faulconstone or sketching *en plein air* on excursions around Sydney with Mrs Palmer or Aunt Louisa. If the weather looked fine, they took up their sketchbooks and easels and picnicked by the waters at Coogee, Bronte, Manly, Clontarf and Botany Bay. They even embarked on a three-day excursion, accompanied by Mrs Drummond and her two daughters, all keen art students, to the sublime crags and waterfalls of the Blue Mountains.

'These misty valleys and majestic bluffs are nothing short of a paradise for painters!' declared Charles, overcome with admiration. Charles was a patient and inspiring teacher, courteous, encouraging, full of passionate enthusiasm and generous praise for his fellow artists Glover, Earle, Evans and Eyre, as well as the talented women botanical illustrators Mrs Louisa Meredith and the Scott sisters.

Meanwhile he and Isobel rejoiced in their knowledge of each other as it grew, day by day. By the exercise of great stealth and discipline, they managed to avoid stirring up any suspicion or scandal regarding their 'friendship'. Isobel was relieved, of course, that no one in her social sphere had guessed her feelings for Mr Probius or his for her. And yet, while she appreciated his gallantry, she also fretted in the private pages of her journal about his 'lack of ardour': *Am I hopelessly wicked for wanting something more? Some sign of affection apart from his courtesy and kindness.* Her 'wicked' prayers were soon answered.

It was early April. The leaves were turning in the garden and the last of the frangipani blossoms had appeared on the tree at Faulconstone. Isobel had almost finished her work on the painting for Mr and Mrs Cooper and would soon have no more excuses to visit Juniper Hall. She loved the time she had spent in its garden in the shade of the Kaffir lilies and evergreen magnolias, sketching the iron arch and gravel path bordered by flower beds and shrubs trimmed into box hedges along the wall.

Whenever he could spare the time from teaching Mrs Cooper's offspring, Charles joined Isobel in the garden. They were usually accompanied by Miss Catherine Cooper, her fellow debutante the night of the ball that, in Isobel's mind, now marked the auspicious beginning of Isobel and Charles's romance. As Charles stood at her side, the air between the art master and his protégé seemed to pulse palpably with the heat of their desire. Meanwhile Catherine played on the lawn with Alphonse, her boisterous cocker spaniel. Every now and then she found an excuse to absent herself, announcing loudly and brightly that she would fetch her dog a ball or a bowl of water. This ruse gave the lovers their furtive opportunity.

And so it came to pass that on her sixth visit to Juniper Hall, with her sketches all done and little time left before Robert the Large and his family had to finally vacate their grand home, Isobel and Charles first kissed. Isobel swore she would never forget that moment: his warm hand on the nape of her neck, her small hand pressed against his chest and then withdrawn to signal her consent, the loveliness of his handsome face so close that she could smell the astringent aroma of his skin.

At first there was the tender, even tentative, touching of lips that fast became more inviting, more overwhelming, more daring and demanding. Isobel felt the steam valve of her heart opening, the heat of her body flaring, the urgent telegraph of her pulse, the flash of flame in her loins like a lamplighter's wick to the gaslight. Behind the blood-red flesh of her eyelids she glimpsed her own face, eyes closed, adrift in a bubble beyond time and care.

Was she lost or was she found? Was this a fall or a rescue? The torrent of her desire surged through her body like the giant grey-green wave of her dream, clearing away all notions of what was proper, crushing in its path the old-fashioned strictures of her girlhood. In her lover's eyes she saw herself anew, in his arms felt both freedom and security, in the blissful oblivion of this kiss felt released.

'I have something I want to show you,' she whispered in his ear. She unbuttoned her blouse and, from beneath her lace petticoat, she showed her lover her cherished secret. The opal dragonfly. How it flashed and fluoresced in the sunlight! Charles gasped with delight.

'Dear God! It is so beautiful.' At the sound of footsteps on the gravel path, Isobel hastened to tuck the pendant back into its hiding place. The couple sprang apart as young Miss Catherine approached with a knowing smirk on her face.

It was a week later during an art class in the morning room at Faulconstone that Isobel unburdened herself of the secret history of her mother's strange gift. Charles listened, fascinated. She did not, dared not, mention her dreams. Not yet. But she did tell him the story of meeting Fanny Macleay in the garden, the Tennyson poem of the dragonfly and Fanny's talk of young girls being 'gobbled up in the jaws of matrimony' by their suitors.

'I hope when we are married,' Charles declared, 'that you, my dear, will always be able to fly as "a living flash of light". Just like the dragonfly in Mr Tennyson's poem! I do not want to be a husband who crushes your spirit and shackles you to the role of Angel of Hearth and Home. God forbid! The thought of such a life fills me with horror.'

After that day, to Isobel's astonished delight, Charles would sometimes whisper in her ear the tender soubriquet he had coined for her, 'Madame Libellule'. Lady Dragonfly.

As he walked across the front lawn of Juniper Hall in the late afternoon, with Alphonse the spaniel gambolling at his heels, Isobel, freshly kissed and fizzing with desire, looked on her lover with eyes of adoration and wonder. What a marvellous, strange man!

It was irrefutable that Charles Probius was unconventional in many ways. He was well known for his colourful but always superbly cut outfits, particularly his daytime ensemble of burnished knee-high riding boots, cream jodhpurs, mustard waistcoat, mint green frock coat and French blue cravat, and his much-admired collection of walking canes featuring the carved heads of birds. He liked to call himself a 'bohemian', having recently acquired the Parisian writer Henri Murger's *Scènes de la vie de Bohème*, celebrating the lives of struggling artists in Paris. He even read favourite passages aloud to Isobel.

Isobel saw clearly that, as an artist and a free spirit, Charles walked on a broader stage than most men: the merchant, the lawyer, the politician and the public servant. His horizons were wider, literally and figuratively. He had lived abroad and mixed with intellectuals and artists of all nationalities and creeds. He had encountered ideas alien to the pinched, narcissistic society of New South Wales, with its endless treadmill of status seeking and its politics of envy, greed and loathing. He had even stepped outside the bounds of the law in a desperate bid to survive. He was a man who, to pursue his calling, had learned to view humanity with an uncompromising and gimlet-eyed clarity. In this way, he saw the inner workings of people's souls: their foibles, vanities, virtues and passions.

How had Isobel been so lucky to be taken up by such a man? she wondered. She prayed that the words spoken by the soothsayer were about Charles. *'I speak of the future. The future not set in stone, not carved in marble. Of what will come if nothing is changed. Of a man that you love who sees you clearly.'* Isobel hoped that Charles was not just a lucky accident but rather a soulmate, whose appearance in her life had been set by destiny.

From their very first meeting, Charles Probius had seen Isobel more clearly than anyone, except perhaps her father. He had glimpsed her secret passion and recognised her talent. He had even talked of her future vocation: '*Some women, with uncommon strength of character and will, as well as prodigious talent, have managed against all the odds to become artists . . . I have a feeling that you could be one of those women. Could I be right?*'

Isobel was determined to prove him right. She surrendered herself willingly to his authority and guidance as her teacher. She no longer attended lessons in Surry Hills with Mr Vasey, her long-time art tutor, a gentle, old-fashioned gent who used the well-worn demonstration-and-copy method, commencing every lesson with a technique or subject that his female students then dutifully copied. 'Cloaks are very useful for hiding badly drawn legs and arms,' Mr Vasey advised. Amateur lady artists like Isobel were stuck with drawing thumbnail landscapes with small stick-like figures in the foreground. They were forbidden to draw from life as the academic painters did; the closest they ever got were miniature portraits at which Mrs Georgiana McCrae, the Melbourne painter, excelled.

As a young woman, Isobel had quickly tired of flowers and miniatures and Mr Vasey's tricks of the trade. Given the views from her bedroom window and Rosemount's gardens, Isobel embarked instead on picturesque landscapes, inspired by Messrs Martens, Earle, Glover and Prout. She worked in ink and watercolours, never graduating to oils or trespassing in the forbidden male territory of the Classical or the Sublime.

Isobel had no illusions. She knew very well that the number of women artists of any talent or note in the colonies was very small.

There was Mrs Sophia Campbell, unorthodox wife of rich merchant Mr Robert Campbell, who painted early views of the town. There was Mrs Georgiana Lowe, wife of the brilliant, mercurial lawyer Robert Lowe, and a fine watercolourist of plants and harbour views, particularly around her charming house at Bronte. There was Miss Mary Allport, a successful Hobart artist and printmaker, who had even had her sketch of the Great Comet of 1843 printed in *The Illustrated London News*. To pay her baker's bills in hard times, Mrs Georgiana McCrae had taken on portrait commissions while Elizabeth Gould, wife of the famous bird taxidermist John, did over six hundred illustrations for her husband's books. The Scott sisters, Harriet and Helena, had only recently finished a magnificent book of moths for their entomologist father. It was easy to see the odds were against any chance of success for a woman artist.

Even so, Charles remained supportive of Isobel's talent and ambition. He had no tolerance for the notion of art as a mere display of feminine 'taste', and art education for women as no more than 'ornamental'. He encouraged Isobel to sketch *en plein air* and take risks with more difficult techniques and materials. He gave her tutorials on how to make lithographs and aquatints. He promised to one day teach her the finer points of oil painting.

'You shall be known as the painter Madame Libellule, the envy of the academicians!' he told her. 'I hope to see the day when one of your works hangs in the National Gallery in London. You shall be a guiding light to generations of women artists.' She kissed him then and loved him for his gallantry and unapologetic high opinion of her worth.

Charles himself was kept busy with several commissions from wealthy clients but had so far had no luck in his quest for a well-paid position as a private art master (apart from his lessons with Isobel, of course, for which he charged much less than he normally would). Mr and Mrs Cooper and five of their brood had embarked for England in April leaving behind their daughter Catherine, who was reluctant to give up a prosperous suitor, and was now in residence with an aunt.

Despite this lack of secure employment, the artist seemed happy enough to stay in Sydney, though he sometimes still talked about his plans to start afresh in Melbourne or even Hobart, where he believed artists were more valued. Flushed with gold, the civic leaders of Melbourne had started making noises about a public art gallery like the Royal Academy in London or the Académie des Beaux-Arts in Paris. Charles prayed that one day Sydney might do the same. 'I look forward to the time when this brash, vainglorious upstart of a town is no longer in thrall to Mammon!' Charles told Isobel during one of their field trips as they looked over the lovely city of sandstone spires and turrets. 'Maybe then its burghers will stop aping their betters back home with their preference for all things English and snobbish contempt for anything done here! That is the only way we will plant the seeds of a cultured society.'

It was not as if artists lacked for sublime and epic subjects in the colony. In June, the people of New South Wales were reminded of the awful terror of Nature when floodwaters carried away most of the settlement of Gundagai on the Murrumbidgee River. Charles read out the dramatic newspaper account to Isobel: '"Eighty-nine people, comprising a third of the town's population, perished in the mighty waters of the flash flood that struck Gundagai on 25th June. The township has all but vanished with only three dwellings left standing.'"

Of singular interest to Charles was the courage of four Wiradjuri men, who risked their lives in bark canoes to pluck over forty stranded white settlers from the roofs of their houses and the raging floodwaters. 'Now that would make a subject for a painting!' enthused Charles. 'A different story to the ones we usually hear, eh?'

In pursuit of the sublime, Charles and Isobel, accompanied by a less enthusiastic Catherine Cooper, braved the cold winds roaring off the iron-grey harbour for a day of sketching at Watsons Bay. Isobel was reluctant at first to revisit the site of her humiliation at the hands of her so-called friends, but she was persuaded by Charles's enthusiasm and her own fascination to witness the vision of The Gap, especially on such a dramatic day.

On the way there, as their carriage rattled past the swamps around Rose Bay, Charles suddenly pulled up by the side of New South Head Road. A black man, huddled in blankets, sat a few feet from the roadside, his right arm extended towards them, hand cupped upwards.

'What's the toll today, Billy?' asked Charles cheerfully, stepping down from the carriage. It was Billy Warrell, known around Sydney as 'Ricketty Dick' and the Chief of Rose Bay. Charles had done a sympathetic portrait sketch of him years ago. Billy looked up, squinting, his eyes rheumy and bloodshot. A big smile spread across his face.

'Mr Charles, eh? Only thruppence for you and the ladies.' His voice croaked. Charles pressed a shilling into the man's palm. The man's smile grew bigger.

'You been looking after yourself, Billy? And how's Mrs Snowball?'

'She be good, Mr Charles. Out fishing today. You going somewhere?'

'Yes, Billy, we're off to South Head. To do some drawing.'

'Bring me back some nice fish, eh? Some nice mussels. For my tea?' Billy laughed a deep, rumbling laugh, slapping his thigh for good measure. 'Got any baccy, Mr Charles?'

'Sorry, Billy. Not today. Take care of yourself, old man. And your wife.'

'Will do, my friend. You too.'

Charles said little for the rest of the drive out to South Head except to gee up the horses or note the loveliness of the vista as they came over the ridge. Isobel could tell he was lost in melancholy reflection and she could only guess at his thoughts. But she suspected they had something to with the pitiful sight of Billy Warrell, his back hunched against the freezing winds and his hand outstretched for a few wretched coins.

Soon after the Major's departure, Grace and Augustus set up house in their elegant villa in the small village of Hunters Hill, with views from its upper-storey windows over the Lane Cove River. Augustus had leased this handsome French-style house from Monsieur Didier Joubert, a champagne merchant, and his brother Jules, who had bought up land on the waterfront of this narrow peninsula, flanked by the Lane Cove River on one side and the Parramatta River on the other. The Didier brothers had imported seventy masons from Tuscany to build large houses from the lovely local sandstone to lease and to sell.

The 'French village' (as it was called) that sprang up there became a precinct for emigrants, political exiles and fortune hunters from France, Switzerland and Italy. While Grace was glad to be mistress of her own fine house, she had not yet become accustomed to the extreme quiet and isolation of Hunters Hill. This idyllic retreat suited the temperament of Augustus, whose presence was only required in town once or twice a week. But for Grace, the peninsula felt a long away from the city proper, even further than Rosemount.

There had been much to do to prepare their new home for public inspection, but by July the married couple felt that they were ready to host a house-warming party at *Villa Dordogne*. An invitation arrived at Faulconstone for Isobel, Anna and Aunt Louisa. While Isobel was curious to see the new house, her dreams were still haunted by sad visions of Rosemount all shut up, its furnishings shrouded in white and its empty rooms home only to moths and mice.

At Isobel's next lesson with Charles he had some interesting news. 'You will never guess,' he said when she entered the room. 'It appears I will be joining you at your sister's party next week.' Isobel visibly startled at this announcement and her face went white. 'My dear, what is the matter?' asked Charles.

'Nothing. I'm fine,' said Isobel. 'I don't know what came over me.'

But the truth was that the strain of keeping her relationship with Charles a secret was taking a toll on Isobel's nerves. Anna had been all sweetness and courtesy when she first met Charles at Faulconstone but ever since she had examined them both with her habitual squint-eyed expression, full of misanthropic ill will. Isobel knew her sister too well. She was convinced that Anna suspected something and would do anything to make mischief and cause Isobel harm. For a split second, Isobel had irrationally assumed that Charles's invitation to the party was proof that their relations had been uncovered—by Anna or Grace or God knows who; prying eyes were everywhere. As soon as her heart began to bolt in terror she realised this was an absurd conclusion and regained her composure.

'So how . . . why?' Isobel looked at Charles blankly.

'Your sister has just furnished her new house with tables, chairs, vases, clocks and all manner of ornaments. So what does she now urgently require over her mantelpiece?'

Isobel smiled. 'A portrait painting!'

'Yes, indeed. A double portrait, I am glad to say. Grace and Augustus and perhaps an adoring fox terrier or two at their feet in lieu of children. I have your guardian to thank for the recommendation.'

'Make sure you charge them handsomely!' insisted Isobel. 'Augustus's pockets bulge with fistfuls of guineas just the way his cheeks bulge with foie gras and truffles!'

'I know. The more I charge, the more they will enjoy the art,' winked Charles.

How strange it felt to know that she and Charles would drink Grace's champagne and eat Grace's food right under her nose while she did not have the slightest inkling of their forbidden love. And how delicious to think that some of Augustus's money that went into Charles's pocket might end up spent on a token of affection for Isobel! The whole notion of this underhand performance tickled her fancy. It might be unworthy, but it felt like a small yet satisfying act of vengeance in exchange for Isobel having to endure Grace and Augustus's marriage while she was still smarting from the cruel blow of Father's rejection of Charles.

On the appointed night, Anna, Isobel and Aunt Louisa set out in the brougham as early as half past five to be sure of arriving in time, picking up Charles from his terrace in Woolloomooloo on the way. Charles looked resplendent in a plush blue double-breasted frock coat, Jacquard-woven silk vest in black and gold stripes, and an ebony cane with a handle carved in the stooped figure of a raven. Isobel had dressed simply in a velvety moss green gown with a high collar, in part to conceal the opal dragonfly on its chain that hung about her neck. Her defiance had assumed a new pitch of daring and danger, at the same time as she felt protected by the sanctity of her dead mother's love.

The horses were tiring as the brougham at last turned into a driveway through a set of ornate iron gates and Isobel, Anna, Aunt Louisa and Charles clapped their eyes on the *Villa Dordogne,* a striking double-storeyed sandstone house with intricate ironwork verandas and green-tiled roof, surrounded by a lush garden and with views over the water.

'It is so beautiful,' gushed Isobel as her sister shepherded their party from room to room, drawing attention to the Italian marble fireplaces and the ornate furniture from Paris. Grace explained how their occupation of the house had been delayed because most of the furnishings were imported. Her moon-faced husband beamed with unapologetic pride.

Isobel kept to herself her impression that the Major would hate everything about the place, not least the French name of this jewel of a house by the water. Perhaps that was even part of its appeal to her newly independent sister. Grace and Augustus had invited several local luminaries including the Joubert brothers, the jeweller Edmond De La Rue and the aristocrat Count Gabriel de Milhau, exiled from his homeland after the 1848 revolution.

It had rained that afternoon and the bush still gave off the rich loamy smell of soaked earth mingled with the lemon tang of eucalypt blossom still heavy on the bough. In the failing light of dusk, the guests could just make out the tricolour of the Second Republic flying above the French consulate located only a few streets away.

'The people of France will live to regret that they have elected another Napoleon to lead them!' declared the Count in conversation with Charles, Isobel and other guests as they stood on the terrace with their glasses of wine and French fizz. 'Before the year is out this President-for-life will have himself crowned Emperor, you mark my words.'

For Isobel, meeting a real flesh-and-blood French aristocrat was like meeting a mythical creature: enchanting and a little intimidating. The Count was a lean, handsome man in his sixties, with yellow vulpine eyes and long-fingered, elegant hands. Fortified by a glass or two of wine, he grew expansive about his life story. As a young man, he had been an émigré in Switzerland during the Revolution that swallowed up all his family's estates and several relations. Come the Bourbon Restoration, he had returned home where, with a keen nose for business, he had joined the ranks of France's new nobility: the bankers, financiers and industrialists. He had welcomed the ascension of the 'bourgeois king' Louis-Philippe, whose reign proved very good for the rich but not such a blessing for the workers and the poor. In June 1848 a volcano of working-class anger had exploded on the streets of Paris and thousands were killed and injured, the cobblestones sticky with their blood, and crows picking at corpses. The Count wrote articles attacking the return of Napoleon Bonaparte's nephew, Louis-Napoleon, who was then elected president. Declared a public enemy, the Count had fled to Australia.

'Australia is blessed to be spared the bloodshed of revolution,' the Count reassured his circle of listeners. 'Until you have seen the ugliness and violence of the mob, you cannot understand what a boon it is to live under an enlightened monarch and the rule of law.'

Isobel noticed the angry twitch in Charles's lips. His usual languid ease had deserted him and, in its place, she detected an uncharacteristic surliness. 'Australia is indeed blessed, sir,' said Charles with a sardonic smile, 'at least for the rich squatters who have as much land as they can seize and as much free labour to work it as they need. Even more blessed are the wealthy directors of the Australian Agricultural Company who wined and dined most of the British Cabinet to grab their half a million hectares of grazing land.'

The Frenchman's wolfish eyes narrowed. 'A fine speech, sir. You are quite the demagogue.'

Isobel studied Charles's face, dark with anger now, and barely recognised her usually placid, charming companion. Charles continued, 'As for being spared bloodshed, sir, the persecuted Irishman, the murdered and reviled Aborigine and the leg-ironed and cat-o'-nine-tail-lashed convict may not see Australia as quite the peaceful paradise that you do.'

The aristocrat sneered. 'You are quite the pamphleteer, sir. Tell me, have you a soapbox at the Quay where we can hear more of your diatribes?'

Charles ignored this cheap mockery. 'If you feel that my opinions are so incendiary and offensive, sir, perhaps you should have not come to a colony where Britain has sent so many of its discontented. The Croppies and the Ribbonmen of Ireland, the Scottish Martyrs, the Patriotes of Canada, the Chartists of England—they are all here, sir. And one day, their voices will be heard. And more self-satisfied aristocrat heads will roll, you mark my words!'

'Pfff!' The Count gave a short, scoffing bark of a laugh and walked away. As the rest of the company drifted back inside, Charles seemed to recover his equanimity and stood a little closer to Isobel, apologising under his breath for his outburst.

'I am so sorry, my dear, if I have embarrassed you! But that— that insufferable man!'

'No, no, please do not apologise, Charles,' whispered Isobel from behind her fan. 'You were right to be angry. The man was a fool. To be honest, it frustrates me that we women are considered unfit to have strong opinions on such subjects. How can we be worthy companions to men if we are expected to remain ignorant of worldly affairs?'

Charles turned his head to smile at her. 'I believe that Mrs Wollstonecraft would heartily agree with you. My dearest Isobel, what a wonderful mystery you are!' He looked at her with such tenderness that it took all their self-restraint not to touch each other as more guests began to gather on the terrace to admire the sunset.

The unfortunate argument between the artist and the Count was soon forgotten in the general atmosphere of self-congratulation that prevailed at Grace and Augustus's lavish party. Quadrilles were danced until well past midnight. Mr Joubert's jeroboams were uncorked and drunk by the case accompanied by the unrestrained consumption of fricasseed fowl, fricandeau veal, pâté de pigeon, cheesecakes, tartlets, gooseberry fool and biscuits rose de Reims. Anna was flattered by being asked to perform on *Villa Dordogne*'s brand-new Italian harpsichord. Aunt Louisa watched the whole affair primly from the sidelines, where she noted how every year the ladies' crinolines grew wider and more voluminous. Ostentatious excess was the spirit of the times, it seemed. All in all, the party was a triumph of cultured taste and unstinting hospitality that endeared the hosts to their neighbours, just as it was intended to.

For Isobel, the evening left one lasting impression: her handsome Charles, outraged on behalf of the common man, a picture of impeccable and high-minded integrity. She added this to the list of the many reasons she loved him.

Following the party at *Villa Dordogne,* there were no invitations to balls or parties or dances and life became rather quiet again at Faulconstone. Preoccupied as she was with Charles and her art lessons, the lack of formal social outings did not overly concern

Isobel, though she did wonder if the ladies of the Benevolent Society fancywork circle would ever meet again for a gossipy afternoon tea or throw a gay supper party or dance at one of their grand houses.

Thanks to Sir Charles Nicholson, speaker of the Legislative Council and an old friend of the Major's, in late August the women of Faulconstone were sent tickets, in the Major's absence, to a 'Steam Ball' at the Australian Museum to celebrate the arrival of the P&O's Royal Mail steamship *Chusan,* which had made the trip from Southampton in a record time of only sixty-seven days.

The cream of colonial society was in attendance including His Excellency the Governor-General, Sir Charles Augustus FitzRoy; nearly all the members of the Legislative Council; Lieutenant-General Wynyard in command of the NSW troops; Colonel Bloomfield and most of the officers of the 11th regiment; and the consuls of all the maritime powers in friendly intercourse with Great Britain. Twenty chandeliers and dozens of sinumbra whale-oil lamps illuminated the main room, which was bedecked in national flags, and the grand assembly of more than seven hundred guests in all their finery stood and raised a toast to Captain Henry Down and his officers of the *Chusan.*

Huge crowds had gathered at the Quay to see the magnificent steamship with its smoke-belching stack and mighty engine that had hurled this miracle of modern engineering through wild storms and precipitous waves at unimaginable speed. At the ball, speeches were delivered, both patriotic and even poetic in tone, that praised the revolutionary 'sorcery of steam'. This remarkable innovation saw the Australian colonies on the cusp of a bold, new chapter of prosperity (thanks to the gold rushes) and of statehood (thanks to a new constitution); it was particularly fitting then that they were in such rapid and close communication with the Mother Country for the purposes of trade and good governance. When these formalities were over, the guests danced to the specially commissioned *Chusan* waltz.

As Aunt Louisa had excused herself from the ball, Anna and Isobel were chaperoned by Augustus and Grace. The married couple were the centre of admiring eyes, Augustus repeatedly congratulated on a recent brilliant legal success and Grace complimented on her latest gee-gaw, a gold Algerian-knot brooch with a bezel-faceted garnet. Isobel discreetly fingered the opal dragonfly, hidden beneath her own gown and *pelerine*, to calm her qualms of jealousy. She was jealous only of Grace's freedom to openly display her husband's love, of course, and certainly not of Augustus himself! Her Charles was ten times, nay, a hundred times the man that this dull, self-satisfied fellow aspired to be.

It should have done Isobel's heart good to be at a party again, released from the daily routine at her aunt's, but the truth was she missed Charles. He had regretfully cancelled tomorrow's art lesson as he was obliged to be out of town for a few days. While Isobel took pleasure in the spectacle of the dancing, the distinguished assembly, the gay dresses and uniforms, and the general bonhomie of the company, she felt bereft. After three dances with three equally charming men, including a naval lieutenant from HMS *Pandora*, she retired to a chaise longue at the back of the room, unable to persist in the charade of blushing debutante a minute longer.

At the supper table she heard an oddly familiar voice call her name. 'Miss Isobel Macleod?' She turned and saw a short, dark-haired man in a splendid vest. It was none other than Mr Simon Davidson, her father's implacable enemy and duelling partner. Despite the scandal of the duel, Mr Davidson had thrived and was earning a reputation as an animated speaker in the Legislative Council and a powerful advocate for modernising the colony's economy.

'Mr Davidson, what an unexpected pleasure!' said Isobel, trying not to blush.

'I am glad to see you out in society, if you don't mind my saying so,' said Mr Davidson, offering to refill her glass at the punchbowl. 'I hear your father has gone to England on urgent family matters. You know how gossip travels here.' He smiled apologetically. 'But I hope there are no untoward circumstances surrounding this sudden departure. Your family have suffered enough these last few months. Please, tell me, how are you faring?'

Perhaps I am naïve, thought Isobel, but the gentleman seems genuinely solicitous. She recalled how chivalrous he had been on the day of the duel: *I believe what you did today was courageous.* She was surprised to find that she felt perfectly happy to talk to him. 'We are all awaiting the report from the inquiry into Father's conduct of his department with great anxiety, as you can imagine,' said Isobel.

'Yes, of course,' said Mr Davidson, looking a touch shamefaced. 'I am sorry if I have been the cause of such troubles for your family. You may find this hard to believe but I did not mean to injure your father's reputation, only to suggest improvements in the running of his department. It was never intended to be personal.'

'I know, Mr Davidson,' said Isobel, though to be honest, she knew no such thing. 'But I fear that if this report goes against

Father it will destroy him. Not just financially, which I think he could possibly survive, but in his spirit, which I doubt he could.'

Mr Davidson was suitably distressed by this remark. Alarmed at her own frank confession, Isobel shook her head and even laughed, perhaps to assuage his mortification. 'Of course, I am under no delusions that Papa is a saint, Mr Davidson. I know he can be diffi- cult, ill tempered and stubborn at times. But I believe he means well. He has made mistakes, I am sure, but never out of malice. At least, I hope not. He does not deserve such public humiliation.' Isobel blushed more deeply. 'I am sorry, sir, I did not mean to make a speech.'

She marvelled at her own courage and eloquence. It had nothing to do with the wine (she had barely drunk any) but more to do with her own frustration with her father and her apprehension about the future. Mr Simon Davidson coloured a little then and his voice grew husky with emotion. 'Miss Isobel, I cannot apologise enough for the pain this situation has caused you and your family. If there is ever anything I can do to help you, I insist you write me a letter, and I will do everything within my power to oblige. That is my solemn promise.'

The gentleman passed Isobel her glass, now refreshed with punch, and withdrew.

It was a strange and memorable moment, Isobel reflected much later, to receive such sympathetic regard from the man whom Father had challenged to a duel. And for her own part, to feel trust in a man who some considered her family's enemy, who had permanently wounded her father with his pistol shot but—much worse—fatally injured his reputation, beginning a process that could well end his career.

How could she regard Mr Davidson with anything less than loathing?

And yet, she trusted him.

Chapter 27

LETTERS FROM ABROAD

SEPTEMBER 1852

Isobel's dream that night began in Rosemount's forest, where she sat on her favourite rustic seat among a sea of orchids, painting. Sometimes, as she lifted her brush to the canvas, she was momentarily blinded by the star-like dazzle of light off the harbour. Out of the corner of her eye she saw an indistinct shape, drifting—walking?—between the trees. Was it a man, looking in her direction? The weight of his gaze lay on her with a quality of intemperate longing and feverish scrutiny. It frightened her a little and she stood up and shouted, 'Hello?'

It was then she heard a girl's high-pitched laughter. Out of the shadows stepped Ballandella, her face and limbs daubed with ochre and white ash. The scene had changed imperceptibly from sunny daylight to dusk so that Ballandella could only be partially glimpsed by the light of a fire that burned fitfully in the middle of the grove.

'Secret blackfella business. I gotta go!' she shouted and ran off into the dark forest.

'Hey, Ballandella! Come back!' yelled Isobel, feeling younger and more vulnerable than a seventeen-year-old should. Or was she little Izzie now, only five years old, heartbroken on the morning she found Agnes taking pillows and sheets off Ballandella's bed?

In the dream, little Izzie ran along an obscure track in the woods—or was it just a pattern of dead leaves that passing animals had trodden black?—shouting after her playmate. The path came out into a clearing of ruined timber: huge, shattered and termite-riddled trunks, like sunken ships barnacled with bright fungi, plated and fleshy and obscenely orange. The trees were gigantic now and towered overhead, their top branches interlocking like a barrel-vaulted ceiling, shutting out the evening sky except for pinpricks of starlight. The wind was chill and bleak, driving dead leaves before it in flurries.

To her shock Isobel suddenly realised, as she noticed half-fallen walls and piles of broken masonry around her, that she was standing in the ruins of Rosemount, her home. Through the trees she saw what must once have been the garden, now a vegetative riot, its ponds a stinking swamp, its glasshouses turned into skeletons limned with jagged glass. All about, she saw fetid tea-coloured pools, which appeared flat and shallow until she tiptoed to the edge of one and looked in. She uttered a shriek of horror. A body, puffed up like a sodden chaff bag, was submerged just beneath the surface: the supine figure of a man, arms outstretched, face ghastly white, lips blue, hair tarnished green and floating around his skull like duckweed. It was impossible to say who he was.

Isobel backed away and began to run through the ruined remains of her family home. Every door and window lay shattered and gaping to the elements. Creepers and moss carpeted the walls and inundated each room like a green tide. Overhead, the twilight sky crackled with lightning, veins of flame beneath the muscled torso of its clouds. Isobel entered the saloon, its spiral stairs choked with a frozen torrent of mud and debris, and its marbled floor under a slick of seawater. Seawater? Here? And there was something else. Staring eyeless up at Rosemount's dome, now cracked open to the heavens, lay an effigy atop a granite tomb. Isobel stepped closer. The graven figure, gauntleted arms crossed in solemn repose, was a medieval knight in full heraldic armour. She looked upon the face of the fallen warrior, flanked by his sword and shield. It was, of course, her father.

It was not an auspicious start to Isobel's day to wake with images from her nightmare snagged like wisps of mist on the corners of her mind. She already knew that today's art lesson with Charles had been cancelled and so she descended to the breakfast room with trepidation, or at best a skulking sense of pessimism, regarding the day's prospects. The overcast morning sky with banks of storm clouds to the east mirrored her mood.

When she entered the breakfast room, Anna was serving herself kedgeree and bacon. 'Good morning, dear sister,' she chirped. The unfortunate history of their relations meant that Anna's cheerfulness on such a morning immediately suggested that she was up to no good. Isobel even wondered at times if Anna, residing only two rooms away, could overhear Isobel's cries in the middle of the night during her tormented dreams. Had she ever uttered her lover's name aloud? It had been six months since the Major left and Isobel had risked everything on a lie to keep her courtship secret and alive. Her fearful vigilance threatened to overwhelm her.

'I am sorry you were unable to attend devotionals this morning, Isobel,' huffed Aunt Louisa as she came bustling into the room. Was this the source of Anna's good mood, that her aunt was cross with Isobel but pleased with Anna? It was entirely possible. 'I have something I must share with you both.'

Isobel felt her pulse surge again. How she craved some peace of mind and surety about her future so that she would not be panicked at every new turn of events!

'What is it, Aunt dear?' Anna asked sweetly.

'Grace has forwarded me a letter she received in the last mail. It is from your father.'

The two sisters took their seats at the breakfast table and became sharply attentive as their aunt unfolded a letter in the Major's elegant, familiar hand. She proceeded to read aloud.

My dearest family,

I hope this letter finds you all in good Spirits and Health. My voyage out was favour'd with fine weather and strong tail-winds for a mercifully smooth and swift passage. Since my arrival in London, I can report that my representations to my patron, Lord Sherbourne, have receiv'd a sympathetic hearing.

*I embark soon on my boomerang-screw lecture tour and have
also met with my printer. All goes well there. But the main
Import of my letter concerns my efforts to find Alice. And
thereby hangs an unusual and, at this point, inconclusive tale.*

Aunt Louisa looked up from her reading. Isobel and Anna wore
frowns of intense puzzlement. Inconclusive? What on earth did
that mean? wondered Isobel.

*My brother Fergus and I were inform'd by the keeper of the
Debtors' Prison in Newgate that the young Baron is severely
unwell with consumption and delirious with a high fever in the
Hospital wing. He has had no visitors in many weeks. With no
known address for his family in London and no communications from them or their solicitors, my brother and I grasp'd
the nettle and travelled by coach to pay a visit to their country
seat in Hertfordshire. From our inn at St Albans we arriv'd,
unannounced, at Gothamberly House. The eighteenth-century
manor is a grand neo-Palladian palace of some 190 rooms
boasting Piranesi fireplaces, stained-glass windows & a library
of more than two thousand books.*

*The sight that greeted us on arrival beggar'd belief. From
our coach, we could see the estate (six hundred acres of rolling
downs, forest, streams and a lake) overgrown with bramble,
gorse, and heather, its weed-chok'd waterways and wood walks
blanket'd in snow. A large herd of wild deer appeared quite at
home in this wilderness. Our coachman left us to walk the last*

mile or so as the drive was impassable from fallen timber and
thick foliage.

Thus we approach'd the mansion on foot and were confronted with the most sombre and pitiful sight imaginable. A grand
house in ruins, its portico enshrouded in ivy and bracken, its
every window a glassless casement, its crumbling pediments
and cornices iced with snow. The front door stood open so we
entered the gloomy entrance hall as silent as a Mausoleum.
The spiral staircase, wide enough to take a carriage and four,
was all fallen in on itself. The sepulchral ambience of the place
felt all the more lachrymose for the heavy hand of decay at
every turn. We went from room to room, each spoil'd in their
own grotesque fashion: frescos of breathtaking beauty eaten
to dust, high domed ceilings split open to the sky, mould and
fungi in luxuriant profusion feasting on the carrion of draperies, furniture, tapestries, and paintings. Nature's conquest of
this once stately hall was absolute. The Baron's famous family
seat is an abandon'd ruin, a lair for rats and crows.

As we walked through the hoary graveyard of the gardens,
an old man approached from a cottage close by. 'I am the
caretaker. Why are you trespassing here?' he challenged. We
explained that we sought the whereabouts of my daughter,
the Lady Crawley, and that this was her last known address.
'The family comes here only once a year to leave flowers
on the grave of the 13th Baron's poor mother, Lady Olivia,
A tragic business.' The lady in question was young Andrew
Twyckenham's grandmother. Encouraged by my pressing
of a guinea into his palm, the old fellow finally let fall the

name of a relative in Cambridge, Lady Agatha Horsham of
Abercrombie Manor, who may be able to assist us. I assure
you that Fergus and I shall pursue this information with the
greatest urgency. Though this strange excursion has provided
incontrovertible proof of the Twyckenhams' duplicity and desti-
tution, I refuse to admit Despair. Alice is a strong, sensible
and mature young woman and, no doubt, a loving mother.
I promise we will find her and her son and bring them home,
safe and sound.

With affection etc., etc.,
  Major A. H. Macleod, Esq.

Isobel's face blanched at this bizarre tale. Had Alice been taken hostage against her will by these penurious aristocrats? Or was she still under the spell of the Baron's professed love? Isobel knew how smart her older sister was. But she also knew from the poets and playwrights that love famously made fools of us all.

Is it making a fool of me as well? Isobel wondered for one anguished moment. Am I as reckless and lovesick and unable to see the plain truth as my poor sister? No, no, not at all. My situation is completely different, she told herself. Charles has never pretended to be anything other than the man of integrity and talent that he so clearly is.

'Do not fret, my dears,' counselled Aunt Louisa, seeing Isobel and Anna's pale faces. 'Angus will not rest until this matter is settled, I assure you.'

Isobel had no doubts about her father's determination to rescue Alice. But what stopped her breath in her mouth, what chilled her blood in her veins, was the vision that her father had painted of the ruined house.

It was the same vision of ruin and decay that her dream last night had shown Isobel of Rosemount. And at the centre of that dream lay the tomb of her father.

The following week, her beloved Charles returned from his affairs out of town and came to Faulconstone for their Monday art lesson. Aunt Louisa wished to hear all about his meeting with a rich squatter at Bathurst who had broad acres and deep pockets but craved the mystique of respectability that Charles could provide with a formal portrait of the gent and his wife. Isobel understood how much Charles despised these bunyip aristocrats and resented that his livelihood depended upon their callow ambition and ill-gotten wealth. But he seemed in good spirits, his face and arms lightly tanned.

'Are you unwell, my dearest? You look so pale and tired, if you do not mind my saying so,' Charles observed when they had retreated at last to the morning room. Aunt Louisa had explicitly instructed Emmet that they not be disturbed by the staff until he was sent to summon them for lunch. Even so, Isobel was in the habit of checking the door and twitching the curtains, terrified that her sister Anna lurked nearby.

'I have not been sleeping well,' Isobel told him, still determined to keep her vivid dreams a secret from her lover. 'I have missed you.'

'I know, my sweet,' he smiled. 'Soon, soon we will be able to announce our happiness to the world. Tell me, have you heard anything from your father?'

Charles had agreed to the Major's supposed request to hide his courtship from public view to keep the family peace, but as it now seemed the two sisters, Grace and Anna, had embraced him (the first far more warmly than the second) he could see no obstacles. He knew that Aunt Louisa was an admirer. These last three months he had made regular visits to *Villa Dordogne* for sittings with Grace and Augustus; as always with portraiture, a comfortable intimacy had grown up between artist and subject to help him capture a sense of their personalities on canvas. It had also laid the foundations for his secure future within this family.

For these reasons, Charles privately hoped that Major Macleod might decide enough time had passed to allow him and Isobel to announce their intentions. But he was to be disappointed. The Major had much more urgent matters on his mind as Charles was to discover when Isobel related the unsettling tale of her father's visit to Gothamberly House. 'Dear me, it is a story worthy of Miss Radcliffe,' said Charles. 'Not to make light of your sister's terrible situation, of course! I hope we receive some better news soon.'

Poor Isobel. Was God, from Whom nothing could be hidden, watching this little drama through His peephole? Was she to be punished for her subterfuge? She felt as if her whole life had become a house of cards, built on deception and able to be brought down by one careless word. She had lied to Charles, to her aunt, to her father and her sisters. But was it her fault really? Circumstances had forced her to such desperate measures. And she knew in her heart it was unjust for Charles to be judged so harshly while Augustus was not punished for his family's shame. Surely God must forgive her that. Maybe others would too.

'Tell me that you still love me,' she implored Charles. 'I have grown so fearful of late. Every day brings me the terror of hearing bad news.'

Charles studied her face with a look of profound compassion. 'Why, my poor *Madame Libellule,* you must not torment yourself this way,' he said in his most soothing tone. 'I love you and shall always love you. There is nothing that can ever change that.'

And then, just as Isobel had feared, the storm came, arriving without warning on the fourteenth of September. Isobel would later learn this was the same fateful date that Field Marshall Arthur Wellesley, 1st Duke of Wellington, died of a stroke. His body would lie in state for two months before being borne through London's streets for the most spectacular state funeral in English history. In November, Grace would receive a letter from the Major telling her of his decision to delay his return to Australia as he planned to stay for the funeral to farewell his commander, the hero of his youth.

But the late morning of the fourteenth would prove momentous for the Macleods for a more immediate and devastating reason than the death of the Iron Duke. The news that day would later seem to mark a fork in the road in Isobel's fate from which she would either walk a path that led to happiness and good fortune or a road to misery and damnation. Of course, it was never that simple, but for a long time that was how Isobel looked back on that fateful day.

That morning a carriage pulled up unannounced at Faulconstone's front gate. Isobel startled at her writing table in the morning room at the sound of its wheels rolling to a halt. She went to the window to see the front gate open and a figure in a hooded cape enter the garden. There was no mistaking its identity: Grace, hurrying along the path beneath the frangipani tree. Just before she mounted the steps to the portico, Grace paused and looked up. Had she felt Isobel's presence at the upper-storey window? In that instant, Isobel saw the white blank of her sister's face, bereft of all colour and life, and she felt the world stagger from its secure axis. Something was terribly wrong.

The bell rang.

Isobel threw on a shawl and hastened to the top of the main stairs. Here she froze for a moment, hearing the voices in the hall below of Grace and Emmet, the butler, who was busily taking her cape. 'I will tell them that you are here, ma'am.'

She tried to stop her mind fixing on any one person as the probable cause of this visit. Was it Alice? The Baron? Or Papa? Or Augustus? What calamitous event would bring her sister such a long way and in such a state? Isobel reluctantly descended the stairs.

Aunt Louisa and Anna were already in the drawing room. The shock on their faces reflected the gravity in Grace's. To be honest, Grace's expression went beyond gravity; it was more akin to horror. Red-rimmed eyes and ashen cheeks, translucent skin stretched tight over the bones of her face, a fixed stare of utter bewilderment, her mouth held grimly shut so as not to trigger another flood of tears as soon as it opened to speak.

'What is it? What has happened?' asked Aunt Louisa, full of fear.

Tears began to slide freely from Grace's eyes then and she did nothing to check them. From her reticule she pulled a folded sheet of paper. A letter. 'From Joseph. It arrived this morning.' Aunt Louisa took the letter, unfolded it and read aloud.

My belov'd sisters,

I apologise for the long silence since my departure from you. When you have read the contents of this letter I hope you will find it in your hearts to forgive me. My hand has been stopp'd every time I plucked up my pen to write you; even now, I can barely bring myself to record what I must tell. Poor, sweet William is dead.

'No, no, no, say it is not so,' cried out Isobel, half-swooning to the floor.

Behind her, Anna began to pace, clawing at her hair. 'Dear God, what have we done, what have we done, what have we done to deserve this?'

Grace stood as silent as a statue. Aunt Louisa's face collapsed into a ruin, her voice trailed away. She bowed her head and murmured, *'I am the Resurrection, and the Life: he that believeth in me, though he were dead, yet shall he live. And whosoever liveth and believeth in me shall never die.'*

'Please, Aunt. What does Joseph say?' pleaded Isobel.

Aunt Louisa read on.

Bear up, dear sisters, in your Grief! I have a sad story to relate. Two weeks into our voyage, our ship was struck by a typhoon off the coast of Celebes. Driven onto rocks and broken up, she sank so swiftly that most souls on board perish'd, among them my dear Brother. We embrac'd in our cabin when the ship struck and prayed together for deliverance but were separat'd in the chaos that ensued. By Divine Providence, I surviv'd the fury of the storm and drifted into a current that carried me into the nearest shipping lane. Here, a passing Dutch merchantman retrieved my broken body from the sea.

While I escap'd Death, I suffered grievous injuries to my person and am grateful to the skilful doctors at the Sinees Sieken Huys in Batavia who saved my life. In my weaken'd state, I laps'd into a coma for six weeks. For a short period of sweet delirium, I imagin'd William sat by my bed, comforting me as he always did . . .

'Oh, this is unbearable!' moaned Isobel. Aunt Louisa continued to read.

By the time you receive this letter, I shall be on a ship back to Sydney. I find I have no stomach for the enterprise that William planned for us. It was mostly his dream to succeed in India and he recruit'd me out of his boundless love. Forgive my bitterness but I believe had Father allow'd me to apologise for my indiscretions and plead my case before him, this whole tragedy might have been avoided. William wish'd to repair the schism between us and invested much hope in this situation in India to overcome Father's disappointment in me.

Ah, Disappointment! The burden that has crushed all three sons of Major Macleod. How can I explain to you the pain that dwells in the heart of a son who is a permanent disappointment to his father? Such a son hopes to win his father's favour while raging against the very vanity of that hope. It was Papa's disappointment that drove poor Richard to his untimely death and now it has killed sweet William.

I pray to God to lift the burden of my bitter anger from me. I know how heavily this news will fall on you all. And on Father. I pray that each of you can find some peace of mind to reconcile you to this loss. Amen.

Your brother,
Joseph

Silence settled like dust over the four women in the drawing room. They were dumbstruck, unable to summon a single word of piety or solace to ward off the full horror of this news. Not William, not William, Isobel said to herself, why should God strike down dear William?

And then the drowned man in her dream surfaced in her thoughts and Isobel felt herself dragged under by a giant, cold wave of absolute terror.

Chapter 28

DUST STORM

SEPTEMBER TO NOVEMBER 1852

The harbour scintillated in the lovely sunlight, its dark green waters swelling with the morning's ebb tide. Isobel stood with her back to the old sandstone grotto, one of her favourite picnic spots in Rosemount's gardens when she was a child. It was here, the morning before her thirteenth birthday, that she had sat in the shade with Winnie, talking of her father's troubles and sketching the harbour view in her journal. That was only five years ago but it seemed to Isobel an aeon.

Isobel was supposed to be at her dance class with Mrs Acutt in Woolloomooloo but instead she had alighted from the coach and walked down Victoria Street to her old home. Anna had been unwell and stayed in bed, so there was no one to witness Isobel's diversion from her usual routine. It had felt so strange to wander along Rosemount's empty driveway past the forest and the gardens, coming into their spring foliage, and the silent house, all its curtains drawn, asleep like a hibernating giant. The image from her dream of Rosemount in ruins, ravaged by nature's trespass like the Baron's family seat, drifted into her mind. When she looked at her home in that dismal light, it now appeared to her as an unloved old man on his sickbed, pale and comatose, teetering on death.

She lingered for a long time in the coach loop outside the house.

It was almost a year since the three sisters had waved goodbye to William and Joseph but Isobel could recall the scene as vividly as if it was only last week. She had whispered in her brother's ear, *'Please read my note, dear William, I beg you. And send me your good counsel.'* His short reply (now tucked away in her writing desk drawer) had come weeks later, urging her to be brave. Oh, what courage I shall need now, sweet brother, more than either of us could ever have imagined! With William gone, Charles was her only good counsel.

As Isobel stood inside the grotto, overlooking the sparkling harbour, she held her mother's last gift, the opal dragonfly, in her hands. These past few months she had worn it about her neck as a talisman of her mother's love and protection. And as a badge of honour worn by a proud daughter in secret communion with her mother. Winnie had been no stranger to duty and suffering but she also knew the value of love. And it was this reassurance that gave Isobel the courage to defy—at least for now—her father's refusal to give his blessing to her courtship.

For the sake of love. A love that would save her.

This is what Isobel told herself as she turned the dragonfly over in her hands. But, just like her mother before her, her attachment to this lovely treasure had become complicated. She recalled Winnie's bewilderment on her sickbed and her words, half-blessing, half-warning, as she handed Isobel the 'powerful gift'. *'I want to give you this but . . . I am afraid to do so . . . I have such strange dreams. Terrible dreams . . . Unimaginable . . . They show me . . . I do not understand what they show me. Or where they come from.'*

As Isobel stared into the shifting flames of the opal—the bright fire in the cold stone—she was struck by life's troubling ambivalences: her love for Charles, conceived in a moment of pure-heartedness, but now only made possible through deceit; her love and respect for her father, once the innocent adoration of a child, now hedged about with doubts and rebelliousness; her childhood worship of Grace and protectiveness of Anna, now poisoned by years of petty antipathies; even her love for her mother, hallowed by death and longing, but tainted by the memory of her heartless rejection of Captain Tranter.

Sometimes Isobel wished she was a child again, who knew nothing of the complications of the adult world. Why had she ever asked her mother to explain her father's unhappiness?

Now she was not interested in the past. She wanted to know about the future. What was it that her nightmares were trying to tell her? If her disturbing dreams were indeed glimpses into a future that revealed *'what will come if nothing is changed'*, as the sooth-sayer had said, then what did she have to do to change that future?

She feared that the Macleods had not yet drunk their fill of misery, that the opal stones had more misfortunes to tell for this seemingly cursed family. Her mother had warned her that if the opal dragonfly *'should ever cause you—or anyone you love—pain or suffering, then throw it away! Cast it into the sea, bury it some-where secret.'*

Isobel stood, her fist clenched about her mother's brooch, willing herself to hurl it into the bright waters. Was that the answer? Could she walk away from her family's woes that easily? Or was she tied to all their fates, her brothers' and her sisters', her mother's and father's? It seemed clear that Charles was her only escape—her dreams had shown her that, had they not? He was the only way she could flee from Rosemount's ruin and her family's downfall. And why shouldn't she?

The social disgrace that Isobel suffered was not of her own making; it was the legacy of a proud, stiff-necked father obsessed with his own reputation and honour. She would not be dragged down by her father's pride. It had already entrapped two of her sisters and, according to Joseph's letter, led to the self-sacrifice of two of her brothers for the sake of their father's approval.

She raised her arm and prepared to cast the opal dragonfly into the harbour. 'Do it, do it!' an inner voice urged. But she could not. 'It is all very well to rage against your father's hubris,' she murmured to herself, 'to talk of disowning your family. But to do it? That is too hard.'

Her heart was breaking. She was Isobel Clara Macleod, youngest daughter of Major Sir Angus and Winnie Macleod. Her past— Grangemouth, Ballandella, Rosemount, her father's fame, her mother's love—were knitted into the sinews of that heart. To cast away the opal dragonfly would be to throw away a part of herself, a vital part. Now that it seemed clear her exile from Rosemount was final, her mother's brooch was all she had left to remember her childhood by. A precious trinket. A token of love. A knot of memories. She could never just throw it away.

Grace promised to write to the Major in England about William's death. There was a good chance that Father would have left England by the time the letter arrived; it was even possible that the mail ship from Sydney and his return vessel would pass each other in the Indian Ocean. The three sisters and their aunt put on their mourning garments, their grieving made sharper for the lack of a body to weep over and to lay in the earth with the ceremony that was its due. There was a small private service at St Mark's at which all the Macleod women broke down and wept openly. Grace placed a black-bordered obituary in the *Herald* with a poem:

> We cannot tend beside his grave, for he sleeps in secret sea.
> And not one gentle whispering wave, will tell the place to me.
> But though unseen by human eyes, and mortals know it not.
> His Father knoweth where he lies, and angels guard the spot.
> No willows weep, no scented flowers bloom o'er the
> watery grave.
> No emblem left of him who sleeps, beneath the silent waves.

Charles had never met William but he knew how deep Isobel's bond was with her brother. He did his best to comfort her without resorting to the pieties of 'eternal sleep' and 'release from suffering' and 'God's mysterious purpose'. William was a young man, full of energy, ambition and faith in his future, and he had been cut down for no good reason.

Isobel wondered if God had winked asleep for a moment at His peephole as he looked down on William and Joseph's foundering ship. How could the premature death of her brother make any sense in God's plans? And then she paused to consider God's wisdom in saving her other brother, Joseph. Was that not a miracle? Isobel's faith was sorely tested. Nor could she forget the old soothsayer's words: *'And now two more brothers. Over water. And a sister. Over water. They are lost to you.'*

And the next blow to come? Unlike William's death, everyone knew what that was. The commission of inquiry into the Major's conduct of his department, chaired by his old nemesis, Mr Macleay, had submitted its report for the Governor's consideration in August. The Macleod family waited anxiously for its publication in the *Government Gazette* in September. On the strength of this report, the Governor would make his recommendation to the Colonial Office as to whether Major Macleod should have his pay cut or be removed from office.

In consultation with Grace, Augustus decided to write a courteous letter on behalf of the Macleod family to crave the Governor's indulgence in delaying public release of the report until the Major's return. The letter explained the extenuating circumstances of the death of the Major's eldest son, William, news of which had not yet reached his father. A letter had been sent to England in the hope that he would receive it before his departure. If not, public scrutiny (and, no doubt, censure) of the Major's career coupled with the shock of his son's death would be a severe double blow on his return.

The Governor sent a gracious reply in which he expressed his sincerest regrets at the family's loss and agreed to delay the public release of the full report until the Major came home. He insisted that the Major must return no later than January. The Governor conceded that the Major's service to the colony warranted the courtesy of his reading the report in full before it was made public and any other actions were taken with regards to his employment.

Over the following few weeks, the agony of grieving for dear William was numbed a little, particularly with Charles's tender attentiveness and kind words, but Isobel was not immune to repeated bouts of weeping and melancholy. 'This is all to be expected, my love,' counselled Charles, quoting the poet Shelley:

> As long as skies are blue, and fields are green,
> Evening must usher night, night urge the morrow,
> Month follow month with woe, and year wake year to sorrow.

'Your love for William will never die, nor will your grief,' said Charles. '"*Winter is come and gone, But grief returns with the revolving year.*"'

Not surprisingly, William appeared many times in Isobel's dreams: as a boy playing cricket at Grangemouth, as a young naval officer on leave from HMS *Iris*, as a well-dressed traveller with bright prospects in India during his last visit to Rosemount. Charles encouraged Isobel to sketch her brother's face from her recollections. This was painful at first, almost unbearable, but she persisted. And with time, this exercise became a salve to her soul and a moment of private communion with her dear departed brother. Much like the way she sometimes sat in her room alone late at night, holding the opal dragonfly up to the candlelight and talking to her mother's spirit.

One morning in early November, seven weeks after the news of William's death, Isobel was sitting in the drawing room with Anna and Aunt Louisa, all three women busy at their reading. Ever since her encounter with the French aristocrat at Grace's house-warming party, Isobel had decided to become better informed about current events on the world stage. Aunt Louisa looked at her with an expression of puzzlement when asked if Faulconstone could take delivery of the *Herald* but had indulged her nonetheless.

On this morning, Isobel was thumbing through the newsprint when her eye was drawn to the following paragraph in the Water Police Court reports:

> *The second inquest before the Coroner today concerned the death of a 38-year old woman, a Mrs Emily Vera Pittman of Gloucester Street in The Rocks, found floating near Pyrmont Bridge by a seaman while making fast his vessel. The deserted mother of seven was last seen alive at the Black Dog the previous night in a drunken state. Asphyxia by drowning was announced as the cause of death by the medical man having*

examined the body. Three of the dead woman's children are already in the Benevolent Asylum; all seven will now be sent to the Protestant Orphan School at Parramatta.

Isobel's hand flew to her mouth. She suppressed the urge to cry out. She looked up at her Aunt Louisa, absorbed in reading her book in the morning light. Could this sad story have been avoided if my aunt had been less suspicious? thought Isobel. Was poor Mrs Pittman condemned from the minute that we walked out her front door?' Isobel was sure that this woman's death—whether from drunkenness or suicide—would simply be proof in her aunt's mind of her unfitness as a mother.

The image of Mrs Pittman's bloated body, facedown in the murky waters under Pyrmont Bridge being hooked out by the water police, haunted Isobel all day. She tossed and turned that night, praying the poor woman's corpse would not turn up in one of her dreams. She didn't. Mrs Pittman's death was just another footnote in the sorry story of Sydney's poor. There would be many more deaths like Mrs Pittman's and, if they were reported at all, they would always be buried deep in the fine print of the court reports.

That morning Isobel was tempted to stop reading the newspapers. What was the point? This endless catalogue of misfortune and misery, violence and deceit. As if to confirm her worst suspicion that newspapers were chroniclers of nothing but human tragedy, the following morning she spotted another notice, even shorter than Mrs Pittman's, which simply stated:

DEATHS

On Tuesday, the 18th inst. at Parramatta, Mr Alexander Macleay,
Esq., MLC, F.R.S., F.L.S. in the 82nd year of his age.

'Did you know Mr Macleay had died?' Isobel asked her aunt, looking up from the paper.

Aunt Louisa nodded. 'Mrs Forbes told me last week. Something about a carriage accident at Government House. The horse bolted and Mr Macleay lost control. His carriage overturned and he died on the spot. Sad business.'

It was obvious Aunt Louisa did not feel at all sad about Mr Macleay's demise. Isobel thought of Fanny, of course. She hoped that her recent marriage provided some refuge from the overwhelming grief of losing a father. But what disconcerted Isobel most of all was the brevity of the death notice, its reduction of Mr Macleay's life to one line, a mere jot in a sea of newsprint. No eulogy, no record of service, no tribute or lamentation. Was this stark record all that Mr Macleay deserved? Isobel expressed her surprise to her aunt.

'Mr Macleay will get his public encomiums and memorial plaques, don't you concern yourself about that,' said Aunt Louisa. 'Men like Mr Macleay always do.'

Aunt was probably right. Mr Macleay had been forgiven most of his sins, his nepotistic relations with Governor Darling and bitter quarrels with Governor Bourke. He had been saved from humiliation and bankruptcy by his son. Only his zealousness and hard work as a public servant and his contributions to natural science would be remembered. His legacy was vouchsafed. The same could not be said for her own father whose reputation was still under siege. Mr Macleay had made sure of that. No doubt when the Major learned the news of Mr Macleay's passing, his only regret would be that the man had not broken his neck much earlier.

'I hope the commission report is not going to be too hard on father,' said Isobel. It had taken a typhoon and a shipwreck to kill her brother William but it might take only four men in a room and some words on paper to fatally wound her father.

'Why is everyone so worried? He'll be fine,' announced Anna confidently. 'He managed to come through the official inquiry into that massacre all those years ago.'

Isobel's eyes widened. 'What *massacre*?' What on earth was Anna talking about?

'Oh, Anna, for mercy's sake!' Aunt Louisa rolled her eyes in exasperation. Trust Anna to blurt out this buried business! It was ancient history that had taken place when Isobel was only four years old. Before Anna could utter another word, Louisa began to tell the story that had caused the family great disquiet at the time.

'There was an unfortunate ... incident ... on your father's third expedition,' said Aunt Louisa, clearing her throat nervously.

'You mean when he brought Ballandella home?' asked Isobel.

'Yes, yes. Some two hundred natives, armed with spears, had followed the Major's party for days. Piper, the Major's native guide, said these savages had made very clear their intention to kill some of the white men.' Aunt Louisa wiped her face with her hands. She sighed. 'So your father reluctantly sent a group of convicts back through the bush to provide protection against a surprise attack. They were given strict instructions not to shoot unless the main party came under attack first. But one of these convicts, a Mr King, fired a single shot and then the rest of the convicts opened fire with their rifles. Several natives were killed crossing the Murray River.'

Isobel shook her head in amazement. Not a word of this story had ever been spoken in her presence in all these years. And then a terrible thought struck her. What had her playmate Ballandella known of this? Even worse, what had she seen? What if these 'natives' were members of Ballandella's own tribe? This completely changed Isobel's view of Ballandella coming to live with them. Father had never said anything.

'So why was there an official inquiry?' Isobel asked.

Louisa scratched her head irritably. The topic obviously upset her. 'Well, you see, the Governor had issued strict instructions that forbade the use of firearms or force *"unless the safety of the party should absolutely require it"*. While your father reported the incident to the Governor before he returned, the Executive Council wasn't satisfied. They formed a panel of inquiry with the Governor, Bishop Broughton and Mr Macleay, the Colonial Secretary.'

Mr Macleay again. No wonder the Major hated this man. It seemed that he had sat in judgement on the Major many times. 'And what did this panel say?' Isobel insisted.

'They took evidence from eyewitnesses, including Piper. It turned out that Piper had been spreading stories about a possible attack for days, getting all the men upset and jumpy. The Executive Council's report regretted the incident and the fact the convicts had not followed the Major's instructions.'

Isobel nodded. This would have done nothing to improve her father's opinion of convicts as brutish and unreliable. Then Anna jumped in before her aunt could stop her. 'Yes, but then the Council also chastised Father for the tone of his report, saying it was not sufficiently regretful.' Anna's face left Isobel in no doubt what she thought about the Executive Council.

Aunt Louisa coughed, anxious to bring the topic to an end. 'Anyway, your father was not formally disciplined and the whole matter was dropped. No mention was made of the nasty incident in the Major's public report in the *Government Gazette*. And the members of the Legislative Council felt so guilty about this shameful carry-on—and so grateful to the Major for his expedition—they published a glowing tribute to him in the *Herald*.'

Isobel knew this public letter of gratitude well, written and signed by men who had benefited handsomely from his explorations. Squatters mostly. Her father was so proud of this letter he had a copy of it framed in his study. It praised the Major for his skills, courage, leadership and resolve *'though harassed by tribes of hostile savages and subjected to the greatest privations and perils'*. This phrase took on a new meaning for Isobel now she knew its context. Aunt Louisa had a set of the Major's published journals on her bookshelves in the morning room. Isobel decided that she must read Father's account of his third expedition.

'Let us just pray that this latest inquiry does not rake over these old coals again!' said Louisa. 'As far as I can see, it is all ancient history and best left alone. Enough said.'

That night, as Isobel half-expected, Ballandella made an appearance in her dream. She beckoned Isobel to follow her through the abandoned gardens at Rosemount, finding a trail in the thick undergrowth and the wild profusion of native grasses and dense trees. As they walked, the forest around them changed from conifers and oaks to ironbark and scribbly gum, peppermint willows and casuarinas. They came out of the forest into bright sunshine, but where Isobel expected to see the green waters of the harbour she was confronted by a broad, brown stretch of water with banks of red dirt. A river.

Now Ballandella began to stamp her feet and shake her fists at Isobel, picking up handfuls of the red dirt and throwing them. 'What is it? What are you doing?' implored Isobel, confused and scared. Ballandella's face was distorted into a scowl of rage. She spat at her old friend and threw another handful of dust in her face. Isobel was crying. 'What is it? What is it?' And then she saw something in the river. Bodies, bodies of black men, circling on the current. It was possibly Isobel's worst nightmare so far.

Not that her daylight hours spared poor Isobel private anguish. She thought about her brother William every day and missed him terribly. Grief was a dark and unpredictable passage. Just when she thought she had readjusted her spiritual compass to navigate the calmer waters of acceptance, a new wave of anger and bitterness would swamp her, plunging her back into the blackest of moods.

How could William have abandoned her like this?

There was one unlooked for and potentially happy consequence of William's passing: the three sisters were brought a little closer in their shared distress. They had all loved William, the great conciliator and umpire who had so often kept the peace when they were younger. Isobel and Anna wept together and Isobel relieved some of the painful burden of her heart in letters to Grace, a mixture of reminiscences and regrets. But this truce between Isobel and her two sisters was not as robust as Isobel would have liked.

Anna's troubled mind was stirred up again by her grief and her private fantasies were raised to a new pitch of suspicion. Isobel often discovered her lurking in the upstairs corridor in the mornings like a bloodhound on the scent. Isobel made a habit of locking her bedroom door and hiding her letters and journals, afraid of Anna's prying eyes. Anna knew something. And if she didn't, she was determined to find out.

It was the second week of November and the sun was already hot and bright. The first flowers had appeared overnight on the frangipani tree, their shell-shaped petals flushed yellow and apricot. Summer had begun. Isobel came down for morning devotionals at half past six with Aunt Louisa, Anna and the household staff.

As soon as she stepped into the room, she sensed that all was not well. Anna had opened the drapes so the room was awash in blinding light. She was arguing with the poor housemaid, Peg, who had been instructed to keep the drapes drawn. Aunt Louisa had spoken a few stern words to Anna—'Calm down, my dear'— but these had only served to incite her more, culminating in her stubborn refusal to play for this morning's devotionals.

'Blast your moaning Welsh hymns!' swore Anna.

Isobel recognised the wildness in Anna's eyes, the snarl of her lips. She was the rabid dog again, cornered and beginning to bare her teeth. The servants had backed towards the door in terror and mortification at seeing their 'betters' behaving so badly. Aunt Louisa's attempts to 'talk sense' into her would only make things worse; Anna hated being lectured to and would bite back with even greater fury.

'Now, you mind your tongue, Miss Anna. This is no way for a lady to behave!'

'Damn the way a lady should behave. And damn you! Someone should cut *your* tongue out, stupid old woman!' shouted Anna, pacing back and forth and clawing at invisible creatures that buzzed about her head. Her demons were well and truly in control today.

'Call for Dr Finch, Aunt,' advised Isobel. 'He's the only one to calm her.'

'How about *you* stay out of it! How about *you* shut up!' Anna picked up a *Book of Common Prayer* on the bench where the staff normally sat. She hurled it across the room, narrowly missing her sister's head. 'You've caused enough trouble already, you have!' Isobel heard the hissing of the volcano, felt its ominous rumble that presaged the torrent of hatred that would now gush forth from Anna's lips.

'Do you think everyone has forgotten about your disgrace, Isobel? Do you? The Finches and the Bradleys? They still talk about us behind our backs. "Those brazen, ridiculous Macleod women!" they say. "They have stooped so low that they now have an ex-convict's son in the family tree." And *you* and that artist, making eyes at each other! You carrying on like a whore right under your aunt's nose! I see what goes on!'

Aunt Louisa's face had gone white with fear. Even Isobel was shocked. Anna's face was contorted into a hideous, spitting gorgon's.

She advanced on Isobel, her mind consumed by madness. 'And now your disgrace has destroyed our father's wits and sent him racing off to England to escape us! It drove away Joseph and William too—you saw how quickly they fled, so full of shame! You are the reason William died! You are the reason Alice won't come home! You are the reason Grace has left me here all alone! You are the root of all our shame, all our pain and misery!'

Isobel knew better than to provoke Anna but this was too much. She stepped towards her and the crazed woman flinched as if Isobel was about to strike.

'No, please, no!' she whimpered.

'Get to your room before I call the police and have you locked up!' shouted Isobel, her hand raised. 'Go!'

Galvanised by these words, Anna ran from the room and up the stairs, wailing, 'Please don't hurt me!' They heard the bedroom door slam.

'Anna has these fits. Please pay no attention to the nonsense she spouts. You must send for Dr Finch. He has medications that will help.' Isobel's face was set in a determined frown, her cheeks flushed, head throbbing. 'I am going out for a while. If I stay I shall only provoke her.'

She pecked her poor aunt on the cheek and hastened to her room to change her clothes and collect her art satchel. In the bedroom nearby she could hear Anna sobbing inconsolably. Isobel did not go to comfort her for she knew that when the madness had her in its grip, she was beyond the help of words. The only whip that could bring her inner devils to heel was fear—at least until Dr Finch came with his sedatives. To be honest, Isobel did not feel much like comforting Anna or saving her from herself. She was sick of Anna's cruelty. They may well be devils that possessed and spoke through her sister but Isobel feared that even so they spoke the truth of her sister's most vile thoughts.

Poor Aunt Louisa. She had been scared half to death. Isobel wondered how much longer such outbursts from Anna could be tolerated before they would be forced to have her committed. No doubt Anna was tormented by the same question.

Isobel needed to get away from the closeted atmosphere of Faulconstone. She needed to feel the breeze on her skin, to inhale the spring flowers and the invigorating smack of salt air, to walk and walk and walk. With her parasol to shield her from the heat, she caught an omnibus back along Old South Head Road and down Darlinghurst Road to what people were now calling Darlinghurst Heights, the home of her long-missed Rosemount. From the top of William Street, she walked past the grand homes of her childhood and their iron gates, avenues of trees, high walls and hedges. She then climbed down the steep flight of sandstone stairs into the valley behind Woolloomooloo Bay.

A fresh breeze whispered soothingly in the needled branches of the casuarinas and the silver-green canopies of the red gums that fringed the bay. Isobel loved the quiet and solitude of this place. Apart from a handful of wharf buildings and a timber yard and slipway for the construction of small ships, the foreshore was largely unspoilt. Isobel found a secluded spot on one of the crags overlooking the water. In the distance she could see the new Gothic Revival terraces being built along Victoria Street high up on the plateau of the Heights.

The lovely farm in the valley that had once belonged to Mrs Palmer and her husband had been broken up for workers' cottages and terrace houses, which sprouted all over the valley like mushrooms after rain. The elegant days of old Woolloomooloo were fading fast. Lining the dirt roads behind the waterfront there had sprung up several brick warehouses and sheds, a scattering of cottages and two pubs, precursors to the bay's new identity as the haunt of shipbuilders, sailors, lumpers and publicans. Even so, it was still a lovely spot.

On her shaded boulder overlooking the bay, Isobel sat, absorbed in her sketching. She had seen a charming pen-and-wash drawing by Mr George French Angas of this same view printed in the newspaper only a few weeks ago. She was interested to see how her own impression would compare and looked forward to showing it to Charles.

Isobel had been in love with this harbour since she was a little girl. She knew all its moods: serene, limpid jade on a spring morning; mirror-smooth and dazzling on a summer's day; leaden and stygian under rain clouds; grey and white flecked in a gale; bombazine-black and silvered under a full moon. The surge and suck of its waters were as vital to her sense of self as the ebb and flow of her own pulse. Isobel was possessed by this harbour.

On Boxing Day this year, Sydney had put on an impressive aquatic show on her beloved harbour. Isobel had come down with her father, aunt and two sisters to join Captain Clark and two hundred other guests for luncheon on the flagship *Young England*, anchored in Woolloomooloo Bay. The occasion was the inaugural Boxing Day Regatta, watched by a crowd of over two thousand that thronged the foreshore from the Domain all the way round to

Lady Macquarie's Chair. The course of each race started from the bay, looped round Fort Denison and the Sow and Pigs Reef, came back around the flagship, looped Fort Denison a second time and the buoys off Shark Island, before returning finally in triumph to the flagship. The holiday crowd cheered and waved handkerchiefs and hats as the skiffs, gigs and dinghies went gliding over the bright waters. On board the flagship, gold medallions were awarded to the winners, loyal toasts proposed and dances enjoyed late into the afternoon thanks to the Volunteer Band. Such a successful pageant, showing off Sydney's harbour in all its majesty, promised to be an annual event.

Today, only a handful of dinghies were tied up near the wharf and five small sail craft zigzagged lazily across the bay. Isobel counted four men down at the wharf sheds, two couples walking along the waterfront and a young man in a boater, lounging on the crags to her left. The jaunty notes of a squeezebox and a chorus of male voices floated out of the Rose and Crown on the corner to her right. A horse meditated on its chaff bag, harnessed between the shafts of a coach in front of the pub. Three dogs formed an irregular triangle in the dusty road. It was a picturesque scene, worthy of her pen and brush.

This furious concentration on her work was how she tried to purge the sadness and anger, pooled like poison in her heart, because of everything about her family: its shameful secrets, its overweening pride, its ancient grudges and new despairs. She wished she could be rid of it all! She would marry her Charles, change her name, maybe even go to Melbourne or Hobart (why not Paris?) with him and begin her life all over again in peace and happiness.

The breeze dropped and the air began to pulse with the heat. Droplets of perspiration beaded on Isobel's brow and the sun cut out her shadow, sharp and perfect, on the rock. It was going to be a hot summer if spring was this warm. But the blazing sunlight did not bother her; instead, it made every colour sing and every shape dance with greater intensity.

Isobel was so lost in her work that she failed to notice the wind gusting across the bay, apart from the odd finger-flick at the edges of her paper. Overhead the sky began to take on a bilious tinge and the waters of the bay to darken. Then she heard a voice on the road below her shouting, 'Brickfielder! Brickfielder! Get inside!'

She looked up and saw that the light over the city had grown acid and rust-coloured. Winds were racing across Sydney from the south, loaded with their freight of red dust and rising into a giant wave as thick as a pea souper. She had to move fast. She began to gather up her journal, parasol and satchel and look about, with some urgency, for shelter.

She did not feel comfortable about approaching any of the workers' cottages nearby. The wharf sheds were probably too far away for her to get there in time. And the pub was out of the question. She knew Charles had a studio above a store in a side street here but she had never visited him there, of course, for fear of scandal. But in an emergency, surely she would be justified in seeking shelter. If only she could remember the address.

The wind was fierce now, bending the trees before it and shredding their leaves to confetti. Isobel ran as fast she could, though the wind kept punching her, causing her to stumble from her course. All the people on the waterfront had scattered, as had the three dogs. Only the horse, blinkered and chewing in its nosebag, stood stock-still against the blast. Isobel looked over her shoulder.

Her heart bolted. This storm was bigger than a brickfielder. It had not just sucked the red dirt of the brickfields from the edge of the city into its lungs, it had taken in a whole desert of rust-red dirt from out of the west and now drowned the sky and the land in ochre. What Isobel saw when she looked back was a wall of dust taller than St Mary's, advancing swiftly across Sydney Cove, obscuring the outline of the city and sweeping up over the Domain. She pulled her shawl over her nose like the kerchief of a bushranger, if the illustrations in *Bell's Life* were to be believed.

At all points of the compass the sky had turned orange, deepening in places to red, the sun shrunken to a shrivelled white pea floating in a blood soup. This was the Apocalypse, the End of Days, more terrifying than the wave in Isobel's dream. From inside this advancing wave of dust came a shrieking unlike anything she had ever heard.

All over Sydney people were hurriedly closing their shutters, drawing their drapes, pulling down their blinds, sealing their windows, locking their doors, scooping up their children and chooks and dogs, and retreating into their backrooms and cellars and basements as the red wave broke over them. It came down on the city like an Old Testament plague, cloaking everything in an eerie silence of choked bells and gummed clocks. It brought the entire city, its busy traffic and bustling human assembly, to a standstill.

There was no escaping the insidious invasion of dust. It poured like smoke under doors, down chimneys, through gaps and crannies, to smear every surface with a lurid powder. Even when the wind passed and its tormented voice died away the dust continued to settle, blossoming like mould on plates and glasses, tablecloths and mantelpieces.

Isobel was caught out in the middle of the street still ten yards from anywhere she could shelter. The shadow of the enormous rolling cloud fell over her. If she did not get inside soon, she would have the dust shoved into her ears, eyes, nose and throat. It was a choice of the nearest cottage or the pub. And then she saw her only salvation. The coach. There was no luggage on the roof, the horse was hobbled, the brakes were locked, the canvas blinds were down and securely tied. Was there a remote chance a door had been left unlocked?

Isobel staggered the last few yards to the coach's step and grabbed the door handle. She had never travelled on one of these new coaches, which were beginning to take over all the Royal Mail routes in New South Wales. Oh, sweet deliverance! The door opened and she tumbled inside just as the dust storm struck. She slammed the door behind her and fell back against the wooden seat. She was safe. Outside, the full-throated scream of the wind was deafening and the blood-red darkness of the great cloud enveloped the coach.

She startled when there came a banging on the coach door on the opposite side. Whoever wanted access was tugging desperately on the handle. This door was locked. She could hear a voice shouting, its message muffled in the blast. Dear God! She could not in good conscience leave a wretched fellow creature outside in this!

She pulled back the bolt. A figure in an oilskin jacket and wide-brimmed hat pulled down low over its face clambered into the carriage with her. Her heart raced at her own act of daring. The stranger was unmistakeably male. She had now allowed this unknown man into this confined space with her, a young woman alone. She prayed that nobody had seen them both enter the coach. It seemed unlikely in the circumstances.

'Thank the Lord,' exclaimed the stranger in a voice oddly familiar. And then the man removed his hat to reveal none other than her Charles. He looked at her with undisguised shock and delight. 'So *you* are my saviour! Of all the people in this city, it should be *you*!'

They embraced and kissed and fell about in peals of laughter at this extraordinary circumstance of their meeting. All about them the storm raged, rocking the carriage as if it was a small ship buffeted in a gale. They could hear the nervous whinnying and snorting of the hobbled horse and the stamping of its feet. The canvas blinds rattled loudly in the window frames but miraculously admitted little dust as they were tightly tied.

'This is providence, my love,' said the artist, holding his soon-to-be fiancée in his arms. 'I have been down by the wharf for some time, sketching. And then I saw the storm coming. The sheds were all locked and this was my only route of escape. I was too slow to make the Rose and Crown so in sheer desperation I decided to try the coach!'

Charles's eyes sparkled with a fierce ardour as he looked at her. His face was lightly tanned by the sun and his hair gleamed gold in the strange burnished light of the storm. There was something different about him, thought Isobel, something magnificent but also a little intimidating. He smelled of the warm sun, and the salt of the harbour, and the tar of the charcoal under his fingernails. And a rich fume on his breath.

'Have you been drinking?' she asked, trying not to make it sound like an accusation, even though clearly it was.

'Not drinking, my love. Just a small dram of something over at the Rose and Crown. To be social, you know? Look, see what I have been drawing.' With the impatient enthusiasm that endeared Charles to her, he pulled his sketchbook out from under his oilskin and flicked through its pages. 'There, look at these faces. Faces of honest toil, bone-deep weariness, everyday care. The faces of working people, Isobel, the people who really run this world, without whose labours we would all starve and go without.'

She looked at the rough faces on the page. They appeared to be labouring men of all kinds, young and old, lined and unlined, dark- and white-haired: sailors, carpenters, shipwrights, lumpers, cabmen, fishermen. Charles had captured the subtlety of each one's character with such virtuoso ease, the merest stroke of his pen denoting a squint of ironic humour, a cynical twist to a mouth or a soulful tilt of a head. These portraits were no more than quick studies but they were masterful even so.

'They are wonderful,' said Isobel, genuinely impressed, though her thoughts were still preoccupied by Charles's confession that he had been drinking in a workingman's pub. Was this something he did often, another secret of her lover's other life?

Charles beamed at her. 'And look at this. See, you are never far from my thoughts.'

He turned the page and there was a portrait of Isobel. The frisson of recognising this beauty as herself had a profound effect. The sketch was exquisitely observed, a drawing you might dream of, neither falsely flattering nor sweetly cloying, but instead a frank, touching vision of Isobel that she immediately accepted as a true image. And at the same time, there was no use denying it, it was a work of worship.

Her heart was flooded with love, her body enflamed with passion. The roaring of the storm echoed the volume of her feelings, the unnerving, fiery light answered the fire in her veins, her skin, her loins. 'Do you love me, Charles? Tell me how much you do,' she sighed.

Charles saw the light in her eyes catch fire, heard the note of yearning desire in her voice. They would have her father's blessing in two months and their secret love would be trumpeted to the wide world and sanctified by a churchman. What shame was there in this?

Charles took her into his arms and kissed her.

The storm outside reached a new pitch of ferocity. To Isobel it sounded like the giant wave of her dreams, the grey-green wall of water that fell on Rosemount like a judgement from God and wiped away all its vanities and delusions, exposed all its secrets and pettiness.

'Damn the way a lady should behave. And damn you!' Anna had screamed at her aunt. Isobel felt the liberating power of her own rage, stoked by the ungrateful selfishness of her family, each one of them in their own way happy to abandon her: her mad sister, her dead brothers, her cruel sister, her distant father. This righteous

anger burned brightly as did her righteous love and shameless desire for Charles. It released her, absolved her, impelled her. Charles was her future. Charles was her destiny. This was what she wanted. She was free of self-reproach and fear and guilt.

'I love you,' she sighed as he kissed her neck, her shoulders, her breasts. And as the blood-red storm rolled over them, as unstoppable as their desire, with its hot light and urgent voice, Charles and Isobel turned a mail coach into their marriage bed.

Chapter 29

GRACE AND AUGUSTUS

NOVEMBER 1852 TO JANUARY 1853

A powerful alchemy of high emotion and physical ecstasy made Isobel invincible. She felt she had weathered the storm of these past few weeks, rising above her nadir of deepest misery. Isobel's heart had not hardened against these distresses—she still shed tears for William and kept a watchful eye on Anna—but she felt safe from being dragged into an abyss of despond. It was not hard to understand why. She was fortified by the power of young love, itself bold and indestructible. It was also, Isobel told herself, her first *real* love. Any traces of her infatuation with Ralph Tranter were all but forgotten. There was no one to warn her about the arrogance of such volatile young love that could not imagine its own end. For now, at least, Isobel was possessed by that most potent of loves: a secret love, known only to a conspiracy of two, hidden from the rude gaze of society, untouched by the world's cynicism.

Isobel hungered for her lover more than ever. As a girl she had been told by her elderly art tutor, Mr Vasey, that her drawings from nature would 'amplify the wonder of God's creation'. While the study of botany was a suitable subject for an educated young woman, there was the awkward fact that Dr Linnaeus had classified all plants by the number and arrangement of their *sexual organs*. Books of 'sexless' botany for women were printed with bowdlerised illustrations and text but these were not the ones Isobel found in her father's study, which acquainted her intimately with the sex lives of the plant world. But, of course, nothing had prepared her for hot-blooded mammalian sex: the savage coupling, the sweet terror, the rough pleasure, the animal urgency, the lustful abandon. Thankfully, Isobel's body now had this forbidden knowledge imprinted in every cell, nerve, sinew and pore of her.

After the dust storm passed, she lay for a short while in Charles's arms before they climbed down from the coach. They were dazed in the clear sunlight, reborn into new skins, a little awkward and self-conscious. People emerged from their refuges to make sure the city was still there, undamaged. Charles and Isobel strolled back along the street, peeling apart the space between them. At last they arrived outside Charles's studio in a narrow terrace house above a grocer's store. They lingered for a while, unsure how to return to their proper and separate spheres. Their eyes told all their longing and, with lovesick looks, they parted.

Her desire for her lover made her giddy with wanting. She fantasised risking disgrace all over again. If only she disguised herself, thought Isobel, she could go to his studio and nobody would know. In her fantasy, Isobel saw herself dressed as a young man again, hair tucked away beneath a cap, breasts and hips and waist concealed inside her dead brother's clothes. *Like Rosa Bonheur,* she thought. *How that would please her lover!* She had endured and survived the catastrophe of social disgrace and it held no fears for her now. She was beyond caring; scar tissue had grown over that wound long ago. Without her lover, she barely knew herself or how to be in her own body. She would go mad without his touch.

To make matters worse, Charles told her he had to go away to Melbourne. He earnestly hoped she would forgive him his three weeks' absence, a trip he had planned months ago. There was already talk of colonial exhibitions to be held in Sydney and Melbourne the year after next in preparation for a second international exhibition in Paris in 1855. Charles hoped to find out more about the Melbourne exhibition, for which a palatial glass-domed hall was to be built on William Street. He had also arranged for a painting trip to Ballarat and Bendigo. His old friend Samuel Thomas Gill was making his name and fortune in the gold-boom capital of Victoria with sketches of life on the goldfields. It was too good an opportunity to miss. Isobel was gracious about Charles's plans, of course, though she also let him know his absence would grieve her.

As if to underline Isobel's retreat into the life of a chaste maiden, Aunt Louisa had reconvened the fancywork circle for the New Year's Day charity bazaar. Isobel's participation was presumed and she joined the weekly meetings of the Mesdames Cornwall, Burdekin, Thierry, Forbes, Herriott, Smart, Long and Drummond. On other days, Isobel sat by the fire with her aunt, her fingers aching with the effort of stitching and crocheting. The fire warmed her pained hands and exhausted body and stirred up memories of evenings at Rosemount with her mother and sisters, bent over needlework and making lighthearted chatter. Such memories were nostalgic cameos, ghosts of a remote and now lost past.

Life resettled into familiar and comforting rhythms at Faulconstone. Dr Finch's pills temporarily quieted Anna's outbursts and she behaved as if nothing untoward had occurred. Neither Anna nor Aunt Louisa was in any hurry to wake that sleeping dog. Anna returned to her music and the house awoke most mornings to the martial strains of Chopin's 'Heroic' polonaise.

Three weeks after Isobel's apotheosis in the fury of a dust storm, a card arrived from *Villa Dordogne* requesting the presence of Aunt Louisa and her two charges. Grace and Augustus had just received a letter from their father in London off the *Chusan*'s sister ship, *Shanghai*, and there was some important news they must share. And they also wished to show off the magnificent portrait, executed by none other than Mr Charles Probius himself, that now hung in pride of place above the drawing room's Italian marble mantelpiece.

When they arrived that evening, Isobel could not help noticing how luminous Grace appeared. Her husband's expression, habitually one of self-satisfaction, was even more beatific than usual. Aunt Louisa and the three sisters wore black in honour of William, of course, but their sombre mood was lightened a little by the prospect, ever hopeful, of good news. Why else would their hosts look so happy? Isobel was also delighted to see Mrs Palmer. A long period of ill health over the last few months had forced poor Mrs P. into a prolonged period of recuperation. Tonight she looked a little frailer than usual but in excellent spirits otherwise.

She commiserated with Winnie's daughters over the loss of William and wished she could have attended the memorial service.

The portrait of the married couple (complete with foxhounds *couchant* at their feet) was duly admired and then everyone was seated for dinner. All glasses were refreshed with wine and a first course was served of asparagus soup, fricandeau veal, lobster tails, fricasseed fowl, beef tongue in sauce piquante, and potatoes à la Maître d'Hôtel.

The absence of the Major at such family gatherings was keenly felt. He was still the keystone in the arch of the family's stability without whose presence there was a vague but persistent unease, despite the natural authority and alacrity with which Grace had stepped into the role of *materfamilias*. She stood and asked for the company's attention. 'I have some important news to share with you all.' She looked around the table with a regal air, as if about to deliver a message *ex cathedra*. 'I am going to be a mother!'

'Grace! Oh, Grace! That is such wonderful news!' The company's cries of delight were mingled with tears of joy.

Isobel leaned over and kissed her older sister and her brother-in-law. 'I am so happy for you both. When is the baby due?'

'Next April.'

Augustus's moonface shone down on his guests with benign pride. 'He will be called Ignatius if he is a boy and Olympia if she is a girl.'

'We are still considering names,' corrected Grace, a trifle cross at her husband's unilateral announcement. 'We have already begun planning the baptism and asking Dr Finch about a wet nurse. So much to think about!'

How like Grace to look on this newborn baby as a complex project to devote her energies to, thought Isobel. One could only hope that somewhere in the plans of these two proud parents there was room reserved for love.

Isobel was not the only one to register Anna's pitiful look of shock as if she had been slapped in the face, her cheeks flushed and eyes fixed in a stare of utter panic. If Anna held any fragments of hope that Grace's historic love for her would survive her marriage then these seemed to be now conclusively crushed by the prospect of her motherhood. Anna could not compete with a baby.

The second and third courses were served and the wineglasses recharged. It was Augustus's turn to stand and deliver news to the gathering. 'I think it is important I tell you something that I learned this week,' he said, clutching his lapel with his right hand in a gesture Isobel was sure he adopted addressing a courtroom. 'Through someone I know at my club, I have found out some of the contents of the commission's report regarding the Major.' He hastened to explain. 'I have reason to believe that certain persons of high rank have been circulating a copy, though thankfully only with a few others.'

There was a ripple of disquiet around the table.

'I assume you want me to share this information?'

'Yes, yes, of course!' came the chorus of replies, though everyone at the table dreaded hearing how the Major had been scrutinised like a dead butterfly pinned under the magnifying glass of a naturalist.

'I shan't go into all the details but the report's findings were critical of several aspects of the Major's conduct of his department:

bad management of budgets, poor delegation of duties, arrogant treatment of inferiors, prioritising the surveying of roads and his general trigonometric survey over land claims by squatters.'

Isobel could feel the blood rising to her face. She hated to think of her father's despair when he read this litany of faults. It would confirm all his worst fears.

Augustus continued. 'The report also found fault with the Major's methods and actual measurements for his general survey, questioning the accuracy of his baselines. There was divided opinion on this point as to how badly it affected the overall accuracy of his Nineteen Counties map.' This went to the heart of the Major's professional competence and would hurt him most of all. 'The recommendations from the Governor are still pending.'

Grace nodded grimly. 'The whole report is a tissue of lies and exaggerations, there is no doubt about that. It is easy to see the hand of Mr Macleay in all of this. His final act of revenge.'

'And now he is beyond any accountability!' mocked Aunt Louisa with a look of angry disdain that echoed the collective indignation.

'So what happens now?' asked Isobel.

'The Major will be asked to respond,' said Augustus. 'While his position is being reviewed by the Governor he will be put on half pay and, if the Colonial Office is not satisfied with his defence of his record, he will be dismissed. He could tender his resignation now but he may lose his pension entitlements.'

Isobel's mind was cast back to the picnic lunch with her mother just before her thirteenth birthday when she had first learned of her father's troubles. Ever since, she had wondered if the price of admission to adulthood was the death of optimism. If someone as hardworking and dedicated as her father was hounded from office, it made a mockery of all hard work and dedication.

'As I told you in my invitation, we have just received another letter from Father two days ago,' said Grace. 'He has decided to stay in London for the Duke of Wellington's funeral, which will be held later this week. He will then return on the *Chusan* and, all being well, be home by the end of January as the Governor has asked. But the other important news contained in his letter is that Father has finally found Alice.'

The table erupted with cries of surprise and joy. 'Oh my, how is she? Is she well? What did he say?'

Grace signalled for them to calm down. 'Thanks to the information they had received from the old caretaker at Gothamberly, Uncle Fergus and Father had a very helpful visit with the young Baron's great-aunt in Cambridge. With further communication from the Twyckenhams' lawyers, they tracked down Alice and Xavier in a small house in outer London. Father reports that she looks well, if a little thin and careworn, but is bearing up remarkably under the circumstances.'

'She was always brave,' said Anna, tears glistening at the corner of her eyes.

'Father says his grandson is a bonny little chap with a strong resemblance to William when he was a baby.' Grace choked back tears at the mention of her brother. 'The long and the short of the matter is that Father has agreed to pay off some of the young Baron's debts. He had fallen seriously ill in prison and his release came just in time to save his life. Father has also decided to invest adequate funds in an account to support Alice and her son for the future.'

There was a gasp from every throat. This was not the news anyone had expected.

'But . . . are Alice and Xavier not coming back with him?' Isobel asked.

'No, they are not.'

Isobel did not understand. This was astonishing. Grace acknowledged her younger sister's disbelief with a nod of her head. 'Alice told Father that, despite everything, she still loved her husband and would not abandon him.'

'But that is—' Anna began to protest.

'There are no "buts" in this case, my dear Anna. As you can imagine, Father made all the sensible arguments but finally he was faced with the stark choice of either helping Alice or not helping her. You know how stubborn Alice can be. Just like Father. I do not think this was an easy decision but it seems Papa has chosen to help her.'

'But where will the money come from?' asked Isobel. 'Especially if he is put on half pay and may even lose his job.' Even as she spoke these words, she suspected she already knew the answer.

There was an awkward pause. Grace and Augustus exchanged significant looks. Augustus spoke. 'Before the Major left I made it clear to him that, if he thought it was necessary, I would be prepared to buy Rosemount. The Major has written to say that, under the circumstances, he has agreed to its sale.'

Anna and Isobel were dumbstruck. Of all the revelations that evening, this was the most shocking and profound (but one that, it appeared, Aunt Louisa had already heard). The two sisters could hardly object to Rosemount staying within the family, but this news confirmed their permanent exile. Rosemount was no longer their home. It would be Augustus and Grace's home. It marked Grace's ascension from middle sister (overlooked and taken for granted) to mistress of Rosemount.

Grace explained that they would cancel their lease at Hunters Hill and hoped to move into Rosemount by the end of the year. Father would live with them until he made further plans. She hastened to add that her sisters would always be welcome. For now, they would both remain at Faulconstone as companions to Aunt Louisa.

Isobel did not feel reassured. Anna looked even less sanguine. But both sisters did their best to conceal their deep dismay and to congratulate Grace and Augustus on their good fortune. It was evident that Augustus regarded his purchase of Rosemount as a gift to the family, an act of self-sacrifice and salvation, and expected heartfelt gratitude. Isobel imagined that William Macleay had felt the same when he took over Rosemount from his own indebted father.

An alarm sounded in Isobel's head as she tried to take in the full import of this momentous announcement. She could not find the words to express her precise fears but Isobel had a strong intuition that, even with Father's welcome return in January, this new arrangement would not be the guarantor of a happy future as they no doubt hoped. In fact, it may well be the cause of more grief.

With the exception of everything in the Major's study, Rosemount's furniture and possessions were sold off at a private auction (by invitation only) in early December. Isobel and Anna were invited to come to the house two days beforehand to choose any pieces they particularly cherished.

On what would prove to be her last visit to Rosemount before it was to be occupied by Grace and Augustus, Isobel arrived with Anna one grey overcast morning. The house had been closed up ever since the Major's departure. Every room was musty with the smell of damp, and dead moths and mouse droppings; and their contents (even the chandeliers and mirrors) had been transformed into an alien geometry of circles, triangles and oblongs beneath white dustsheets.

As she stood in the echoing saloon under the dome, Isobel could not help thinking of the silence that had reigned here the morning after her mother's death. In Winnie's monumental absence, the chairs and tables, the cushions and vases, the needlework baskets and antimacassars, everything familiar had appeared absurd and obscene. These things had only been receptacles for meaning when Winnie was alive, when her hand had touched them, when her eye had ordered and admired them. In the same way, the house now felt like the empty stage of a theatre, waiting for the props to be cleared away for the next play.

Grace and Augustus hoped to christen the house as their new home with a family dinner on Christmas Eve. How strange, thought Isobel, that only a year ago they had toasted Grace's engagement at such a dinner. How much had changed. Her own love for Charles had barely ripened and the fate of Alice was unknown, as was that of her brothers. She recalled the spirit of her father's toast that evening, if not the exact words, blessing Grace and Augustus's union and anticipating the scene at this year's table with *one united and blessed family.* The chasm between this vision and the present reality was hard to ignore. Isobel's father would still be abroad and the memory of William's death would rob the occasion of any cheer.

And there would be no Charles.

His letter a week ago had craved Isobel's indulgence as he was now planning to spend most of the summer in Victoria, probably to the end of January. He sent his most profuse apologies and protestations that he would make recompense for this long absence *'at such a challenging time for you, my dearest'.*

Charles and his companion, Samuel Gill, had spent three very productive weeks in the Victorian goldfields where *'such diverse and rich scenes of humanity in all its guises and moods'* proved irresistible to the artist's eye. *'It is hard to do justice in words alone to the spirit of brotherly love that prevails here despite the hardships. I truly believe that out of this busy, makeshift conurbation, this self-ruled fraternity of stout-hearted men and women, will be born a new society where the citizenry will claim a fair share of the common wealth produced from their own sweat, toil and dreams.'*

Charles's letter explained that he and Samuel had just set out on a field trip into the Flinders Ranges. Thanks to Samuel's growing reputation as an artist, they had been invited to join a surveying party dispatched by Lieutenant-Governor La Trobe to mark out new pastoral leases. Six years ago, Samuel had been the draughtsman on an expedition into this country led by the ill-fated Mr John Horrocks, who had died from his wounds when his gun accidentally discharged while he was seated on a grumpy camel. The rugged countryside was still a wilderness, not yet overrun with sheep and cattle. The two artists now camped under the stars and in the lilac light of early morning painted huge mobs of kangaroos grazing in the wild. Charles greedily drank in all this beauty and worked hard. *'You will forgive me when you see my sketches—this country is a paradise!'*

Isobel imagined that Charles and her father would have much to talk about when they met. But there was, she could not forget, a huge obstacle to surmount: the looming prospect of Isobel's lie being exposed. Back in March she had told Charles that her father was *in favour of the match, with no objection to their courtship in principle.* She had gone on to elaborate her lie with a truth: *'He would still like to meet you in person and discuss your proposal for my hand in marriage.'* Charles had certainly not forgotten this date with his destiny. *'I await your father's return impatiently when I shall claim you as my darling wife. Soon, soon, my sweet!'*

What could Isobel do now? If she said nothing to Charles then the fact of their secret courtship since Father's departure would be laid bare at his meeting with the Major, as would her deception. The consequences were too terrible to contemplate. Charles would feel duped and betrayed and her father would be furious and never approve of the match. Her lie would bring about the very thing it was designed to prevent.

Isobel had no choice. She had to tell Charles the truth. She knew he valued honesty so highly he had taken it as his name. But she also recalled the mischievous spark in his eyes and his tone of voice when she suggested they keep Aunt Louisa in the dark about their love trysts: *'Dear, oh dear, you are asking me to dissemble? . . . You are more wicked than I thought, Isobel Macleod.'* She hoped that

Charles would be sympathetic to her determination to lie for love. He of all people would understand the necessity, especially for the weak and disenfranchised, to break society's rules at times. What power did she as a woman possess, as the property and possession of men, fathers and husbands alike, except to dissemble?

Isobel had a firm faith that Charles's passion and his patient, kind and dedicated love for her—already proven beyond any doubt these last months—would overcome his scruples. Isobel also earnestly hoped that the last ten months had afforded her father enough time to inquire into Charles Probius's reputation in order to make up his own mind. Charles and the Major were both, in their own spheres, men enraptured by this country's beauty and promise. Surely theirs would be a meeting of compatible souls and minds?

Despite all these reassurances to herself, Isobel still anticipated the return of her father and her lover with a disconcerting mix of joyful anticipation and fearfulness. She knew she was fast approaching a crossroads that would determine her future path to happiness or despair. Every night she half-prayed that the opal dragonfly's dreams would give her a sign to illuminate the road ahead. But she waited in vain for the reappearance of the man in the rowboat, rowing neither away nor towards her, to tell her of her fate.

Christmas proved a dreary, even trying affair, despite Grace and Augustus's generous hospitality. Both Anna and Isobel were ill at ease at the ornate French winged table in Rosemount's dining room as they sat either side of Aunt Louisa and opposite dear

Mrs Palmer. 'A toast to our family and its imminent reunion!' proposed Augustus, still basking in his own good estimation that he was the heroic saviour of Rosemount.

In making the house their own, Grace and Augustus had crammed the spacious rooms, once the domain of sober tables, chairs and chiffoniers in mahogany and cedar, with their new furniture: lavishly carved and plumply upholstered French chairs and chaise longues, dark-wood and gilded gueridons and desks in ebony, walnut and tulipwood. Everywhere one looked were Indians from North America, blackamoors from Africa, and bare-breasted, winged women from Egypt, seated, bowed, upright, in postures of submission and support. Aunt Louisa's eyes bulged with disbelief.

Isobel smiled to imagine what Charles would make of it all. Whatever political reservations Augustus might have about Louis-Napoleon's Second Empire, these did not seem to interfere with his and Grace's taste. Isobel also wondered how the Major would tolerate living among such trappings of French decadence. She suspected that the decor would drive her father to seek alternative accommodation sooner rather than later.

Apart from its questionable taste, the presence of all this unfamiliar stuff in such an intimately familiar setting was deeply unsettling for Anna and Isobel. Their childhood home was almost unrecognisable. They did their best to appear supportive of their sister's new ownership of Rosemount and yet, despite their smiles and nods, Grace could feel her sisters' discomfiture and in their faces saw the silent accusation of her and Augustus's usurpation.

Isobel was thankful that her busy days with the fancywork circle in preparation for the New Year's Day bazaar took up so much of her time and attention. Despite her zealous devotion to the cause, Isobel apologised to Aunt Louisa that she did not feel well enough to attend this year. While it was true she had been unnaturally fatigued these last few weeks, the real reason was her fretting about the future. The last place she could bear to revisit was where she had heard the dire predictions of the soothsayer: '*You will find what you are looking for. But everyone you love will be gone.*'

She received two more letters from Charles during January. He planned to be back in Sydney on the last day of the month. '*Do you know yet when your father returns? I wish to make an appointment to see him the minute I am back. When I have his formal consent, we can post our banns at St Mark's and share with the world the news of our blissful love. I am sure that your sisters and your aunt will be more than reconciled to these glad tidings.*'

Isobel had written to Charles about her longing for his return and how she could only keep herself distracted from thinking about him with her needlework and her drawing. '*I too have been drawing,*' she wrote, '*mostly botanical studies as I wish to sharpen my skills of observation there. I am coming to understand more deeply every day how Art and Science are twin sisters in our humble endeavours to comprehend God's creation, to see the hidden patterns of His handiwork that will reveal nature's mysteries for our enjoyment and our use.*'

There was one detail that she omitted in her news to Charles: Grace and Augustus's purchase of Rosemount. Why did she hesitate to mention such a momentous change? She did not dwell on the reason. She simply decided that it was a topic best left for his return.

The day finally came for the Major's arrival in the last week of January. The family gathered at the quay with feelings of relief and gladness in their hearts as the *Chusan* steamed into the harbour. A majestic plume of smoke signalled her arrival on the horizon greeted by a chorus of 'hurrah's, repeated several times as she made her stately progress through the Heads. The ship's appearance was still a welcome novelty and cause for jubilation, and a raucous throng lined the cliffs and jetties of Port Jackson to cheer her in. The mail she carried was more precious than any other cargo in her holds (including thousands of pounds sterling) and her decks bristled with naval cannons and swivel guns as protection against the pirate junks of the China and Java Seas.

Isobel's heart leaped at the sight of this ship, which bore home her beloved and dearly missed father. Despite the strange portents of her dreams and her nervousness about the future, Isobel was determined to be optimistic and to hope that, with her father's auspicious and safe return, harmony and good sense would prevail.

Chapter 30

THE RETURN

JANUARY TO FEBRUARY 1853

Isobel fought back tears as she embraced Papa.

'Ah, Isobel, it is so good to see you.'

She thought he looked much older than the past ten months could account for. While there was still that purposefulness and vigour in his bearing that was so familiar to Isobel, she also sensed a deep fatigue. It was there in his whole manner, slower and more hesitant than usual, and in his speech, less voluble and assertive. It was there in the slight stoop of his shoulders, the thinning of his hair and whiskers, the slack skin of his neck, the pallor of his face and the soft pouches of flesh beneath each eye. But perhaps it was simply that his prolonged absence made clear to Isobel just how much her indestructible father had aged these last years without her really noticing.

Back at Rosemount, Isobel noted a tremor of alarm pass almost imperceptibly across her father's face as he entered his home, now so very changed. And, of course, there were other, more profound shocks to come. The family anticipated that Grace's letter had not reached him in time so the subject of William's death had yet to be broached; to soften the blow the Macleod family had dispensed with their mourning clothes for one day. Grace had agreed to tactfully take Father aside and break the terrible news to him later that night. A copy of the commission's report waited in the study but none of the family was in a hurry to mention it. *Sufficient unto the day is the evil thereof.*

While his luggage was unloaded and unpacked, the Major settled into a chair in the drawing room and called for a rummer of punch and a plate of cold collations. He had suffered terrible stomach pains (a bout of seasickness?) and a persistent cough in the last week and had not eaten properly for all that time. He was brimming with news and seemed greatly cheered by having his family gathered around as an eager audience.

'I gave addresses on my ship's screw to the Institution of Civil Engineers in London, the Royal Military Academy at Woolwich, and the Royal Dockyard Schools at Portsmouth, Devonport and Chatham,' the Major told them proudly. 'I even met with Mr William Patterson from the Great Western Steamship Company.' Mr Patterson was one of Britain's most famous boatbuilders, who had worked on Mr Brunel's mighty passenger ship *SS Great Britain*, the largest ocean-going vessel afloat with an iron hull and screw propeller.

Isobel was glad to have her father home. She hoped that William's death and the commission's report would not cause him to regret his homecoming, though she feared what heavy blows they would be for him to bear. It was also evident to Isobel that the meeting with Alice had unsettled him. He had been deeply moved to see his eldest daughter so vulnerable and proud. She had told him that the fall of Gothamberly House and the family's fortunes had begun years ago with a shameful tragedy, barely ever spoken of: the murder of Lady Olivia at the hands of an adulterous and insanely jealous lover. The house's ruin dated directly from this grim episode. The 13th Baron Crawley, Andrew's father, was so haunted and shamed by its memory, he had all but abandoned the house. It was a tale certainly worthy of Mrs Radcliffe, as Charles had observed.

It was obvious to everyone present that it had taken all the Major's strength of will and force of love to leave Alice and his sweet grandson behind. Papa explained that Alice's husband had grown so grievously ill that leaving him in debtors' prison was tantamount to a death sentence. The Major had been appalled at how little kindness or interest Andrew's parents took in their son's fate. It was clear that the poor fellow had for a long time been a victim of his father's heartless control, forced, against his will, to sink his inheritance into his father's risky ventures. He had also been sent to Sydney for the express purpose of securing land grants and a marriage with a well-off colonial family as no family in England would ally itself with the scandal-plagued Twyckenhams.

As it happened, Andrew had fallen deeply in love with Alice and now wished to sever relations with his parents if only his debts could be settled. He promised to make a new life with suitable employment to support Alice and Xavier as a responsible father and husband. 'I came to know the man, to see past the charade he had been obliged to perform, and found it in my heart to embrace him, despite everything that has happened.'

The Major took out an envelope and opened it. 'A letter from Alice to you, her sisters.' He handed it to Grace, who read aloud.

My sweet sisters, Grace, Anna and Isobel,

Please forgive my long silence. I think of you daily and miss you all very much. I have not found the heart to write earlier as life has been a great trial with no good prospects of Improvement and I did not wish to burden you. I am sure Papa has explain'd the circumstances of my decision to stay. What may be hard to understand is why I am so loyal to a man who must appear proud and deceitful in your eyes. I hasten to reassure you he is far from that. His love for me shows him to be the most tender and considerate of men. Since childhood he has been relentlessly bullied by his father into upholding the Family Honour.

But the truth is that Andrew is a kind and sentimental man who loves his own son dearly. He also loves me and would do anything to spare me such suffering. I know how much this terrible situation tortures him.

For me to take the escape route offered by Papa and abandon Andrew now would surely destroy him, in spirit if not in body. I cannot express my gratitude to Father deeply enough that he has cast aside his rightful suspicions and anger and chosen to help where help was most sorely needed. Andrew is determin'd to repay this Debt in any way he can and shall forgo his hereditary title – which is no more than a shackle of shame to him – in order to win his freedom. He is a changed man now that he has renounced his bonds of fealty to his father who used him cruelly. I will write you all again soon.

Please find enclosed a drawing of little Xavier who is over-joyed to see his father again.

With all my love and best wishes for your future happiness,
    Your sister, Alice

Everyone was deeply moved by this testament of love. It also showed their father in a magnanimous light, able to overcome his anger and give this desperate young man a second chance, all for the sake of his daughter Alice and his grandson Xavier. Isobel hoped it augured well for her father's meeting with Charles; maybe Papa would be more kindly disposed towards him now.

The Major looked pale and exhausted after all this talk and decided he should have a nap. 'There is much news still to share,' he told his family. 'But there is plenty of time.' Anna, Isobel, Aunt Louisa and Mrs Palmer embraced him again and took their leave.

Later that evening, Grace knocked gently at the Major's door to tell him the news of William's death. 'It was better that he hear it directly from me than from someone else's lips. I could not risk that.' Grace told Isobel later that her father had been struck down by the news as though poleaxed. She feared for a moment that he had suffered a stroke for he sat in his chair, stony-faced, muttering 'kismet' repeatedly like a man possessed. And then he barked angrily, as if berating himself, 'No, you fool. It is all your fault.' Grace heard him sobbing all that night and pacing the floorboards in his room. The following morning, he asked to be taken to see William's headstone in the graveyard at St Mark's. Grace obliged. He laid fresh-cut flowers and one of his campaign medals on the stone and walked away. How strange, thought Isobel when she heard Grace's account later. Was the medal a gesture of paternal regret, a private salute to his dead son?

The second onerous duty that day was to read the commission's report. The Major sat in the study for hours with the door locked. He had received and taken comfort from reassurances from his patron, Lord Sherbourne, that the Colonial Office would take a dim view of this so-called official commission of inquiry and the report that his old enemies had cooked up to discredit him. He composed a long letter to the Governor in which he disputed many of the report's findings and defended his conduct.

The following morning, he went to the city for a brief meeting with His Excellency. The Governor welcomed him home, conveyed his condolences and graciously received the Surveyor-General's letter of response. 'Your deputy, Mr Perry, will be able to brief you on developments in your absence.' That same day, the Major visited his accountant and his solicitor to review his affairs.

Dr Finch came by Rosemount later that afternoon and examined his old friend. The tremor in his right hand had never gone away and was most pronounced when he was tired; today it troubled him more than usual. His pulse was weaker than it should have been, his face appeared dreadfully pale and he was short of breath even when sitting. He neglected to tell the doctor about the traces of blood on his handkerchief that morning following another violent bout of coughing. The doctor advised that Sir Angus take up the load of his many duties slowly and gradually; a long sea voyage often proved vexatious to the spirit and taxing on the body, not to mention the terrible shock of grief the Major had sustained at the news of William's death. 'Rest is what you need, my friend.'

The Major thanked Dr Finch for his advice, promised to have him as a guest for dinner soon, and promptly returned to work the following day. There was still so much to be done and, despite the report's criticism that he failed to delegate work to others, the Major insisted on visiting a road-repair crew in the Blue Mountains the day after to personally check on their progress.

In the meantime, another ship had docked at the quay that morning from Port Phillip. Isobel stood alone, her face hidden in the darkness of a hooded cloak, anxious not to draw attention to herself. She was meant to be visiting Mrs Palmer but she had come here instead. As the gangplanks went down, Isobel searched impatiently for her lover's face in the noisy egress of passengers. At last, what a welcome sight! With his unmistakeable swagger, and that noble profile and golden hair, he crossed the wharf, swinging his cane, and looking about for his darling Isobel. Their reunion after two and a half months was as tender as she had imagined it. They found a moment alone behind a brougham, hidden from public scrutiny, to steal a passionate kiss. 'Dear God, how I have missed you!' Charles growled at her.

'I am due at Mrs Palmer's in an hour,' confessed Isobel, 'but I had to steal some precious time with you. I could not wait a moment longer.'

Charles laughed. 'Ah, my dearest love, how good it is to see you. I have so much to show you. And to tell you.'

Charles spoke to the petty officer and paid for his luggage to be taken to his studio. 'It can be left with Mr Dawson, the shop-keeper, down below. He knows me.' This business concluded, the happy couple strolled along the quay, rejoicing in their reunion and the sheer loveliness of the harbour on such a sunny morning. The shining green waters and teeming panorama of the quay were a rapture to Isobel's eyes. And to her ears, the bell-clanging, gull-crying, wagon-trundling tumult seemed a jubilant hymn of praise. And yet in all this exultation, Isobel's heart ached with fear.

'So is your father returned from London? When can I see him?' asked Charles.

Isobel could not put off the dreadful truth a moment longer. She must make her confession. She must do it before her lie destroyed her future.

'There is something I have to tell you, Charles,' she said. 'But I am almost too afraid to speak. I fear you will be very angry with me.'

Charles stopped walking then and looked at her. 'What is it, my dear? You look so pale. Please tell me. You frighten me as well. Is it bad news?'

'I hope you do not receive it as such,' she said. 'I ask you to consider my desperate situation when I tell you what I have done. And I beg your forgiveness in advance. Whatever crime I have committed, I did it out of my love for you.'

Charles studied her face with a look of utter bewilderment.

'I lied to you, my darling,' said Isobel.

Charles stared at her. 'When?'

'I told you my father favoured our match. I told you he approved of our courtship in principle, and that we must keep our courtship secret to spare my sisters. All lies. Father did not give his blessing to our courtship. He said he could not do so until he was satisfied you were a respectable man in the eyes of society. Because you have been a convict. He told me he would inquire about your reputation and may agree to meet with you when he returned.'

'I see.'

'I felt so betrayed when he said all this. So angry! I hated him for his hypocrisy. He was happy to let Grace marry Augustus whose father stole thousands of pounds of feathers and silk! But he hesitates to forgive you who, out of hunger and despair, took the paltry contents of a woman's purse. I realised then that my belief that honesty is the best policy was a mistake. It had only been rewarded by my father's hypocrisy and heartlessness!'

Charles appeared at a loss for words. His face was grave and still. His eyes were downcast and his expression impossible to read. Isobel continued her confession, unable to turn back now. If this was to be the end of her love, her happiness, her only chance at a future in which she could fly like a flash of light and discover her own true nature, then so be it. She would tell him the truth and be damned for it.

'I knew it was wrong to lie. That it was an offence to you, to God, to my whole family. And I knew that my lie would be discovered and would grievously hurt the people I have deceived. And yet I still prayed that Father would come to see things differently. You and he share so many interests, so many fine qualities. I know when you meet you will like one another. Were it not for a petty crime long ago there would be no obstacles to our marriage, I am sure of it. I lied because I could not bear to lose you, Charles. You are the only good that has come into my life in these last few years.'

Charles looked up at her then. There was a great tenderness in his regard.

'We have kept our courtship secret from everyone. And yet, as my teacher and friend, you have already won the hearts and good opinion of my family: Aunt Louisa, Grace, Augustus, even Anna when she is not ill. The only heart that waits to be turned is Papa's.'

Isobel was crying now. 'I have no right to ask you any favours, I know. I have deceived you. If I were a man, I would not be forgiven such deceit. And yet . . . I love you, Charles. I love you so much that I am willing to imperil my immortal soul. And to risk the wrath of my family all over again. I am beyond caring about reputation and honour. What are they worth if you must trade away true love and be condemned to misery for their sake!'

Isobel's voice had risen to a pitch of indignant anger. Now she dropped her voice and spoke quietly, her hands folded in supplication. 'So this is what I ask, dear Charles. I beg you to find it in your heart to forgive me. I pray that we may still have a chance at happiness. Father is not the proud man he once was; life's blows have bowed that stiff neck and tempered that pride with humility. He may well look on your offer of marriage with fresh eyes. That is if you have any love left in your heart for one so wicked!'

Isobel wept then. Charles clasped her left arm and drew her closer, oblivious to the curious stares of passers-by. 'Listen to me, Isobel.'

She looked at his serious, handsome face. Dear God, how she would miss it! How could she live without this man in her life? The man in the rowboat gripped the oars and she heard them splash as they hit the water. Which way would he row? Towards her or away?

'Listen to me,' he said again. 'You have nothing to be ashamed of. You did what any true lover would do to save herself! I do not judge you for that. You have my solemn promise that this changes nothing between us. I yearn for our life together, two souls dedicated to the same ends: beauty, love, freedom. I will meet your father and ask for your hand in marriage.'

'Oh, Charles!' Isobel was overcome. She felt herself close to fainting but Charles's firm grip had her by the elbow and guided her to the nearest seat. Her tears blurred the blazing harbour light that seemed to envelop her like a blessing. She had risked everything, gambled everything on this confession. Honesty had won through in the end.

And its most fierce champion, Mr Charles Probius, would lay this sinful lie aside and send a note urgently to Rosemount for a meeting with the Major the following morning.

That evening, Aunt Louisa and Isobel visited Rosemount. The Major, still very pale and with his chest racked by spasms of coughing, welcomed his daughter into his study – his only refuge now in a house changed beyond recognition. On an impulse, Isobel decided she wanted to show her father a watercolour she had finished that day. It was a view of Woolloomooloo Bay, worked up from the sketches she had done weeks earlier on the day of the dust storm. He was very pleased to see her and they sat in his study for the best part of an hour. There was, of course, another even more pressing reason for their meeting.

'Your mother would be so proud of you, my dear Isobel.' The Major held her hand affectionately. He picked something up from his desk. 'I have received a note from your suitor. Mr Probius.'

Isobel blushed, mindful that she must feign ignorance. 'What does it say?'

'He wishes to meet me early tomorrow morning here. In the gardens.'

'I see.'

'He seeks your hand in marriage.'

Isobel looked her father full in the face then. He looked at her with curiosity. 'So tell me, do you still have feelings for this fellow?'

'I do, Papa. I do.' Isobel struggled not to shed tears. She did not want to alarm him.

'Well, I shall look forward to our meeting with great interest. I believe I have acted properly with regards to the welfare and happiness of your two sisters. I am gratified that this man has not changed his attitude towards you even after all this time. It bodes well, I think.'

Isobel's face burned now. 'Oh, Papa.'

'You shall have my answer tomorrow, Isobel.'

'Thank you, Papa,' said Isobel and kissed him on the cheek. She had reasons to be hopeful. She had only to pray that all would go well on the morrow.

When she looked back the Major was studying the watercolour she had left on his desk. A view of Woolloomooloo Bay.

Later that evening, the Major put on his dress uniform with his campaign medals and Macleod clan tartan. While he did not feel at all well, he was determined not to miss that evening's important occasion. Two hundred eminent men had been invited by the Governor to attend an anniversary dinner to celebrate Mr Hargraves' discovery of gold at Bathurst two years ago. His position as Surveyor-General might be under review ('under threat, more like,' the Major snarled) but Sir Angus's service to the colony had earned him a place at that table.

The saloon in the Royal Hotel in George Street was bathed in the brilliance of four gaslit chandeliers. The banquet table and its epergnes, stocked with fruit and flowers, glistened opulently. There were many speeches about the colony's grand future, evoking soul-stirring visions of Sydney Harbour choked with steamships, all laden with money and migrants, and the banks bursting at the seams. Mr Thomas Mort, owner of Sydney's largest dry dock, proposed a toast to the city's traders who were destined to become 'like those of the once magnificent cities of the Mediterranean— merchant princes!' This was greeted with lusty cheers. Amid all this self-congratulatory bonhomie, Major Macleod felt a quiet glow of satisfaction at having played such a vital role in the colony's prosperity.

Early the following morning, the Major met Mr Charles Probius for a walk through Rosemount's gardens. Except for the artist's unfortunate past, there was a firm foundation already in place for a congenial meeting of minds, a happy commingling of kindred spirits. The artist admired the Major's sketches and maps and had read the published journals of his expeditions. The explorer and mapmaker in his turn had a set of the artist's lithographs and knew of his portrait work. The two men discussed their respective encounters with natives, a topic on which they shared many observations and insights. The Major complimented the artist on the sensitivity and subtlety of his portraits of indigenes. The artist complimented the explorer on the courage and tact with which he had negotiated with tribes in the hinterland and his keen interest in their customs and language. And then Charles Probius formally requested Isobel's hand in marriage. Isobel would have to wait until the following day to learn the outcome of his request.

The Major then changed his clothes, packed his instruments and boarded a coach to the Blue Mountains where he would meet one of his assistant surveyors at the Gardner's Inn at Blackheath. A road gang was conducting repairs on Victoria Pass and the Major wished to supervise the work personally. He arrived late that evening and camped up at the Pass with the foremen overnight. The following morning he arose early to inspect the labourers' work.

The Major had fond memories of this part of the Blue Mountains with its views to the plains beyond; it was here, as a young man, he had first encountered the wild country beyond Sydney Town and it had changed him. The truth was that the Major was never happier than when he was outdoors on horseback, his artificial horizon in his saddlebag, taking readings. He revelled in the subtle splendour of sky and bush; the smell of rain-soaked earth in the evenings or bush blossom in the heat; the epic majesty of red desert, grey-green scrub, wild grasses the colour of parchment, groves of white eucalypts, the ramparts of purple mountains. From habit, the Writer began to dream of words, the Artist to envisage shapes, translating this scenery into poetry and image. The Surveyor imagined something else again: an invisible grid laid across the countryside like a stencil, flattening it into abstraction to reveal its hidden patterns.

All three—poet, artist, mapmaker—performed these mental labours without which no man could comprehend, own, use, understand or value this land. Maps, songs, diaries, poems, paintings, stories: Angus Macleod understood that the land did not exist without these mental labours. It had no meaning, no form, no framework, no context without Angus Macleod's sketches and journals and maps. Of course, he acknowledged that God was the creator of this strange, unforgiving country and that he, Angus Macleod, was merely His instrument in discovering and mapping it. But at God's behest, he had brought this land within the grasp of civilised men from the Governor and his Executive Council down to the farmer, the digger and the pastoralist who followed in his bullock tracks and trod his roads.

His expeditions had revealed tens of thousands of acres of fertile grazing land to the south and north. They had been a mixed blessing when it came to expanding the map of human knowledge; some people said other explorers—Mr Sturt, Mr Oxley, Mr Hovell and Mr Hume—had done a better job in that regard.

And it was true that these expeditions had come with a heavy personal cost. But that was all in the past, dead and buried. The roads he had surveyed and constructed would remain his proudest legacy, the Major told himself. These were the arteries that kept the colony alive, the channels that carried settlers and farmers, and the network of its commerce and communication, long after the coming of the railroad, the telegraph, and the river and coastal steamers.

Just past mid-morning, with the frost barely thawed on the black ground in the shadows of the trees, Sir Angus felt so unwell he was persuaded to return to the inn at Blackheath. Here, a doctor was called to examine him. The Major was now struggling to breathe and his lips bubbled with phlegm speckled with blood. The doctor told him he had caught a chill, which was quickly turning to bronchial pneumonia or worse, and insisted he go back to Rosemount immediately and summon his own physician.

Racked with violent coughs, the Major was ferried back home in a coach. He arrived just on dusk. Dr Finch was summoned straight away and battled to control his patient's fever and stop the virulent spread of infection. But the Major's lungs were drowning in a dirty froth of sputum and blood and every breath was a monumental effort. It was obvious that the Major had been sick for weeks. Weakened by his long sea voyage and the shock of the news on his homecoming, the Major's spirits and body were failing fast.

'Fetch the family,' Dr Finch urged Grace. 'He does not have long.'

Isobel, Anna, Aunt Louisa, Grace and Augustus gathered about the dying man's bed. Father was beyond their help and care.

His mind rode out across light-bleached plains. He was finding his way to a bright new territory that no man had mapped. The pendulum, the engine, the heart of the colossus slowed and finally stopped.

Isobel's father died at a quarter to midnight.

Chapter 31

SHAME

FEBRUARY 1853

As she stood by his bed and looked down on her father's face as shiny and white as wax, Isobel could see no future past the next second, minute, quarter hour. With her father gone, she mourned again for Richard, for William, for Winnie. Isobel was now an orphan, irrevocably, irreconcilably lost. She wanted to stand here, suspended forever between her girlhood, her youth, her happy days at Grangemouth and Rosemount, and her future, the vast unknown.

She dared not move, breathe.

She had risked everything the morning of the duel—her reputation, her peace of mind, her sisters' and friends' love—to save her father from the deadly bullet. And for what? So that, less than eighteen months later, he would be struck down by pneumonia? She remembered the words of the old soothsayer, the augury of the opal dragonfly: *Everyone you love will be gone.* Winnie, Richard,

William and now Papa. Where would she ever find comfort? Aunt Louisa insisted on reading passages from *In Memoriam*:

> Thou wilt not leave us in the dust:
> Thou madest man, he knows not why,
> He thinks he was not made to die;
> And thou hast made him: thou art just.

Yes, soon, soon, she would bow her head and acknowledge God's merciful wisdom, His guiding hand in all things. But not now. Now she would rail against cruel Fate, her fists raised against an empty, senseless sky. She would howl out all her pain, drown in an endless flood of tears. She would be the swimmer, ducking her head under freezing black water, letting her body's heat leach out, numbed by its icy chill.

Grief would be her sole companion.

Charles came to Faulconstone the following morning. As always, news travelled fast in the colony and he had already heard of the Major's passing. He left his card with the butler and asked him to convey a message. 'If neither of the ladies are fit to have company, I perfectly understand and will return whenever I can be of service.'

It was a thoughtful gesture but unnecessary, as Isobel was eager to see Charles. Only he could tell her how the meeting with the Major had concluded. It was too late for her to hear the verdict from her father's own lips.

'Isobel! My darling! Did your father tell you . . . ?' he asked as soon as he entered the room and rushed to embrace her.

Isobel shook her head. 'He was too ill. He said nothing.'

'Oh cruel fate! That such deep sorrow should accompany such great joy! Your father is . . . was . . . such an honourable and sympathetic gentleman, it grieves me that I did not have the chance to know him better. To think that death has robbed me of so fine a father-in-law!'

'So he . . . ?' Isobel's eyes widened with wonder.

'Yes, yes. He gave his consent!' cried Charles. 'We found so many matters of mutual interest to discuss, I believe we would have become the firmest of friends. While he was abroad, it appears your father corresponded with eminent colleagues here and in England who spoke well of me. I was able to furnish him with ample evidence of my financial bona fides. He also said he had examined his own conscience and could see no obstacle to our happy union.'

'He was delirious when they brought him in,' said Isobel, 'and then he could barely speak at all. I do not know if he even knew we were there. How I wished I had been able to . . .' She began to weep at recalling the agonies of the deathbed. Charles took her in his arms. 'I cannot tell you how it gladdens my heart to know he approved!' smiled Isobel bravely through her tears. 'I knew he would see you for the fine man you are.'

'Should we tell your aunt? If you wish to delay the announcement of our engagement, I will understand. Under the circumstances.'

'No, no,' cried Isobel. 'I have waited so long already. We are already married in flesh and spirit, are we not? Let us sanctify our union as soon as we can.'

'Very well, my love,' said Charles, embracing her again. 'Just as you wish.'

Aunt Louisa was summoned and told the astonishing news. She burst into tears and hugged them both. 'I am so happy for you, Isobel, my dear. But so sad at the timing of this news. If only your father could have lived to see you wed, my dear niece!'

'I hope I have your blessing as well, Mrs Blunt, now that you are Isobel's legal guardian. I am willing to show you everything that I showed your brother.'

'Mr Probius! Of course you have my blessing,' smiled Aunt Louisa. 'I have grown to admire and—if I may speak freely—very much enjoy your cultured and considerate company, sir. I believe you and my niece will make a very good match. Your reputation speaks volumes. And I have your word of honour as a gentleman as to the contents of your meeting with poor Angus. I have no doubt he embraced you warmly as a son-in-law.'

And so plans were put in place to formally announce the engagement of Charles 'Probius' Ludiger and Miss Isobel Clara Macleod. Aunt Louisa would send out letters to all the family and a lunch would be hosted at Faulconstone or Rosemount in honour of the engagement. In about four months' time, the banns would be posted once a respectable period of courtship had been concluded. The happy couple were free to see each other in daylight out of doors, unchaperoned. They could take walks in the garden or along a beach, attend parties and suppers, go for a ride or share a coach as long as their behaviour was decorous. They were even permitted such intimacies as a hand around the waist or a chaste kiss. In this way, all the formal protocols were duly observed and the world was none the wiser that Isobel and Charles had committed a sin in the eyes of God and lied to everyone in Isobel's family and in society at large with no hint of shame.

The Major's funeral was held a week later at St James' and a special notice was published in the *Government Gazette*: 'The Governor, with a desire to shew every respect for the memory of Sir Major Angus Macleod, invites all the civil officers of the Government to attend the funeral. Sir Macleod will be buried with full military honours.'

Through her veil of tears, Isobel watched 'the great and the good' file into the church with pious nods in the direction of the mourning family. They included His Excellency the Governor, of course, and members of the Legislative Council as well as Mr Perry, the deputy surveyor-general (who would probably take her father's place at least for now), and the heads of other departments. She tried to quell the bitterness that rose in her heart at the thought that some of these men had been her father's enemies, had spread vile gossip behind his back, had written the report intended to wreck his career, had destroyed his self-worth and his health. And here they sat in their sanctimonious smugness to pay tribute.

Among the Major's papers, Grace found a poem that he had apparently penned in the days since his return. He had entitled it 'Farewell', presumably to be published once his retirement was forced upon him by the Government's unfavourable report; it seemed that he had made the decision to leave Sydney forever and return to England. The poem made references to Victoria Pass, named for Her Majesty, and built with the sweat and blood of 'the banished' convicts, as well as to his expeditions into the hinterland (his 'centaurs') and the deaths of both his sons. What had been intended as valedictory verses had now become the Major's own epitaph. Grace stood in the lectern and read it to the assembled elite of the colony, her face proud and serene:

> Deep, deep in thy rocks, O Australia,
> I carved out my sovereign's name;
> By the side of the banished but faithful,
> I climbed up the steep hill of fame.
> Farewell to thy deserts, Australia,
> My centaurs who swept o'er them are gone;
> Their bones bleach on hill and in valley,
> Their dust in the hot wind is blown.
> Cold under the grasses of Camden
> And deep beneath wild ocean's waves,
> My two sons whilst serving Australia,
> Have both found untimely graves.
> With bittersweet memories, I leave you
> Source of pride and of pain o'er the years
> Yet I leave thee in sorrow, Australia,
> Thou field of my toils and my tears.

As the poem was read, Isobel studied the faces of the men around her. Was there any shame in these hard faces, any regrets that they had hounded this fine man to his death? She could not tell. There was only one man she regarded with respect here. Her future husband.

In November, Papa had joined the teeming thousands on the streets of London as Wellington's funeral car passed by, his four nested coffins laid on a velvet pall, surmounted by heraldic escutcheons and drawn by twelve horses. Behind it came two mourning coaches followed by a cavalcade of British knights and aristocrats, and Wellington's regiments and battalions, a procession that stretched so far along Pall Mall that it took over two hours to arrive at St Paul's. As she stood in St James' the morning of her father's service, Isobel wondered what feelings had stirred in his breast to see the hero of his youth laid to rest and to contemplate the passing of his generation of war veterans. Did he feel that his hour of courageous service had also marched on?

The Major's military honours were, of course, a more modest affair than the Iron Duke's, but executed with meticulous ceremony and solemnity nonetheless. His coffin was draped in a flag, his sword and hat placed upon the bier and his body borne on a gun carriage, accompanied by cavalry officers, to the church. Soldiers of the 11th Regiment fired a salute over the grave and the last post was played by a solitary bugler at the graveside to signify that the dead man's duty was done and he could now rest in peace.

A wake was held at Rosemount for family and friends. As Isobel passed through the crowd of sympathetic faces, wearing their kind smiles and bestowing their words of comfort, her mind was drawn back to a memorable evening when she was only six.

She had stood with her sister Anna in the ballroom at Grangemouth and watched the glamorous assembly applaud her parents at their wedding anniversary ball. Her parents had looked so young and proud that night as they waltzed under the brilliance of the chandeliers. Isobel had later recalled the whole scene as if it was a painted illumination, a tableau bathed in the golden light of nostalgia: one of the last times her family had been truly carefree. She also recalled the shifty-eyed looks and low mutterings when her mother had appeared, defiantly wearing her 'unlucky' opal dragonfly brooch, and Mr Macleay's mask of pathos when he beheld its bewitching beauty. Was this night the origin of all the evil that had followed? Was the opal really unlucky? Or had it merely served as a talisman, like a magnet to iron filings, to draw out the secrets of her family's souls?

She fingered her mother's brooch, concealed beneath her mourning weeds. She had worn that same brooch to her mother's funeral. And to her sister's wedding. And now to her father's funeral service. Would she ever be able to wear it openly, without shame or secrecy?

Among the crowd of mourners, Isobel spotted a figure standing apart. It was a young man, his hair prematurely white. His crippled left arm dangled at his side with its hand stiffened into a claw, and his face seemed stricken by a permanent spasm of the left cheek below the blank marble of a blinded eye. He looked oddly familiar but she could not place him at first. And then, with a sudden shock, she realised it was her brother Joseph, so terribly altered!

She had not seen him at the church service; it was possible he had chosen not to attend for fear of being recognised. She went to him.

'My dearest Joseph, how good it is to see you again! I cannot find words to express my joy!' cried Isobel, kissing him on his unaffected cheek. She felt his body flinch as if it pained him to be the subject of such intimacy. He studied her momentarily before replying.

'You look well, dear sister,' he murmured in a strained, formal tone. 'I hear congratulations are in order. You are to be married. I must meet the lucky gentleman who is to have the honour.'

It was not hard to guess why her brother looked so uncomfortable. His falling out with the Major was a matter of public record. To his own sisters he had confessed his bitterness, even going so far as to blame William's death on the Major's disappointment in all three of his sons. And yet here he was, presumably to join with his family in their grief if not to pay his respects to his father. Isobel's heart was full of confused feelings: joy at seeing Joseph alive, distress at his physical and spiritual injuries, fear of his anger and dismay when he learned about the fate of Rosemount. Everything she wanted to say opened a door onto a painful topic and she struggled to speak her mind.

'Yes, of course. I hope you will like him. Do Grace and Anna know you are here?'

'Yes. I wrote to Grace last week when I saw the death notice in the papers,' said Joseph. 'I understand there is to be a reading of the will later in the study.'

Isobel was saddened to hear the sour note in her brother's voice, and to observe the hardness in his face. Joseph had been the most thoughtful and quiet of her three brothers, often found in a secluded corner reading one of the Romantic poets or a volume of polit- ical philosophy by Thomas Paine, William Godwin or another of those radical 'English Jacobins' that his father despised. While Richard was the classics scholar and William the scientist, Joseph had been drawn to poetry and philosophy to imagine a more just world. Partly to please his father, he had undertaken the law but had grown disillusioned and turned to politics and journalism instead. Isobel had privately admired Joseph's independent spirit and often wished she had his courage. Perhaps, after all, she did.

'Have we met before?' asked Joseph on being introduced to Charles Probius.

'Well, if we have, I must apologise for not recognising you,' said Charles.

Isobel noticed a strange look of disquiet creep into her brother's features. She was mortified at Joseph's coolness. Her fiancé was courteous and empathetic, however, before he was drawn away into another conversation.

'I think I have met your fiancé before. In Melbourne. A few years ago,' said Joseph. 'But I cannot remember where. How much do you know about him?'

'Enough,' Isobel replied, dismissing Joseph's insinuation. But her cheeks burned as she turned away. 'Excuse me, Joseph. There are many people I must speak with today. I am sure you understand. We'll talk later.'

There were many familiar faces in the throng of mourners that eddied from room to room in the great house. Aunt Louisa and Isobel had woven simple but pretty wreaths out of wildflowers (wattle, boronia, pink spider grevilleas, fuchsias and bush-peas) and hung them about the frame of an oil painting of Major Macleod that stood next to a portrait of Winnie in the drawing room. Isobel and her aunt had thought that these native wreaths made a fitting tribute to the Major's heartfelt attachment to the bush.

Another unexpected figure from the past emerged from the crowd of guests and approached Isobel: Major Ralph Tranter. He appeared pale and anxious. 'It is the greatest pity that we should meet again under such dreadful circumstances,' said the soldier, his eyes glistening. 'I offer my humble condolences, Miss Macleod, knowing they are but a drop in the ocean of your grief. I was a great admirer of your father's, as you know. I also remember how much he meant to you when you were younger, if I may be so bold.'

This speech seemed to tax poor Ralph Tranter's emotions greatly for he stammered and blushed a great deal as he uttered it and appeared to struggle against tears. Isobel was quite taken aback at the depth of his feelings. 'Please, do not distress yourself on my account, Major Tranter. Your words are most kind, a real balm to my soul. I thank you.'

Major Tranter looked at her, his eyes glazed with tears and suffused with such tender longing and regret that her heart fluttered with alarm. The poor, wretched man! What had come to pass to make him look on her so? He attempted a smile to acknowledge her gracious reply but it failed utterly. His lips trembled and, unable to speak, he bowed his head and retreated as quickly as he could, back into the crowd.

Later in the proceedings, Isobel spied Anna, her face carved white as alabaster, a beacon of maddened grief, in conversation with Joseph. She wondered what bile Anna poured into his ear and Joseph into hers as they stood, an angry, conspiratorial knot in the corner of the drawing room. One of the saddest faces of all was Aunt Louisa's. Even the consolation of her Methodist faith and its assurance she would meet her brother again in the Radiant Kingdom did little to ease her wounded heart. She sat with the fancywork circle, disconsolately sipping tea and ignoring the scones and other pastries that well-meaning guests pressed upon her.

When the black sea of sympathisers had finally trickled away back to their coaches and carriages, the extended family—Grace, Augustus, Isobel, Charles, Joseph, Anna and Aunt Louisa—were the only mourners left in the echoing house. Rosemount felt emptier than ever today for, despite its expensive new guise as the abode of Mr and Mrs Augustus Cooper, it was still, to most minds, the home of Major Macleod. For Isobel, the Major's absence haunted every room as palpably as if he was a spirit in limbo. It would take time for all her intimate memories of him to desert this place.

The family gathered in Father's study where the solicitor, Mr James Whitton, and the accountant, Mr Simeon Lawson, awaited them. It was time for the reading of the will. Chairs had been arranged in a semi-circle around the Major's large mahogany desk and everyone took their seats, as if filing into the family pews at church. Because he was not a beneficiary of the will and legally not yet a member of the Macleod family until he wed Isobel, Charles was asked to wait in the drawing room, which he was happy to do.

'This is the last will and testament of Major Sir Angus Hutton Macleod, filed in the probate court of New South Wales a week ago,' intoned the solicitor in a solemn singsong voice. 'I must inform you that, while he drew up the original will himself, the testator changed the terms by a codicil signed and witnessed in my office on his return from abroad. In this codicil he named, in the absence of his deceased son William, his son-in-law Augustus Cooper as his executor. It is at Mr Cooper's request that this meeting has been called to inform Sir Angus's heirs and beneficiaries of the terms of the will, the manner in which the estate is to be divided and what encumbrances on the estate must be resolved before that can happen.'

With his benign shining moonface, Grace's husband occupied the chair between the accountant and the solicitor. 'As Sir Angus's executor it is my solemn duty to take an inventory of all the Major's assets and call upon any creditors to make their claims against the estate. Once these matters have been settled, the Major's assets can then be distributed according to his express instructions.' Isobel looked around nervously. What nasty revelations were hidden in this document that would divide this unhappy family even more bitterly than it was divided now? She shuddered to think.

'At the time of Sir Angus Macleod's death, this house, its grounds and all its outbuildings had already been the subject of a bill of sale to his daughter Grace and her husband, myself, for the sum of twelve thousand pounds. They therefore do not form part of this estate.' Augustus coughed nervously and Isobel shot a glance at her brother Joseph, who chewed his upper lip in anguish but said not a word.

Augustus continued. 'The Major requested that it be known that from the sale of Rosemount, five thousand pounds was set aside to settle the debts, in part, of the 14th Baron Crawley, husband of the Major's eldest daughter, the Lady Alice Twyckenham, and a further two thousand pounds was set aside in an account to pay an annuity to support her and her son, Xavier John Angus Twyckenham, and to form part of this boy's inheritance when he achieves majority.'

Isobel was astonished to hear these large sums being sacrificed for the sake of Alice's marriage. 'There remains in the estate two farming properties in Camden with their livestock and improvements as well as three terrace houses purchased more recently in Woolloomooloo. Apart from these properties there are sundry artworks, artefacts, journals and books, coaches and carriages, and a stable of fine riding horses, estimated at a value of about two and a half thousand pounds.'

Augustus cleared his throat a few times and the shine of his moonish face dulled a little. 'Unfortunately, I have to inform you of some sizeable debts that have been incurred that are still incumbent upon the estate. These include substantial bills owing to printers in London for the Major's journals, mortgages and monies for work still outstanding on the new houses in Woolloomooloo and monies for work already completed on the country estates.'

Isobel could feel the surge of her pulse and a wave of panic that threatened to overwhelm her. In his calm, measured voice, this lawyer, with the soul of an ascetic and the face of an epicurean, was announcing the dismantling of her family's fortune.

'While his wife, Winifred, was entitled to a widow's pension, this entitlement was extinguished by her death and no other official provision has been made for the family.' Isobel could not credit the penny-pinching meanness of the government and the Colonial Office after all her father's years of service.

'The most serious encumbrance on the estate is the large sum raised and spent on the Major's screw-propeller scheme, which appears now to promise no financial returns. Nobody has come forward to take up this project and so substantial monies are now due to many investors and suppliers, engineers and others involved in sea trials here and in England.'

There were gasps from the family as this news fell on them as an unexpected blow. Augustus continued. 'To settle these outstanding debts, it is proposed to sell two of the terrace houses in Woolloomooloo and relinquish most of the residue of the Rosemount sale.' An awful silence reigned in the Major's study. All the Surveyor-General's grand visions were now dust; his fortune, so painstakingly built up over decades, was dissipated.

'This will, of course, affect what assets remain to be distributed to the Major's beneficiaries according to his wishes. They are as follows. That his beloved sister, Louisa Blunt, receive the sum of one thousand pounds and sundry personal items of sentimental value including letters and diaries. That his eldest daughter, Alice, receive an annuity from the account he has established for her and his grandson, Xavier. That his second daughter, Grace, receive the title to one of the Camden properties. That his third and fourth daughters, Anna and Isobel, share the title to the other Camden property to revert in whole to Isobel on the death of her older sister

Anna. That the income from rent or sale of the remaining terrace house be divided between these two sisters. His sons William and Richard's entitlements reverted to the estate on their deaths as they were not survived by spouses or children. To Grace he has left one thousand pounds, his sword and his portrait; to Anna one thousand pounds, the Broadwood piano and all his sheet music; to Isobel one thousand pounds and his sketchbooks and all his field journals.'

'And for me?' A voice came harsh and loud from the back of the room. 'For his disowned and despised second son? Nothing? Nothing! Not a penny?'

Augustus's face turned bright red. 'I am sorry if there has been some misunderstanding, sir, but I had assumed that your father communicated to you his intention to disinherit you.'

'Don't you *sir* me, you hyena!' shouted Joseph, now standing and flailing his good arm at the three men at the table. 'I see how you and my sister have swooped down like vultures and picked apart the carcass of my family's inheritance. I am the Major's flesh and blood, *sir*! I am his son! My two brothers were sacrificed to my father's heartlessness but I will not be! You will receive letters from my solicitor, *sir*! This will and testament is nothing but a vicious instrument of my father's sickly, hate-filled mind! I will see you in court, *sir*, you and this family, and damn you all!'

And with that the crippled man fled from the room, leaving the company in a state of profound shock, the women broken down in tears and everyone's happy prospects in ruins.

With the dramatic exit of her brother Joseph, Isobel would have been justified in thinking that this sorry day of her father's funeral had reached its nadir of pathos. But she would have been wrong. Fate had in store even worse scenes of anguish. All semblance of family peace and unity would be smashed before nightfall.

Charles did his best to comfort Isobel following the shock of Joseph's outburst, advising her to stay calm and not anticipate the worst. He had an appointment within the hour with one of the city's most distinguished businesswomen who had sounded him out a few days ago about a portrait commission as well as a possible appointment as an art master for her daughters. Charles could see how much Joseph's behaviour had grieved Grace and outraged Augustus, and now Anna appeared to becoming agitated. He thought it wisest that Isobel absent herself from Rosemount as soon as possible.

'Promise me you will go back to Faulconstone as soon as it is practicable,' he told her. 'I believe nothing more can be resolved here today.' He kissed her on the cheek and took his leave. While Augustus was occupied with the solicitor and the accountant, the four women withdrew to the drawing room to counsel each other after the distressing scene next door. Aunt Louisa excused herself as she wished to inspect the items in her brother's room that he had nominated as part of her bequest.

Anna began to pace back and forth. She had been agitated all day, skulking about the crowd of mourners, her face twisted into a sour expression of disgust and distress, withdrawing into a corner with her brother Joseph to vent her anger. Some of this may have been excusable, or at least understandable, in light of her grief at her father's funeral. But the truth was she had been growing more restless over the last week. When Charles and Isobel announced their intentions to become engaged, Grace and Augustus had been gracious and warm in their congratulations. Not so Anna. Her face had hardened to stone and her manner chilled. She could barely spit out the words 'I am very happy for you'. Ever since, she had kept her distance except to glare at them both with looks of uncensored scorn.

Isobel could tell another typhoon was coming, another explosion of anger. But what Isobel could not foretell was that this vicious outburst was to be the death blow she had feared all along, the cataclysmic convulsion that would bring her whole world crashing down like the Rosemount of her dreams, broken by a giant wave.

'So you must be happy now!' hissed Anna, at liberty to give full rein to her rage now that Charles was not there to protect Isobel. 'Your handiwork is all but complete: the utter ruination of this family. Joseph near-drowned and crippled thanks to your disgrace, which drove our two brothers to run away and unhinged poor Father's mind. And now this! Joseph, so troubled that he threatens us with legal writs!'

Isobel closed her eyes, refusing to listen to Anna's ranting. Grace began to soothe Anna as usual. 'Now, now, dear sister, we are all upset by what has happened.'

'Are you blind?' screamed Anna. 'Are you all *blind*? Cannot you not see how Isobel deceives us? She is a spider spinning a *web* of deceit. A thief, a liar and a whore! I see everything. *Everything!* How she played on Mother's affections and twisted Father to her will. How she took advantage of William's good nature. And Joseph's gullibility. How she and that artist have been steeped in sin for months with their kissing and moaning behind Aunt's back. How she stole what you, Grace, wanted most of all, the gift of Mother's love!'

Before Isobel could defend herself, her mad sister ran at her and tore at her black blouse with her long fingers. Grace blanched in terror and reached out to restrain Anna, but too late to save Isobel. Anna clutched at Isobel's throat, wrenched free the chain from about her neck and, with a triumphant shout, held aloft Isobel's secret trophy: the opal dragonfly.

Anna began to laugh. 'You see! You see! She has made fools of us all!'

Isobel looked at Grace, her face transfixed with horrified disbelief. 'I can explain, Grace. It was mother's wish . . . her strict instructions . . .'

But Isobel's words failed her. She knew she had lost. There was nothing she could say that would save her now. Grace's worst suspicions were confirmed, as was her unflagging belief that Isobel was the preferred daughter who stole away Winnie's love; the cheating, slippery sister who had used her role as go-between to entrap Captain Tranter; the same monstrously selfish and perverse creature with her claws so deeply hooked into Father's heart that she had thought it was her job to save his life!

'You witch! All this time.' Grace looked as crazed as Anna. 'I knew you lied!'

Isobel's face reddened and she felt the burn of tears. But these were not tears of self-pity; they were tears of rage. She would not be made to feel guilty for what she had done. She would not apologise for the years of humiliation and cruelty her two sisters had made her suffer. She advanced on them both, her face transformed by a fury no one had ever witnessed. 'Enough!' she screamed. *'Enough!'*

Anna shrieked and cowered near the fireplace. Looking as if she feared actual physical violence, Grace ran from the room to seek help from the men in the study.

'You are the one who is blind,' said Isobel as she closed on Anna, her back pressed against the mantel. 'Do you think Grace will save you? Do you think she wants *you* around to spoil her perfect life? Do you think she hasn't already signed the papers to have you put away in the madhouse? *Nothing* can save you now, you, stupid, stupid woman!'

Isobel slapped Anna's face so hard she heard her teeth grind and a red stain glowed across her cheeks like a birthmark. In shock, Anna dropped the dragonfly, lifting her hand to soothe her face. She whimpered then with a look as pathetic and frightened as that of a small child. It did not take much to convince Anna of the terror that already lurked in her heart. A sob broke from her mouth as Isobel lunged forward to retrieve her mother's brooch. Anna shielded her face and cried out. Wailing piteously, she ran from the room, across the main hall and out the front door into the darkness of nightfall beyond.

'Anna! Come back! Come back, Anna!'

It was Grace's voice, urgent and fearful. 'Quick, after her!' she said, turning to the servants. Grace and Augustus stood in the doorway of the drawing room. Trembling with rage, they both stared at Isobel. They had heard every word of her speech.

'Filthy liar!' said Grace, her voice low and menacing. 'How dare you try to poison my poor sister's love for me! Anna is right. You are a liar and a thief. Your contempt and hatred for this family is the root of all the evil that has befallen us.'

Isobel did not reply. She had heard all these accusations before, knew every note of this symphony of recrimination. The same old tune, the tired old story, again and again.

And then Augustus stepped forward. The moon of his face shone red and his expression was more thunderous than Isobel would have thought possible. He did not roar or bellow. Instead he hissed like a steaming kettle.

'Get out of my house,' he said. 'And do not come back.'

Chapter 32

EXILE

FEBRUARY 1853

Now Isobel was truly in exile. Under a clear, starry sky, she trudged along Rosemount's driveway to the main road. Her right hand ached from the force with which she had slapped Anna's face. She should be ashamed but she was not. Her fury impelled her along the winding drive like a woman possessed. Let Grace explain the whole catastrophe to Aunt Louisa, thought Isobel. If her aunt fretted over her disappearance, so be it. Damn them all!

By command of whatever guardian angel watched over her, Isobel saw the omnibus that headed down William Street approaching the front gates. She climbed aboard and, in no mood to be with company, ascended to the upstairs seating where she could be alone. A breeze fanned her, cooling the blood-heat of her face. She felt her pulse begin to slow as she contemplated the soothing darkness and the measured pulse of starlight.

If God was at His peephole tonight, what did He see? A heartless and wicked woman who had deliberately terrified her sister? Or a long-suffering, scared woman who had finally struck back at her tormentor? Of course, Isobel preferred to think it was the latter. But she realised that the rightness or wrongness of her feelings was not what was important now. She had awakened ancient and overwhelming resentments in her sister Grace and had also insulted the integrity of her husband. She was banished from Rosemount for good.

Isobel was still in numbed denial that today she had put her dear father into the cold earth, and that she would never see his face or hear his voice again. Death had taken away the keystone of her family, and within hours of his burial Grace, Joseph, Anna and Isobel were at war with each other. Both Isobel's parents and two favourite brothers were dead. Alice was on the other side of the world and might as well be. Isobel was all alone.

Except for Charles. He was her refuge, her rock. She must go to him. She alighted from the coach and followed the dirt road through the valley to Woolloomooloo Bay. There were no street lamps so she walked along the verge, guided by the line of paler road against the darker edge. The night was warm with soft breezes off the bay and yet the amber firelight in windows and homely smell of smoke made the houses she passed seem cosy.

What a sight she must have made in her heavy crepe mourning dress, and her black bodice and veil, straight from her father's funeral and wake! As she lifted her hem to step over a puddle, her black stockings and black silk petticoats were revealed. Fleeing from Grace and Augustus's house without a second's thought as to where she would go, she still had on her jet jewellery: a ring, and a pendant that held a lock of her father's hair. And pinned to her bodice the opal dragonfly, its chain broken and discarded, glistening at her breast. In the darkness Isobel was a phantom, blackly invisible as she passed cottages and terraces. Without parents, Isobel was no longer a dutiful and loving daughter and she had yet to become a dutiful and loving wife. What was she now? A ghost slipping between worlds.

'Evening, ma'am,' came rough male voices in the gloom, their owners touching their caps. As she neared the Rose and Crown she could hear a rowdy chorus of men singing.

> The Currency Lads may fill their glasses,
> And drink the health of the Currency Lasses;
> But the lass I adore, the lass for me,
> Is a lass in the Female Factory.

A dog whined in a nearby backyard, a baby yowled at an upstairs window. Isobel was assailed by smells that she did not associate with her daylight visits here: the stink of cabbage cooking and meat frying, of coal smoke, tobacco, beer fumes. She turned her face away as she walked briskly past an alleyway where a man, presumably drunk, urinated against a wall.

Over the road she could see a light on in Charles's studio. Was he home then from his appointment with his patron? It seemed too early but she did not want to stand for long too close to the smells and clamour of the pub. In the light that spilled from its windows, Isobel saw the figures of three women on the street opposite, dressed in such a manner as to suggest they were not simply enjoying the evening air. Not wishing to arouse their interest, Isobel walked away smartly, her heart in her mouth, towards the wharf overlooking the bay. She lingered a moment there, catching her breath and watching the black waters slop and slap against the piers. It comforted her, this harbour music with its familiar liquid lullaby.

She recrossed the street then and went in at the side door of the narrow terrace where Charles had his studio. The grocery shop was still open even at this late hour, its exhausted owner half-dozing at his counter. After all the drama of the day, she too was bone weary. She mounted the cramped stairs and knocked at the door. On the other side, she heard two voices, a conversation broken off. 'Hold on a moment!'

The door was flung open and Charles stood there with his arms spread wide in greeting. His face drained white at the sight of his fiancé. 'Isobel?' Half-question, half-reproach. 'What—what are you doing here?'

'Can I come in?' Isobel asked peevishly, wondering what delayed the invitation.

Charles froze, his hands limp by his sides, his shoulders hunched. 'Is that—is that a good idea? I mean—people will talk . . . our engagement . . .'

'I think it is a bit late to worry about that,' said Isobel tartly. She was puzzled at her fiancé's awkwardness and lack of warmth. Questions crowded her mind. Who was he expecting so eagerly? Why did he seem so embarrassed to see her? Who was the other voice in the room? He was behaving very oddly, hanging at the door, his face haggard.

And then she felt sickened with panic. She recalled Joseph's odd reaction to meeting Charles at the wake: *'I think I have met your fiancé before . . . How much do you know about him?'* What was he hiding? Was it possible that her fiancé was expecting a visit from a *woman*? Or, even worse, was there a woman in his studio right now? Was that why he looked so trapped? Don't be a fool! she counselled herself, but could not throw off her fear.

'I want to come in, Charles! I have been thrown out of Rosemount. Anna, Grace, Augustus, they have all conspired against me.'

Without warning, another man's face appeared at the door. He was younger than Charles, heavily bearded and decidedly drunk. 'So is this the pretty young lady in question?' he asked, surveying Isobel from head to toe.

'Yes, Richard, this is my *fiancé*, Miss Isobel Macleod.' Charles placed a steadying hand on his companion's shoulder. 'You know, I told you all about her.'

Richard nodded his head in an exaggerated manner to signify he understood.

'Righty-o, then.'

'And I am about to escort her home,' announced Charles firmly. 'You can explain everything that has happened on the way,' he said to Isobel. 'This is no place for a young lady to go wandering about at night. I am only glad you came to no harm.'

Isobel pouted. She hated being treated like a child. And she could tell something was not right. Charles seemed to be in great haste to get her away. 'Let me get my coat.'

Charles hurried from the door to fetch his coat and hat. His inebriated friend smiled at her. 'I'm sorry you can't join us for a drink or two.' He blinked and looked at her again more closely. 'Someone died?'

'My father.'

'Oh, that is a pity. My sincerest cond— condolescences,' he lisped drunkenly.

Charles returned. He seemed to have regained his composure. He kissed her on the cheek and wrapped his arm about her protectively. 'Let's get you home, poor lamb.'

Isobel looked her lover in the eye. 'You haven't heard a word I've said, Charles. The fact is I no longer have a home.' And with that acknowledgement of the truth, Isobel collapsed into her lover's arms and wept as if she would never stop.

In the cab on the way to Faulconstone, Isobel poured out her anger and grief. Charles listened with his usual patience but also seemed a little distant. Relieved as she was to be in his custody, she could not dismiss a nagging sense of unease. What had she interrupted at the studio? Charles told her Richard was an old friend and they were expecting a third gentleman to join them. Was that not explanation enough?

Not surprisingly, Aunt Louisa was in a state. Her swooning spirits had only been revived with the aid of salts upon hearing the news of Isobel's outburst and then disappearance. With great reluctance, she had returned to Faulconstone, but not before insisting her coachman drive her about the streets of Darlinghurst Heights and Victoria Street in a haphazard search for both her nieces. When this hunt had proved fruitless, she had come home and sat in a state of extreme nervous agitation, awaiting Isobel's return. 'I thought you were dead,' she told her niece, mopping the tears from her cheeks.

'I am sorry to have been the cause of so much distress, Aunt,' apologised Isobel. Nearly two hours had passed since Anna had fled Rosemount and there was still no word of her whereabouts. Her aunt told her that Augustus and two servants had ridden out to look for her at the neighbours' houses while a third was sent to the nearest police watch house to alert them. It was possible she had made for the Bradleys' or Finches' but the unpleasant truth was that there were few people Anna trusted or liked.

Aunt Louisa thanked Charles Probius for his honourable conduct in escorting Isobel home. She promised to let him know how matters were resolved as soon as they had an answer. Charles parted company with them, his departure marred by an uncharacteristic awkwardness. Much as she wished to feel her trust fully restored, Isobel could not ignore the lingering disquiet in her heart.

Isobel slept fitfully that night. Her nightmare returned, beginning with the scene of her climb to Rosemount's rooftop as the floodwaters rose to submerge the house. As if her dream could be any more disturbing or uncanny, tonight she dreamed that the waters closed over the rooftop dome completely. For a last few desperate minutes, Isobel clung like a shipwreck survivor holding on to the upturned hull of her stricken ship. In the waters all about her floated the splendid wreckage of the house. Out on the horizon, she could still see Charles hunched over the oars of his rowboat, which, no matter how strenuously he worked at the oars, appeared to move neither away from nor towards her. And then close by she saw the oddest thing, a tiny rowboat, no bigger than a basket, floating. She reached out to grab it but with no real hope that it would save her. Rosemount's dome was swallowed up by the dark waters and she was left, flailing and screaming, convinced that she would drown.

Isobel woke, bolt upright, gasping.

She pulled the opal dragonfly from beneath her pillow and held it in her hands. She ached for Winnie's loving arms, the reassurance of her words, the balm of her voice. Winnie would see Charles Probius's character clearly. She would know what to do.

She stared at the cold fire of the opal stones. Some days she was still tempted to walk to the nearest beach and hurl the blasted thing into the sea. When her spirits were low, she would half-convince herself the dragonfly was more than a spinner of dreams, a window on the future. She believed then it was a cursed thing that exerted a malicious and destructive influence over her life. She knew that this was blasphemous and absurd but still she struggled against the impulse to get rid of it. 'Forgive me, Mama,' she whispered in the dark, making her confession to the insect in her hand, her precious link to Winnie. 'Forgive me.'

She thought of her outburst at Anna and recalled the spasm of murderous rage she had felt then, easily able to imagine with no compunction Anna lying dead in a ditch. Was this the new Isobel, transformed by suffering and despair, who had shed the husk of her old self? A violent, vengeful creature she did not recognise?

She slipped the dragonfly beneath her pillow and lapsed back into a dreamless sleep.

The following morning, with the sun still low on the horizon, a coach pulled up outside Faulconstone. A cloaked figure approached the front door and pulled the bell cord to announce her arrival. It was Grace. There was little doubt that she had not slept a wink, but her face betrayed more than sleeplessness. The blank-eyed stare of horror, the pallor of her skin, the furrows of pain in her brow, and the grim set of her lips were all too reminiscent of the day she had arrived, unannounced, to deliver the news of William's death. Both Aunt Louisa and Isobel felt heartsick at the sight of her. Had something happened to Anna?

'The police have found a woman. At The Gap,' said Grace. She almost choked on the words. 'I have been asked to go down to the morgue on George Street to identify the body.'

'At The Gap?' gasped Isobel. How could she forget the awful majesty of that place? On that memorable day at Watsons Bay, Isobel had stood near the cliff edge, looking down on the restless waters crashing over the ruin of fallen rocks. Isobel knew that The Gap's gloomy reputation as a spot favoured by suicides was beginning to grow.

'Yes,' replied Grace, staring into Isobel's face with a look of unwavering malice. They both understood the unspoken accusation levelled at Isobel. 'She is *our* sister. I insist you accompany me.'

Tears streaked Aunt Louisa's face but she said nothing to contradict Grace's demand. Isobel knew she had no choice. If Anna had indeed killed herself, then the blame, rightly or wrongly, would lie on Isobel's shoulders.

'Very well. Let me get dressed,' she said and hurried to her room to fetch her coat and bonnet. Her mind reeled as she imagined her sister's broken body being tossed in the black waters below The Gap.

Grace and Isobel did not exchange a single word during the coach trip to the Coroner's Court and the 'Dead House' at the end of George Street, next door to the Water Police Court in The Rocks. Augustus sat up front with the coachman; he believed Anna's death, if that is what they were about to confront, was a private matter between sisters.

When the coach arrived and they alighted, Isobel could not help recalling the sad news of Mrs Pittman, the victim of her aunt's uncharitable suspicions. Had her body been brought here, fished out of the harbour near Pyrmont Bridge? Death made no nice distinctions when it came to social position, thought Isobel, as they entered the ugly building. With its bare stuccoed walls and cold draughts, the Dead House was unprepossessingly functional. A lugubrious clerk with soft, long-fingered hands greeted the party and took them into a small room to sign some paperwork. 'There were no personal items to help with identification. So we appreciate you coming here,' said the clerk in a well-practised speech.

Grace's body began to shake. In an effort to hold back a fit of sobbing, her chest and limbs convulsed violently. Augustus clasped her in a clumsy attempt to offer comfort. She flung his arms away and composed herself with a deep breath. They entered the chilly brick room, where Isobel could hear water running into a trough. A swarm of black flies seemed to buzz around her head and she could feel her body grow light. She was close to the point of fainting. This torture was to be her punishment just as Grace intended. She was being forced to confront her own guilt and share in Grace's pain.

A solemn man in a leather apron stood at the entrance. On a long table in the centre of the room a body lay under a white sheet. All that was visible was a woman's foot, white and blue-veined like marble, protruding from the hem of this shroud. 'Now, ladies, please take a deep breath,' said the mortician apologetically. 'I shall pull back the cover now.'

The sheet was peeled back and they both contemplated the face of the dead woman. It was the second corpse they had looked upon in the last two weeks. But where their father had slept in a peaceful repose, this was a vision of violent death. The head hung at an unnatural angle to the body, probably due to a broken neck, and the face was distorted by its time in the water, with bloated cheeks, a distended tongue and the skin beginning to turn violet-blue. The body and face had been washed clean but there was still evidence of yellow bruising and the jagged line of a fracture to the skull.

Both sisters uttered pitiable shrieks. Grace rushed to the trough to retch. Isobel staggered back and reached out for something to steady her. The mortician caught her in his arms as she began to faint. The buzzing blackness cloaked her for a moment and then lifted.

It was not Anna. Even with the horrific alterations of death, the hair, the shape of the face, the features in general did not resemble Anna's. Isobel felt a spasm of angry resentment. Why had Grace brought her here? Was it pure revenge? She was overwhelmed with revulsion and terror on seeing this dead woman's face but then flooded with relief. And yet another ghost hung over this scene. William, her brother, who had died at sea. To think that his beautiful face had undergone the same transformation. No, no, this could not be borne.

'I'm sorry,' whispered Isobel as they exited the cold room. But Grace did not acknowledge this apology. Everything about Grace's bearing and expression radiated unremitting hatred towards her younger sister. She refused to look at her, refused to hear her, refused to notice her presence in any way. They rode back to Faulconstone in silence, broken only by fits of Grace's quiet weeping.

Isobel's shame was all encompassing and her banishment was now complete.

Chapter 33

FATE

MARCH 1853

Two weeks passed with no news of Anna. Grace and Augustus sent out a circular to all the police watch houses, hospitals, the Benevolent Asylum, the Lunatic Asylum, the House of the Good Shepherd and the Sydney Female Refuge to see if any women matching their sister's description had recently been admitted or sought shelter. The case had also been reported in several newspapers, appealing for help in locating her and even offering a reward. The fear was that Anna had become so unhinged that she might not even remember her own name. What now appeared equally possible was she was so afraid of Isobel's threats and Grace's intentions to be rid of her that she had gone into hiding and did not wish to be found. But where?

Isobel struggled with her feelings of responsibility in all of this. She refused to accept that Anna's state of mind and her flight from the house were wholly of her making. Nor did she characterise her lashing out as calculated or malicious. Anna had wanted to harm her and had in fact succeeded in doing so. Isobel had only acted in self-defence. The discipline she normally exercised around her sister's madness had been worn down to a nub by grief and exhaustion. Yes, in that moment of pure rage, she had wanted to frighten Anna out of her wits and to repay the hurt Anna had inflicted on her. Surely God would forgive that.

But not if Anna was dead.

Even with the crisis of Anna's disappearance unresolved, Isobel's focus shifted elsewhere. The excruciating first shock of her father's death was beginning to numb a little, leaving her with an eternity of time to grow accustomed to his absence. Even so, just as it had with William's death, grief would every now and then overwhelm her with the full force of the truth that he was gone, and with him the boon of his love and protection.

Three days after the reading of the will, a carriage had arrived at Faulconstone from Rosemount bearing two tea chests. The first contained Father's sketchbooks and field journals, part of his bequest to Isobel, and was carted up to her room. The second chest, packed with items of sentimental value to Louisa, was sent to her aunt's room.

Isobel took her time inspecting the contents of her tea chest, sitting on her bed and slowly leafing through the stack of her father's sketchbooks. Some were from his time as a young soldier in Spain, others were more recent including landscapes of Victoria Pass in the Blue Mountains and watercolours and pencil drawings of scenes all over New South Wales. There were bridges, rivers, mountain ranges and copses of slender gums; quick ghostly studies of natives massing with spears or settlers in cabbage-tree hats leaning on rifles in attitudes of indolence or reflection, depending on your point of view. 'Oh, Papa,' she sighed, smiling at the large green caterpillar and the undulating snake, both drawn in splendid isolation on their blank, creamy pages. And there was the candid study of a soldier lying on the turf, stealing a few minutes' reprieve in the pages of a book, her favourite sketch of Papa's from when she was a girl. Tears poured freely as she turned these pages. Healing tears.

She had been deeply moved when she heard that Papa had bequeathed her these sketchbooks. They had talked of them while walking in the gardens at Rosemount when he had congratulated her on her first commission. *'I flatter myself I had a hand in encouraging your talents for drawing when you were younger,'* he had said.

She understood her father's impulse to leave her these. But why had he left her the field journals as well? These contained the day-to-day entries he had made every evening by the light of an oil lamp or the fire of his campsite during his perilous excursions into the interior. They were the source from which he had composed the official accounts of his expeditions, later published in London. Why on earth had he passed these into her keeping?

She stacked the journals up on the floor of her room, a pile of honey-coloured paper in dark green and red-veined marbled covers. As she did so, she noticed her father had written what must be a dedication on the title page of one of the journals. It read:

To my dearest Isobel,

I leave this true record in your hands. You will know what to do.

With a father's undying love,

Angus H. Macleod.

The note was written in a hurried hand and dated two days before his death: his final message to her. Isobel was so shocked she dropped the journal as if it burned her. 'Why, Papa?' she cried out. 'Why?' She could not fathom the reason her father had written this message to her. Did he have some intuition he would die soon? And were these books some form of deathbed confession consigned to her care? None of it made sense. But whatever the reason for this bequest, Isobel felt a terrible burden had been placed on her. It seemed both her parents had chosen to leave their youngest daughter with a troublesome inheritance: her mother's gift of the clairvoyant dragonfly and her father's 'true record' of she knew not what. What had Isobel done to deserve such a dubious privilege? Was she supposed to be grateful for their trust?

Despite her misgivings, Isobel resolved to read these journals so that her father's request might become clear. She even hoped that, perhaps, they would help her in her grief.

Charles visited Isobel every day that he could find time from his busy schedule. The wealthy businesswoman he had hoped for as a patron had commissioned a portrait of herself and her husband;

Charles still awaited her decision to appoint him as a drawing master. Isobel welcomed all good news. She needed it like a drowning man needs flotsam to cling to for survival.

'I do not think we should delay the announcement of our engagement any longer,' she told Charles three days after Anna's disappearance. 'And I want to set a date for our wedding as well. I am sure Aunt Louisa will help us with all that.'

Aunt Louisa was still in a state of shock about what had occurred at Rosemount the night of her brother's funeral. But Isobel had gone to her and explained the strange circumstances of her mother's gift (or at least a version that would not strain belief), telling her how dear Winnie had made her promise to keep this heirloom a secret. 'She knew what grief it would cause between her daughters if I did not. It seems she was right to be afraid.' Having witnessed some of Anna's lunatic behaviour for herself, Aunt Louisa was more than willing to give Isobel the benefit of the doubt when it came to Anna's vile accusations.

'Do not concern yourself, my dear,' counselled Isobel's aunt. 'I am sure this will all blow over. We are all out of our minds with grief. Such times are sent to try us!'

Isobel knew that the timing was not propitious for announcing her engagement and planning her wedding but she yearned to run as fast she could towards her happy future, free from her family's misery. Grace and Augustus had originally offered to host a wedding breakfast at Rosemount; it was unlikely that was ever going to happen now. She did not care. She wanted to marry Charles, with or without Grace's blessing.

'But what about Anna?' asked Charles. 'How can we go ahead when we don't know what has happened to her?'

Isobel turned her face to him, eyes blazing. 'Charles, I have taken care of Anna's feelings ahead of mine my whole life. I will not let her cheat me out of my wedding day.'

If Charles was shocked, he gave no sign. 'Very well, my darling, as you wish.'

Anna was discovered six days later. She must have wandered down the far side of Woolloomooloo Hill and ended up sleeping in a paddock at Rushcutters Bay near the blacks' camp at the edge of Barcom Glen estate. The sad figure of the deranged woman in her mourning weeds had won the sympathy of the natives. She traded away her jewellery for food and drink and the blacks built her a crude humpy to keep off the rain. She was lucky that it was a mild autumn with no frosts or heavy storms. It was the offer in the papers of a monetary reward for her discovery that led to one of the local blackfellas notifying the police.

When the constables found Anna, she was lying beneath a pepper tree, drunk and asleep. She told them her name was Ballandella and her adopted father was Major Macleod, who had saved her from her tribe. She had half-sisters who no longer loved her and had driven her away. She insisted this was now her home. She did not answer to the name of Anna Macleod. 'She died years ago,' she said. She was a pitiful sight: her hair filthy and matted, her face black with dirt, her arms covered in suppurating sores and scratches, her mourning clothes torn to rags. She resisted all attempts to remove her at first but grew weak with weeping and was taken away to the Tarban Creek Lunatic Asylum.

The matron, Mrs Digby, wrote to Grace Macleod stating that '*a woman matching your sister's description has been admitted*'. The letter explained that '*she has been examined by two independent doctors who have issued medical certificates and an order for admission had been granted from a magistrate to protect her from further harm to herself*'. The matron wished Grace to confirm her sister's identity as soon as possible and warned her that she might find her altered state shocking.

Grace reported all of this later to Aunt Louisa. She and Augustus decided it was safer to visit Tarban Creek without Isobel as she was sure Anna would become agitated in her presence. Purpose-built as a hospital for the insane on Bedlam Point overlooking the Parramatta River, the asylum was a solemn collection of barrack-like buildings. Grace and Augustus found the atmosphere more fitting to a place of incarceration and punishment than rest and recuperation. The grounds were surrounded by high walls and the courtyards (for exercise and outdoor 'recreation') were narrow and permanently in shadow. Once inside, they were shocked at how small, dank, overcrowded and dismal were the dormitories and cells.

Concerned as they were by the conditions of the asylum, Grace and Augustus had to admit that Anna was in no fit state to return to their care or Aunt Louisa's. When they entered the ward, she cowered by her bed, wild-eyed and muttering. Grace was inconsolable when confronted by this pathetic, unrecognisable creature. She still refused to answer to Anna, insisting her name was Ballandella.

What had broken in her sister's soul that she would impersonate the little black girl Father had brought home all those years ago? Was this her way of feeling more valued—as Isobel's preferred play-mate? It was both remarkable and sad to think that these childhood injuries possibly still had such a grip on Anna's mind.

Even Isobel's heart was mollified a little when she heard about Anna from Aunt Louisa, now the only source of news from Rosemount. Poor mad Anna. Had there ever been any hope for her? Was she always fated to end up like this? Isobel's own life now teetered precariously on a knife's edge between the condemnation of her family on the one side and the happiness and love promised by her marriage with Charles on the other.

When she was younger, Isobel had always assumed her life's story was already written. As the youngest daughter of Sir Angus Macleod, her fate was clear: to be 'gobbled up in the jaws of matri-mony' by a man from a 'good' family, either from the colony or the Old Country. Marriage, children and then grandchildren would all follow in orderly, middle-class fashion, the same narrative as her mother's. But, ever since that fateful morning of the duel, Isobel's life had not faithfully followed this pattern.

With all the strange events of the last two years, it was not surprising that Isobel often reflected on the nature of fate. Were the blows that rained down on her family to be understood as divine punishments or were they no more than a series of terrible acci-dents? And what of her dreams? How was she to understand them: were they proof that the future was set in stone or the complete opposite, warnings to help Isobel navigate a happier path? Winnie said she did not know what the dreams meant. But Isobel was sure that her mother hoped the dragonfly's gift of foresight would be a boon not a burden for her daughter.

As she unpacked Papa's tea chest, Isobel came across a slim notebook from his time as a college student in Edinburgh. She skimmed its pages, crammed with youthful scribblings and notes on all manner of subjects. She was not in the least surprised to find that one of his favourites had been phrenology, the popular science of the human brain that had become all the rage for members of the intelligent middle class, her father included.

In the same way that a surveyor could map a landscape to understand its geographical features, phrenologists claimed they could map the regions of the brain to understand the qualities of an individual's character. For men like her father, clever, talented and ambitious, this was a philosophy that liberated human potential. He had written: '*With the right training tailored for our individual brains, we can improve ourselves in every conceivable way and aspire to excellence in all our pursuits. Education and not aristocratic privilege is the path to rank and fortune. No longer will advancement be the inherited monopoly of the rich.*'

As she contemplated her uncertain future, Isobel wondered to what extent her own character had been formed when she first came into the world, written in the map of her brain. Did this mean she was as easily classifiable as a flower or an insect in some Linnean equivalent of human types? Female (*Caucasian, British descent, Christian, Evangelical*): charitable, pious, well-bred, educated, good character, excellent health, pleasing appearance, propertied family, upper middle class, socially prominent, well-connected, promising prospects.

What would happen to Isobel if, like a flower or an insect, she was suddenly removed from an environment into which she had been born, formed and nurtured? Would she inevitably wither and die? Or would she adapt and become someone different?

Little did Isobel know how pertinent these reflections would prove one day in the not too distant future.

Chapter 34

MARRIAGE

APRIL TO MAY 1853

Isobel could see no reason to delay her wedding and did not want to tempt fate to throw even more obstacles in the path of her happiness. In early April, on a warm sunny day, the marriage of Isobel and Charles Ludiger was celebrated at St Mark's, a modest but felicitous affair followed by a wedding breakfast with a handful of friends in the garden at Faulconstone. As she had anticipated, neither Grace nor Augustus attended. Joseph also declined but sent a short note. *'You will always have my love. I trust Charles will be an honourable husband who will make my dear sister happy.'* It was not a resounding vote of confidence in her future.

On Isobel's side of the church, her matron of honour, Aunt Louisa, sat with the ever-loyal Mrs Palmer and three members of the fancywork circle, Mrs Drummond, Mrs Long and Mrs Smart. On Charles's side of the church sat Miss Catherine Cooper, determined to show support for her teacher and her fellow debutante (and to defy her haughty brother, Augustus), joined by three of her sisters. Catherine must have written to her parents with the glad tidings as a letter of congratulations arrived on the *Chusan* in June. *'What a handsome portrait of marital bliss you two must make!'* wrote Robert the Large in his hard-won copperplate.

Among Charles's group of bohemian friends was his best man, the heavily bearded, mysterious gentleman known to Isobel only as 'Richard', and the artist-engraver Mr Austin. The church was more than two-thirds empty but Isobel was not overly concerned. The only absences that truly affected her were those of her parents, her brother William and Alice, to whom she had written with her good news. Otherwise she was overjoyed to finally make her wedding vows to her beloved Charles.

At last her life was set on its proper course.

There were tearful farewells at Faulconstone. Some sentimental items of furniture chosen from Rosemount were conveyed to Isobel's new home, as were all her worldly goods: clothes, journals and sketchbooks, her desk easel and boxes of colours, a fine antique wardrobe from Faulconstone that Aunt Louisa presented as a wedding gift, and the tea chest of the Major's journals and sketchbooks. The latter were placed on bookshelves in the studio with Isobel making a vow to commence reading them as soon as she had set up house.

From Charles's own savings and a trifling sum that had been advanced to Isobel from her father's still unresolved estate, the young couple paid rent on a small but pleasant terrace in Woolloomooloo within sight and sound of their much-loved harbour. It had an upstairs room sufficiently large for a studio, a small parlour and adequate dining room, and quarters for two servants. When the upstairs windows were opened wide, sunlight flooded the studio, and warm, salty breezes carried the cry of gulls and noise of marine traffic off the bay.

The hope was that when the Major's estate was settled, Isobel and her husband might be able to move into the larger terrace house nearby that had been bequeathed to her and Anna in their father's will. The interest on Isobel's thousand pounds would also bring in a tidy annual income. When Anna was finally recovered from her fit of madness and discharged, she would probably be sent to one of the family farms at Camden to live out her days in the relative quiet of the countryside.

To Isobel's joy, married life began auspiciously. The happy couple fell quickly into a routine of painting in the mornings, breaking for a modest lunch, taking a walk around the bay or through the Domain in the early afternoons before Charles called on clients and Isobel wrote her journal. They came together for dinner every evening except on the odd Friday, when Charles met up with fellow artists for a meal. Isobel invited Mrs Palmer, who was her neighbour in Woolloomooloo, and Catherine Cooper, if she was free, for cards and supper. When they could afford it, she and Charles went to plays at the Royal Victoria Theatre on Pitt Street, race meetings at Bellevue Hill, and lectures at the Australian Museum and the Mechanics' School of Arts. At weekends they would head to a beach with a picnic lunch or embark on a painting trip to Parramatta, Windsor, the south coast or over the Blue Mountains.

'Where shall we go today, my love?' Charles would ask, arms outstretched, as if to embrace the world in all its infinite richness. 'Beachcombing at Manly perhaps? Coogee?'

Isobel would kiss Charles's noble brow, lovingly stroking his temples or curling a finger around one of his lush stray locks. 'Wherever my lord and master commands!' She would giggle then and Charles would laugh, folding her in his arms. He was so unlike the template of the sober, authoritarian husband and she of the quiet and obedient wife that they both liked to make a game of married life, playing their roles like children in dress-ups, mimicking their parents.

Isobel's heart had not felt this light and carefree for so long. Every morning she sat and combed her dark hair in her cheval glass, smiling at her own reflection. Ever since she had moved in under the roof of her new home, her nightmares had gone, vanished! All that heavy burden lifted. She enjoyed peaceful nights of sleep undisturbed by fateful dreams.

Some days she felt so emboldened, so free from care, she proudly hung her mother's gift and love token about her neck on display for all to see. The opal dragonfly. No longer a harbinger of doom, it was now worn as her badge of honour as a married woman. Mrs Isobel Clara Ludiger. 'Madame Libellule', the artist.

What had begun in a coach under cover of a dust storm was resumed in the marriage bed proper. How Isobel revelled in that! And yet. And yet her lover's ardour that she had experienced that first time was never fully revisited, though she could not understand why. It was certainly not from any lack of desire on her part. Perhaps it was the dull safety of the marriage bed, hemmed about with convention and duty or the humdrum demands of daily life. Was that what robbed Charles's passion of the savage hunger that had been there in the whirlwind of the dust storm? Was it precisely the forbidden and risky nature of that first encounter that had inflamed him in a way that married sexual relations could not?

But she had found love—true, bountiful, impregnable, steadfast love—and that was more than compensation. Despite all the trials and shocks of the recent past, Isobel felt she had escaped her family's disapproval and the legacy of their shame. She had come through so many troubles and had at last found the refuge she had craved, a place where she was loved simply for who she was. She was happy.

Isobel barely gave a thought to the grand dinners at Rosemount, the riches of her father's house, the parties and suppers and dances that had once been her life's endless round. These seemed now as insubstantial as dreams, gossamer visions that belonged to another time, fading away already to memories. She ate more simply now, slept in a smaller room in a far more modest house, did not hanker after new ribbons for her bonnets or a silk shawl or a pair of new gloves. She gave up all dance, music and language lessons except, of course, her art lessons under Charles's tutelage. She did not drop her calling card at grand houses or pay her respects to well-bred ladies or hold afternoon or morning teas or attend society lunches. Her only connection to her immediate past was her attendance at church every Sunday (seated at the back, well away from Augustus and Grace) and fulfilment of her promise to join Aunt Louisa's fancywork circle for the annual bazaar. She marvelled at how easily she had cast off the husk of her old life and adapted to this happier, simpler existence.

Her reward was that life with Charles was exciting, even if, sometimes, challenging and confronting. Fascinated by what he called 'the faces of the street', Charles would bring home human strays, men and women he found in pubs, taverns and alleyways to be subjects for his portraits. He told Isobel that their features spoke to him of 'spiritual suffering and beauty'. If they were poor, homeless or simply drunk, he would pay them for their time with food or beer, or, if he had any to spare, a florin or two. 'Rembrandt did the same. He had a keen eye for faces.'

He even encouraged his wife to join him in the studio to sketch or paint these complete strangers. Sometimes it was just their face. At other times it was their whole torso, undraped to reveal bare arms and shoulders, muscled chests, gnarled hands and mottled feet. Even naked breasts. Isobel was shocked at first, struggling to overcome her habitual gentility. But once inside the hallowed space of the studio, she quashed her self-conscious modesty. Charles explained that these sketches were not for public display. They were executed purely for the pleasure of observation and a means for instruction and experiment. Isobel became less inhibited and her timidity gave way to unbridled enthusiasm.

Little by little, she learned from Charles that Art transcended the bread-and-butter demands of the market and good taste. She began to see that, for him and his circle of friends and acolytes, it was a calling, a way of life, a pilgrimage. Charles continued to encourage and nurture Isobel's talents and teach her new ways of seeing, new techniques of execution. He introduced her to his bohemian circle, one by one so as not to intimidate her, and, to her delight, she felt accepted and taken seriously. Her work was admired, discussed, reflected upon alongside her husband's and the work of others. She became known and hailed as 'Madame Libellule', Lady Dragonfly, and signed her work as such.

One evening, Charles came home, rubbing his hands with glee. He summoned Isobel to the parlour. 'Someone has just bought your latest study of Woolloomooloo Bay for his own private collection. You will never guess who.'

Isobel looked at him in amazement. 'Who?' He grinned. 'Charles! Tell me! Who?'

Charles's grin grew even wider. 'None other than Mr George French Angas, that's who!' At a salon at the Royal Hotel that evening, Charles had shown the artist his wife's most recent pen-and-wash study of the bay. 'The man slapped down five pounds on the spot. "It is exquisite and I must have it," he declared. "Tell the talented lady, we must meet."'

Far from being diminished or threatened by the recognition of his wife's talent, Charles was excited. This excitement assumed a new dimension late one afternoon when he arrived home to discover Isobel in the studio, working at her canvas and so totally lost in concentration that she did not even hear his approach.

The day had been exceptionally warm. Even with the windows thrown open, the air in the studio was stifling. Tired of persistent drops of perspiration running down her face and trickling along her limbs and hands, Isobel had shed her normal skirt and blouse. In a moment of impulsive and devil-may-care daring, she had borrowed a pair of Charles's work trousers and an old cotton shirt. She had also tied up her thick hair and tucked it under a battered canvas hat. Now she could apply her brush and control each stroke without fear of her fingers slipping or of being blinded momentarily, blinking away droplets of sweat.

Catching a glimpse of herself in the cheval glass, she startled at the memory of her disguise on the morning of the fateful duel over two years ago. But this was different, Isobel told herself. This was not pretence or subterfuge; it was, rather, a blurring of the separate spheres, a rising above sex. Here she was, an unashamed female artist dressed in the garb of her male counterparts, unapologetically crossing into their forbidden territory of the epic and the sublime. Her first landscape in oils! This was the true nature of her transgression: as an artist, Isobel chose not to be defined by her sex, knowing that her creativity flowed from a sensuality and a spirit that transcended male and female.

Charles entered the room and gasped. Isobel turned and smiled at him. 'Madame Libellule!' he sighed and took her in his arms. 'A living flash of light indeed!' He kissed her deeply then, and, with their mutual passions ignited, they stumbled towards the bedroom. Thus ensued such sweet, rough, untrammelled bliss! The ardour of their first love-making in the hot, blood-red light of a dust storm had returned, doubled and redoubled. There was no more that Isobel could ask for: her life was near perfection.

In this way, married life continued as a source of daily surprise and gratification. But like any artist's precarious existence, it was not without its trials. While he still received commissions, Charles had not yet managed to find a secure teaching position with a wealthy family. While gold lined the pockets of some families, the huge drain of labour and customers to the goldfields was still playing havoc with Sydney's economy. Money was not always in steady supply.

One morning over breakfast, Charles asked Isobel if there was any news of the legal proceedings in the probate court. As there was now no communication between Isobel and Grace, it was Aunt Louisa who had told her that Joseph had filed a long list of objections to his father's will. 'Augustus says cases like these have been known to drag on for years. We can only hope for a speedy resolution,' said her aunt. Apart from the sentimental articles Papa had bequeathed and some small sums of money advanced on the will, the rest of the Major's estate could not be settled on his heirs until all these matters were reconciled in law. Isobel debated with herself whether to tell Charles the bad news but decided that it was better it came from her than elsewhere.

He nodded gravely. 'I am sorry to hear that,' he said. A touch coldly, she thought. Isobel felt the sharp prickle of resentment. She wanted Charles to reassure her that this was of no consequence to the happiness of their marriage. Was she being peevish?

Despite this shortage of cash, Isobel's life felt bright and peaceful most days. Just like the glittering green waters of Woolloomooloo Bay in the autumn sunshine that warmed her face as she stood listening to her much-loved harbour. Fears for the future might still lurk beneath this calm, sunny surface and perhaps more storm clouds of discontent hovered out on the horizon. But for now, Isobel decided to take pleasure in the quotidian loveliness of her new life.

❧

Every day she entered her studio, her father's field journals sat accusingly on the bookshelf beckoning to her: *I leave this true record in your hands. You will know what to do.* But truthfully, she felt no inclination to open her father's books. Despite pleas from poor Aunt Louisa for her and Grace to 'make peace', Isobel wanted to shut the door on Rosemount and her family and all its sad history. Was she being selfish? Her life with Charles was her one bid for happiness and she did not want to taint or imperil it with memories of the past.

She missed her father, of course, but her feelings were not solely those of grief and regret. At times her thoughts about him had tended in another direction. If it was not for her father's stubbornness, Joseph would not be contesting the will and stopping his siblings from now claiming their inheritance. It was her father's pride that had led to the duel and Isobel's fall from grace, the trigger for much of the bitterness that followed. It was her father's vanity and overweening confidence in his boomerang-screw scheme that had drained the family coffers. It was Father's refusal to heed advice that led to him catching the chill that killed him. The more she thought about her father in this light, the longer the list of her resentments grew.

In this dark mood, Isobel even thought about tossing all her father's field journals into the fireplace in the same way she was tempted to cast Winnie's opal dragonfly into the sea. Why was she, Isobel, chosen to be the keeper of her family's secrets while Grace got to be the mistress of Rosemount? Why on earth would she want to have these stinking albatrosses hanging about her neck? Better to throw the past away, cast it off, bury it, forget it all. Make a fresh start.

But something held her back.

And then one afternoon, while Charles was still out meeting with a client and she would have normally sat down to write letters or make entries in her own journal, Isobel was overtaken by curiosity. She pulled the first field journal off the shelf and began to read. By her side she kept the published accounts as well (Aunt Louisa had given her a set, signed by the Major). These accounts were the more polished narrative that had been composed from the short entries recorded in the field journals. The immediate impressions. The 'true record' according to her father's message, whatever that meant.

Almost against her will, Isobel was drawn, little by little, into the story these daily journals told. Sometimes the entries were no more than dry observations of fact (the weather, distances covered, compass bearings, geographical features) recorded in terse, workmanlike prose. But at other times there were passages written in poetic and patriotic outbursts of strong feeling. *'We had at length discovered a country ready for the immediate reception of civilised man, and fit to become eventually one of the great nations of the earth . . . Of this Eden it seemed I was the only Adam, and it was indeed a sort of paradise to me.'*

As she read, the familiar sounds of the street and the bay were dimmed almost to silence to be replaced with the clamour of bellowing bullocks, creaking drays, shouting men or the cheerful thunder of cockatoos breaking cover en masse with the promise of nearby water. Isobel's view through the window was overwhelmed by the blinding haze of outback sunlight, clearing to a vista of parched red desert or distant purple hills or the more welcome prospect of a broad, snaking river with its lovely fringe of trees.

Isobel was particularly impressed at her father's physical toughness and courage as a young man. In charge of a team of surly, ill-bred convicts (all promised tickets of leave at expedition's end) and with only an assistant surveyor for civilised companionship, the Major led his large, cumbersome party of horses, cattle, sheep, bullocks, wagons and handcarts, piled high with provisions, into rugged, inhospitable country, most of it unknown and uncharted. When it rained, the heavy wagons sank up to their axles in mud or became bogged in riverbeds. Trees were cut down to make improvised roads where none existed. Most days, the Major rode out ahead of the main party with his native guide to find water (the lack of which would spell certain death) and to scout for a safe campsite protected from attack by blacks and with adequate grass and a nearby river for the stock. Meanwhile, his assistant surveyor and the convicts used chains to make their measurements, surveying the landscape they traversed each day, while every night the Major checked these figures and recorded their progress.

Isobel came to appreciate that the qualities that caused the Major such grief in public life—his stubbornness, his pride, his excessive confidence and conviction that he alone was always right—were exactly the qualities that served him well as an explorer.

Apart from the privations of hunger, thirst and disease, Isobel was most struck by her father's encounters with the natives. The Major would walk out alone ahead of the main party, unarmed and bearing only a green branch as an emblem of peace, to sit or kneel upon the ground in front of a stirred-up gathering of blacks, waving their spears and fists. Even with his guides (Jemmy or Mr Brown or Tackijally) there was no guarantee these encounters, without common language or custom, would end peacefully. As these men from vastly different worlds stared at each other across a chasm of mutual incomprehension, anything seemed possible. On his first expedition, two convicts accompanying the assistant surveyor, Mr Finch, had been killed by 'murderous savages' and their depot plundered. On the second expedition, the colonial botanist Mr Richard Cunningham, brother to the chief scientist at Kew Gardens, became lost in the bush. His body was later found, speared and horribly mutilated. It was not surprising that fear stalked the Major's expeditions at every step.

Whether motivated by theft or sheer savagery, these killings profoundly changed the Major's attitude to the blacks from one of sincere admiration to disappointed rage. His generous notions about noble, cultured natives, estimable for their musical corroborees by firelight, their skilful hunting and knowledge of the country, their hospitality and willingness to help, were all but wiped out by these cold-blooded treacherous acts. Now the blacks' invisible presence in the bush—signalled by notches in trees or voices in the dark or smoke in the sky—was the cause for anxiety and, at times, even terror.

As Isobel read her father's private field journals for his second expedition, this time along the Darling River, the atmosphere of foreboding became palpable. Encounters with the 'Spitting Tribe', as her father named them, grew ever more menacing as they communicated their displeasure by throwing dust, chanting war songs, and setting fire to the bush. They also boldly entered the expedition's camp, pilfering supplies and jostling the men. When the Major's expedition passed into Barkindji territory, the numbers of natives stalking the party swelled over several days and grew more vocal and restive, particularly those led by King Peter, chief of the Barkindji or 'Fishing Tribe' as the Major called them.

Some months ago, Isobel had read her father's published account of the tragedy that then occurred. On the very day the Major had decided to turn home, he heard a shot fired down by the river where five drivers were watering the bullocks. He quickly dispatched three men to investigate while he made preparations to defend the camp. More shooting was heard. An hour later, the men returned, one of them wounded and bleeding. They reported a quarrel had broken out over possession of an iron kettle with King Peter, who then struck a convict with his waddy. A second convict shot this man in the thigh, provoking an attack by a large group of blacks. In the melee that followed, a native woman, with a child on her back, was shot and killed, as well as a spearman who came to her defence. While the Major regretted the incident and felt 'a painful sympathy' for the orphaned child, he did not blame his men for defending themselves. Despite this exoneration, he also wrote: *'My honour and character were delivered over to convicts, on whom I could not always rely for humanity.'*

To Isobel's surprise, this observation in the published version of this violent encounter was missing from her father's field journal. And to her even greater astonishment, the field journal told an altogether different story from the one in the Major's published narrative. In this other version, her father recorded that on their return to the main campsite, the convicts had told him that it was the native woman who had been the principal cause of the quarrel, arguing with the convict bullock drivers over an iron kettle. She had then called on King Peter, her chieftain, to attack the white men. In retaliation, she had been shot in the legs and lay, wounded and bleeding, by the water's edge. It was then that one of the convicts killed her as she lay helplessly on the bank.

Isobel dropped the journal to the floor, dizzy and sick with horror. She tried to banish this appalling image from her mind but could not. To murder a woman, a young mother, in cold blood: how could anyone be capable of such brutality? It could have been Ballandella's mother shot there by the riverbank. Or Ballandella herself. This cruelty was monstrous beyond words. But what was almost as shocking to Isobel was that it was obvious her father had deliberately kept this atrocious murder secret.

I leave this true record in your hands.

Isobel struggled to breathe. Sweat dripped from her hairline and coursed down her neck. Though the casement was flung open, the room felt as if the glaring heat of the interior had invaded and now made her skin itch and ooze. She knew very well that her discomfort was more than physical: she felt soiled by this crime, the execution of which her own father could possibly be excused direct responsibility for but not its concealment.

You will know what to do.

What was she supposed to do? Make this knowledge public? Was that what her father hoped, so he could be judged posthumously? *He* was beyond punishment; such a revelation would hurt his children more than it could hurt him. She picked the journal up, determined to put it back on the shelf and never open it again.

As she did so, an envelope that had been inserted beside the back cover dropped to the floor. With a feeling of dread, she opened it and read its contents:

Major A. Macleod—Sir,

I shall not mince words, sir, as you and I know the matter of which I write. Thanks to Mr Charles Sturt who recently follow'd in your footsteps down the Darling and heard the stories told by the local tribespeople there, I have learned the Truth of what occurred on your two previous expeditions through that territory. That Truth cannot be hidden any longer. I challenge you, sir, to make public the facts as you know them. There is no kind way to put this: you lied to the Governor and the Executive Council in your reports and in your official accounts. This is not the honourable conduct of a gentleman. Please understand that I have the greatest admiration for your record of service but this cannot stand unchalleng'd. You and I both know what bloody and unjust cruelty has been inflicted on the blacks of New South Wales in our merciless dispossession of their land. I am sure you would agree that the perpetrators of such acts of brutal violence must be held accountable. I sincerely hope that you will correct the public record regarding these tragic incidents. I would hate to have to press the matter further as we both know what that could mean for your tenure of office.

Yours sincerely etc. & etc.,
    S.D.

The room spun and Isobel had to grip the arm of her chair to anchor herself. There was no mistaking the identity of the writer. It could be none other than Mr Simon Davidson. But that was not the only thing to cause Isobel's heart to race and her head grow light.

The date! She looked again in dismay. Could it be possible? The letter was dated *13 September 1851*: two weeks before the fateful duel between Mr Davidson and her father. Isobel's mind reeled then with all the implications of the timing and import of this letter, which was a barely concealed threat to expose her father to public ruin if he did not reveal the truth about his expeditions. Was *this* the real reason her father had taken up arms against Mr Davidson? It seemed obvious that if the Major had succeeded in killing Mr Davidson under cover of a gentleman's duel then there was a distinct possibility this scandalous secret would have been buried with him.

Was that her father's plan after all? And had she, Isobel, accidentally defeated this plan by interrupting the fatal proceedings? Isobel was horrified by the possibility that her father had been willing to compound his original sin of concealing a murder by killing the man who threatened to unmask him. She felt as if she did not know her father at all. And then she remembered the look of cruel triumph on his face the night he dealt a crushing blow to his nemesis, Mr Macleay. Her love and admiration for her father was sustained only by deliberately ignoring this side of his nature.

Her mind was now crowded with more questions, of course. Why had Mr Davidson not pursued the matter further once the duel was over? And, stranger still, why had her father not destroyed this letter?

Was it possible that he had left it here by design for her to find? Was his atonement after death to be Isobel's responsibility then?

Isobel hastily returned the journal to its shelf as if it was a loaded shotgun that might discharge at any moment. No more of her family's shameful past, no more! She would not read another word. Why, Father, have you done this? she railed to herself. What had this atrocious murder on a riverbank long ago and this quarrel between two men to do with her?

Nothing. Nothing at all. Isobel refused to have her happiness destroyed by secrets.

Chapter 35

SECRETS

MAY 1853

As it happened, the idyll of Isobel's married life with Charles, despite all her efforts to keep it safe, would run its course for only two months. Two months of unforgettable bliss.

In the first week of May, Isobel had her nightmare again. She was disappointed, of course, because up to that point she had experienced no nightmares in her new home. She had begun to hope that the powers of the opal dragonfly no longer held sway here and that the separation from her family and Rosemount was the key to her peace of mind.

But she was wrong.

The dream of the drowned Rosemount rooftop resumed where she had last left it with the silver waters closing over the dome. On the corner of the surrounding courtyard wall stood her playmate, Ballandella, as she had done before. 'Minhi!' she shouted, hailing

485

her little sister, and held up in her hand something that shone in the pale moonlight. 'Come, Izzie. Wash away your sin!' What was she saying: calling her to a baptism?

Ballandella danced along the wall, yelling and shaking her hands in the air. 'Come on, Izzie! Come, come!' A cloud passed before the face of the moon and for a second or two the dark waters appeared as red and sluggish as blood. 'Time to go!' shouted the little black girl and jumped into the claret-coloured sea.

In the distance, the hunched figure of Charles still worked the oars in the frozen rowboat. Isobel called to him. 'Charles! Over here!' And then she saw the tiny rowboat close by, the one she had seen before, no bigger than a basket. It bumped up against the dome and she leaned down to look inside. There lay a baby, tightly swaddled and red-faced from crying.

Isobel awoke in a sweat and ran from the bedroom. She rushed down the stairs, illuminated by moonlight through the window on the landing, and into the bathroom where she vomited. Dear God, she prayed, this cannot be true. She did not need a doctor to tell her. She was pregnant. Of course she was.

And she also knew the precise moment of this baby's conception. While she and Charles had practised withdrawal since, in that first act of abandon, they had thrown all caution to the proverbial winds as the drama of the dust storm all around them had created an atmosphere of dreamlike unreality. How could she have been so stupid? And her wilful stupidity had continued. Over the last four weeks or so, she had felt flutterings like hunger pains and waves of nausea and had chosen to pay them no attention. Even Charles had commented on the growing pouch of fat around her waist, which she could not explain, as she ate sparingly. A baby had been unfolding in her womb for the last six months and was now beginning to quicken. Isobel realised that she should have begun showing weeks ago; while her belly had tightened and thickened considerably in that time, it had not distended into the tell-tale profile of a pregnancy.

They had both behaved like fools! Isobel tried to calm her breathing but her head swam with all the catastrophic consequences that flowed from this. Charles and she had discussed children, of course, but as a possibility in the remote future. Neither of them was in any great haste to become a parent, though they understood this was expected of them as a married couple. How would Charles respond then to the news that he was to be a father?

But that was the least of her worries. The most pressing concern was how this would stir up another whirlwind of public outrage. There was no hiding the timing of this disaster—a baby conceived out of wedlock—or avoiding the consensus that Isobel was morally dissipated, a fallen woman.

She kneeled on the floor and leaned her head against the marble washstand.

Mercifully, Charles was still asleep. She could not summon the courage to tell him. Perhaps she would never tell him. Perhaps she would find a doctor to help rid her of the unborn child. She had heard Augustus talk some months ago about how British law had abolished the death penalty for 'post-quickening' abortions. Even so, the offence of procuring a miscarriage was still punishable by transportation for the term of one's natural life, or a long prison sentence. 'Too good for them!' Augustus had scoffed in his usual superior tone.

That she could even momentarily contemplate the destruction of her baby, a prospect repugnant to all her principles, showed the depths of Isobel's despair. Had she not had enough ignominy heaped on her head? This would only confirm the public view that she was, to use Grace's word, 'perverse'. Oh, how easily she imagined everyone—her sisters, Aunt Louisa and the well-bred women of the fancywork circle—turning their faces against her. 'She was always trouble, that girl,' they would say, rewriting history. 'Once fallen, forever socially dead'—that ironclad rule had returned to haunt her. Except that Isobel was twice fallen. What hope was there for her restoration? None.

Her present happiness was so new, so fragile, she was prepared to do anything to preserve it. At least for now. She would secretly seek Dr Finch's advice on her pregnancy. Perhaps she would write to Alice to unburden herself. She might even seek counsel from dear Mrs Palmer, her neighbour who lived only a few streets away. Seemingly overnight, Mrs Palmer had become so very old and frail, stricken with multifarious pains and afflictions. But she was the only person Isobel could imagine being able to offer compassion without judgement.

But now, right now, her baby would remain her secret.

Isobel knew that secrets had a way of eating at the foundations of love, friendship and trust. As she felt the stirrings behind her belly and said nothing to Charles, so too her mind stirred with dark thoughts that she kept hidden from everyone.

Under the pretext of an afternoon tea with Aunt Louisa, Isobel went to an appointment at Dr Finch's rooms in Macquarie Street. She trusted that Dr Finch's professional discretion (as well as his affection for her late father) would protect her from shame. Upon applying the cup of his stethoscope to her belly, he announced in his habitual sober manner: 'Two heartbeats. Yours and your baby's.' Was there news more exquisitely mingled of pain and joy? Isobel thanked him, fighting back tears. Dr Finch insisted that she make another appointment soon as she was now in her third trimester and should be watched. Neither of them spoke of the glaring fact of this baby's conception out of wedlock though Isobel detected a suitably tragic note in Dr Finch's voice.

'There is a delicate matter that is difficult for me to raise,' stammered Isobel, a blush rising to her cheeks, 'My . . . *circumstances* have somewhat altered since my father's death. I may have to consider securing the services of a midwife.'

Dr Finch's face darkened. He held up his hand to ward off the very notion. 'If it is a matter of finances, Miss Macleod, then think no more about it.' He looked down at her with a smile of beneficence. 'Midwives may be all very well for, shall we say, a *particular* class of women. But I will not stand by and allow the daughter of an honourable friend to be exposed to the perils of poor hygiene. I am sure we can come to some satisfactory arrangement.'

She acknowledged his kindness and began to take her leave. Clearing his throat with theatrical extravagance, Dr Finch called her back. 'On another delicate matter, please excuse my asking, but have you told the father'—he quickly corrected himself to avoid any unseemly implication—'*your husband* about this yet?'

Isobel's blush deepened. 'No, not yet. I was waiting for your confirmation.'

There was more throat clearing. 'Of course. I only ask as I am aware that some women in your situation, if you do not mind me saying so, decide to conceal the fact for as long as possible. I hope you will not find my advice obtrusive but from my experience of these matters, I have found this is not the wisest course.'

'I understand, Doctor,' nodded Isobel. 'I am grateful for your advice.'

But as she stepped out into the sunshine and the bustling multitude on Macquarie Street, her mind reeled at the thought of having to confront Charles.

And the world.

If God was indeed watching at His celestial peephole, He must have viewed the immediate sequence of events that followed Isobel's visit to Dr Finch with grim irony. Isobel hurried to her next appointment at the Misses Smiths' café on Pitt Street for afternoon tea with her aunt. There she was greeted with the startling news that her sister Grace had been delivered of a healthy baby daughter two days ago (and over a week past her due date). Olympia. It seemed that Augustus's choice of name had won the day after all.

'Olympia! It sounds so regal!' cooed Aunt Louisa. 'Ah, your dear father would have been so proud.' She wiped a tear from the corner of her eye and smiled bravely.

The cruel coincidence (and stark contrast) of this joyous public announcement with Isobel's own secret shame was almost too much to bear. She did not begrudge Grace her maternal happiness but she did resent the imbalance in their fortunes. The birth of Grace's child would be welcomed with general celebration while the news of Isobel's would only invite gossip and censure. She could not imagine any possible reason why Charles would refuse to acknowledge the child as his own but still she felt haunted by fear.

'Do you think that such a happy occasion might be . . .' Aunt Louisa chose her words carefully, '. . . grounds for a reconciliation between yourself and Grace?'

'That lies within Grace's power, not mine, Aunt,' said Isobel tartly. 'As I have had no word from her these last few months, I have severe doubts about the chances.'

'Have *you* written to her, Isobel?'

While she understood her aunt's grief at the schism in the family, Isobel was not pleased by her nagging tone. 'And what should I say, Aunt? I am so sorry to hear that Anna's mind is still beyond all remedy—for which I know you blame and hate me—and that you did not find it in your heart to write to me about your daughter's birth. Presumably I am still banished from Rosemount. I hope you are both well, your loving sister, Isobel.'

Aunt Louisa looked hurt at this rebuke. But Isobel was beyond taking care of everyone else's finer feelings when they seemed so uninterested in taking care of hers. An awkward silence ensued before the conversation resumed on less personal topics.

The afternoon tea ended awkwardly and abruptly. Isobel was feeling nauseated and increasingly agitated by her aunt's sulkiness. 'Please excuse me but I have to pick up a package at the post office before I return home.' It was a white lie; some books for Charles had arrived from Melbourne but there was no urgency to collect them.

Isobel hurried away, flustered and sick at heart. Walking briskly along busy Bridge Street heading towards the post office on George, she passed the sandstone obelisk in Macquarie Place. This elegant monument had been erected by the Governor back in 1816 as the anchor point at the geographical heart of Sydney *'to record that all the public roads leading to the interior of the colony are measured from it'*. She paused for a moment of reflection and her mind filled with the image of her father, the master road maker. The memorial made no mention of the terrible price that had been paid for conquering 'the interior of the colony'; its lovely, smooth sandstone and formal lettering obscured the shameful spilling of blood behind that brave enterprise.

Isobel picked up the mail and took the next omnibus up William Street. As she sat nursing the package in her lap, listening to the team of horses blowing and straining as they trudged the steep hill to the ridge, she looked back at Sydney's sandstone buildings with their Gothic spires and belltowers stark against a cloudless sky.

On a day like this, it was easy to imagine a noble future for this city. Only last year a ceremony had been held to found a university, surely the mark of a civilised metropolis. And yet, with the revelations from her father's journals, Isobel's thoughts about her hometown became more embittered. This was a city built on lies and secrets, a city that refused to face its demons.

Having cut short her afternoon tea with her aunt and hastened to the post office, Isobel arrived in her street two hours earlier than she was expected. She wondered whether Charles was still out with his client or had returned early too. It was such a beautiful afternoon she was tempted to take a walk around the bay alone. She needed some time to herself to sort through all her troubled thoughts. Yes, that is what she would do—drop the package off at her house, change her clothes and take in the peaceful prospects of the bay.

She unlocked the front door and left her package on the table in the parlour. As she ascended the stairs she thought she heard someone in the rooms above. It was the servants' day off so there should have been no one home.

'Charles? Charles is that you?' she called, her heart racing a little.

She opened the bedroom door and the sight that greeted her eyes was beyond her imagining. Her life would never be the same again. The idyll of her marriage was ended.

Standing before her, frozen in horror, was her husband, his shirt half-unbuttoned. And lying naked on the bed was Richard, the bearded and mysterious gent she had first met at Charles's studio back in February.

Isobel reeled against the wall on the landing.

'I'm pregnant, Charles!' she screamed. 'I'm pregnant with your child!'

Chapter 36

FORGIVENESS

JUNE TO JULY 1853

Later that night, Isobel sat alone in the parlour with only the light of one lamp to keep her company. She would probably fall asleep here in her chair as she could not bring herself to return to the marriage bed that had been polluted by she knew not what abominations.

Charles's lover (if that was the right word) had dressed and fled the house. The scene of recriminations that then ensued lasted what seemed an eternity. Charles sat with his head buried in his hands or stared at the wall, his face chalk-white, running his fingers madly through his hair. His mood veered from tearful expressions of remorse and vows of expiation to outbursts of reproachful anger at being deceived into a penniless marriage with the additional burden of an unwanted child.

Then his mood would change tack just as quickly again and he would weep and beg Isobel for absolution. 'Oh, my darling, please forgive me, I beg you. I still love you with all my heart and soul. Nothing changes my love for you.'

Isobel could only feel dismay at such a deep betrayal. Had she been wilfully blind? Aunt Louisa had been so reassured by Mr Probius's dandyism (and, in her mind, lack of interest in women) that she had been happy to leave Isobel alone with him. But there was no doubt about Charles's sexual passion. Surely that was not something a man could dissemble!

Charles knelt at Isobel's side and clutched her hand, wetting it with his tears. 'It is a perversion of my nature to have feelings of attraction for women *and* men, I cannot deny it. But you are my wife and my muse and my life's companion! It is you I *love*.'

'But him! How could you, Charles?' accused Isobel. 'Your best man at our wedding? Was it him you thought of when you said, "I do"?' Her face was dark with fury. She could have spat on Charles, so great was her disgust. But to do so would have destroyed her own feelings for him completely, and she found that despite everything she still did not want that if it could be helped. But how could she ever forgive him?

'How long has this man been your paramour? Before we met? Have I been your gull, your dupe, this whole time, a cover for your forbidden love?'

'No, no. That is not true. Not at all!' he protested. 'Yes, I knew him before. In Melbourne. But when I fell in love with you, I tried to end our liaison. I told him I loved you, wanted to marry you. That he and I had no future. He became so distraught, I feared he may harm himself. I was too frightened to tell you my dreadful secret. I did not want to lose you.'

'So instead you conducted this affair in our house? In our bed!' Isobel was shouting. She clenched her fists and struck Charles repeatedly about the head. He put his hands up to shield his face but did not restrain the rain of blows. His punishment was deserved. 'Mr Probius, indeed! You are nothing but a shameless liar! And to think how guilty I felt for the lie I told you. For love! Not for some unnatural lust!' Isobel broke down at this point and wept helplessly. Charles did not comfort her. He hardly dared touch her.

'Yes, yes, I confess it is an unnatural and abhorrent lust!' he whimpered. 'I promise you on my soul it will never happen again. I was weak but I can change. Please give me another chance. I could not bear for our love to be thrown away for such a meaningless transgression. I have sinned and I will seek repentance. For our love, Isobel, I will endure any punishment. But not the end of our marriage. Please let me save that!'

Charles's pleading was so abject and heartfelt that, despite herself, she felt pity for him. She did not understand the nature of his desires but she wanted to believe that this perversion did not in fact cancel out or contradict his genuine feelings for her. Men drank and gambled and stole because they could not help themselves and such men found salvation.

'I will remake the bed,' said Charles, looking guiltily in that direction. 'And I shall sleep in the studio tonight.'

Isobel sat alone in the parlour, turning over all the events of the last two years in her mind. Was she being punished for something *she* had done? Or was her punishment for a hereditary shame that must be expunged? That idea filled her with a vertiginous horror. At last she fell into a deep and mercifully dreamless sleep. She did not wake again until the maid shrieked when she found her in the parlour the next morning.

'Oh, ma'am, I thought you was a ghost!'

When Charles came downstairs he had packed a bag and said he would spend a night or two at a boarding house nearby. 'I do not want to stay here as a provocation to your anger and aggravation to your heartbreak. Perhaps Mrs Palmer could come and keep you company. When you are ready, I hope I can find some way to repair our marriage.'

'What are you going to do?'

'First, I am going to write a letter to Richard and put a stop to the whole thing. I will never see him again, I swear on my life.'

Charles had tears in his eyes as he closed the front door and walked away. Isobel washed and dressed in fresh clothes. She had no appetite so she left the house soon after her husband and set out on a walk along the bay past the Rose and Crown, the warehouses and shipyards, and Mr Punch's hotel with its tower.

Despite Charles's demonstrations of what appeared to be genuine remorse, Isobel's heart was hollowed out by a sense of utter helplessness. Charles had been her rock, her refuge at a time when the comfortable world she had inhabited as a young woman was broken up and lost like so much storm-tossed wreckage. Any hope and self-esteem she had rescued from this catastrophe were attached to her love for Charles and his for her. If that love was founded on a lie, a delusion, what did she have left?

Nothing. Only pain and regret.

She normally found the salt air and the bright water a balm for her soul. The harbour view offered a largesse that dissolved all the troubles in her heart or at least diluted their pain. But today she found no such solace. She stood, a lone figure in her spring bonnet and cape, at the far end of the wharf, her eyes fixed on the dark green waters at her feet.

Isobel contemplated what the world would be like without her. Except for the child still unborn inside her, who else in her life would miss her? Her sisters, Anna and Grace? Hardly. Her aunt? While she professed some affection for her niece, Louisa Blunt had survived the death of her husband, George, and had three daughters of her own to cherish. Dear Mrs Palmer? She would be broken-hearted but she would not grieve for long; given her poor health, her days were surely numbered. Her brother Joseph? He might have some regrets but he was not himself anymore, utterly changed by suffering into a self-obsessed and vengeful person she did not recognise. Her playmate Ballandella? Their friendship had ended years ago and she had no reason to think Ballandella would mourn her passing more than any other general acquaintance.

And Charles, her lover, her husband, her mentor? Yes, he would no doubt grieve for a time and probably be overwhelmed by guilt and self-pity. But with her death, Isobel would remove herself and her unwanted child from his life as the two obstacles to whatever relationship he enjoyed with Richard. Free-spirited Charles would soon make a new life for himself. The one person Isobel would truly regret hurting was her sister Alice. But she was far away and had a husband and son to devote her life to. She too would survive her grief.

Isobel stood, turning the opal dragonfly over and over in her hand, its stones as cold as ice despite their fire within. How many times had she rehearsed in her thoughts tossing it into the sea? If it was indeed the progenitor of her dreams then it had prefigured Charles's divided love—the man in the frozen boat, rowing neither away nor towards her—and the conception of her child—the infant bundle in the tiny rowboat. Would she see herself in her next dream, a floating corpse, arms outspread, like her brother William? Was this her fate?

She imagined herself then, falling into the harbour. It would be so easy to do. Right now. Two, three steps. She saw herself descending into its emerald liquid depths, suspended for a moment, her dress inflated bell-like, her eyes looking up, mesmerised by the dazzle of green light above. It was so peaceful, so quiet, an elegiac vision of surrender. And then she saw herself sinking, watching the bright surface recede far above her and the crushing walls of water all about her growing darker and darker, the thudding of her heart louder and more insistent in her ears until she blacked out.

Angry thoughts intruded. I'll show them!

This would be her revenge against Grace, Anna, Joseph, even her own parents, who cared so little they had abandoned her. She was tempted to leave a note that would expose all their secrets and cruel failings. Isobel's death would create yet another scandal to plunge the family's name deeper into disgrace. Having risked her own life and reputation to save her father's, Isobel now chose to bring dishonour on them all for their heartlessness. She felt a grim satisfaction at that prospect. She would also punish Charles for his cold-hearted deceit; maybe she would let the strong light of public scrutiny flush out his grubby little secret. And her death would be an act of mercy as well. She would spare her poor child the indignity of being born into such a cursed family.

She broke down and wept. She wept for her own child self who had played so happily at Grangemouth with her friend Ballandella. She wept to recall her meeting with Fanny Macleay and the dragon-fly by the ponds at Rosemount. She wept to remember her mother toasting her thirteenth birthday: *'May your future bring you all the happiness you deserve, Isobel, my love!'* How had her life come to this dark place?

As she took a step forward to look down into the green water, she heard a voice shouting, 'Stop! I beg you, stop!'

She halted, turned her head in the voice's direction and saw a man running towards her, silhouetted against the morning sun. Who on earth was this? As the figure drew closer she recognised it as Major Ralph Tranter, jacket unbuttoned, flapping behind him as he ran. His face was a picture of distress, eyes ablaze, pale forehead and ashen cheeks. He held out his arms as if to restrain her. 'Please, I beg you!'

'Major Tranter . . . what is it?' She was at a loss for words.

'I . . . I thought you . . . you looked so terribly unhappy,' he said, looking abashed now, not quite sure what to say. 'I was frightened you were going to . . .'

'Jump? In the water?'

'I'm sorry if I misunderstood. It's just that . . .' The Major wrung his hands. 'You see, I was having lunch over there and I . . . I saw you passing by and followed you a little way to greet you. But then you seemed so lost in thought standing here. And so I . . .

I stopped and watched for a moment. You looked so terribly . . . please forgive me, Miss Macleod . . .'

'Mrs Ludiger,' corrected Isobel. With the palms of her hands, she wiped the tears from her face, still red raw from weeping. What a pathetic sight she must make!

'Yes, of course, Mrs Ludiger. I apologise for alarming you. I feel so foolish. There was just something about your . . . the way you were standing . . .'

'I thank you for your solicitude, Major Tranter, I really do,' said Isobel blushing deeply, still barely able to look him full in the face. It was true she had changed her mind about ending her life in the harbour but it was also true that the Major had perceived her despair. She was grateful if a little ashamed. 'I still grieve for my father, Major Tranter. Still think about him every day. It is hard, I am sure you understand.'

The Major nodded vigorously. 'Please forgive my outburst. And my idiotic behaviour. I wish you some relief in your deep sorrow. Time is a great healer, they say.' He looked pained. 'Though I know some afflictions may never be fully eased.'

Isobel was touched by her former suitor's concern.

'Please do not apologise, Major Tranter. Your outburst was motivated by the most generous and gentlemanly of feelings. And I thank you for it.'

'Mrs Ludiger, if you should ever need my help, please let me know.' He pulled a card from the inside of his jacket and handed it to her. 'I am at your service, dear lady.'

Isobel smiled at him and the Major bowed in return and, without another word, turned on his heel and left. As he retreated, Isobel, in spite of herself, pondered how her life might have been different if she had married the chivalrous and kind-hearted Ralph Tranter.

The weeks that followed were among the hardest for Isobel to endure in her short life. She had suffered so many blows these past few years and yet it was this sinking below the waves of her last rock of salvation in a vast, friendless ocean that was the most bitter blow to bear. Rightly or wrongly, Isobel had counted on her marriage to Charles to save her. And now her mind teemed with doubts. Had this man ever loved her? How could she ever trust him again?

Charles returned after two days, repentant and full of sorrow. He swore that he still loved her and never wished to do her any harm. He told her that Richard had already left for Melbourne and that he, Charles, would never see or speak with him again. He acknowledged that he was a sinner, accursed with unnatural desires, and prayed God would cleanse him.

She could tell that Charles was truly afraid and she pitied him. While she had lived a protected life, hedged about by ignorance of the wider world, Isobel knew that Charles's was a crime punishable by ostracism and social ruin, and possibly even death by hanging. Aunt Louisa, the source of so much information about the vices of the underclass, had told her about Lady Macquarie's Chair. This scenic spot by the harbour, a short walk from the Domain, had for a long time been notorious for 'perverse liaisons' between men. If arrested, such men could expect to be hanged if convicted of 'unnatural acts'; there was no pity and much disgust and hatred for these 'sods' and 'mollies'.

'While such acts of depravity continue, this colony will never be free of its convict past,' her aunt had declared. Everyone knew such relations were common among convict men; spyholes called 'squints' had even been cut into the walls at the Hyde Park Barracks so the guards could keep an eye on the inmates to prevent acts of degeneracy.

Charles would find no clemency in the court of public opinion for his 'perversion'. His wife spoke words of forgiveness but there were no feelings to match them in her heart. She and Charles were like two drowning swimmers, clinging to each other in desperation, too frightened to loosen their grip. They both needed this marriage to survive.

Their only hope now was that Richard would keep the sordid affair secret and that they would somehow stumble on, acting out the charade of a happy marriage until perhaps, in time, the pretence would become reality again. Isobel told him she had no intention of killing or giving away their child and that they would have to weather the storm of disgrace of a conception out of wedlock when the time came. Charles said he was not intimidated by society's prejudices. He vowed he would stand by her no matter what the consequences.

An uneasy reconciliation was achieved. But fine words were one thing; fine actions were another. Despite her protestations of forgiveness, she found her husband's touch repugnant and rejected his most tender shows of affection. Charles vacated the marriage bed and retreated to the chaise longue in the studio. There was no hiding these arrangements from their two servants and, fearful of their gossip, they invented the pretext of Charles falling ill.

Isobel struggled with her feelings of distrust and despond. Because her artistic efforts were so strongly associated with her teacher and mentor, Charles, she found no pleasure in picking up her pencils or brushes. Robbed of this diversion, she cast about for something else to preoccupy her mind so it would not dwell on thoughts of despair. Her eye alighted again on her father's field journals.

Having decided her unborn child must live, Isobel began to muster the courage to face the future, no matter how trying. If she was to continue the family line, whatever the cost, she calculated that she owed this child the truth. It seemed to be what her father wanted too, or why else would he have delivered these journals and Mr Davidson's damning letter into her hands? *I leave this true record in your hands. You will know what to do.*

The other, more mysterious impulse that drew her back to these journals was the intimacy they afforded her with her absent father. She had rehearsed in her head all the reasons to hate him for his legacy of shame. And yet she still loved and mourned him. These journals gave her a remarkably candid view of her father's character: his strengths and failings, his courage and generosity, his wonder and delight, his loathing and fear. They read like a confession, showed her his heart. He had submitted himself to her judgement. Surely that was the ultimate act of self-sacrifice, of trust. Even love.

With a father's undying love . . .

She opened the journal for his third expedition, his push to explore the lower Darling River where it joined with the Murray.

This was the journey on which he had discovered Ballandella and her mother, and found such well-watered grazing land that he called it *Australia Felix*.

At first the party travelled through country occupied by white farmers. The Major observed the sorry results of settlement: whole districts depopulated of blacks through disease and extermination, the survivors now scattered as refugees in strangers' country.

The Major had employed a Wiradjuri guide, Piper, and found the natives to be civil and useful for much of his journey along the Lachlan River down to the Murrumbidgee; maybe they had heard of the Major's fearsome reputation. But now the party approached the same Darling River country where the convicts from the second expedition had murdered a mother from the Fishing Tribe, the Barkindji.

The Barkindji began to follow the expedition in large numbers, carrying spears. By the last week of May, the Major was convinced that they intended to attack either in force or to pick off his men one by one. He split his party in two, keeping some convicts with the wagons and sending a second group to lie in wait, hidden in the bush.

One of this 'ambuscade', the convict Mr King, defied the Major's orders to wait for an attack on the main party and opened fire on a group of Barkindji men coming up behind. This triggered a wild spree of shooting as natives then tried to escape, swimming across the river. Major Macleod and his men at the wagons ran down to the riverbank and joined in the shooting. Seven natives were killed including their chief, King Peter.

Isobel was taken aback at her father's lack of any guilt when he wrote: *'Much as I regretted the necessity for firing upon these savages and little as the men might have been justifiable under other circumstances for firing upon any body of men without orders, I could not blame my men much on this occasion; for the result was the permanent deliverance of the party from imminent danger. Such was the fate of the barbarians who, a year before, had commenced hostilities by attacking treacherously a small body of strangers. I gave to the little hill which witnessed this overthrow of our enemies . . . the name of Mount Dispersion.'*

Such an unsullied name, thought Isobel, untainted by blood or death.

Far from regretting the encounter, her father seemed to welcome this provocation by the Barkindji as he had feared his own sympathy for the blacks might have endangered his men. He had written: *'I was indeed satisfied that this collision had been brought about in the most providential manner; for it was probable that, from my regard for the aborigines, I might otherwise have postponed giving orders to fire longer than might have been consistent with the safety of my men.'*

Isobel was in no doubt that the deaths of seven natives were only a few drops of blood in the great ocean of bloodshed that accompanied the conquest of the hinterland by white settlers. Even so, the killings should have been avoided and had been in direct defiance of the Governor's orders. She remembered what Anna had told her: how the language of the Major's report of this incident to the Governor was criticised for *not being regretful enough*. The Major's heart had been hardened against these 'treacherous savages'.

Isobel knew all this already. What she did not know until she read this field journal was that a passage had been removed from the Council's official report and her father's published account. It described how his men had chased away the Barkindji warriors, *'pursuing and shooting as many as they could'*. The convicts had not just fired to disperse the initial attack; they had chased the blacks and killed as many as possible. Her father's direct involvement in this shooting spree was not clear from either of his accounts.

Now that she had read the field journal, Isobel was alarmed to find out that her father also justified this massacre, this *'fate of the barbarians'* shot in the back as they ran away, with his assertion that this tribe had previously *'commenced hostilities by attacking treacherously'*. But that was not true! And Father knew it was not true. His own journal revealed that his men had shot a Barkindji woman in the legs and executed her in cold blood as she lay wounded on the riverbank.

Mr Davidson knew this too and had been determined to expose it. There is no kind way to put this, Isobel thought to herself in a welter of distress: her father had lied to the Governor and the Executive Council. And what's more the Council had admonished the Major in the mildest terms for this massacre and suppressed all mention of it in his public report in the *Sydney Gazette*.

Her father's previous admiration for the Aborigines had now turned to coldness and anger. It was obvious that he felt betrayed by the 'treacherous' behaviour of the Barkindji. As Isobel read on, she noticed that the Major now distinguished two types of blacks: the open-hearted and civil blacks who had lost their homelands to the white man and made peace with the invader; and the greedy, brutal, untrustworthy and aggressive natives who had yet to be dispossessed. But to Isobel's mind, none of this excused her father's lie about the two heinous acts of violence by white men against the Barkindji.

And then she had a thought that had never occurred to her before. She now wondered if her father's adoption of Ballandella into his family was an act of redemption for these crimes. Or was it intended to demonstrate his faith, severely challenged but not yet relinquished, that the natives were not barbaric by nature and could be civilised? Whatever his motivations then, her father had now handed her the truth, perhaps as a posthumous act of contrition. But what was she supposed to do? Was she meant to seek forgiveness for her father?

As she sat in her chair in the parlour, the journal lying open in her lap, she looked out the window at the street beyond, bleached in the sunlight. Forgiveness was so hard. Isobel herself had hardened her heart against her cruel sisters but she still secretly hoped for their forgiveness and acceptance. Most difficult of all was finding the forgiveness in her own heart that would melt away the years of resentment she felt towards Anna and Grace. How else could the past be mended, her world made whole again?

Now that her own father sought to set the record straight, did he also hope to be forgiven? And who could give that absolution? Surely it had to be the Fishing Tribe, the Barkindji themselves. Maybe it was time to write to Ballandella again, to find out what she knew, to tell her the truth.

And, of course, there was the greatest obstacle to Isobel's future happiness, barred by the hardness and distrust in her own heart. How would Isobel ever find *that* forgiveness?

For Charles.

Chapter 37

EXECUTION

JULY 1853

Before the month of July was concluded, the strain of maintaining the charade of Isobel and Charles's marriage was taking a heavy toll. Isobel continued to have strange dreams, with visitations from Ballandella and her father and even Major Tranter, clutching his purple orchid and declaring his loyalty to her. Charles in his frozen rowboat never got any closer to Isobel in these dreams; in fact, she was sure he drifted further towards the horizon.

Isobel struggled with her own feelings of loyalty, desperate to restore the bliss of her marriage with Charles. She had thought about seeking advice or even just a sympathetic ear from Mrs Palmer or Catherine Cooper (now engaged to be married). Major Tranter had also offered her help, as had Mr Davidson. But she felt such shame about her husband's perversion and her own pregnancy she could not bring herself to confide in any of them.

She was showing now, her belly swollen beneath her petticoats and crinolines with her baby due to arrive in only three weeks' time, and so she remained confined to her bedroom. She wrote to Aunt Louisa and the fancywork circle to tell them she was unwell and in the care of Dr Finch, who in fact came to the house regularly for discreet visits to check on the health of mother and child. Charles was solicitous, of course, and expressed his tender and joyous anticipation of becoming a father. It was Isobel's fondest hope that the birth of this child would prove the keystone in their future happiness, uniting Charles and Isobel in protectiveness of their son or daughter against the sordid opinions of the world.

'Charles, do you still love me?' asked Isobel.

'I do. The question is: do you still love me?'

Charles looked at her strangely when she replied, 'Of course, I do,' as if her answer was too pat, too quick, too easy to lay before him, like some homely sampler.

One night in the last week of July, Charles arrived home for dinner nearly two hours late. The cook was beside herself trying to keep the meat from drying out and rescue the vegetables. Isobel heard the front door open and the manservant greeting his master. 'Can I take your coat, sir? I see it has started raining.'

When Isobel entered the dining room, she could tell straight away that all was not well. Charles had been drinking. She smelled the sour fumes rolling off him and did not fail to notice the slow blink of his eyes and unsteadiness of his gait. Under his breath, he sang a martial song, an anthem of revolution, from his youth.

Ah! ça ira, ça ira, ça ira

Le peuple armé toujours se gardera

Le vrai d'avec le faux l'on connaîtra

Le citoyen pour le bien soutiendra

Ah! So fine! It will be, it will be!

A people armed will always keep themselves both safe and free!

We'll know what's right from wrong, and true from false,
    yay, verily!

Each citizen supports the good—for all humanity!

'Charles?' Isobel could not clearly read her husband's mood, an unsettling mix of surliness and abandon. Divested of his coat and hat, he stumbled towards the table and seated himself heavily in his usual chair.

'So here I am, your faithful husband, having done his duty to earn his wife's respect and love.' He surveyed the plates of dried-out meat and charred vegetables that had been hurriedly served up. 'And here is my reward. A modest meal prepared in my modest house.' He clapped his hands imperiously. 'Come, come, where is my wine?'

'Please, Charles, I think . . .' Isobel trailed off, hurt by his cruel words.

'Oh no. Have I offended you, my dear?' Charles grabbed the wine decanter from the manservant and clumsily spilled some into his glass. 'Please forgive me.' His mouth curled bitterly. 'Oh, I forgot. You don't do that, do you? Forgive.'

Isobel ran from the room.

'Isobel! Come back! Come back here!'

She ran into the hallway where Charles's weather-beaten cloak and plush riding jacket, stained with rain, hung on the hooks by the front door. Something caught her eye: an envelope stuffed into his jacket pocket. A warning tolled in her mind. Do not! She was about to cross another line, which could only bring grief. She grabbed the envelope and ran to the parlour.

'Isobel! Come back, will you?' Charles shouted from the dining room.

Had she not learned her lesson? Was she determined to invite more trouble into her life? What could be here that would not be bad news? She ripped open the envelope and took out the letter. She was Truth's warrior, fearless, reckless, unstoppable.

She read:

Charles, my Adonis, my Apollo,

My heart burns for you, my body hungers for yours, my lover, my love. Come away, come away, I beg you. What is the use of living a lie? You of all men, Charles, were not fated to be the prisoner of drudgery. Your marriage offers nothing but a life sentence of poverty, duty and pretence. You must be true to yourself, Charles! How else to be free?

I have booked our passage for Melbourne: the Condor, boarding ten o'clock, departs two o'clock, Friday week, Circular Quay. You have so many friends in Melbourne, the Paris of the south. Not like Sydney, this grubby temple to Mammon, this marketplace for peddlers and politicians. We can start again just as you did before, Charles. New names, new faces. No one will find us. I count the minutes until we are together again.

R.

Isobel cried out, an inarticulate utterance of outrage and distress. Her husband had lied again. Richard was still in Sydney and they were still in contact with each other, maybe even in person. And now her husband was planning to desert her and his unborn child. Charles Probius, the man of honesty, was a fraud, a liar, a heartless monster!

He stood in the doorway, unsteady, red in the face. His eyes fell on the letter in her hand. 'How dare you!' he bellowed and lunged at her. 'That is none of your business!'

She retreated, frightened but still angry. 'Isn't it? Are you going to leave me, Charles? Is that what you would do?' she yelled at him. 'Is that the kind of man you really are, Charles Probius? A coward and a liar?'

'Don't you lecture me!' he roared. 'What do you know of real men?'

She had crossed a line by reading her husband's private mail. And now, licensed by her indiscretion and by his own tongue loosened with wine and the accumulated misery and anger of the last few weeks, Charles crossed a line as well. His lips curled into a snarl, reminding Isobel of her sister's madness.

'What do you know of the real world, my Lady Dragonfly? Living in your lovely fortress of privilege on Woolloomooloo Hill. Your family—ha! Playing at being aristocrats while pretending to be friends of the deserving poor and the dispossessed native.

So genteel, so pious, so proud. While your whole pretty world is built on the sweat and pain and misery of real men and women. Servants, convicts, soldiers, murdered blacks.'

He lunged again and fell against the chiffonier. Two porcelain figures reeled and crashed to the floor, exploding. 'Come, Isobel, my love! You want to know the truth?'

Isobel did not want to hear the truth, not from the mouth of this foul, drunken man. This was not her Charles, her devoted husband, this was someone else who had assumed his face and spoke with his voice. A demon. He was mad like Anna, his mind consumed by delusion. Or was she the deluded one?

'Behold the mighty Macleods, so steeped in dishonour and disgrace, mocked and reviled by everyone. And all looking for a way out. Especially you, strange little Isobel. How easy you were to hook on my line, so proud and eager to be praised that you swallowed my flattery all in one bite. Twenty-five pounds for a painting at a ladies' charity bazaar!' He slammed his fist on the table like a gavel and laughed. 'Such a small deposit on a rich girl's inheritance!' His mood darkened again. 'But it turns out I tricked myself. I was the self-deluded fool after all. Duped by the Macleods' grand estate and fancy house! And by you as well, Isobel, lying to me about your father's blessing of our courtship!'

Isobel backed away as Charles drew closer, his face distorted into an expression of such hateful rage that she thought she would surely die at his hands tonight.

'Well, it's time you knew the whole truth, Isobel my dear! Your father *never* changed his mind! He *never* gave me his blessing! Did you really think he would? Major Angus Macleod? We met as I said in the gardens at Rosemount. And we talked, yes, like two civilised gentlemen, two men of education and taste. But he did *not* bless our union! He would *not* unstiffen that proud neck and allow his precious daughter to share the bed and the shame of a lowly emancipist!'

Isobel's head swam in stultified horror and disbelief. She simply could not credit what she was hearing. Her father had *not* blessed their marriage? Charles had lied to her and to Aunt Louisa? Was that possible? Charles had gambled everything on one monstrous deception when the Major died, so the truth could never be revealed that he did not wish Isobel to marry Charles Probius. 'I have repaid your lie with one of my own, dear Isobel!' Charles lunged again and this time he caught Isobel by the elbow. 'But I am afraid there is no future here for me! One kiss before I go, my sweet. Just one!'

He toppled then, catching his foot on the table leg and dragging defenceless Isobel with him. She screamed and her face glanced against the table edge as she fell. As her body collided with the floor, she thought of her baby, not herself. Her hands involuntarily hugged her belly to protect her child. She tasted blood at the corner of her mouth. Her cheek had split where it fetched the sharp corner of the table. It now bled freely.

Charles's body lay sprawled on the carpet. With a grunt, he rolled over and looked at his wife. His face paled. The spirit of madness seemed to flee his eyes.

'What have I done? What have I said? I am losing my mind!' he cried. 'Please, Isobel, please forgive me. I don't know who I am, what I am saying! I did not mean a word of it!'

He reached out to touch her and she flinched. Forgiveness had been difficult before; it was impossible now. He could not unsay the dreadful things that had been said. Their life together was no more than a charade, a play, a tragic farce.

They both then heard the pounding at the door and the voice beyond, demanding entry. 'Probius! Probius! Open up! Open up or I shall break down this door!'

Ignoring his master's orders to the contrary, the manservant opened the door. There in the doorway, his face half-lit by the lamp above, stood the figure of Major Tranter. Behind him, the rain fell in steady sheets. 'Probius! You will answer to me, sir. For your treachery. For dishonouring one of the finest women in the colony.'

Isobel looked up, amazed. What fresh nightmare was this? What did Ralph Tranter know of her shameful secrets? Why was he here to defend her? She feared that he too had been drinking. She could hear it in the slight slurring of his words, and the uneven volume of his voice, strident and shrill and too loud, even for speaking over the din of the rainfall. Despite this, Isobel thought that she should be pleased to see him, her rescuer. She needed help, certainly. Her husband had clearly lost his mind and was a danger to her and himself.

'Come, sir, I have someone here who will be your second,' shouted the Major.

What? Isobel's thoughts raced in a panic. A second? Dear God, let it not be true! Was the Major here to challenge her husband to a duel? Was it possible that history was to repeat itself in such a horrendous way? It was not to be borne. Isobel rose from the parlour floor and hurried to where the Major stood in the hall, his cloak pooling water at his feet.

'Good heavens!' cried the soldier on seeing her wounded cheek, now dripping blood. 'Has he dared to strike a woman? And such a woman as you, my dear Isobel!'

'No, no,' protested Isobel, 'It was an accident, I swear. He meant me no harm. You must calm down, Ralph. If you bear me any loyalty at all, you must desist, I beg you. There is no need for you to challenge anyone.'

'I knew you would defend him, Isobel, my love,' declared the Major. There, he had said it. He had confessed his love for her, this woman he had always desired, had never stopped desiring. He had been a fool to think he could trade such sweet ardour for a loveless and respectable marriage. He was not ashamed to confess his love.

Isobel blanched. This was both her worst fear and, at one time long ago, her fondest hope, confirmed in two simple words: 'my love'. Oh, how many times she had heard those words abused of late. She shook her head, unable to find her own words to express her alarm.

The Major saw the distress he had caused and did his best to restrain his torrent of feeling. 'Do not be afraid, Miss Macleod,' he said, clearly rejecting her married name. 'I am here to defend your honour,' he reassured her. 'I do this out of the respect that is your due, Madam, and not only for the love I bear you.'

The figure of Charles appeared in the hallway. He stared blankly at the soldier. 'Who are you to dare address my wife in this way? In my own home? Get out!'

This outburst provoked an equally violent reaction from the young soldier. Tranter removed his pistol from its holster and pointed it straight at Charles's head. 'By orders of the Governor in Council, you are under arrest, charged with the crimes of buggery and assaulting a woman. You will hang, you filthy scoundrel, which is unfortunate as I would prefer to have the privilege of blowing your brains out myself!'

The soldier surged forward and seized the now trembling Charles by the collar, half-choking him as he pulled and pushed him through the front door. All the while Isobel desperately entreated her ex-suitor to release her husband. 'Stop, Ralph, I beg you, stop!'

In an awkward shuffling dance, the two men, locked together in a rough embrace, and the wretched woman, pleading for her husband's liberty, emerged onto the street. Here, the rain fell in an unceasing drizzle. Less than four yards away there was parked a coach with two soldiers in uniform, standing as if on guard, at the nearest door.

'Come, sir, it is time to answer for your crimes,' shouted the Major as he pushed the miserable artist into the street. With a sharp shove, Charles fell to his knees.

'I thought you were arresting me. I must speak with my lawyer!' he protested.

'We shall settle this matter as gentlemen first,' said Tranter, pulling a second pistol from under his cloak. 'Though no sodomite and wife-beater deserves that name!'

'Why do you call me these names? I am nothing of the sort!' Charles was weeping now, his tears indistinguishable from the rain that wet his face and smeared his untidy blond locks to his pate. He was a pathetic, bedraggled sight. Isobel's heart was filled with pity though she knew she should hate him for his monstrous duplicity.

'Perhaps this will remind you!' said Tranter. The two soldiers by the coach, no doubt the Major's subordinates, obediently opened the cab's door. One of them leaned in and bodily tugged a man, crouching in the darkness within, out onto the street.

It was Richard. Even with his heavy beard, it was obvious from the cuts and bruises on his face that he had been punished. Bent over on his knees, he rocked back and forth, keening like a distraught widow at a funeral. 'No, no, no, no.'

Isobel felt a surge of disgust rise in her gullet. Were all the men in this town drunkards and cowards? This vile creature had conspired to rob her of her husband and her unborn child's father. She had no pity for him.

'I saw this piss-maker in the Rose and Crown. And overheard him boasting about his plans to make off to Melbourne with his lover! Turns out that the lover in question is none other than the husband of this fine woman.' The Major addressed these remarks to the figure of Charles, kneeling before him, with the air of a magistrate about to pass sentence.

'What's more,' Tranter continued, 'far from feeling any guilt or shame, this nasty piece of work expressed nothing but contempt for his lover's wretched wife who, he claimed, had tricked her husband into a loveless marriage. And trapped him even further with a child!'

'Lies! Lies!' shouted Richard. Isobel saw now that her husband's lover had both his hands bound behind his back. The soldier to his left casually struck the pathetic sot across the neck with the butt of his rifle, knocking him onto his face in the mud.

'No! No!' cried Charles. He clutched his own head as if he had received the blow. 'Punish me, not him. I am the one to blame.'

Major Tranter stepped forward and dragged Charles to his feet. 'Oh, you will answer for this, sir, do not worry about that. We shall settle this like gentlemen to defend the honour of this peerless woman. You know the rules, sir, surely? "Any insult to a lady under a gentleman's care or protection is to be considered as a greater offence than if given to the gentleman personally." So you shall answer as if you have done me insult and worse.'

The two soldiers lifted Richard up by his armpits and hauled him, half-walking, half-stumbling, across the street to where Charles now stood, bewildered. 'Here is your second, sir,' said Tranter. 'I am sure he will serve you well.' The Major cocked his own pistol before doing the same with the second firearm. He handed the loaded pistol to Charles, who refused it. 'Come, sir. Are you a coward? Take the gun, man. Or I shall be forced to put a ball through your skull right now and be done with it!'

All this while, Isobel stood, frozen in disbelief and terror, watching this scene unfold on the street in front of her house. The macabre irony did not escape her. Here she was again, trapped in the middle of men's madness, forced to intervene or watch a man she loved be murdered in front of her eyes. 'Stop this, I beg you, stop this!'

She broke down and wept, plucking at the Major's arm to elicit his pity. How she hated herself for being so weak! She would end this farce with the sacrifice of her own life. There was no other way. She saw it now. She had no future, her story was over. She saw how it would be done, rehearsed it inside her head. She would run to embrace Charles and take the deadly shot that was meant for him.

In the meantime, the manservant had gone to the rear of the terrace, climbed out a back window and sprinted as fast as he could in the rain towards the nearest police watch house. Lights had come on in neighbouring houses and there were clearly visible shadows of people at their windows. But no soul was brave or foolish enough to interfere in this private quarrel, especially where soldiers were involved.

'Please calm yourself, my dear.' Tranter took Isobel firmly in his arms and steered her back to her front door. 'This is not a matter to concern a lady. You must go inside now and leave us to settle this affair.'

Isobel struggled in Tranter's arms but his grip was firm. Quicker than she realised what was happening, he had pushed her into the hallway and shut the front door. One of his men had already picked up a length of timber from a stack of wood that lay in the street where work was being done on a fence. The soldier jammed the beam under the door handle, preventing it being opened, and stood guard over the entrance.

Isobel was trapped inside. She ran to the front parlour and pulled back the curtains. Her mind was in a whirlwind of terror, the same terror she had experienced two years ago when she had hidden in the paperbark grove with James and watched her father face death. She tried to open the window but the latch was rusted shut. She pounded the glass with her fists and screamed at the man who would kill her husband. Isobel's protests were all but silenced behind the front parlour window. She could not hear a word that was uttered on the street and could barely see what was happening in the thickening rain.

'No, no, please no. Not again! Not again!' Her voice became hoarse.

Tranter returned to where Charles stood, body slumped, head bowed, the very picture of pathos. Isobel could tell he was weeping openly by the rise and fall of his shoulders. He knew he was going to die.

The soldier pressed the second pistol into the artist's trembling hands. As if reminded at the last minute of his obligations as a man, and acting almost involuntarily with that weary resignation of one condemned to death, Charles took the gun. Tranter turned and walked away from him, measuring out the correct distance for a duelling ground. The second soldier had taken up a position between them as the umpire, raising his right arm to signal.

Isobel screamed mutely behind the glass. Who should die: Charles or Ralph? This was insanity. This was what men did to each other and the ones they loved. How could the world continue in this way, forcing women to witness such wanton destruction and stupidity?

For a second, Isobel wondered if her husband would shoot the Major in the back and try to make his escape. It would have been a futile and cowardly act, unworthy of a gentleman, of course. But she would have hardly blamed him. Instead, he stood his ground, his head tucked into his chest, his arms hanging lifelessly at his sides.

Richard fainted, folding up like an umbrella and toppling to the ground. Isobel would not allow herself this luxury. She would bear witness to poor Charles's death. She would be able to testify later when it was needed. From one point of view it could be argued that she, Isobel Clara Ludiger, nee Macleod, was the cause of this murderous ritual. She would not flinch and look away.

The rain fell so heavily now it formed a shifting veil of water over the whole scene. Isobel thought of all the nightmares that had tormented her these last two years: the man drowning in the surf as she ran along a beach; visions of her childhood home inundated and destroyed by water, the terror of the great wave wiping away all the precious trinkets of her family's wealth and status; the blood-red river where bodies floated, and the eerie ocean where Ballandella swam away, where Charles sat, hunched, frozen at his oars and where her baby was delivered in a rowboat no bigger than a basket. She knew that, through this rain-veiled parlour window, she now watched the final act of a drama that had begun the night she woke at Rosemount in her moon-drenched room, listening for her father's footsteps.

Tranter took up his position and raised his pistol. Over the thunderous drumroll of the rain, Isobel heard the umpire shout, 'On my signal!' His arm dropped.

Charles did not raise his pistol. At the last minute, he turned his head and looked to where Isobel stood at the window. She could not see his face behind the rain. But she knew what he was thinking: Forgive me.

And then the pistol ball struck and Isobel saw her husband's body jerk and spin and fall to the ground, lifeless.

Chapter 38

THE TRUTH

AUGUST 1853

Major Tranter was put on trial, found guilty of murder and hanged. Isobel's name was in every newspaper, with her described as the 'grieving wife of the murder victim', the ostensible reason for the duel and the key eyewitness. But her testimony was not solely relied upon. Many eyes had watched and many ears overheard what took place that night. In addition to the events of that fateful evening, there were also reports of Major Tranter's troubled marriage, his gambling debts and bouts of drinking, and his obsession with the woman he had once courted and always loved. With little evidence of shame, he confessed that he had stalked her secretly for years, hiding in the gardens at Rosemount, in the streets of Sydney Town and Woolloomooloo and by the barracks near Faulconstone. Isobel recalled the many times she had felt the weight of some stranger's gaze on her with an unshakeable and unsettling sense of being watched.

The Major, whose mind was greatly perturbed, said very little in his defence when offered the opportunity to speak except to admit, as if it was a self-evident truth to excuse his behaviour, that 'I loved her.' The Major's widow, Mrs Charlotte Augusta Tranter, nee Bathurst, moved back to England. Rumour had it that she remarried within the year.

Isobel had sat in the courtroom, her hands folded protectively over her swollen belly. She still wore mourning weeds for her father and her brother William. Every sordid detail of her counterfeit marriage and scandalous family was aired for public scrutiny and opprobrium: her prenuptial pregnancy; her ex-convict husband's unnatural liaisons with his drunken, dissolute lover; even her sister Anna's lunacy and the ignominious end to her father's career. This was all picked over by the ghoulish press whose speculations included whether her unborn child was in fact Major Tranter's and that she and he had conspired to murder the famous artist Probius. While the legal proceedings were supposedly intended to prove Major Tranter's guilt, Isobel could not help feeling that it was *she* who was on trial.

Isobel bore all this with a stoicism that surprised her. It was only later that she realised she had spent much of this time in a state of numbed shock, listening to the speeches in the courtroom as if they were dramatic monologues in a theatrical production.

As she had anticipated, everyone from her past life turned against her, even Dr Finch and Aunt Louisa, either out of hatred or shame or merely anxiety to distance themselves from scandal. Catherine Cooper sent her a note of condolence but, newly married, could not risk being contaminated by association with this now thrice-fallen woman. The Bradley women and the Finches, all her teachers and former acquaintances, and the ladies of the fancywork circle too kept their distance and all but vanished from her life.

The only person in her ever-shrinking circle who remained loyal and even accompanied her to court was Mrs Palmer. 'I will never abandon you, my sweet Izzie, for yours and your dear mother's sake.' Dear Mrs Palmer. She sat in the public gallery every day, pressing a handkerchief to her teary eyes as she watched poor Isobel's humiliation.

The trial took two days to conclude. When the judge had pronounced the death sentence, the Major's wife had astonished everyone present in court, including Isobel, with a howl of rage and despair. This performance was followed by an even more melodramatic assault on the steps of the courthouse in which she tried to claw at Isobel's face and had to be restrained by constables, a denouement that the press delighted in describing in lurid detail.

Isobel was soon confronted with the aftermath of her husband's death. He had accumulated debts of one kind and another so that she found herself virtually penniless and owing rent on her terrace. With no compensation for her loss and no progress in the probate court regarding her father's will, Isobel did not know where to turn. Mrs Palmer gave her a paltry sum from her own mean savings but Isobel's pleading letters to Joseph and Aunt Louisa were met with an obdurate silence. She wrote to Alice too in a last desperate bid for help but the letter was returned 'unknown at this address'. While Grace did not acknowledge the letter she wrote her, four days later a sum of money in an envelope from Rosemount was delivered by a post boy.

With this she paid off the rent owing on her and Charles's terrace. Isobel had thought about moving into Mrs Palmer's tiny cottage a few streets away to be a companion and, soon enough, a nurse in her final days. Mrs Palmer would have welcomed such an arrangement but she was overruled. Her cottage belonged to her eldest son, John, who refused to have such a 'dangerous fallen woman' living with his mother. Instead, poor Isobel scraped together enough to pay the rent on a smaller, shabbier terrace in another dingy street of Woolloomooloo. To make some cash, she sold most of the furniture and dresses that she had brought with her to Woolloomooloo, save only a few precious things, of course, including her mother's brooch, her father's field journals and sketchbooks, hers and Charles's sketchbooks, and her own journals and unfinished paintings.

As she watched all these familiar possessions pass out of her life, she thought of the funereal procession of wagons and coaches loaded with treasure that she had watched leaving Woolloomooloo Hill when she was a small girl. She thought of the families bankrupted by the depression and forced to become refugees from their villas and mansions. Now it was her turn. She too was a castaway, a shipwreck survivor washed up by the tide of misfortune on an unknown shore. Her few precious possessions were her only links to the past.

Two days before the hasty and modest funeral of Charles Probius, buried in the cemetery at St Stephen's in Newtown and farewelled by a small circle of friends and admirers, Isobel had received a letter that she now looked on as a last link with that past life. It was from Mr Simon Davidson, member of the Legislative Council, the outspoken critic and enemy of Isobel's father. She had written to Mr Davidson after finishing her father's journals and finding herself in a quandary as to what to do next.

What were her father's intentions? *I leave this true record in your hands. You will know what to do.* Part of her could not believe that the Major, who had always been so proud and insistent in pressing his claims for recognition and fame, would wish to destroy his posthumous reputation. On the other hand, now that he was beyond worldly judgement, perhaps he thought it only just that the record be set straight. Who would it hurt but his children? Which is why, perhaps, he had left it in Isobel's hands to decide.

In a moment of reckless and malicious revenge, Isobel imagined the terrible blow she could deliver to her proud aunt and her superior sister Grace. With her memories of the exodus of so many rich families from the Hill, she had also recalled her own family's triumph: the purchase of Rosemount arising from Mr Macleay's bankruptcy. As a little girl she had been struck by the nostrum 'one man's fortune was another man's ruin'.

So who had profited from Isobel's fall from grace and the tragic downward trajectory of her family's fortune? It seemed to her that the only beneficiaries had been Grace and Augustus, who now lived in Rosemount in perfect bliss with their daughter, Olympia, untouched by misery and poverty. How sweet then to let them taste some of Isobel's disgrace!

Though great was her temptation, Isobel knew such sentiments were despicable. And yet she still hungered to know the truth of her father's past. There was only one way to find out for sure. So she wrote to Mr Davidson, revealing she had inherited and read her father's private journals as well as the letter that Mr Davidson had sent him two weeks before their duel. She concluded, *'I entreat you not to hide the facts as you know them for my sake. Please be honest with me, I beseech you, and provide me with the unvarnished, uncensored truth, no matter how painful it may be to hear.'*

This was the reply she received:

Dear Mrs Isobel Ludiger,

I have read your letter with some degree of astonishment as you can imagine. I had no idea that your father would now risk linking his proud name to the truth he went to such pains to keep hidden. And yet it seems that he has left the door open to uncovering that Truth. I have good reason to remember what an exceptional young woman you are so it does not surprise me that your father has entrusted you with his legacy. Out of respect to your courage and love for him, I shall tell you what I know.

As I wrote to your father, Mr Charles Sturt had partly follow'd in the footsteps of Major Macleod's second expedition down the Darling River. Sturt was surprised to discover how welcoming the Barkindji people were, contrary to your father's descriptions of them as 'murderous savages'. They told Mr Sturt what he believed to be a true account of the tragic

*events that occurred at the hands of Major Macleod's men.
This account is different from the one that the Major used to
justify the later massacre at Mt Dispersion. I must warn you
that it concerns some of the most depraved aspects of human
nature. But you have asked for the 'unvarnished, uncensored
truth' and so I shall tell you.*

*A young Aborigine named Topar, aged eleven at the time of
the tragedy, told Mr Sturt what he saw that day. Two convicts
had gone down to the river to fetch water and saw a native
with his wife and child by the riverbed. One of the 'whitefellas' then went to the riverbank and, with threatening gestures,
frighten'd away the native man who swam across the river
to escape. The white man then tried to force himself on the
poor native woman who resisted strenuously. In a fit of anger,
he drew his pistol and shot the woman in the thigh. He then
raped her. When he had finished, he killed her and her child
with a tomahawk. The second white man shot at the man
swimming in the water but missed. The three other convicts,
sent by the Major to investigate, fired at the retreating native
but their bullets only struck trees.*

*When he returned to Sydney, Mr Sturt consulted me about
these revelations. I agreed to take responsibility for making
the truth public as Sturt wanted to avoid any accusations of
destroying the reputation of a rival explorer. I wrote to your
father giving him the opportunity to correct the public record.
He refused.*

*What was then the right course to pursue? I knew that your
father had recently lost his son in an accident and his wife to*

illness. While I believed in the justice of my request, I also felt pity for your father. I reminded myself that he may well have been lied to by his men. He had hitherto always shown respect for Aboriginals and intolerance for aggression towards them. I also took into consideration his family name and the future of his children.

It was these thoughts that stayed my hand when I went to write to the Governor. Instead I chose to make public a lesser offence—his flagrant overspending of the departmental budget—to chastise him. Perhaps I regarded it as a 'shot over the bow' hoping he may still confess to the true nature of the events. Instead he challenged me to a duel.

As you know, I was later deeply ashamed to see you, the Major's brave daughter, witness our contest of arms and risk her own life for love of her father. I was glad then that I had decided to keep Topar's story secret. Was that the right decision? I still do not know.

I lay out these grim facts before you and leave it in your hands to decide the right course. Burn this letter and your father's journals and say no more about it. Or have the truth published and let posterity be the judge. I urge neither course but trust you will find the answer in your heart and conscience.

Your admiring and obedient servant etc. & etc.,
  Simon W. Davidson

Secrets within secrets.

The images this letter conjured made Isobel's temples throb and bile rise into her throat in her horrified disgust. Putting the letter aside, she hung her head and wept with shame to think of the violence that had been visited upon this poor woman and her child. Rape, shooting, murder. What were these men not capable of? Isobel's hand cradled the unborn child she carried as her horror shook her to her core, her body racked with tremors of fear and waves of nausea.

Isobel had learned in a more general way that the frontier had brought white settlers and blacks into conflict but, like so many other people in Sydney, she had turned a deaf ear to such stories. Others, far from feeling guilty about such atrocities, had vociferously demanded the extermination of these 'depraved savages' and called for the proper protection of farms and stations. Isobel was also ashamed that she knew nothing of her father's private torments. He had faced all these challenges alone without the knowledge or sympathy of his wife or children. It was his duty, of course. 'Just be grateful, my dear, that you were not born a man,' her mother had said, all those years ago, when Isobel had asked about her father's 'troubles'.

Nothing excused the convict's devilish and murderous behaviour, and nothing excused the lies that covered it up. Nothing excused the violence that had then issued from those lies that begat, in turn, yet more lies. What did her father actually know of these events? Isobel wondered. She could not say. But the fact that he had kept Mr Davidson's letter, slipped inside his journal, suggested he wanted the truth to come out. Did he feel responsible? Was that why he had left this trail for Isobel to follow?

Isobel recalled then her conversation with her father in the garden at Rosemount so long ago, when she had sought his blessing for her courtship. He had made a confession even then. *'I too am not without regrets. I too have made mistakes. Terrible mistakes.'*

With this new letter from Mr Davidson, Isobel could feel all the old comfortable certainties of her life slipping away. *'My father was made a Knight of the Realm because he is good at drawing maps.'* She had happily applauded her father's heroic explorations and mapmaking and road-building that had opened up the country for occupation. She had never spared a thought for the real cost of this settlement, in blood and sorrow and death. She had played with little Ballandella in the gardens at Grangemouth, Isobel's much-loved home, and never stopped to consider how this girl and so many like her had lost *their* homes.

Yet it seemed her father knew the cost of what men like him had done in the name of civilisation and progress. In the journal for his fourth and last expedition, Isobel had come across this passage: *'We cannot occupy the land without producing a change fully as great to the Aborigines as that which took place on Man's fall and expulsion from Eden.'*

Was this something to be proud of?

Isobel knew how it felt to be expelled from the Eden of her home at Woolloomooloo Hill, but that fall from grace was nothing compared with the bloody extirpation that Ballandella's tribe and many others had experienced at the hands of men who followed in the wake of her father's exploration, on his roads and with his maps.

To Isobel, knowing the truth seemed to bring nothing but regrets.

Aunt Louisa's harsh moralising had trumped her Christian compassion and charity. In her final letter to her wayward niece, she expressed her regretful disbelief, and disappointment in 'one for whom I had such high hopes and deep affections'. She enclosed twenty-five pounds (paying off the debt her aunt felt she owed Isobel for the Botanic Gardens painting, and thereby neatly cutting all ties of obligation). Her one other concession to kindness was to recommend Isobel to the Benevolent Asylum, which had a 'lying-in' wing devoted to the care of deserted and widowed mothers with infants.

It was here in the last week of August that Isobel gave birth, with the help of two midwives, to a healthy baby girl. She named her Winifred, after her mother, of course, and cried with a piquant mix of joy and sadness to behold this beautiful infant and think how much her namesake would have adored her. So little she was and so late had she arrived in the story of Isobel's fading life as the youngest daughter of Sir Angus Hutton Macleod! As she held the newborn in her arms, Isobel knew that this Winnie would grow up in a very different world from that of Grangemouth and Rosemount. That world had already begun to assume the soft, blurred edges of memory, almost of myth.

In the asylum she was allotted a bed for the first three months of motherhood. In the lying-in wing, Isobel nursed little Winnie. The staff came and went, tending to their charges, in the long, gloomy dormitory with its high windows and rows and rows of iron beds and cots. Soon she would be expected to help with the washing and cleaning of sheets and blankets, and the cooking in the asylum kitchen. When they were fit enough, all the women here were expected to work to earn their keep. There was to be no special exemption for Isobel.

It was intimidating, verging on terrifying, at first. Isobel had never experienced such a close crush of other humans in one room; she was overwhelmed by the heat of so much flesh. Most of all, she was oppressed by the noise and the smells: the high-pitched wailing of babies, the rough, raucous talk of the women with their slack-mouthed laughter and swearing, the stale odour of sweat, the fug of foul breath, and stink of sour breastmilk, vomit and urine. Isobel's body tried to shut itself away from all this, stopping up her ears and nose, while her mind pretended it was all a passing nightmare that would be gone by morning. But it wasn't. This was her new life. Little by little she would readjust.

Everyone had a sad story to tell here: deserted, widowed, raped, beaten, convicted for being drunk, slatternly, unemployed, vagrant, sick, destitute. Isobel's fall and expulsion from *her* Eden counted for little among so many stories of injustice and woe. She would be lucky to find a sympathetic ear for her tale of misery. Isobel could not hide what she was: an educated middle-class woman fallen on hard times. There were those who seemed to take exception to her presence as if she was taking charity away from the real 'deserving poor'.

'Well, it's alright for some, ain't it?' whined a young woman with broken teeth and a hard, lean face, too used to pain and hunger. 'Loads of jam and puddin' all her life, nice silk and linen dresses, plenty of wood on the fire in winter, big 'ouse and all the pretty things she could ever want. And just 'cause her family can't be bothered to bail her out when she's got one in the oven, she takes a bed from one of us poor starving bitches!'

To Isobel's surprise, two other women leapt to her spirited defence. 'Ah, shuddup and quit ya jabberin'. It's not 'er fault! I betcha she was one of those ladies 'oo made fancywork to keep this place goin', didn't ya love?'

Isobel nodded. 'Yes, I worked on the bazaar last year to raise funds.'

'See, I told ya so. So why shouldn't she get a bed here like the rest of us when times are tough? Don'cha listen to Mary here, she's a nasty old mollisher, that one!'

One morning, Isobel saw a new face in the bed opposite. A young woman, careworn, exhausted, her hair as dry as straw and skin all tanned by the harsh sun. She seemed strangely familiar, a face from long ago. She held a newborn bub in her arms and sang to it.

Isobel came over and introduced herself. 'My name is Isobel. I have a feeling we have met before.'

The woman looked up, wide-eyed and amazed. 'We have indeed, Miss. I'm Sarah. I used to work at Rosemount as a housemaid.'

Isobel almost broke down and cried to find a familiar face from her past in this friendless, unhappy place. She admired Sarah's pretty little girl—Polly—and asked what had befallen her and James since they last saw each other the night before the Major's duel. Sarah hesitated at first but once she began to talk, she seemed glad to unburden herself.

'Well, as you probably know, Miss, James and I tied the knot at St Martin's and headed out for Sofala with grand plans for our future. When we got there, there was this sea of tents as far as you could see; tens of thousands of us. I'd never imagined anything like it! So we stumped up thirty shillings for our monthly licence and staked our claim. James and his brother Caleb worked on the diggings every day but most of the easy pickings on the river was all gone by the time we got there. And the mining companies had moved in to dig for the deeper gold.' Sarah sighed, her face tinged with deep sorrow.

'Life was hard at first, I can tell you: everything in short supply and overpriced, lots of sly grog, drinking and fighting, even on Sundays. And, of course, the flies, the rain, the cold and heat. Things settled down but it was the licence fees and the crooked "traps"—police, that is—and their "digger hunts" that really did for us! Poor James spent two nights in the lock-up for not having a licence, fined five pounds each time by the magistrate. Still, we battled on.'

Sarah's eyes misted. 'The final straw was that law they passed last year making everyone—diggers, shopkeepers, blacksmiths, doctors—every business on the goldfields pay their filthy thirty shillings a month.' Her chin jutted aggressively 'There was a big meeting, a thousand of us, up at Sofala to make our views known. This was all the doings of those rich squatters on the Council and, above all, that devil himself, Mr Wentworth—excuse my language, Miss. The next day things got ugly. They burned a dummy of Mr Wentworth and broke some windows. With a bit of luck, the Governor and his Colonial Secretary will back down.'

Isobel broke in. 'So why are you here with Polly? Where's James?'

Sarah's face grew dark and tears coursed down her cheeks. 'When things got bad, James took to the drink. He fought a lot with Caleb, who'd had enough and took off. After I fell pregnant with Pol, he began to gamble: cards, backgammon, anything. He was not my James anymore. He got into a terrible fight with a man he cheated. He was stabbed and died.'

'Oh, Sarah!' Isobel's heart was pierced with pity. She had liked James, admired his spirit. And she felt indebted to him for sticking his neck out, refusing to abandon her at Lachlan Swamps. *'I've come this far. I'm not leaving you alone now.'*

Out of spite, Grace had dismissed Sarah and James the following morning without any references. Isobel did not blame herself then as James had made it clear he wanted to help her and that he and Sarah had cast their lot in with the westward torrent of gold-diggers. Even so, she felt wretched now, trying to pick apart her own liability in the fate of Sarah and James from their own bad luck. Whichever way she viewed it, she felt a compelling sense of debt to Sarah and her late husband. She wanted to make amends somehow.

Ever since Charles's funeral and her quitting their house, Isobel had been forced to think about her future. She was without any friends, apart from the aged and ailing Mrs Palmer, whose time on this good earth could be counted in months, if not weeks. Isobel was also 'skint', as Mrs Pittman had explained to her and Aunt Louisa, with limited ready cash and no income, and no inheritance or financial help of any kind in the offing. As soon as she left the asylum she would have to find a way of earning money to feed herself and her child, a novel and intimidating prospect for a woman of her upbringing.

She entertained the idea of hiring herself out as a drawing teacher. The main obstacle was her tainted reputation and lack of references. Who would employ a fallen woman, so mired in scandal as Isobel, to teach their offspring? Thanks to the trial and the newspapers, not to mention all her previous unfortunate history, there were few wealthy families in Sydney who did not know her name. Maybe she would have to move to Melbourne and make a fresh start there as she had sometimes planned with Charles. But as a woman alone with a small child, she was condemned to be regarded with suspicion and looked down on as morally lax and untrustworthy. Maybe she should chop off all her hair and adopt the guise of a man again, like Rose de Freycinet and Rosa Bonheur, so she could restart her life and find well-paid work? There were women who did just that but Isobel feared she did not have the nerve to sustain such a life-changing transformation.

Sarah too had no references or prospects of work, nor did she have any family in Sydney. She was a single mother with a baby to feed, but young and strong like Isobel and possessed of many talents. They were two women alone in the world. Surely they could help each other? When Isobel told her own sad tale to Sarah, the young woman was deeply moved, and expressed the greatest sympathy for her former mistress's plight. She had a good heart, did Sarah and, despite everything she had suffered, an indestructible faith in the future.

'When we leave here, I have a house I rent in Woolloomooloo and a little money,' said Isobel. 'I would be grateful if you and Polly would consider moving in with me.'

'As your maid?' asked Sarah, her face brightening.

'As my friend,' said Isobel, giving the young woman's shoulder an affectionate pat.

Sarah's face broke into a smile and she blushed a little. 'Why, thank you, Miss.'

'Please, call me Isobel.'

WINNIE

Chapter 39

THE DRAGONFLY LADY

1905

I want to tell you about my mother. Your grandmother. You already know how she fell from grace, from the heights of Woolloomooloo Hill to the depths of Woolloomooloo Bay, not such a long way as the crow flies but nothing short of a chasm. How she renamed herself Clara to leave the past behind. But the story I want to tell is about how stubborn and brave she was. How, despite the odds, she managed to find contentment, and even happiness.

My father, as you know, was Tobias Woodhouse. A man married to the sea but devoted to his wife. Not an easy life for either of them. They met, quite by accident, at a Quakers' meeting in Surry Hills, my mother's first time there. Tobias was a midshipman then, nearly finished his apprenticeship and hoping to take his examination for lieutenant. He had decided to give up the grog and find the light. A mate had told him about the Quakers ('good people and not too churchy'). Clara liked the look of him. Aged twenty-seven, he was three years older than her when they met and still had all his hair then, dark and wavy. But he was not *too* handsome; Clara had been cured of that. She joked that it was her love of uniforms that sealed the deal. 'I always had a weakness for a man in uniform, goes back to my father. And my brother William, who was in the navy,' she'd say.

When they met, she was living in a terrace in Woolloomooloo with her sister Sarah. Yes, great-aunt Sarah. Not her actual sister, of course, but it suited them both to be 'sisters' for the sake of the neighbours and to avoid any gossip. The same reason your grand-mother changed her name. Here, this is a photo of me and Clara, both dressed up in our fanciest clothes. Little Winifred. Winnie. See how pretty I am, sitting on my mama's knee. Black glossy hair, just like her. And this one is of Sarah and her girl, Polly. Yes, Aunty Pol. My cousin. Or at least that's what we tell people. Isn't she a beauty? Copper-red hair and such delicate, pale skin.

Until she met Tobias, life was very tough for Clara. 'Not that it was all sunshine and roses after that,' she'd tell us. She and Sarah did whatever they could to pay the rent and make ends meet. Sarah took in laundry, mended and made slop clothing. Clara did fancywork on consignment, supplying shops and bazaars with all manner of goods, crocheted, knitted and embroidered. Her first love was painting and she had such a good eye and nimble fingers, her fancywork was well regarded. But if it didn't sell, well, she didn't get paid. She worked late into the night, stitching by the light of a candle to save money on oil.

She rarely talked about her Aunt Louisa, who she had lived with for two years before her first marriage. Louisa was her father's sister, a Methodist do-gooder and a tough old bird who cut off her niece without a penny when Clara fell pregnant with me and her first husband died. Louisa died from an infected ulcer only a few years after that. But she did pass on one gift. 'She taught me everything I know about fancywork. My bread and butter now!' Clara would laugh to remember how much she had dreaded fancywork when she was younger. 'Couldn't stand all that fiddly stitching! And now it puts food on the table.'

She learned so many bitter lessons about what it was like on the other side of the street when her life changed. She found out that when the society ladies put on one of their fancywork bazaars to raise funds for charity, they flooded the market with so many fancy goods that hundreds of poor women like her, who worked on consignment, did not make a penny for weeks on end. 'What a crazy, upside-down world!' she'd say.

Six months after they met, Tobias and Clara got married. Tobias was happy to have Sarah and little Polly as part of his household. He was away at sea for long stretches and could see how much his wife and her 'sister' cherished each other's companionship and shared the workload of keeping house. There were lots of families like that where we lived, with nine, ten, twelve people all crammed in together in a few small rooms.

Three years after my parents got hitched, along came my baby brother, Angus Hutton Woodhouse. Three adults and three children, with the addition of a boarder when the cash ran short, all living in one cramped, musty terrace house with a small yard out the back, a washshed and a dunny. The ceiling in the main bedroom sagged, mould bloomed on the kitchen wall, and the drains became blocked in the summer. But it was home.

The 'Loo was no longer the sleepy cove, with its mangroves and mudflats, its melaleucas and casuarinas, that my mother had painted when she was only eighteen. The quiet valley where Clara's most loyal friend, Mrs Palmer, and her husband had planted their orchards was unrecognisable now. Mrs Palmer did not live long enough to see all the changes; she passed on a few months after I was born. 'The one true heart in this whole town stopped beating,' said Clara whenever she talked about the death of her dear friend. When I was little, I used to love looking at my mother's ink and watercolour *A View of Woolloomooloo Bay* that hung over the fireplace in the parlour, like a window onto the past.

Many years after she'd painted it, they drained the mangrove swamp behind the bay and the valley filled up with workers' cottages, springing up like weeds. Most of the older larger places were turned into boarding houses or started to fall apart, with rotting floorboards and ceilings made out of brown paper. Then they built the long half-moon of the timber wharf round the bay, which, when it was deepened, became crowded with clippers and coal ships and steamers, and the little boats of Sydney's fishing fleet. Before too long the 'Loo sang to the buzz of sawmills and timberyards, the hammering of boatbuilding sheds, the cries of fishmongers, and the whistles, shouts and cooees of sailors and lumpers out for a lark at the pubs, brothels and billiard rooms. And all about, the streets filled with rows of terrace houses with their hunchbacked, shingled roofs and narrow windows.

It was a pretty rough neighbourhood when I grew up there, I can tell you. And this was even before the days of the larrikin thugs of the Push and their nasty street fights. The prostitutes hung in the doorways in a state of half-undress and even paraded up and down the streets with no bonnets on, openly inviting men to sample their wares. I can remember seeing one of the constables pushing a drunken doxy to the lockup down Forbes Street in a wheelbarrow, screaming her lungs out in language no Christian child should have to hear!

Our neighbours were all sorts. Some of the women were on the game, others did factory shiftwork or worked as maids in the private houses of the rich. Mrs Latimer and her three daughters ran the corner store and made enough to own a piano in the backroom behind the shop. Clara sometimes gave music lessons, often to earn a little credit at the store, and entertained the family and customers with performances of Chopin or cheery music hall numbers. She told us what a fine pianist Anna had been, her poor mad sister who died in Tarban Creek Asylum when I was six.

Meanwhile, up on the ridge, the estates with their grand houses that my mother knew so well when she was a little girl continued to be split up and sold off to sharp men with wads of cash and an eye for the main chance. Here and there appeared townhouses and villas, including the great Gothic pile of Maramanah with its gables and turrets and showy ironwork. A few fine terraces went up along Victoria Street, which we could see from down in the smoky valley of the 'Loo and could reach, much later on, up the steep Butler Stairs.

I knew Mama had grown up on the Hill, as she still called it, in the 'big house', Rosemount. She was careful not to go on about those 'golden days' too much for fear of making me, Angus and Polly sick with jealousy. From the back streets of the 'Loo, we looked up at the plateau with its high, mossy wall of rock and its tall trees and white buildings as it floated above us like something out of a dream. It was not a place for the likes of us.

One day when we caught the ferry over to Watsons Bay, I saw Mama looking all misty-eyed across the water at her old home. Her sister Grace and her husband had three children by the time Angus was born: Olympia, Edward and baby Ellen. With the gold boom and some wise investments, they prospered. Their names were often in the newspapers, either regarding Augustus's law business or political ambitions (he stood for the Legislative Council twice with no success), or in the social pages. Grace and Augustus never allowed my mother to darken their door again.

It was only much later I found out that every now and then a man would come by our house and deliver a packet of money wrapped up in old newspapers. It was an under-the-counter payment, a charitable donation dropped in the collection plate on the quiet to assuage whatever guilty conscience Grace still had about her impoverished, disgraced sister. It was delivered and received on the understanding that Izzie would never make any claims on her old family or come haunting them. My mother was too proud not to keep up her end of the bargain. But she took the money. She was not too proud for that. She needed it.

I tried to imagine what life had been like for Clara when she was still Isobel, 'little Izzie', all cultured and poised and in her finery. Not that she had changed so very much in her manners as far as I could tell. She still liked to read and borrowed books from the circulating library. She sketched and painted whenever she could spare the time and the money for a box of colours and pencils. Polly, Charles and I were always bothering her to do a little picture for us, a thumbnail sketch of our street or a view of the bay with its boatsheds, jetties and Jem Punch's busy hotel on the corner. Or even a portrait of us children. We loved those sketches most of all, my mother's hand moving lightning fast and her eyes darting up and down as our faces appeared like magic out of the blankness of a page.

One day Angus and I went with her on one of her rare weekend 'drawing trips'. We watched her at work, sitting on the grass, sketching Fig Tree Baths and the bay beyond while we played jacks and ate jam sandwiches. Mother looked so at peace that day I even asked her, 'Tell me, Mama, why does this make you happy?'

She looked at me quizzically for a moment and then smiled as if pleased to have worked out her answer. 'I have everything I want, right here. My children. My drawing. And my harbour.'

Most of the locals thought she was eccentric; that wasn't the word they used, of course. Her nickname was the Dragonfly Lady because of the fancy brooch she wore whenever she went to a meeting for worship with her Quaker group on a Sunday. In all the years we lived in the 'Loo, it amazed me that no one tried to steal it from her. She walked the streets with no fear, even in the dark days of the Maritime Strike and the Push. Everyone knew her.

She tried to bring us up properly, Polly and Angus and me. We went to the Ragged School and later Plunkett Street. But Clara also made a point of teaching us at home. Reading, writing, sums, even a few words of French. If I'd tried on any of that 'parley-voo' stuff at school I would've got my teeth knocked out! I'm afraid to say I was not a model student. I was not a model anything. I was a bloody tearaway, to tell the truth. Clara did her best to keep me in line but I had some kind of demon in me. I was angry at everybody. With Father away at sea and Clara and Sarah with their hands full, I fell into bad company.

I became what the coppers called a 'street Arab', one of a gang of layabouts, eight- to twelve-year-old girls and boys both, roaming about the 'Loo and all the way over to Darlinghurst and the Domain, climbing fences, taking pot shots at birds and cats and dogs, larking about at the Fig Tree Baths, singing bawdy songs, harassing the prostitutes and the drunks, begging for farthings and threepenny bits off the sailors, breaking windows and beer bottles, and even pinching stuff like fruit off the barrows and lumps of coal off the carts.

The thing I remember with the greatest shame was the day I pinched Mama's brooch. It always fascinated me, that thing. She'd told us the stories of how it was supposed to be bad luck. Maybe it was, after all that had happened to Mama and her family. She explained that opals were such brittle stones they were hard to cut and mount. Jewellers who cracked or scarred them were made to compensate their owners; it was said that one French king even cut his jeweller's hands off as a punishment! She told us of Mr Walter Scott's creepy book and how it spread the word about the opal's curse. We loved these spooky tales, of course. But by the time Isobel turned twenty-five, the opal was back in fashion thanks to Queen

Victoria herself, who took a shine to it and gave out lovely opal jewellery to her daughters as wedding gifts. Now opals were worth a fair few bob!

Whatever the reason, I decided that Clara's obsession with her dragonfly brooch was madness. Here we were living on bread and dripping, mutton, tripe, oysters or fish straight out of the stinking harbour. The house was falling down around our ears and our landlord never lifted a finger to fix anything. And there was my dreamy mother, waltzing about the streets of the 'Loo as if she was some genteel dame from Potts Point or Elizabeth Bay. It was merely a matter of time before someone knocked her on the head with a sand sock or a brick and made off with her opal insect!

I would lie in bed at night thinking about what we could buy with the proceeds from selling or pawning that damned dragonfly. A roast chicken in gravy, something we had once a year at Christmas if we were lucky. A pineapple! I had seen one once. Now, what would that taste like? Clara said they were so highly prized as decorations for the dinner table when she was growing up that you could even hire one for the evening! I have to say, the few things that Clara told me about her life with the Major and her sisters were hard to credit.

I used to watch her sometimes at night when she would sit by the fire with the brooch in her hand. She seemed to stare at it for hours at a time as if it would reveal a secret. It reminded her of her mother, she said. My namesake. As far as I could tell, it just made her sad. I would be doing her a favour to get rid of it. So one night, I snuck upstairs and spied through a crack in the door. She kept her brooch with a few other bits and pieces in a tin box.

But where did she hide the box? That was the question. So on this particular night, I watched closely through the crack as she pulled a brick out of the bedroom wall and pushed the box inside before replacing the brick. I now knew its hiding place.

The day I stole the opal dragonfly was one of the hottest in months, if not years. Mother had fallen asleep in the front parlour and Sarah was out in the shed, washing. I wrapped the brooch in an old bit of rag and slipped down the back lane. There was a pawnshop over on Brougham Street. The owner was an old Jew, Mr Solomon Levy. He knew our family on and off for years as my mama often pawned the odd trinket for some ready cash.

'Mama sent me over with this,' I lied. To cover my crime, I even wrote a short note, copying my mother's handwriting as best as I could from one of her shopping lists. I was a forger and a thief. Mr Levy read the letter and squinted at me quizzically.

'What have you got?'

I took the dragonfly from its rag. Mr Levy's eyes just about jumped out of his face.

'Where did you get this?' he gasped.

'My mother was given it by her mother.'

Mr Levy shook his head mournfully. 'I can't take this. Does your mother know you have it?' He studied me with that same quizzical squint.

'You have the letter,' I protested.

'Yes, yes. But I need to speak with her first,' he insisted. 'My, my, such beautiful workmanship. And these stones. I have never seen anything like them.'

Despite the vicious talk on the street about Mr Levy, it seemed he was an honourable man and would not take the brooch without my mother's authority. I was furious. My plans were in tatters. 'Well, if you don't want it, I guess I'll take it to someone who does!'

I could feel the struggle in him. The piece was obviously very valuable and there was little doubt that Mr Levy could make a very tidy sum if he took it and found the right buyer. But his conscience got the better of his business instincts. 'I think you should take this home. And tell your mother to see a jeweller in the city.'

I was about to storm off. There were no other pawnbrokers in Woolloomooloo but there were surely some in Surry Hills. I could probably even get a good price off some of the sharp men who hung around Punch's hotel or the Rose and Crown. There were always fences prepared to take stolen goods down here in the 'Loo.

'Hold on a minute,' said Mr Levy as I reached for the door handle to leave.

He asked for the brooch again and inspected it closely with his jeweller's eyepiece. 'Very well, this is what I'm prepared to do. I give you a chit to say I have the piece. And I make a down payment of, say, one pound. I want one of my colleagues to take a look at this rare item to make sure we can agree on a fair price. Yes?'

One pound! That was a fortune to my ears. What could I not get with one pound? I took the chit and the money and raced off. On the way home, I stopped off and bought a pie and peas from the pie cart near Mr Press's boatshed. The pieman's eyes bulged at the sight of the florin I flourished in my sweaty hand. I was rich!

Of course, that slippery old Jew had done the dirty on me. Afraid that I would hock this beautiful brooch on the street or to a less scrupulous pawnshop, he tricked me into handing it into his safekeeping. That evening he came by the house and told my mother everything. She was mortified. I was summoned and told to pay back all the money. I had already spent two shillings and sixpence on sweets and a hat that I had hidden under my bed. I was a shameless fool!

It was the angriest I ever saw Clara. She gave me two spoonfuls of castor oil and put me in Coventry for a week. Not a word. And then, when my father got home on shore leave, he gave me a thrashing. With his belt. He'd never hit me before. Thrashings were strictly for Angus, but this time he made an exception. It took me the longest time to forgive them.

I am so tired, my dears. I must get some sleep now. I will tell you more tomorrow.

Night, night.

Chapter 40

DREAMS

1905

Come, sit here, Phoebe, my love. And you here, Joan. I dreamed of you both last night, living back on the Hill in your terrace houses. Your grandma Clara used to have the strangest dreams. She told me once that they showed her the future. That this was the gift and the curse of the opal dragonfly. Not the future fixed like an insect in amber but a future that will happen if nothing else is changed. She had dreams about me too. Terrible dreams about dungeons and caves. She tried to warn me. But I was twelve and angry and determined to punish her.

My days as a 'street Arab' got me into more and more trouble. I am ashamed to say that I drifted into the company of petty criminals, doing odd jobs, pickpocketing, going 'cockatoo' to watch out for the 'jacks', passing goods. And then one day I got picked up for soliciting. My first time. Thought I was pretty flash, I did, making eyes at the drunks outside the Rose and Crown. I was lucky some of the regular whores didn't tear my eyes out.

I ended up in a bad place, just as my mother feared. Biloela it was called, a girls' reformatory on Cockatoo Island, one of the largest islands in Port Jackson. Its trees swarmed with white cockatoos that screamed like banshees day and night. Us 'bad girls' were cooped up like chickens in a cage behind a galvanised iron fence. We shared this island with a girls' industrial school right next door, a shipbuilding yard, and a nautical school ship for training destitute boys, the *Vernon*, anchored offshore. What a strange, horrible place it was. The ship and the industrial school were for orphaned and homeless boys and girls, victims of ill fortune who were to be 'saved' by training as seamen and housemaids. But us reformatory girls were vicious criminals and said to be beyond all hope.

We went out of our way to prove them right. It was bad enough that our prison was so cold, dismal, and overcrowded we had to sleep on a hard floor with only a thin blanket and bedroll for comfort. Our superintendent, Mr Lucas, was a cold-hearted, sadistic brute. He and his wife had volcanic tempers and habitually mocked and insulted us. Those he singled out for punishment spent time in solitary confinement in a dark, dank room with nothing but stale bread and water from a bucket. Worst of all, he assaulted us when his blood was up, slamming poor Mary's head into a sandstone wall and beating others until their bodies were black and blue. I escaped his fists but I lived in a state of terror.

That's how I spent my sixteenth birthday, looking forward to a dinner of greasy stew and vegetable scraps and a tongue-lashing from one of the matrons, and contemplating the lovely harbour through a grated, narrow window with no glass. A bit of a difference from my mother's harbour views from the gardens at Rosemount, where she spent her idle hours sketching and eating cherry lollipops. I won't lie. I resented my mother's plummet from a life of wealth and privilege up on the Hill to the sordid, pinched life we had down in the valley. At times I hated her for it. I blamed her for all my misery.

This whole sorry episode at Biloela came to an abrupt end when two reformers, the Hill sisters, came to talk to us on behalf of a commission into public charities. Lucas and his wife were sacked. Within a month I was transferred to the industrial school and eventually got a position in service with a good family, the beginning of my path to a better life. It was years later I found out that Clara had written to an old friend, a Mr Simon Davidson, who had served for a short while as the Premier of New South Wales; thanks to him, the parliamentarians decided to investigate the evils taking place on the island.

It took some time but Mama and I finally made our peace. I forgave her for no longer being the rich daughter of a family on the Hill and she forgave me for being a she-devil. Poor Mama, I was so unkind to her. She had her own demons to struggle with. Her strange dreams continued. Nightmares, many of them, warning her of terrible fates that might befall Angus and Polly and me. Or her husband, Tobias, whose life was hostage to the merciless ocean. All courtesy of that blasted opal dragonfly that she would not give up for anything.

⚜

The strangest dream of all was the one that took her out to Windsor. Night after night, this dream showed her a figure, silhouetted against the setting sun. She could not make out the details of this person's face in the dying light but she was convinced, as one often is in dreams, that she knew this person. In the background was a church and a graveyard with a big river in the distance. The figure waved at her as if beckoning her to approach.

This dream did not leave her for months. And then one morning, quite by accident, she saw a picture in the newspaper of St Matthew's Anglican Church in Windsor, with its shingled, copper-domed spire more like a lighthouse than a church tower. 'That's it!' she cried. 'That's where I have to go!'

By this time, my mother had turned forty, her hair beginning to grey, her body to settle into a stocky, almost mannish frame, made strong and muscular by many hours of hard work. Long gone was the aristocratic girl of her youth. After a life of such suffering, she was not a woman easily defied. And so, with great reluctance, her loyal companion Sarah agreed to go on a wild goose chase to the town of Windsor by the Hawkesbury River.

Why on earth are we here? thought Sarah as she and Clara entered the grounds of St Matthew's on a sultry summer's afternoon. The red brick of the church glowed in the late afternoon light. Rain clouds flocked overhead and the sky was ruddy and bruised. Without any clear thought as to why, Clara felt herself trembling. The cemetery around the church was empty except for a lone figure, head bowed in front of a headstone ten yards away. Slowly, as if sleepwalking, Clara approached her. Sarah tarried by the church portico.

The figure was a woman, her head covered in a long, shapeless cloak. Clara thought it odd that someone should be dressed so warmly on such a hot day. The woman turned towards her and Clara saw her dark skin. An Aborigine.

'Isobel,' the woman greeted her.

Clara thought she might faint from shock. The black woman's face was lined and worn, her hair almost completely turned to grey. But there was no mistaking who it was.

Ballandella. Isobel's childhood playmate.

'I have been dreaming about you, Isobel,' she said.

Isobel did not know what to do. She felt her child-self stirring inside her and an insane impulse to skip across the cemetery lawn and embrace her friend. Isobel's heart was so full she barely knew what to say. So many memories overwhelmed her.

'Ballandella,' she said, feeling the familiar word in her mouth after so long. Where had she been all this time? Isobel had written many letters to her old playmate care of Mr Nicholson's farm in the Hawkesbury but to no avail. Ballandella never replied. There were stories she'd married an Aboriginal man there, that they had children. Isobel had promised herself to write one last letter to Ballandella after reading her father's journals, to find out what Ballandella had seen, what she knew. But somehow that letter never got written.

'I have been dreaming about you,' said Ballandella again. Her eyes fixed on the opal dragonfly that Isobel wore pinned at her breast. Isobel had felt compelled to wear it to this mysterious meeting. 'I have been dreaming about that dragonfly. My mother told me the story. I only met her once after your father took me away. But she told me the story.'

'What story?'

In the distance, lightning flickered through the dark, roiling clouds. Silently. A fresh wind got up and snatched at Ballandella's long cloak.

'The story of how your father came by the opals. Did you never stop to wonder, Izzie? Did you never think to ask him where he got them?' Ballandella gave her a baleful look. Isobel's soul withered a little under that gaze.

'I—I—well, no.'

'You know all those clever maps your papa made, Izzie, all those roads he built? Did you know they followed the walking tracks used by us blackfellas? Think about it, Izzie. He used native guides. They took him the only way they could, one day's ride between waterholes. Makes sense. Whitefellas would've died otherwise. They took him the traditional ways, our routes that go all over the country. Plenty of water and good hunting in the right season. The routes we blackfellas used for trade, for ceremony, for walkabout.'

Isobel had never thought of this. It did make perfect sense.

'So that's how your father found these opals. Sacred stones. For ceremony. The black one from up north in Yuwaalaraay and Gamilaraay country. The white one from near my country, Barkindji and Ngiyampaa country. So how do you think he got them?'

Isobel was at a loss for words. She had a feeling the answer was not going to be flattering to her father. 'A gift?'

'No, not a gift. When your father's men killed that woman and her child by the riverbank, they found something. The man who was with that woman, he carried these stones. He was carrying them to a ceremony. When they shot at him, he dropped them as he fled.'

Ballandella looked to the horizon. The rain clouds were coming fast. 'Didn't your papa ever tell you what happened?'

'No.'

'Your father found these stones on his men when they came back. Came back from murdering a woman and child. He said, "Give me the stones." Such lovely stones. They make people want them, they are so lovely. And he agreed to keep silent about their murder, didn't he, Izzie? That was his promise to them.'

Isobel began to cry. Secrets within secrets within secrets. This was unbearable to hear. Her mother's gift was a blood sacrifice, not a love token. To buy her father's silence. To cover up the great shame of his expedition. To save his name.

'This is the story everyone knows on the Darling,' said Ballandella. 'It is time for you to make amends, Isobel.'

'Oh, Ballandella, please. Please forgive me. Here, here take it.' She began to unpin the opal dragonfly from her blouse. Raindrops were falling, fat and silvery. The lightning forked over their heads and the sky growled.

'Too late for that, Isobel. You whitefellas took 'em and made 'em yours. Took 'em out of the ground, took 'em out of our country. Made 'em into something else, eh?'

'So what should I do?' Isobel was weeping now.

'Tell the truth, Izzie. Tell the truth like your father wants you to. That's what you have to do now.'

'Come on, it's going to pour!' Clara heard Sarah calling out and looked back over her shoulder.

'Coming!' Isobel cried.

When she turned back again, Ballandella was gone.

The lightning illuminated the newly laid headstone by which she stood. She looked on the inscription:

May she rest in peace
Ballandella
Born 1834—Died 1874

Chapter 41

ENDINGS

1905

It was Sarah who finally told me the story of the trip to Windsor. Just before she died. 'Your mother was as white as a sheet, she was, and trembling,' she told me. 'I'd never seen nothing like it. She told me the whole tale. Not straight away for fear I'd think she was mad as a meat axe!' Clara never said a word to me about it. Never has.

I heard that a few years back some kangaroo hunters stumbled on opals at White Cliffs in Barkindji country. Men went mad and staked their claims in desert as barren as the moon and so hot they lived in holes underground like rabbits. Later, a boundary rider found black opals at Lightning Ridge and started an opal boom as crazy as the gold rushes years before. The world got a taste for Australian opals and the miners came to dig up the sacred stones from this opal-hearted country.

When she got back from Windsor that day, Isobel had made up her mind. She took some of her father's field journals off the bookshelf and wrapped them up in cloth and string. I was recruited to accompany her a week later when we took an omnibus into the city. There we entered the huge warehouse owned by Mr George Robertson, a bookseller from Melbourne. I was not a keen reader back then but even I was impressed by the immense variety and volume of books of all kinds on shelves stretching from floor to ceiling and in erratic piles all over the floor. The vast space had that peculiar musty smell composed of mouldy book leather, yellowing paper, dust, and the multiple dried-out corpses of insects.

My mother approached the young fellow at the front counter and asked to speak with the manager. 'Can I ask what it is about?' he asked.

'I have some rare books I wish to sell,' said Mother and placed her package on the counter.

The sallow youth looked mildly interested. 'Well, Mr Robertson is in the back office if you want to speak with him.'

'Very well,' said my mother, clearing a lump in her throat.

Mr Robertson was a friendly chap and eagerly inspected the contents of Mother's package. 'So you are Sir Angus Macleod's daughter, if you don't mind my asking?'

Mother blushed slightly. 'That's right. He bequeathed the full set of his field journals to me. And his sketchbooks.'

Mr Robertson looked especially interested at that point. 'There are more journals? And sketchbooks?'

'Yes, sir. There are.'

'I think there is someone you should meet. He should be somewhere among all these books. He comes here nearly every day.'

Mr Robertson smiled and asked Mother and I to wait while he disappeared into one of the gloomy aisles. About five minutes later he returned followed by a pale-faced gentleman in well-cut but slightly shabby clothes, his lush beard neatly combed as was the lick of dark hair over his high, glistening brow. To me his eyes appeared piercingly bright but not unkind, accompanied by a delicate, uncertain smile. Overall, his face conveyed a mild, almost shy, expression.

'Ladies, may I introduce Mr David Scott Mitchell,' said Mr Robertson. 'He is one of the most scholarly, well-informed book collectors in the city if not the whole country. He has already amassed many thousands of books pertaining to the history of the colony. I suspect he will be interested in what you have brought me today.'

'May I?' asked the mild gentleman, taking a lorgnette from his vest pocket, tethered there by a long cord. He approached the stack of field journals with an air of reverence, opening the first volume with the fingertips of his right hand as if touching something both sacred and fragile.

Mr Mitchell then turned the pages for several minutes in a rapt silence. He picked up the second and third volumes and did the same. The only sound that could be heard in the giant warehouse of books was the fluttering of pigeon wings somewhere high above us and the odd cough and splutter of men hidden away in the depths of the store.

'I am a deep admirer of all your father's works,' he said at last. 'His maps, his published journals, his treatises on many subjects. He is simply one of the most important figures in the history of the colony, Miss Macleod.'

'I am Mrs Woodhouse now. But I thank you for your kind words,' said Mother. I could tell she was fighting back tears.

'You say you have more of these journals?' asked Mr Mitchell.

'I do indeed, sir. A complete set for all four of his expeditions. I also have most of his sketchbooks beginning from his time as a soldier in Spain.'

Mr Mitchell gave an explosive gasp of wonder. 'Well, well, well!' He could not disguise his joy, which replaced his shyness with an expression of boyish glee. 'I believe I must pay you a visit, Mrs Woodhouse, if you would be so kind.'

'I promise you that Mr Mitchell will remunerate you handsomely, Mrs Woodhouse,' smiled Mr Robertson with an expansive gesture. 'He is very particular in that regard, a most ethical and scrupulous fellow. My only regret, of course, is that I have done myself out of a tidy profit. But there are higher things at stake, are there not, Mr Mitchell?'

'Indeed there are.' Mr Mitchell handed my mother his card and they agreed on a suitable time and date for his visit. He noted her address in his little black pocketbook.

Mr Mitchell kept his promise and came to our humble abode in Woolloomooloo about a week later. With her habitual gentility, my mother scrubbed and tidied the house to a sparkling cleanness not witnessed in a long time and set the stack of journals and sketchbooks on the parlour table as if arranging a vase of cut flowers. I noticed that Mother double-checked a particular envelope (addressed to her father) was properly tucked into the back of one of the volumes, securing it with a dressmaker's pin to make sure it did not slip out.

Mr Mitchell did not bother to hide his delight at these treasures. 'Mrs Woodhouse, you have made this bibliophile a very happy man, I can reassure you. I promise you these will be looked after as lovingly as if they were my own family's precious heirlooms. I hope that my collection may provide future generations with a comprehensive picture of the development of this fine colony of ours. And who knows? Maybe even a public library one day where any man or woman may freely study and learn the story of where they have come from and the place where they now live.'

'Are you interested in art at all, Mr Mitchell?' my mother asked.

I thought Mr Mitchell might faint on the spot when Mother brought out the private sketchbooks belonging to her first husband, Mr Charles Probius. The scholarly gentleman's face became flushed as he leafed through these candid pictures of men and women, so closely observed and masterfully executed.

'I can see no reason why these should not be seen now,' Mother explained. 'Most of these people will have died, I expect. And they are so beautiful!' With a touch of pride, she pointed out several that were her own work.

'You . . . you are Madame Libellule?' asked Mr Mitchell. Mother smiled and nodded. Mr Mitchell bowed his head in a nod of sincere respect. 'I have several of your pen and wash studies and two watercolours. I hope you are still painting, Ma'am?'

'A little, now and then.'

That afternoon visit by Mr Mitchell changed my mother's life in many important ways. She seemed more happy and carefree than she ever had before that day, as if she had fulfilled some promise to herself, some burdensome task that she had resolved to finish. 'My father can now rest in peace,' she said to me one day. 'The truth will out.' And that is all she would say on the subject, dismissing my questions with an enigmatic smile.

The substantial sum of money that Mr Mitchell—a man of considerable means—gave her that day was deposited in a bank account, the first my mother had ever opened in her own name. The first twenty years of her marriage to my father were filled with many episodes of genuine happiness but our household struggled to make ends meet. The next twenty years or so would be much kinder financially. Mercifully the handsome deposit in Clara's account increased over the years and was not lost in the bank crashes of 1891. Instead it enabled Clara to buy a modest flat after her poor husband, Tobias, died in the plague year of 1900. She still lives there now, as you know.

The other blessing of that visit was that Mr Mitchell spread the word about my mother's reputation as an artist. Within the year she had collectors knocking at her door to look at what she was working on. All this helped us as a family as well. Mother gave up her fancywork on consignment and took up her brushes and colours. 'My Charles would be proud of me, I think,' she sighed the first time she sent her canvases off to the framers for a small exhibition. 'It is a shame he is not here to see his handiwork.'

It's funny to think how stories end. My mother—born as Isobel and reborn as Clara—was a fine young lady, an educated and cultured daughter of a rich colonial family. It was painful for her to leave all that behind. To fall rather than to rise: now, that is a much harder fate to bear than the reverse. To adapt and survive in such a new, alien world must have taken more courage than I can ever imagine. She knew that nobody in Woolloomooloo would feel sorry for her. She was marked out by the way she spoke, the words she used, the way she walked, everything about her. The Dragonfly Lady.

'I crossed a chasm and had to change,' she told me once. 'But that chasm was as nothing compared to the one my friend Ballandella had to cross. And she survived despite the terrible price she had to pay.'

Clara could not bring herself to part with her beloved dragonfly, her only link to her past. Instead she gave it to me as a wedding gift when I married your father. I was so moved, knowing how much this brooch meant to her. 'Don't give it to Mr Levy, the pawnbroker,' she smiled when she handed it over. I was forgiven, at last.

I have the dreams now. Have had them for years. Such strange and powerful dreams. I shall not burden you with the details, my loves. Suffice to say, I foresaw your births, my beautiful daughters. I foresaw Tobias's death. And your own father's, God bless him. I did not always understand the dreams. But I got so used to them I could not imagine life without them. And just like Clara, the dragonfly and its visions made me feel close to my mother.

The depression of 1891 came on like the giant rolling wave in one of Clara's dreams when she was a young woman. It wiped away much of Grace and Augustus's wealth. By then they had passed Rosemount to their daughter, Olympia, and her husband, Mr Oswell. They too had their fortune decimated and, in a scramble for cash to pay off their debts, cut up the last few portions of Rosemount's grand estate and sold them.

It's funny to think how stories end. The great house of my mother's childhood now stands all by itself on a little island, not much bigger than the house itself. The Oswells demolished the service wing at the back and threw a high wall around the house for privacy with a small garden, a fountain and a square of lawn. This had once been the largest estate on Woolloomooloo Hill. Now it's no more than a tiny block of land in the middle of busy roads and sidestreets.

Poor old Rosemount. Like a dusty diamond in a pile of dull pebbles, alone and aloof, hemmed in by cottages and terraces. Today, there's only a handful of the villas and mansions left that had been built for Governor Darling's 'vision splendid'. Mother thinks this is such a funny ending. The horse-drawn carts and the trams still find it a hard grind going up William Street with its ridiculous incline to the top of Woolloomooloo Hill, all thanks to that stubborn man who defied your great-grandfather, Sir Angus Hutton Macleod. Such a clever fellow! They called the crossroads there Queens Cross for a while, in honour of Her Majesty's Jubilee, and then just this year gave it a new name, Kings Cross. Looks like it might stick.

It's funny to think how stories end. Clara's story—Isobel's story—has come around in nearly a full circle. Rosemount Hall went up for sale a few years back and the new owner, a keen art collector, didn't know what to do with the old place. He stored some of his private collection in the back rooms (Bunnys, Longstaffs and Lamberts) and let many of the rooms out for a peppercorn rent as studios to some of his favourite artists, mostly young men.

With one exception.

In the front room that was once her bedroom when she was a little girl, your grandmother, Clara Woodhouse, also known as the artist Madame Libellule, has set up her studio. Most mornings she raises the blinds to let in the sun and the dazzling light off the harbour that lights up her childhood memories. Some days she even wanders down to the old grotto in the small park opposite that is all that remains of the Rosemount estate. Much of the view is beginning to disappear behind buildings but she sits there with her paints and sketchbook and studies the play of light and shadow on her beloved harbour. Miss Isobel Clara Macleod, youngest daughter of Major Sir Angus Macleod, has returned at last to her home.

And you, my loves, have found jobs in the city and rooms on Victoria Street. Who knows what the future will hold? My dreams don't tell me anymore. But I feel hopeful.

Here, come closer. I have something I want to give you. It is a promise I made to Clara, to Isobel. It is a promise I believe she made to her mother, your great-grandmother, Winnie. It is a gift for the pure-hearted. I give it to both of you. To share. There has been too much bitterness between sisters in this family, too much jealousy.

Come, look. It is so beautiful. The bright fire in the cold stone. Do not be afraid. Let yourself dream.

It is an opal dragonfly.

SOURCES

While this book is a work of fiction it has its roots in historical research. The character of Major Sir Angus Hutton Macleod is modelled on Sir Thomas Livingstone Mitchell, Surveyor-General of New South Wales, who completed the Nineteen Counties map (a complete survey of the colony) in 1834. He was knighted for his services to the colony in 1839. He clashed with Governor Darling over his alternate route over the Blue Mountains (Victoria Pass) and with other governors he served. Governor FitzRoy later wrote: 'It is notorious that Sir Thomas Mitchell's unfortunate impracticability of temper and spirit of opposition of those in authority over him misled him into frequent collision with my predecessors.'

Mitchell conducted four expeditions into the interior: the first to the Gwydir and Barwon rivers in northern New South Wales in 1831–32; the second along the Bogan and Darling Rivers in

1835; the third in 1836 along the Darling River to the Murray and south-east to Portland (changed in the novel to 1838); and the fourth into Queensland in 1845–46. On the second expedition, a skirmish resulted in the deaths of three Aboriginal people including a woman. On his third expedition, a violent encounter with the Barkindji resulted in the deaths of seven Aboriginal people at Mount Dispersion. On this same journey, Mitchell sketched the widow, Turandurey, and her child, Ballandella, who joined his party; the injured girl was then taken back to Sydney where she lived with the Mitchell family until they went to England in 1837.

Mitchell published two accounts of his expeditions and invested in sea trials of a boomerang screw-propeller (1851–53). On 27 September 1851 he fought a duel with Stuart Donaldson (later New South Wales Premier). Both his French pistols are now kept in the National Museum of Australia. The satirical poem (modified and titled 'A Matter of Honour' for the novel) appeared in *Bell's Life* on 4 October 1851. He died of a chill in 1855 while awaiting a Royal Commission report into the conduct of his department. The other poems in the novel (the two lampooning William Macleay and Mitchell/Macleod as well as the poem read at Macleod's funeral) are all slightly adapted versions of real poems, the latter written by Mitchell himself (he lost two adult sons).

I read the two standard biographies *Thomas Mitchell, Surveyor General and Explorer* by J.H.L. Cumpston (1954) and *Sir Thomas Livingston Mitchell and his World, 1792–1855: Surveyor General of New South Wales 1828–1855* by William C. Foster (Institution of Surveyors, N.S.W. Inc., 1985). I also read Mitchell's accounts of his second and third expeditions in his *Three Expeditions into the Interior of Eastern Australia,* two volumes (T & W Boone, London, 1838).

Particularly helpful was *The Civilized Surveyor: Thomas Mitchell and the Australian Aborigines* by D.W.A. Baker (Melbourne University Press, 1997) and Baker's essay 'Wanderers in Eden: Thomas Mitchell compared to Lewis and Clark' (Aboriginal History 1995, 19:1). *The Civilized Surveyor* provides close comparative readings of Mitchell's expeditionary field journals and his published accounts; I have followed Baker's scholarship closely with regard to the murder of an Aboriginal woman and child on the second expedition and the Mount Dispersion massacre on the third.

Jack Brook's essay 'The Widow and the Child' (Aboriginal History 1988, 12:1) is the only scholarly piece I could find about Ballandella. Brook writes that she 'was a welcome stranger' to Mitchell's children while the family resided in Sydney. Her guardian noted that she '"seemed to adopt the habit of domestic life *con amore,* evincing a degree of aptness that promised very favourably".' She and her mother are identified as Wiradjuri in this essay (as well as other sources) but they are also both described as Muthi-Muthi. I have identified them as Wiradjuri and have fictionalised Ballandella's life with Isobel and later.

Isobel is inspired in part by Mitchell's youngest daughter whose diary tells of family life after her father died: *Blanche: An Australian Diary 1858–1861* (John Ferguson, 1980). This intimate, lively account helped me find Isobel's voice and also suggested several incidents including the social outing at Watsons Bay. The State Library of New South Wales holds a great deal of material on Thomas Mitchell (including his sketches and water-colours), some of which informs this novel.

Rosemount is a closely observed fictionalised version of Elizabeth Bay House, 'the finest house in the colony' built by Governor Darling's Colonial Secretary, Alexander Macleay. Macleay's portrait in the novel is broadly based on the historic figure but with fictional aspects (for example, the date of his death is four years later than July 1848). His son William did take over the house from his financially distressed father but it stayed in the Macleay family and was never sold to the Surveyor-General, Mitchell. The Mitchell family lived at Carthona at Darling Point and when Thomas died, they moved to Craigend Terrace on Woolloomooloo Hill. The two historic figures did clash, notably over Macleay's interference with Mitchell's plans for William Street.

My thanks go to Sydney Living Museums for a private tour of Elizabeth Bay House. Relevant sources were *Elizabeth Bay House: A History and Guide* by Scott Carlin (Historic Houses Trust NSW, 2000), *Fanny To William: The Letters of Francis Leonora Macleay 1812–1836* edited by B. Earnshaw and J. Hughes (HHT NSW/Macleay Museum, University of Sydney, 1993), *Taste and Science: The Women of the Macleay Family 1790–1850* by Elizabeth Windschuttle (HHT, NSW, 1988) and the lavishly illustrated *House* by Robyn Stacey and Peter Timms (HHT, NSW, 2011).

Charles Probius is an adaptation of colonial artist Charles Rodius (1802–1860), a noted portrait painter including of Indigenous people of New South Wales. Mr 'Robert the Large' Cooper, owner of Juniper Hall, Mrs Palmer, wife of Governor Phillips' commissary-general, William and Fanny Macleay (children of Alexander Macleay), the

French painter Rosa Bonheur, exiled Frenchman Count Gabriel de Milhau, Sydney Aboriginal identity William Warrell, colonial artist S.T. Gill and the book collector David Scott Mitchell are historic figures. Many events described in the novel are closely adapted from real events including the New Year's Day Grand Fancy Bazaar in the Botanic Gardens (January 1852), the Boxing Day Woolloomooloo Bay Regatta (1852), the SS *Chusan* Steam Ball (August 1852), and the Hargraves anniversary dinner (1853).

For background research on the period I am indebted to Peter Cochrane's award-winning *Colonial Ambitions* (MUP, 2006) and Tanya Evans' (also award-winning) *Fractured Families: Life on the Margins of Colonial New South Wales* (UNSW Press, 2015). For an understanding of women colonial artists, I relied on the excellent *Picturesque Pursuits: Colonial Women Artists and the Amateur Tradition* by Caroline Jordan (MUP, 2005).

I was fortunate to find Annette Shiell's wonderful *Fundraising, Flirtation and Fancywork: Charity Bazaars in Nineteenth Century Australia* (Cambridge Scholars Publishing, 2012). Sources for life in 1840s to 1850s Sydney included *Southern Lights and Shadows* by Frank Fowler (1859), *Sydney in 1848: Copper Plate Engravings from Drawings by Joseph Fowles* (1849) and of course TROVE newspaper archives, the Dictionary of Sydney and many contemporary artworks. Dr Catherine Bishop's very readable (and award-winning) *Minding Her Own Business: Colonial Businesswomen in Sydney* (NewSouth, 2015) also provided valuable insights.

I was excited to discover just in time Paul Irish's *Hidden In Plain View: The Aboriginal People of Coastal Sydney* (UNSW Press, 2017), which filled in important gaps about Sydney's early and ongoing

Indigenous presence as did Grace Karskens' *The Colony: A History of Early Sydney* (Allen & Unwin, 2009).

And last of all I pay my respects to the writers Marjorie Barnard and Flora Eldershaw for their prize-winning debut novel *A House is Built* set in colonial Sydney from the 1830s to 1850s (Harrap & Co, 1929), to which I pay homage with scenes in my novel at Hunter's Hill.

There are too many sources (online and in print) to specify for research on subjects as diverse as music and dancing, dandies, cross-dressing, jewellery, opals, fashion, Woolloomooloo, The Rocks, Hunter's Hill and Watsons Bay but I will make special mention of the entertaining and informative 'The Cook and The Curator: Eat Your History' (http://blogs.sydneylivingmuseums.com.au/cook/).

ACKNOWLEDGEMENTS

I owe thanks to the writer Patti Miller for a house-swap that gave me valuable research time in Kings Cross, Potts Point, Elizabeth Bay and Woolloomooloo for taking photographs and wandering the streets for atmosphere. I am also grateful for helpful suggestions from my neighbours, Richard White and Catherine Bishop, both distinguished historians.

Thanks also to the staff at the Sydney Living Museums for their dedication and the guided tours of Elizabeth Bay House and Susannah Place in The Rocks. My thanks also go to Cathy Brown from the Moran Arts Foundation for a private tour of Juniper Hall in Paddington.

I am deeply grateful to my agent Selwa Anthony for her ongoing support and wisdom and for the critical insights and enthusiasm of my publisher at Allen & Unwin, Annette Barlow, and my editor,

Simone Ford. Many thanks to Nada Backovic for her exquisite cover. My thanks also to Christa Munns and all the hard-working team at Allen & Unwin, who I hope will always continue to believe in Australian stories and support Australian writers.

I dedicate this book to my daughter and her bright, creative spirit. My greatest thanks go to my brilliant and talented wife Claire, who shares with me the endlessly fascinating, always challenging journey of writing novels. Without her literary companionship and insights, her faith and encouragement, and our shared belief in the whole project, this book would not exist.